1792–1814: The Epic Begins...

Meet Jeremy and Zebulon Brand. Handsome, headstrong, as proud as the new nation they are helping to build. Brothers, about to become bloody enemies in the rivalry for the love of an unforgettable woman . . .

Rebecca Breech. Beautiful, willful, ambitious. Her life is about to become part of our history, entwined with the men and women who forged America's early years . . .

John and Abigail Adams . . . Thomas Jefferson . . . James and Dolley Madison . . . Lewis and Clark . . . Aaron Burr. Americans all. Lovers, rivals, builders, fighters . . . united by passion and destiny.

BLESS THIS HOUSE is their story, it is our story, and it is one of the greatest stories ever told . . .

1792 THE AMERICAN PALACE • BOOK 1 1814

BLESS THIS HOUSE

Evan H. Rhodes

BERKLEY BOOKS, NEW YORK

The author wishes to acknowledge
the valuable help of George S. B. Morgan
in researching the material for this novel.

BLESS THIS HOUSE

A Berkley Book / published by arrangement with
the author

PRINTING HISTORY
Berkley edition / June 1982

ISBN: 0-425-05457-8

A BERKLEY BOOK ® TM 757,375

PRINTED IN THE UNITED STATES OF AMERICA

For William R. Grose

Preface

"FROM THE White House today, the President asked for a declaration of war against . . ."

"The White House reported that economic indicators are down, and that the nation is in the grip of a severe recession . . ."

"The White House issued an urgent request that the world's superpowers . . ."

The White House—home and nerve center of the most powerful nation on earth; policies formulated here and courses of action taken shape all our lives.

From its earliest beginnings, the building has been imbued with an almost mystical quality. For it was, and has remained, the visible symbol of the nation's quest for the most perfect, and perfectible, form of government for all its people.

Throughout our history, Americans have been drawn to the White House, to redress wrongs, to celebrate, or to mourn. Women have marched down Pennsylvania Avenue to the President's Mansion to demand the vote, veterans to plead for jobs. Ku Klux Klansmen have paraded past its portals for white supremacy, blacks for equal rights. In 1945, General Eisenhower led a victory march along the famous avenue from the White House to the Capitol, to celebrate the end of World War II. Eighteen years later, Kennedy's funeral cortege passed by this route. And here, the largest peaceful gathering in the history of the world bore witness against the Vietnam War.

Through the years it was called the Palace in the Forest, the American Palace, the Great Castle, the President's Palace, the Executive Mansion, the President's House, and the White House; it was not until Theodore Roosevelt's time that the long-popular name "The White House" was officially inscribed on the Presidential letterhead.

Most of the Presidents who've lived there have had mixed feelings about their residency. Thomas Jefferson described his tenure as "a splendid misery." Andrew Jackson called it "dignified slavery." And Harry Truman labeled it "the Great White Prison." Yet men fight and claw their way to gain the highest office in the land, hoping thereby to secure their place in history. As Bernard Baruch said when the gravely ill Franklin Delano Roosevelt ran for an unprecedented fourth term, "I've seen men pull themselves out of the grave to live in that building."

Every President has left his imprint on the mansion—the mediocre left only faint impressions that have faded into obscurity, the truly great men, their indelible brands. All strove for greatness, but only a few achieved it. And a few rare men attained a stature and a universality that transcended their times.

Though the White House is the home of the President and his family, it has come, by extension, to represent the home and family of every American. For in this dwelling owned by *all* the people lives the *one* man they've elected to lead them. A love-hate relationship between the leader and the electorate has burned strongly for more than two hundred years. Within its hallowed walls reside the recollections of who we were, and where we came from, and the image of what we may reasonably hope to expect from the future.

How did this all come to be?

Who designed this house destined to occupy such a formidable place in world affairs?

Why was it built in a forested, uninhabited, swampy area carved out of Maryland and Virginia?

Which President's administration was almost ruined when his secret liaison with his mulatto mistress was exposed, a slave mistress who'd borne him five bastard children?

When and why was the White House looted and burned, and was there indeed heavenly intervention in the torrential hurricane that saved the building from certain destruction?

Who leveled the dread curse against the building, a curse that said that every President elected in a year ending in zero would die before he finished his term of office? To date, this curse has proven to be horribly true.

What was the social and sexual scandal—a charge of bigamy—that almost brought down a President?

Which of the White House hostesses imagined herself a queen and had a court of "ladies-in-waiting"?

Why was the building ringed by fortresses and besieged by fellow Americans? When were there *two* White Houses vying for power in the nation?

Which President might have been saved from a mortal gunshot wound had his aides followed Thomas Edison's instructions?

Which of the First Ladies was rumored to have had a liaison with another woman while her husband continued a twenty-year relationship with his mistress?

Which President boasted that he had to have a woman "three ways" before he was ready to discard her?

Why do two hundred reporters keep a daily vigil at the White House, reporting every bit of gossip and news? And how and why has this building become the symbol of freedom to all the world?

"We live by symbols," said Abraham Lincoln, and nowhere in the land is there a more recognizable or potent symbol of power and freedom than America's house of destiny, the White House.

This, then, is its story, and the story of the men who shaped it, and helped shape the destiny of the nation and of the world.

“I pray heaven to bestow the best of blessings on this house, and on all that shall hereafter inhabit it. May none but wise and honest men ever rule under this roof.”

—PRESIDENT JOHN ADAMS

ADVERTISEMENT

WASHINGTON, *In the Territory of* **COLUMBIA**

A PREMIUM OF

FIVE HUNDRED DOLLARS

or a Medal of that value, at the Option of the Party, will be given by the Commissioners of the Federal Buildings, to the Person who, before the Fifteenth Day of July next, shall produce to them the most approved PLAN, if adopted by them, for a PRESIDENT's HOUSE, to be erected in this City.... It will be a Recommendation of any plan, if the central Part of it may be detached and erected for the present, with the Appearance of a complete whole, and be capable of admitting the additional Parts, in future, if they shall be wanting. Drawings will be expected of the Ground-Plats, Elevations of each Front, and Sections through the Building... to explain the internal Structure; and an Estimate of the cubic Feet of Brick-Work composing the whole mass of the Walls.

March 14, 1792 **The COMMISSIONERS.**

PART ONE

Chapter 1

THE BLOW caught Jeremy Brand on the side of the head and sent him sprawling. The ten-year-old boy fell against the massive cornerstone hanging from the block and tackle in its tripod sling. Jeremy had only a second to stare at the blood from his scraped arm soaking into the sandstone block, before his master, Mathias Breech, lunged at him again.

"I'll teach you to squander good honest time," Breech bellowed in his whiskey-thick voice.

Jeremy scrambled away from Breech's powerful windmilling arms. A long year of being an indentured servant had taught Jeremy how to avoid his bullying master, but he despaired of ever being able to finish his seven-year term of service.

"Wasting your time drawing those stupid pictures," Breech said, grabbing for a handful of the boy's long flaxen hair. But Jeremy managed to break free. "Get over to me this instant and take what you deserve, or it will go harder for you when I do catch you!" Breech shouted.

Jeremy dodged around the tripod holding the ponderous block of stone, keeping it between himself and Mathias Breech. All the while, he kept searching for a way to escape. Directly behind him lay an enormous excavation, a hundred by two hundred feet, dug deep into the rich loamy red-brown earth. About eighteen acres in the forest were being cleared, though the workers had been given the morning off because of the ceremonies. Scattered about were brick kilns, stacks of lumber, bags of sand and mortar, blocks of stone, and ramshackle cabins thrown together to house the laborers.

Immediately beyond the clearing lay a miasmic wilderness of swamp and forest wedged between the Potowmack River and its Eastern Branch. It was all part of the ten-mile-square territory recently carved from the states of Virginia and Maryland and destined to become the site of the nation's new capital. But now wolves still roamed the area, and an occasional black bear raided the livestock pens; a bounty was paid for each pelt brought in. Stands of dark green pine and elm marched down to the Potowmack, the trees thinning then to the pale limpid greens of weeping willow near the river's banks. Jeremy had seen the nests of copperheads and rattlesnakes that infested the swamps, and had almost been eaten alive by the mosquitoes.

With a lightning lunge that belied his ponderous girth and forty years of profligate living, Mathias Breech cornered Jeremy. The boy stood his ground, his frail hands clenched into fists, his reedy body tensed. His thin angular face, normally bright with curiosity, was now contorted, and anger darkened his intense blue eyes. His sun-streaked shoulder-length hair, cut in bangs, hung straight to his shoulders. He looked overly tall for a lad almost ten and a half, and might have been well-formed, but constant undernourishment made him look as if he hadn't quite grown into his gangly body.

"You've no reason to punish me! I didn't do anything!" Jeremy exclaimed, as he'd cried out all these months whenever Breech got drunk or lost his temper.

Mathias Breech raised his beefy hand, but before he could strike, his arm was caught by a solid-looking man who'd just arrived at the site. Mathias whirled and came face to face with James Hoban, the architect of the mansion about to be built.

"Have you no sense of decency, man?" Hoban demanded, as, exerting his strength, he forced Breech's arm down. Hoban was tall, with the florid complexion of the Irish and a temper to match.

Hoban, in his position as chief building superintendent, was an important man, and Breech dared not offend him. Breech's voice took on a subservient whine: "The boy is a wastrel and not worth his keep."

As a supplier of stone and building materials to the small towns of Georgetown and Alexandria, Mathias earned a decent enough living, but the construction of this mansion could make his fortune—unless, of course, Hoban took it into his thick Irish head to buy from a different stone merchant.

Breech's manner became even more deferential. "I've tried to teach the boy to mind, but let me take my eyes off him for

a second and he's off daydreaming. I asked him to prepare the corn, wine, and oil for the ceremony, told him how important it was, but did he heed?"

"I did," Jeremy said. "They're right there near the cornerstone."

Hoban walked to the tripod, and Mathias and Jeremy followed. "What the lad says is true," Hoban said. Then he caught sight of the black-and-blue marks on Jeremy's arms and cheek and he scowled. "No matter that the boy is your property, Breech, I won't tolerate such treatment here." He turned to Jeremy. "Have you been mistreated?"

Jeremy toed the earth. It went against his grain to tell tales, so he said nothing.

Trying to make a better case for himself, Breech said, "I'll show you how else he wastes time." He pointed to a sketch of a building drawn in the ground. "Let him sneak a moment from honest work and he's forever drawing these silly pictures. He did this one with my good measuring stick. Got mud all over it!"

Hoban studied the drawing. "You did this?" he asked sharply.

Jeremy shuffled and finally nodded.

While waiting for the cornerstone-laying ceremonies to begin on this glorious autumn Saturday, October 13, 1792, Jeremy had amused himself by sketching the building that would be erected here—the palace that would one day be the home of the President of the United States.

In his every spare moment, Jeremy had memorized the winning design, drawing it over and over again. He thought the rendition he'd done this morning was especially good, though it did look somewhat grander than the original.

Since the newspaper advertisements had appeared in New York, Boston, Philadelphia, Baltimore, and Charleston a few months previously, the country had been abuzz with the competition to design a suitable dwelling for the nation's President. Many plans had been submitted, including one by a bridge-builder whose bridges invariably collapsed, and another by an advocate of windowless rooms. Rumor had it that even Thomas Jefferson, George Washington's secretary of state, had submitted a plan under the pseudonym A-Z, for that design looked remarkably like Jefferson's home, Monticello.

Finally, the commissioners in charge of the project, along with President Washington, chose a design by James Hoban, a thirty-four-year-old architect. Hoban, born in Killarney, had studied architecture in Dublin, had come to America shortly after the War for Independence, and set up practice in Charleston, South Carolina. The first prize was five hundred dollars, or a medal of like value. Hoban had chosen the medal.

Hoban turned at the sound of approaching carriages. "We'll speak of this later," he said to Breech and Jeremy. "Now get on with your work, the two of you."

Dignitaries began to arrive, the commissioners of the newly-formed Federal City, Freemasons from Lodge Number Nine in Georgetown some two miles away, and several local landowners. The horses slogged their way along the hundred-sixty-foot-wide rutted pathway that had just been cut through the alder swamps and would eventually be named Pennsylvania Avenue. With the heavy autumn rains and rising estuary tides, the roadway had practically become a bog, and all along its length catfish swam in the tidal pools.

The leaders of the Georgetown and Alexandria communities

clambered down from their carriages, excitement charging their conversation. Devroe Connaught and his wife Elizabeth had come; Elizabeth, a high-strung woman of strong passions, was at least twenty years younger than her husband, and the lack of love was fast sapping her dark, fragile beauty. Devroe, a vain, portly, uncertain man with bandy legs, always insisted that their four-year-old daughter Marianne accompany them, believing her presence a testimony to his virility.

The spinster Victoria Connaught—Devroe's elder sister and the real leader of the American branch of the clan—was helped from her carriage by her seventeen-year-old nephew, Sean Connaught, visiting from England. Sean, the second son of the titled branch of the family, detested America and Americans.

"Ridiculous," he exclaimed, glancing around. "These stupid provincials want to locate their capital here? Philadelphia is bad enough, but this swamp is insane." He slapped at a mosquito that drew blood.

"I too take a dim view of these proceedings," Victoria Connaught said as she adjusted her powdered wig. She was a fleshy woman given to many chins; the lowest one was supported by the mound of her bosom. Yet she managed to comport herself with the bearing of an aristocratic Tory. "I've never given up my dream that the colonies will one day rejoin the mother country," she said.

"Who could possibly want this wilderness infested by savages?" Sean asked, his eyes sliding to the two Indians who stood nearby.

They were braves from the Algonquin and Susquehannock tribes, which considered this land theirs by right of prior occupancy. One suspicious Indian leaned over the excavation pit, wondering what new crime against his people these white men might commit.

"I know exactly what you mean," Victoria said, patting Sean's arm. "Still, the land does contain enormous riches." Victoria had first emigrated to the New World because her impoverished branch of the family had little standing in England. Though she'd grown wealthy here with tobacco and cotton plantations worked by gangs of slaves, her English relations, including Sean, considered her something of an embarrassment. Consequently, she took on more airs and graces than even the real Duchess of Connaught, and passed as minor royalty among these uncouth Americans.

Robert Brent arrived; he owned the Aquia quarries in Virginia, where the sandstone for the palace was being quarried. Mathias Breech hurried over to him and with an obsequious bow said, "As I promised you, I've hired new wagons and flatboats to transport the stone from your quarry. I can't thank you enough for letting me have the contract," he added, then babbled on with fawning inanities.

Robert Brent cut Breech short and turned to Colonel John Tayloe, the richest and most influential planter in the district. "Do you have any further news? Why hasn't President Washington come to the dedication ceremonies? Or Vice-President Adams?"

"I don't know why," Tayloe said. "But no matter. The new capital *will* be situated here, and that's bound to change all our lives—surely for the better."

Victoria Connaught overheard this and fluttered her fan with annoyance. "Colonel, I thought that you would have more sense! What we have here is yet another example of George Washington's folly. Our peaceful land will be crawling with politicians and their sycophantic followers. Instead of meddling with politics, Washington would have done us and the world a service if he'd stuck to the things he was good at—surveying land, and romancing rich widows."

Everyone's head turned as a rider came galloping toward the building site, his snorting, wheeling horse kicking up sprays of mud. Before he had fully reined in the black stallion, the handsome twenty-year-old man dismounted, the fluid motion marking him as a natural horseman.

When Elizabeth Connaught recognized the rider, the blood left her face. She clutched at the bodice of her magenta satin dress. The intensity of her reaction wasn't lost on her husband, and Devroe's lips thinned into a bitter line.

The rider strode toward the gathering. Nature and fate had conspired to make Zebulon Brand a superb physical specimen. He stood fully six feet tall; his shoulders were broad, his eyes a dark moody brown, hooded by heavy winged brows that met at the bridge of his slightly aquiline nose. His thick black hair was tied in a queue. His smile was infectious, fully demanding a smile in return, and his manner so ingratiating that few could resist him.

The early autumn air was still warm and Zebulon wore his maroon velvet riding coat slung loosely over his shoulders. His solid thighs fairly burst from his fawn-colored breeches, and his knee-high antelope boots—received as a present that week in Philadelphia—had cost a small fortune.

The moment Jeremy saw Zebulon he ran to him and grabbed the hem of his jacket. "When, Zebulon?" Jeremy demanded.

Though Jeremy was as fair as Zebulon was dark, as slight as the other was broad, a strange but marked similarity existed between them, for they were half-brothers. Zebulon Brand looked down at his brother. "Ah, Jeremy, how well you look."

"When?" Jeremy repeated, despair ringing in his voice. "When will you buy back my indentureship papers?"

Zebulon's brooding eyes seemed to cloud with sadness. "Jeremy, if you knew how it pained me to tell you this—" He shook his head and all of Jeremy's hopes plummeted.

"I expected to earn the money from this last shipping venture. Everything was going well; the sloop was loaded with slaves from the islands, and a bountiful crop they were. But three days out of port we were stopped by a British frigate, and they seized our ship. Luckily, I escaped impressment myself, but we lost everything."

A year before, in part using the money from indenturing Jeremy, Zebulon had become involved in the slave trade. He imported Negroes from the West Indies and sold them to the planters and merchants in the Chesapeake Bay area. The Connaughts had bought half a dozen, which is how he'd first met Elizabeth. He'd also supplied Breech's stone works with two or three strong backs. Then Breech, anticipating the need for more slaves, had put money into another such venture of Zebulon's. But this was the vessel the British had captured. Undaunted, Zebulon had cast about for other ways to amass a quick fortune; with the new capital being relocated here, that opportunity had presented itself.

Jeremy listened, numbed, as Zebulon's words built a stockade around him, one from which he'd never escape.

"Be of good cheer, Jeremy," Zebulon continued. "I guarantee that in a matter of months you'll be free. This very night in Georgetown—" He looked around conspiratorially. "I can only say that I'm about to turn the Brand fortunes around." Zebulon's arm swept grandly over the heavily wooded rolling hills turning red, orange, and gold with autumn. "One day, you and I shall see a great city rise here, and I mean to make the Brands a part of it."

Another carriage clattered up, and Zebulon broke into a broad grin when he recognized its lone occupant. It was Mathias Breech's thirteen-year-old daughter, Rebecca. Zebulon left Jeremy abruptly and started toward the carriage. Jeremy stared after his brother, and then with a cry sprang onto his back. Zebulon's knees buckled under the sudden attack, while Jeremy tore at him like a bobcat. With a sharp motion, Zebulon flung the boy into the mud. As Jeremy jumped to his feet, James Hoban ran up to separate them.

"There, you see!" Mathias Breech said triumphantly to Hoban. "Perhaps now you'll believe me. The lad is an ungrateful wretch, with the temper of a devil!"

Jeremy fought to get at Zebulon but Hoban seized him by the scruff of the neck. "Mind now, boy, or I'll have you thrown in the stocks."

"But he—"

"Enough!" Hoban said, shaking Jeremy. "We have more important business here today than common brawling."

With a scowl at his brother, Zebulon straightened and went directly to the carriage, which was already surrounded by other young blades of the area. The Negro footman opened the door and Rebecca Breech stood framed in the doorway.

"She's passing fair," Sean said to his aunt Victoria. "How old is she?"

"Just thirteen," Victoria sniffed, "and already a common flirt."

"She carries herself with an air of someone much older."

"Well, a girl matures early here, and is often married and bearing children before she's out of her teens," Victoria replied. But Sean didn't hear her; he too had gone to the carriage.

For the afternoon ceremonies, Rebecca Breech had chosen a hunter-green riding outfit; her maid Letitia told her it would highlight her complexion and her titian hair. When she wore this color, she discovered it also made her hazel eyes a more luminous green. Rebecca was quick-witted, knowledgeable beyond her years. She could be high-spirited or reserved, capable of selfless acts of Christian kindness, and also of crushing cruelties. To the youngbloods in Georgetown she was growing into a desirable catch. To her father, who stood in awe of her beauty, she seemed an enigma, poised between innocence and womanhood. Only one person knew the innermost desires of Rebecca Breech—Rebecca Breech herself.

The young men offered their hands to help her descend. Her eyes flicked over them, lingering on Sean Connaught, and dismissing him for his haughtiness; then she spied Zebulon. The beginnings of a smile played over her lips. Surely Zebulon was the most attractive man in the district. His reputation with the tavern wenches, the scandalous rumors surrounding him and Elizabeth Connaught . . . Her gaze rested on him a moment longer, Zebulon moved forward expectantly, but with an artless gesture Rebecca gave her hand to her father.

Mathias Breech glowed with satisfaction, coloring to the roots of his black hair. He grasped Rebecca's waist, lifted her high, and deposited her on the ground. "You're my darling, and there's not a man in these parts worth your salt. Nothing but a count or a duke will do for my girl."

Jeremy stared at Rebecca, hoping for the slightest sign of recognition. The only thing that made his indentureship bearable was the prospect of catching a glimpse of her. Sometimes she'd come to the warehouse, ostensibly to call her father for dinner, but always knowing that the workers would stare after her. Once she had even deigned to look at him, and he'd walked around in a daze. But if she noticed him now, she made no sign of it, and his heart plummeted.

The gathering crowded toward the building site. Zebulon sidled close to Mathias and Rebecca.

"Do you have it?" Mathias said under his breath.

Zebulon nodded.

"Excellent," Mathias said, barely able to contain himself. "I'll send a rider to Baltimore to tell Villefranche. He should be here in a few days."

Then Colonel Tayloe and Hoban joined them, and Zebulon said quickly, "I've just come from Philadelphia. They say that

President Washington deeply regrets not being able to attend the ceremonies."

"Aye, the commissioners pleaded with him to come, but he claimed pressing affairs of state," Hoban said.

"Well, things are tense in Philadelphia; the Barbary pirates are demanding more tribute, and England and France are at war again," Zebulon said.

Breech made a deprecating motion with his hand. "Nothing but excuses. You know the rumors as well as I. Washington is smarting under the charges that he's becoming too imperial a leader. Imagine Vice-President Adams insisting that Washington be called 'His Highness, the President'?"

"But Washington refused that, didn't he?" Zebulon said.

"Only because he preferred to be called 'His Mightiness the President'!" Breech exclaimed. "Everywhere, people are whispering that we've merely exchanged one George for another. So if Washington came today to dedicate the palace he'll one day occupy, you see how ill people would take it!"

"But the palace won't be completed for another eight years," Zebulon said. "Surely Washington will have stepped down by then."

Breech's hoarse laugh gave way to a paroxysm of coughing and spitting.

"Father, stop that," Rebecca said sharply.

Mathias Breech nodded his apologies to his daughter, then fixed Zebulon with his gimlet eyes. "Sometimes when you act like a young fool, I wonder why I ever got involved with you. Listen, if you had a chance to become emperor of this nation, would you step aside?"

Zebulon thought about that for a long moment. "That's a question none of us can answer. But we do have our new Constitution."

"A worthless piece of paper meant to force the states into giving up their rights so that one man might rule. Power, my lad—learn the lesson well!—once a man has it, he's loath to give it up."

Zebulon cocked his head and nodded. With all his simple ramblings, Breech was not so far wrong. The Federalists in the government, a group including Alexander Hamilton, John Adams, and Washington himself, believed in the rule of a monied and propertied aristocracy, a strong central government with the reins held tightly in its fist. Thomas Jefferson, on the other hand, the dreamer who believed in the perfectibility of every man, felt that if given the opportunity, men could govern themselves. And though Washington had tried to do everything possible to prevent the country from splitting into political factions, that was precisely what was happening, with Hamilton and Adams leading the Federalists, and Jefferson the titular head of a party called the Democratic-Republicans. Zebulon knew where his own sympathies lay; no matter which political party rose to power, he was determined to be on the winning side.

Jeremy rubbed his sore tailbone, chafing under the injustice being done him by Mathias Breech and his brother; and now he was angry with another man, James Hoban. One day I'll be as big as they, he thought, then we'll see. Then with the resilience and curiosity of youth, he forgot his own problems and concentrated on the fascinating dedication ceremonies.

The building site had once been the burial ground of the Pierce family; it was abutted on one side by the cornfields of Davey Burns, and on the other by the tobacco farm of Samuel Davidson. Members of two Masonic organizations, Lodge Nine from Georgetown and Lodge Twelve from Annapolis, formed a hollow rectangle, and the Grand Master, led by the Grand Swordbearer, marched through the file of men. They were followed by the three city commissioners, Thomas Johnson, Daniel Carroll, and David Stuart.

Solemnly, the Grand Master gave James Hoban the large silver cornerstone plate inscribed with the date, October 13, and the year of Masonry, 5792. Also on the plate were the names of the commissioners, President Washington, and James Hoban.

Jeremy stared wide-eyed, as the ground corn, wine, and oil were rubbed onto the plate, to the accompaniment of Masonic chanting. This was followed by a rifle volley from a hastily assembled group of farmers pressed into service as an honor guard, commanded by the one lone policeman of the entire ten-mile-square District of Columbia.

The minister then preached a short sermon and, at its conclusion, raised his eyes to heaven. "We are gathered here on this day in October, in the year of our Lord 1792, the three hundredth anniversary of Columbus's discovery of this land, to commence building this mansion, a mansion that will house the President of the United States and his family. And as this nation was conceived under God, with the proposition that all men are created equal, we do so invoke the Lord's blessings on this house. May it stand for the ages."

As soon as the ceremonies were over, everybody began hurrying off; the swarm of mosquitoes made it impossible to tarry. The carriages headed to the Fountain Inn in Georgetown, where a reception had been planned.

James Hoban approached Mathias Breech, who was busily gathering tools and equipment. "Clearly sir, you are ill pleased with your indentured servant," Hoban said.

"A lazier or more surly lad has yet to be born," Breech agreed with a shake of his head in Jeremy's direction.

"What would you take to let him go?" Hoban asked.

Breech's eyes shifted warily. Even as a lad, Jeremy was strong, and Breech knew he would grow stronger; there were many years of good service in him. "I wouldn't think of burdening you with such a lout," he said.

"I need someone who can fetch and carry for me, someone I can teach to draw," Hoban said, "and the lad's renderings are passable. I'll give you whatever you paid for him, plus a pound more."

Jeremy looked wildly from one man to the other. "I won't be sold like some dumb animal!"

"Be quiet, boy," Hoban said, then turned back to Breech. "You know that what I offer is more than fair."

Breech was caught in a trap of his own making. He wanted to keep the boy; having a ready outlet for his temper made things that much easier for him. But he couldn't afford to antagonize Hoban, not with the lucrative contracts he dispensed. That might cost Breech far more than the lad was worth.

Hoban saw the indecision on Breech's face. "It's settled then," he said. He called to Eli, one of the slaves hauling the blocks of stone to the site. "Leave be for now, Eli, and see to this boy."

Eli shrugged out of his rope harness and with his shackled

feet shuffled to Hoban. The slave was in his late teens, with the chiseled features, thin lips, and slanted eyes of the Masai people of East Africa. His throbbing muscles seemed carved in his ebony body.

Hoban shouted to Blutkopf, the foreman of the crew, "I have need of Eli until nightfall."

The German grunted, not at all pleased.

Then Hoban said to Eli, "See that this lad has a decent meal, then bed him down in the storeroom in my cabin. Most likely I'll be back by the time the sun sets." Hoban grasped Breech's elbow. "I'll have the boy's belongings picked up tomorrow, and we'll settle the paperwork then."

With an admonition to Jeremy to behave himself, Hoban rode off to the festivities in Georgetown. Mathias Breech followed shortly thereafter. Jeremy, his head spinning from this sudden turn, was left alone with Eli. Although exhilarated that Mathias Breech no longer owned him, he was also frightened of his new circumstance. But one thought and one thought only burned in his mind: he would throw off the shackles of any master, and make good his escape.

Chapter 2

JEREMY LOOKED around the clearing. Eli watched the boy as one might watch a bird about to take wing. "I know what's in your mind," he said suddenly. "To the north is Baltimore, but the road is well traveled. Across the river, that's Alexandria, but the currents be too swift for you. But even if you did manage to escape, they'd be after you with muskets and their dogs."

"They wouldn't waste their time with somebody like me," Jeremy said.

"Oh, it's not you," Eli said, shaking his head. "If the masters allow one person to escape, then there's hope for the rest of us. So every runaway got to be brought back, or killed."

"I'd sooner risk that than be known for a coward," Jeremy said, sticking out his chin.

Eli broke into a broad grin that showed his flashing white teeth. He opened his thin cotton shirt so that Jeremy could see the old whip scars. "Twice I ran away, and got this for my troubles. No, there's another way."

"How?" Jeremy asked, interest sparking his eyes.

"Ah, that I haven't yet found out," Eli lied.

"Who's your master?" Jeremy asked.

"A young man named Zebulon Brand. He was here today." When he saw Jeremy start, Eli asked, "Do you know him?"

Jeremy nodded. "He's my brother."

"He's not so bad as masters go," Eli said. "My owner before Zebulon was the one who whipped me. Zebulon rents me out to the work crew here for a right tidy weekly wage."

Now that the visitors had left, work resumed on the construction site, and the sound of hammer and chisel echoed across the clearing. "If you be working with Mr. Hoban, it's best you know about everything that's going on," Eli said and led Jeremy around the eighteen-acre site.

The basement of the President's Palace was being dug; other slaves in a bucket brigade were bailing out the groundwater that had collected through seepage and rainfall. In another area, a crew of Scotsmen worked their two-man saws, cutting the blocks of sandstone roughly to size. Farther on, Irish masons dressed the stone with their hammers and chisels, bringing the building blocks to their exact dimensions. German laborers cut lumber, and stoked the brick kilns that had been erected right on the grounds. Chickens and roosters pecked away at the pile of straw, and a goat walked nimbly atop the stacked lumber.

The air was filled with a polyglot of voices; most of the craftsmen had been imported from Europe. The new nation was still far too young to have produced artisans skilled enough to build such a sophisticated structure.

"Are you hungry?" Eli asked, and Jeremy nodded. The slave led Jeremy into the forest where woodcutters felled trees, clearing paths that would one day be the avenues of the new city. The carpet of leaves, humus, and moss cushioned the boys' footsteps as they trudged through the stands of alder and oak, maple and locust. They came to an intersection of another path and Eli pointed along its sight line.

"That's Jenkin's Hill," he said. "And when Major L'Enfant started planning this city, he saw that hill, and got all excited. He said it was like a pedestal awaiting a monument."

"How do you know that?" Jeremy asked dubiously.

"Why, Master Hoban told us. He keeps a notebook of everything done and said here. They're going to start work on the Capitol building next year."

They reached the bank of the Potowmack and saw a gang of about thirty slaves unloading the barges tied up at the wharves. Boats brought in huge blocks of Aquia sandstone from the quarries in Virginia, other barges carried clay and straw for making brick, and still others were stacked high with timber. The slaves chanted in rhythm as they worked, a low mournful murmur that echoed across the swamp from dawn to dusk.

Eli's face hardened as he listened to the lament. "Good enough only to do their dirty work," he said under his breath. "Try to learn something better and you get the back of their hand." Then he controlled himself. "What do you feel like eating?"

"I've some hardtack in my wallet," Jeremy said.

Eli snorted. With a wary eye out for snakes, he waded into the stands of rushes lining the riverbanks. Overhead, gull and tern dipped and swooped, fishing for the herring and shad in the teeming river. Eli gestured for Jeremy to be quiet, then picked up a rock. He stood motionless for a long moment while river trout ventured close to his shackled feet. But Eli had his eye on a flock of wild ducks that had just landed on the sun-sparkling waters. He watched until the current brought them closer, and then threw the rock. The flock rose with a cry of alarm, but one bird had been hit. As it floundered, Eli dove after it; he tripped on his shackles but managed to grab the duck. With a quick jerk, he wrung its neck. "Some day I'll do that to Blutkopf," he whispered.

Later, he and Jeremy sat around the campfire watching the duck broiling on the spit. Eli was favoring a foot that had been rubbed raw by the shackles, so Jeremy picked some leaves from a slippery elm. "Let me rub this on your ankles, it'll keep the irons from scraping too much."

"You shouldn't be doing this, touching a black man," Eli said, grabbing his hand. "If anybody saw you—"

Jeremy jerked his hand away. "You're right, I forgot." But then he thought for a moment and finished applying the leaves. "If you hadn't caught the duck, then I'd be going hungry. Come on, are we ready to eat?"

Eli carved a wing and breast from the bird and Jeremy ate hungrily. "Mathias Breech never allowed us such a feast," he said through a mouthful. "He thought that keeping his help just a little hungry would make us less able to rebel."

For a sweet, they gorged themselves on wild rosehips that Eli picked. Satisfied at last, Jeremy leaned back on his elbows and watched the sunset. The rays flared across the horizon, heightening the flame colors of the foliage.

"It could be a beautiful place," Jeremy murmured, "if only . . ."

"A man was free," Eli whispered, finishing Jeremy's thought.

"How is it that you're here?" Jeremy asked.

Eli stared beyond the river. He rarely talked about his past life, but clearly, this boy had a good heart. "I come from a land ruled by the Masai," he said softly. "A great warrior race, known for their bravery. We knew of the Arab slave traders, but they never dared invade our land. Those that did—well, they were never seen again."

As Eli talked, staring at the distant Virginia shore, Jeremy took a piece of wood from the fire and held it until the charred edge cooled. Unbeknownst to Eli, he began to make a series of rapid sketches on the smooth inside surface of a piece of bark.

"Within our own tribe there were warring factions," Eli said. "My father's clan supported a chieftain who lost. To prevent any further uprisings, our clan was taken to Mombasa and sold to the slave traders there. British ships then took us on an ocean voyage of many, many months, to a cold city where it rained all the time, a place called Liverpool. There my father died of rage. I was put on an American ship bound for Baltimore and sold on the slave block to a planter in Virginia. I was fifteen by then, and trying to escape, every chance I could. My master became so angry that he sold me to the first person who made him a reasonable offer. That was Zebulon."

Eli caught sight of the sketch Jeremy was drawing and snatched the piece of bark from him. His dark eyes opened as he saw his moods reflected in the drawings, the fine-bridged nose that flared wide at the nostrils, the sadness and determination caught in the set of his full mouth and eyes. "You have captured my spirit," he said, a trace of awe in his voice. He started to hand the sketches back.

"Keep them," Jeremy said, "they're for you."

Eli's eyes lit up. Then he jumped to his feet. "Come, I'll take you to Hoban's cabin."

Though Hoban had permanent lodgings in Georgetown, he'd built a tiny two-room shack near the construction site; to obtain whatever privacy possible, he made sure it was some distance from the other shacks housing the craftsmen. Hoban used the cabin when he worked late on the job, or if the weather prevented him from traveling to and from Georgetown.

Eli opened the wooden door. Jeremy looked around the tiny cabin furnished with the barest necessities; a deep fireplace for warmth and cooking meals, a crude table and two chairs, and a pallet that lay in the corner. The second room was smaller still and almost completely stacked with firewood. A bucket and a rush broom hung on pegs. Jeremy spied a window opening about two feet square that had been cut into the planking and covered with oiled paper; it kept out the drafts but let in the light. A cloth dipped in honey hung nearby to snare the ubiquitous mosquitoes.

"Small enough to cage a beast," Jeremy muttered, "but not me."

Eli shifted his weight from one foot to the other. He could be severely punished for becoming too familiar with a white person, even a boy, but his fear evaporated in the face of his curiosity. "And how do you come to be bound to Mathias Breech? He's got a mean temper, that one."

"My brother sold me as an indentured servant," Jeremy said glumly.

"Can such a thing be, one brother to sell another? Did you steal something?"

"I never!" Jeremy exclaimed hotly.

Eli waited patiently until Jeremy calmed down. Then the boy said, "It happened a year ago. Our father died of a lingering illness, mostly from wounds he took fighting at Yorktown with General Washington."

"I'm sorry to hear that," Eli said softly. "I know what it means to lose a father."

Jeremy nodded. "I didn't realize that until he was gone. He was a good man—stern, but fair, though he never had too much affection for me. Zebulon was always his favorite."

Eli looked at him inquisitively and Jeremy continued, "You see, my mother died when I was born, and though my father never said anything to my face, I think he blamed me. If I was late doing my farm chores, or didn't learn my lessons, he was forever telling me, 'You must make something of yourself so that your mother's death won't be in vain.'"

"You lived on a farm?" Eli asked. "Our tribe only raised cattle, and hunted lions."

"Really? Did you ever kill one?" Jeremy asked.

"I was sold before I came of hunting age. But one day I will kill something just as dangerous."

"What?"

Eli looked away. After a pause he said, "Tell me about your farm."

"It was small, less than twenty acres, but part of it fronted on Chesapeake Bay, and that was wonderful. Though Pa's health failed each year, he worked the land from sunrise to sunset. Zebulon and I helped as much as we could, though Zebulon never liked it much. His head was forever filled with schemes to make us all rich, so we could move to a big city like Baltimore, or Richmond."

"The two of you look so different," Eli said, "he as dark as night, and you as light as the day."

"We have the same father but different mothers," Jeremy explained. "Zebulon is Pa's son by his first wife. While Pa was off fighting in the War for Independence, Zebulon's mother was killed when the British raided the Chesapeake Bay, so he has no love for the English. Then some years later, my father met my mother . . . But like I said, Zebulon was always first in his eyes." Jeremy hung his head.

"He was everything I ever wanted to be. He could break a wild horse faster than anybody, he could catch the wind and win any sailing race. Everybody loved him, everybody. But none more than me."

Tears sprang to his eyes and he fought to control himself.

"But then why?" Eli asked.

Jeremy gulped and brushed his eyes angrily. "One day while Zebulon was off on one of his business dealings, my father had a seizure, coughing and gasping for breath. I rode all through the night to get the doctor and bring him back. He purged and bled Pa, but he weakened further and died." A dry tremor wracked Jeremy's thin frame and Eli touched his shoulder gently.

At last Jeremy controlled himself. "My brother and I didn't have much money; everything was sold to pay my father's debts. There wasn't even enough to give him a decent Christian burial. Then Zebulon said that the simplest way to solve it was for me to be let out as an indentured servant. A month or two at the most, he said."

Eli blinked. He couldn't understand why somebody would willingly sell himself into bondage. "You agreed to this?"

"He swore that he'd buy back my papers as soon as he had enough money. Besides, could I let my father be buried in a pauper's grave? Anyway, Zebulon was now my guardian, and he could do what he wanted. He took me to Breech because he'd had some earlier dealings with him. Then one night Breech got drunk and began yelling at me for something I'd done. He said that Zebulon had sold me for seven years! Seven years! I thought Breech was lying, just to make me more miserable."

"Yes, I've seen him do such things," Eli said. "That man has a meanness in him."

"When I confronted Zebulon this afternoon, he admitted that he'd lost all the money. But that I must be patient because he had a new scheme to make us all rich. Something about the capital. But I don't believe him. Now Hoban owns me and Zebulon will never buy me back, never."

He turned his head away but couldn't hide the tears that streamed down his face. His voice caught in his throat as he whispered, "What makes it worse is that I trusted Zebulon . . . I loved him."

Eli put his arm around Jeremy's shoulder and waited until he'd calmed down. Then he said, "We both be working here, so we'll get a chance to talk more, I know it. But now I best be going. It's getting on to dark, and Blutkopf, he uses his whip if he catches any slave out then."

Eli paused at the door. "A warning. Blutkopf collects a bounty on all runaways he brings back—alive or dead. So whatever you have in your mind to do, think twice." With a final wave, Eli left.

Jeremy waited until dark before he ventured out. When he did, Blutkopf's dog, a mastiff with a nail-studded collar, charged him, barking furiously. Jeremy just made it back to the cabin and slammed the door shut. He stood there, heart pounding, then began to wander around the two small rooms, trying to figure out a way to escape. Finally, the exhaustion of the day overcame him and he fell into a troubled sleep where he ran from snarling mastiffs and pursuing men, all of them with the face of his brother.

Chapter 3

IN THE reception room of the Fountain Inn, the festivities were in full swing. All the dignitaries who'd attended the cornerstone-laying ceremonies were there, and they'd been joined by many residents of Georgetown. Twenty toasts had been drunk: to the fifteen states—Kentucky and Vermont had recently joined the Union—to President George Washington, to Vice-President Adams, to Lafayette, to the fair daughters of America. As the afternoon sun arched toward twilight, it appeared that soon no one would be able to stand up. The rooms were paneled in light pine, with deep booths along the walls; signs were tacked on the exposed beams of the low-ceilinged room, warning, "DUCK OR BUMP."

Zebulon threaded his way through the boisterous crowd, with a ready word for the planters and merchants, a flashing smile for their wives and eligible daughters. He searched for Rebecca Breech and found her in a corner, her father hovering over her.

"Rebecca, I declare, every time I see you, you grow more beautiful."

Breech elbowed Zebulon in the ribs. "I don't want you hanging around her. Just stick to business. And this time your scheme better be good."

"You have a new enterprise?" Rebecca asked eagerly.

But Mathias Breech interrupted. "Come along now, Rebecca, it's time to leave." Mathias had consumed a prodigious amount of wine, and his teeth were stained a dull purple.

Rebecca slipped out of the booth and Zebulon managed to brush his arm against her. She smiled at him, her sweeping golden-tipped lashes framing eyes that looked like glowing topaz.

Zebulon leaned close to her. "I wish you'd stay."

"I wish I could," she said, sounding more like a schoolgirl than the young woman she was trying to be. "But father—well, he's in a foul temper because he had to sell your brother's indentureship to James Hoban."

Zebulon tensed and gripped the edge of the table. "Mathias, you promised you'd keep him for the full term!"

"I couldn't help myself," Breech said. "Hoban boxed me into it. If I hadn't agreed, he'd have canceled my contract."

Zebulon ground his fist into the tabletop. For some unknown reason he was overcome with a wave of misgiving. As long as Jeremy had been safely under Mathias's thumb, he hadn't concerned himself too much with him. But now . . . "What's this Hoban like? Do you think he's a decent master? After all, the boy is my brother."

Breech snorted. "A lot you care, or you wouldn't have sold him in the first place."

"It was the only way out of our dilemma. I wasn't about to spend the rest of my life as a dirt farmer, living and dying the way my father did."

As Mathias bulled his way out, Zebulon managed to grab Rebecca's hand and kissed it, letting his lips linger on her warm skin. "My evening is ruined," he murmured.

"Oh, I'm sure you'll find other things to amuse you," she said, her eyes flicking toward another part of the tavern.

Zebulon followed her gaze and then quickly turned away when he saw the distraught face of Elizabeth Connaught. Lord knows she was beautiful, desirable. But though Devroe Connaught might be unable to fulfill his conjugal obligations, he was still a crack shot with dueling pistols. I've got too much at stake now to be caught in the snare of love, Zebulon thought, especially of a love long gone.

Mathias Breech and Rebecca left and Zebulon sank into the booth, pondering the news about Jeremy. He felt a mixture of guilt and annoyance, but then he'd always had confused feelings about his brother. When Jeremy was very young, Zebulon had treated him somewhat like a puppy, roughhousing with him, and accepting the boy's adoration as his due. But the moment Jeremy began to exhibit a mind of his own, the moment their father's attitude softened toward the boy, then Zebulon saw him as a threat. Foolish to feel that way about a boy who could scarcely do him harm, yet it was true. Perhaps it was because he couldn't bear to be supplanted in the affections of his father, of anybody for that matter.

More wine, rum, and ale were consumed, the conversation grew louder, people talked about the ever-present dangers of a slave insurrection, about the new capital, and about land speculation. Then Devroe Connaught mentioned another piece of news that was so startling that the entire assembly paid close attention.

"The news just came up from Georgia, and they're claiming that this invention will absolutely change the fortunes of the South," Devroe said.

"Something better happen, and soon," said Colonel John Tayloe. The colonel grew cotton and tobacco, and bred the fastest racehorses in the South.

"You all know how long it takes a field nigger to pick the seeds out of a boll of cotton," Devroe continued. "A good slave can clean about a pound of cotton a day."

"Aye, and we lose money on the food and shelter we give our slaves," Davey Burns cut in. Burns, a burly Scotsman, had a reputation for speaking his mind. When President Washington once chastised him for refusing to sell his land to the government and thus standing in the way of progress, Burns had retorted, "Talk about progress—you'd still be a poor surveyor today if you hadn't a married the rich widow Custis!"

Devroe Connaught went on, "This man from Massachusetts, Eli Whitney, has invented a device, a cotton gin, he calls it. It's a simple wooden box with a hand-cranked cylinder studded with hooks. When you turn the cylinder, the hooks catch the cotton fibers and pull them through the narrow slots. The seeds can't pass through and fall to the bottom of the box. Any simple-minded slave can increase his production from one pound a day to close to fifty!"

A murmur of disbelief went through the tavern, but Devroe insisted it was true. "This machine may well save every one of us from ruin."

"Say what you will about those Northerners," Colonel Tayloe said, "from Benjamin Franklin to this Whitney, they do have a genius for invention."

"Do you realize what this will mean for our trade with England?" Devroe asked. "Their mills in Manchester and Bristol keep begging us for more cotton. Perhaps this will finally free us from the economic yoke of the North."

Zebulon chafed under the rising chatter. What did he care about some silly little box? He had far more important things on his mind. He'd spent every last cent he owned on the pieces of paper that lay folded in his breast pocket. But these documents could make his fortune. And in a matter of days. The excitement generated by that possibility coursed through his body, arousing him in a manner both painful and embarrassing.

From the corner of his eye he saw Elizabeth Connaught gesturing frantically at him, but he paid no mind. Pity, she'd once known how to bleed him of these humors, and the memory of their clandestine meetings aroused him even more. But what had begun as a pleasant dalliance had degenerated into a debilitating affair.

He'd met her originally at his first slave auction, where he'd sold her a scullery maid. Their attraction had been immediate. Days later, when he learned that her husband had ridden off to a tobacco auction in Virginia, he visited the Connaught plantation in the hills above Georgetown, ostensibly to see if Elizabeth was satisfied with her new slave. Victoria Connaught was there, as watchful as a jailer, but after her second mint julep, and the heat of the day, she'd dozed off.

Elizabeth quickly led him to a large closet, the imminent danger of discovery added an irresistible spur, and in the suffocating darkness he'd taken her. Elizabeth, full-blooded, was miserable with Devroe, and she and Zebulon made wild, irrational plans to run away. The danger mounted as they continued to meet secretly, when she visited her seamstress in Alexandria, when she paid a call on her doctor. They could never steal more than a few minutes; Devroe was as jealous as he was impotent, and kept a tight rein on his wife.

The fact that the entire Connaught family were British sympathizers gave Zebulon an added, if somewhat grim, satisfaction. For her part, Elizabeth was too consumed by her own needs to pay much attention to politics. Then Zebulon began to notice a certain "queerness" in her actions. He discovered that her erratic moods weren't an affectation, but the mirroring of a deeply troubled soul. Given to quixotic outbursts of tears and sloughs of despond, all for no apparent reason, her moods turned black indeed if Zebulon was unable to keep an assignation. Finally, her cloying ways had so soured him that he told her he was through, and that was when she threatened to kill herself. Devroe had somehow found out about it and delivered an ultimatum: Stay away from his wife or suffer the consequences.

Zebulon stretched and yawned. His journey from Philadelphia had left him bone weary, and he decided to call it a night. He climbed the narrow staircase to the top floor. He'd tried to rent a chamber where he wasn't forever bumping his head, but the innkeeper wouldn't extend him credit. All Zebulon owned in the world was his horse, his young slave Eli, and the clothes on his back, and those had been a gift from a grateful widow in Philadelphia to whom he'd brought much joy during his sojourn.

Zebulon took off his clothes and laid them neatly on the chair; he wanted them to look as fresh as possible for his meeting tomorrow. He flung himself across the bed, opened his wallet, took out the papers he'd brought from Philadelphia and studied them.

"By God, this will really do it," he exclaimed, and once more became aroused. He was still bemused, studying the papers, when minutes later the door swung open and Elizabeth Connaught slipped into the room. Her eyes looked oddly unfocused and a slight tic trembled her lip.

"Damn!" Zebulon started to get up but she threw herself on him.

"You must take me away! You promised," she cried. "I'm a prisoner in that house, I'll go mad!"

"You little fool, your husband's downstairs," he gasped, and thrust her from him.

"He doesn't know, he doesn't care," she said. "He's occupied in a game of billiards." Her consuming need gave her strength and she pressed against him, her fevered arms circling his naked waist.

Though some distant voice warned Zebulon of the madness of this, the memory of what they'd known overwhelmed him. And she was beautiful, the black hair and eyes, her full breasts and long shapely limbs. Then his body moved with a will of its own. Quickly, he had her out of her voluminous skirts, and then her chemise. Her endearments mingled with the coarse words he muttered in her ear, words that shamed her, but also made her more impassioned. She responded like some wild thing, biting every part of his body, leaving red welts on his chest, stomach, and thighs.

With a hoarse cry he coupled with her, her body stiffened and her eyes closed as he entered, and soon they were in a tangle of arms and legs, moving swiftly, building, and when she thought she'd go mad with the ecstasy, Zebulon stopped, and with a deft motion flipped her over and mounted her as his stallion would a mare. He clapped his hand over her mouth lest her moanings be heard in the inn, and all the while the danger made their lovemaking that much more fierce. Then came the moment when Zebulon also lost control and they flowed one into the other in a hoarse muffled scream.

She lay curled on her side, eyes closed, body lightly bathed in sweat, her fingers raking the patchwork quilt. Then reason returned and she sprang out of bed and began to dress.

She looked in the cupboard mirror and hastily rearranged her hair. She dipped a cloth in the pitcher of water and applied the compress to her face, hoping to bring down the color in her cheeks. As he led her to the door she said, "When will I see you again?"

"Never," he said.

She reacted as if he'd slapped her.

"I told you last time. You no longer please me."

Her laugh sounded like something between a challenge and a gasp, and then she whirled and clawed at his face. He parried her second blow, then thrust her reticule into her hands and pushed her out the door.

Voices from the tavern floated up to them and she thought she heard her husband calling for her. Distracted, she didn't fight when Zebulon grabbed her arms and propelled her toward the stairs.

"We shall see who has the last word on this," she whispered, the hatred patent in her eyes.

Chapter 4

TWO DAYS later, Zebulon got word that Mathias Breech's business associate had arrived and he mounted his horse and cantered through the streets of Georgetown. The main thoroughfare was lined on both sides with solid brick houses, and more were going up every year, further evidence of the small seaport's prosperity. Georgetown's only nearby competition came from Alexandria, which lay across the Potowmack in Virginia; with the new capital about to be built less than two miles away, the future of both ports seemed bright indeed. Wagons loaded with tobacco, cotton, and timber rumbled through the rutted streets down to the wharves, where tall-masted ships waited to take their cargo to Europe.

Zebulon reined up at the Breech house, a substantial brick building in the Georgian style with white pediments over the white shuttered windows and a cranberry-glass fanlight crowning the oaken door. Mathias Breech's late wife, Suzannah, had been a woman of some refinement, and she'd insisted on these architectural details because she'd read that the finest houses in Baltimore and Philadelphia were built this way.

Letitia, a thin dark-skinned house slave, answered Zebulon's knock and led him through the wide foyer to the drawing room. He smiled when he saw Rebecca sitting before the crackling fireplace. She looked angelic in a bleached muslin afternoon gown with a demure neckline and long sleeves caught at the wrist with beige ribbons.

Mathias Breech paced back and forth across the polished oaken floor in a state of dyspeptic agitation. "Our man will be down shortly," he said. "Claims he has to refresh himself after the trip from Baltimore."

"Will you have tea?" Rebecca asked Zebulon.

He nodded and watched her as she served. There wasn't the slightest unsureness in her movements.

When Mrs. Breech died the previous year, Mathias pressed Rebecca into service as his hostess. Rebecca had adored her ailing titmouse of a mother and railed against the abuse she suffered from Mathias.

"Mother, how can you let him treat you that way?" she'd demanded. "I hear what happens when he comes home drunk night after night, and treats you like—like you were some animal!"

Suzannah Breech blushed furiously and murmured, "But my dear, that's the lot of a wife, that's our cross."

"It doesn't have to be," Rebecca insisted. "Where's the justice in it? You were the one that started father in his business. It was your dowry, your inheritance, your property, and you had to give it all up the moment you married him."

Suzannah winced and passed her hand wearily across her abdomen. "But my dear child, that's the law, and women have no recourse." Then she managed a smile. "And I would do it all again, my heart, because it brought me you."

Rebecca flung herself at her mother and embraced her fiercely.

"Don't judge your father too harshly," Suzannah murmured. "He's more unthinking than unkind, and he does love you more than anything in the world."

Rebecca knew that was true. And indeed her father proved to be compassion itself when her mother finally succumbed to the growth in her stomach. Rebecca cried, cried until she'd no more tears left, then cried from some hidden wellspring for the cruel fate of simply being born a woman.

But her tears also hardened her resolve that she would never allow herself to be treated that way by a man. The fear of such a fate, and her resolve, lived side by side deep within her.

Rebecca passed the teacup to Zebulon, who grasped her fingers as they both held the saucer. "Careful," she said, "you're liable to burn yourself."

"I'll risk it," he said with a smile that brought out his dimples.

"Ah, here he is now," Mathias Breech said as Audubert Villefranche entered the room.

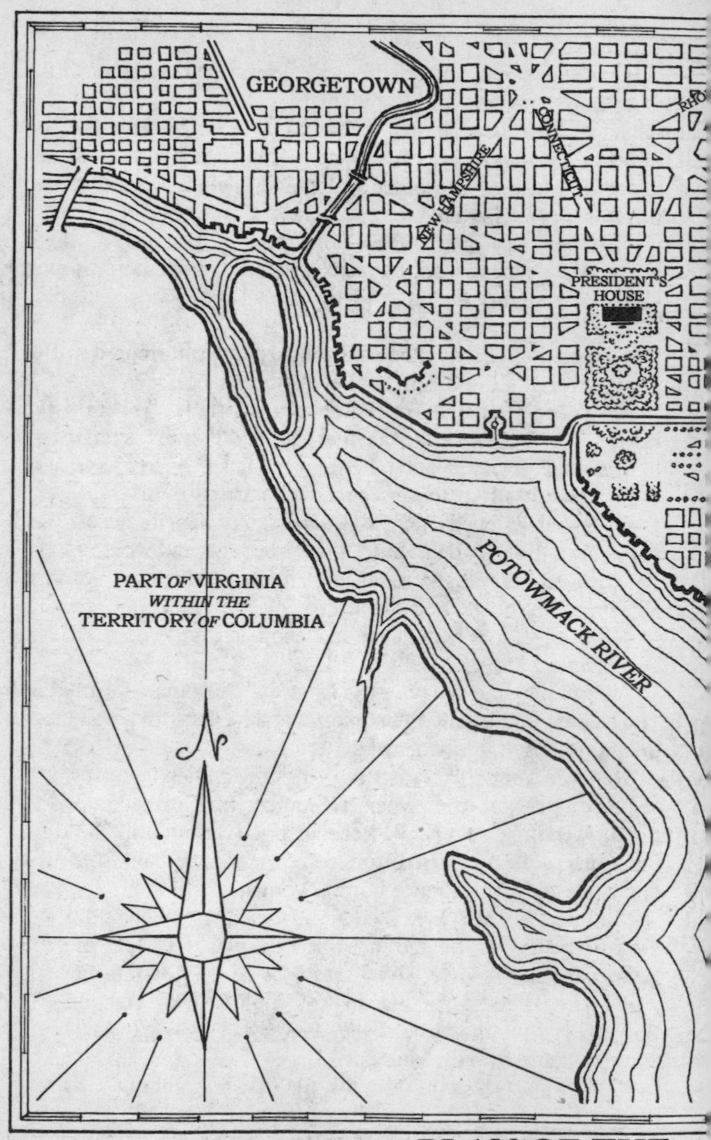
GEORGETOWN
NEW HAMPSHIRE
CONNECTICUT
PRESIDENT'S HOUSE
POTOWMACK RIVER
PART OF VIRGINIA
WITHIN THE
TERRITORY OF COLUMBIA

PLAN OF THE

FEDERAL CITY

Zebulon was taken aback by the foppish Frenchman in his late thirties, who drifted into the study on a heavy cloud of ambergris perfume. Villefranche gazed over the tidy study, appraising the firemark on the china, the hallmark on the crude colonial silverware, finding it all wanting, but nevertheless adding it up in his abacus mind. Chronic adenoids gave his voice a piping quality. He regarded Zebulon from beneath heavy-lidded eyes and then yawned with stultifying boredom.

Mathias Breech turned to his daughter. "Rebecca, I think it's best that you left us now."

The corners of Rebecca's mouth turned down in a pout, but Mathias insisted and closed the door after her. Breech poured them all a round of port, then said gruffly, "Well, Zebulon, what do you have?"

Zebulon took a gulp of the wine for courage. "Gentlemen, what I'm about to show you can make us all very rich." He took the papers from his wallet and laid them out on the refectory table.

"*Alors*, what is this?" Villefranche asked.

"A map of the proposed layout of Federal City, our new capital," Zebulon said.

Breech leaned forward, trying not to show his excitement. "Is it authentic?"

"Absolutely," Zebulon said. "This is Ellicott's rendering of the plan drawn after Pierre L'Enfant's original concept."

"Major L'Enfant?" Villefranche asked. "But I have made his acquaintance in Philadelphia. He is a madman!"

"Perhaps, but he's also a genius," Zebulon said. "President Washington himself chose him to design our new capital."

Major Pierre L'Enfant, an inspired, volatile Frenchman, had been profoundly influenced by his times. His design was of a heroic city of princely vistas and grand radial avenues superimposed on a grid of streets. His entire geometric plan reaffirmed the rational humanistic concept of an ordered world so prevalent in the courts and universities in Europe. Though such a city might cost untold millions to build, L'Enfant would settle for nothing less than his vision.

Villefranche slapped his white leather gloves against his puce breeches. "But I have seen this L'Enfant stalking the streets of Philadelphia, looking as grim as Death and Famine,

Pestilence and Plague. He excoriates President Washington with his every breath."

Zebulon nodded. "They had a falling out last year. Like many a genius, L'Enfant was also erratic; when he started to lay out Pennsylvania Avenue, from the site of the proposed President's Palace to that of the Capitol Building, a farmhouse happened to be in his line of vision, and so he ordered it demolished. Finally he became so erratic that President Washington had to dismiss him, and appointed Andrew Ellicott in his place. Only half a dozen of these plans were printed, showing where the government buildings might be located."

Breech took a magnifying glass from his waistcoat pocket and inspected the map. Streets and lots were numbered. It looked authentic; he'd tried for months to get hold of one of these maps, but they'd been withheld from the general populace for fear of speculation. "How did you come by it?" he asked.

"With great difficulty and even greater expense," Zebulon said evenly. He thought it best not to brag about his coup. Some weeks before, he'd journeyed to Philadelphia for just this purpose. He went to the company printing the maps, Thakara and Vallance, where he met and cultivated the apprentice, an impressionable youth who was flattered by his attention. One night, after a particularly heavy drinking bout, he persuaded the young man to enter the shop and run off a map from the engraver's plates, and then paid him handsomely for the pirated copy.

"To business then," Breech said. "What are you asking for this?"

Zebulon covered the map with a blank sheet of paper. "It's not for salc."

Breech sat back hard in his chair and Villefranche exclaimed, "*Zut!* Why then have I come all these miles to this forsaken place?" He rose to leave, but Zebulon stayed him.

"I propose a syndicate," Zebulon said. "An equal partnership among the three of us. All we need do is buy up certain choice parcels—for example, where public buildings are proposed—and we can make a killing."

Villefranche pulled a lace handkerchief from the cuff of his silk shirt and dabbed at his long nose. "These plans, they remind me somewhat of Versailles."

"It was laid out to approximate Paris, but on a grander scale," Zebulon said.

Villefranche looked at him as if he were mad. "This wilderness? How will it ever become a city?" Villefranche had been a favorite at Marie Antoinette's court, and had just escaped the revolution with his head, and his wife's jewelry. Selling a few pieces at a time, he'd managed to establish himself in the New World, but dreamed only of returning to Paris as soon as the bourgeois madness was over.

"A city will grow here if President Washington has anything to say about it." Zebulon said, feeling his blood rise at Villefranche's condescending attitude.

"Ah, yes, your Washington," Villefranche said. "One cannot understand why he chose this godforsaken place at all. My clothes, my bedding, everything has been damp with swamp fog since I arrived. I have been in your New York, and even Philadelphia; provincial, compared to Paris, but then what city is not? But at least Philadelphia has sidewalks, a water system, the barest amenities of civilization, though I did have to flee for my life when the yellow fever plague struck. But this place—*quelle horreur!* Nothing but wild animals and wild red people. Why not build your capital in a city already established, rather than in a swamp?"

For half a pence Zebulon would have smashed the Frenchman's face, but he needed Villefranche's funds. And much as Zebulon hated to admit it, the man was not as much a fool as he seemed. He would bear watching.

"Then there is the question of your government's stability," Villefranche continued. "Most of the civilized countries believe that it will never last."

"What rot!" Zebulon exclaimed. "Our country's never been stronger. We've even adopted a sound Constitution."

"Constitution?" Villefranche repeated with a deprecating shrug. "A mere piece of paper. But over what does your government rule? I have studied your 1790 census. You have a population of only four million, which includes six hundred and forty thousand slaves, and sixty thousand free Negroes. You manufacture very little; the basic livelihood is eked out from dirt farming. And rumor has it that the cost of your War for Independence, a hundred million dollars, was so staggering that you will never be out of debt. So how will you get anybody to invest in a penniless nation?"

While Breech and Villefranche argued the feasibility of the plan, Zebulon reflected on the events that had made all this come to pass.

Immediately after the Revolutionary War, the burning issue had been whether the federal government should assume the individual states' remaining war debts, a staggering sum of twenty million dollars. The North, having for the most part financed the war, wanted the government to do just that, and their cause was pressed by the secretary of the treasury, Alexander Hamilton. The South, whose spokesman was Thomas Jefferson, the secretary of state, strenuously opposed this, and the growing schism threatened to tear the young nation apart.

Jefferson and Hamilton were bitter rivals, yet both wished to preserve the Union, and one night over dinner in New York, the two men struck a hard bargain. Jefferson agreed to use his influence to have the South support the federal government's assumption of the debt—provided that the nation's new capital was located in the South. Hamilton detested that idea, but he knew it was imperative that the country be put on a sound financial footing. Grudgingly he agreed to Jefferson's proposal.

In order that no one state have legal jurisdiction over the capital, a ten-mile square of land was carved out of Maryland and Virginia. And so the capital city destined to become the most political city in the world came about at its very outset from a political compromise.

Aided by another bottle of port, Breech managed to persuade a reluctant Villefranche of the soundness of Zebulon's plan. After considerably more wrangling, the three men shook hands. For their end, Breech and Villefranche would put up the money necessary to buy the land; Zebulon would purchase the lots he thought most valuable and hold them for resale at inflated prices.

"In which direction do you believe your capital will grow?" Villefranche asked.

Zebulon uncovered the map. "The area around the Capitol Building, to be sure, and certainly the lots on the riverfront."

Villefranche studied the map with his lorgnette. "Where are the falls of your Potowmack River?"

Zebulon pointed to an area about five miles upriver. "Just about here," he said.

"Then that is where your capital should have been built, above the falls. Any competent military commander knows that. Why build directly on the coast within gun range of an enemy fleet?"

Breech broke into a slow, sly grin. "Ah, but you see, Frenchman, our esteemed President owns a great deal of land right here. Why, he even runs the ferry service across the Potowmack to Alexandria. Do you get my meaning?"

"Bien sur," Villefranche said. "One can be President and a good businessman also, *non?"*

Zebulon sprang to his feet. "That's a damned lie! There's not a more honest man on the entire continent."

Zebulon had grown up with George Washington as his boyhood hero. He was nine years old when he saw his mother killed as she tried to defend their farm against British soldiers marauding for food. His father was away, bivouacked with General Washington at Yorktown, where a combined force of sixteen thousand American and French soldiers, supported by the French fleet, had surrounded General Cornwallis and his army of eight thousand.

Stunned by his mother's death, Zebulon loaded his small skiff with hardtack and water and sailed more than a hundred miles down the Chesapeake Bay to the Yorktown peninsula to tell his father the tragic news. There he was met with more bad news, for he found his father lying wounded in a crude field hospital, with bullets in his leg and chest. But he was alive, thank the Lord, and several days later there was cause for further jubilation when Cornwallis surrendered. "We've seen the last of this terrible war," his father had whispered, tears in his eyes.

General Washington had commandeered a horse and wagon for Zebulon and he drove his father home, a rough journey over almost nonexistent roads. He was filled with pride that he had gotten his father safely home. But within a month, Zebulon's world was shaken when his father married again—"More to have somebody take care of him than anything else," Zebulon tried to convince himself. But coming so soon after the death of his own mother, having a stepmother rankled him.

He had little use for this poor frail girl from New York who'd met his father while visiting some distant relatives on the Chesapeake, and he shed few tears when she died shortly after giving birth prematurely. The baby, Jeremy, was taken in by the wife of a local farmer.

During those early years, before Jeremy was old enough to live with them, and they had no one but each other, Zebulon and his father couldn't have been closer. They spent long evenings in front of the fire, always talking of the great event in their lives, the War for Independence. The elder Brand filled his son's head with tales about George Washington's valor until the general assumed the proportions of a mythic hero.

Zebulon pointed his finger at Villefranche. "President Washington believes that this city can become not only our capital but a flourishing seaport as well, and that's why it must be built on the tidal estuary. Of all the Atlantic seaports, this site offers the best access to the Ohio valley and to the west."

Villefranche sighed and stood up. "Well, men will always find reasons to support their own interests. And one day, you may all come to regret your President's choice."

Chapter 5

ZEBULON LEFT the Breech house in a euphoric mood. He planned to ride to Federal City right then and survey the land. He went to the carriage house and unhitched his horse. He'd seen the spirited black stallion at the racetrack auction a year ago last November, and though he could ill afford him, bought him when he learned the stallion's name: Baal. "I've always wanted to ride the devil," he said, stroking the white flash on the horse's jet-black muzzle.

A noise at the second-story window caught his attention. He looked up and saw Rebecca. She was undressing . . . He held his breath when he saw her naked arms and the swell of her budding breasts. He stood motionless as she slipped out of her skirts. And though the window sill was too high for him to see, he imagined her narrow waist, the flawless skin, the mound of Venus for which he would have sold his soul.

Despite the chance that Mathias Breech might overhear him, Zebulon called up to her. But she made no sign of having heard him. She moved to the window, paused, then slowly closed the shutters.

"She did hear me," Zebulon said under his breath. "The vixen will drive me wild. But I shall have her, I swear. And what's more, I'll do it before any other man's been there."

Wheeling Baal, he gave the stallion his head. Once outside Georgetown, Zebulon galloped along the road to Federal City. Behind him, the huge ball of the sun slowly slipped below the horizon. He was so preoccupied that he hardly noticed the black carriage that he passed on the road. Two men sat inside the carriage; between them were a maddened woman and a child.

Devroe and Elizabeth Connaught had been out riding with their daughter, Marianne, and their nephew Sean, when they'd seen Zebulon gallop by. "There goes the blackguard, without a care in the world," Devroe said.

Sean's hand tightened on the reins and said softly, "Is he to go unpunished?"

Elizabeth's hand flew to her mouth. "Oh, Devroe, please, he means nothing to me. Drive on, I beg you."

"Can you deny that Sean saw you coming down from the servants' quarters in the Fountain Inn?" Devroe spat. "And Zebulon Brand had a room up there."

"Devroe, I swear, I'll never see him again. Now let's go from here or something terrible will happen."

"To him, you may be sure," Devroe said.

Elizabeth's glance darted from her husband to her daughter. "Devroe, for the sake of all that's holy, not in front of the child."

Devroe looked at Marianne, huddled frightened against her mother. He hesitated, but Sean cut in, "In England, a gentleman believes it his sacred duty to demand satisfaction when his wife—for his wife's honor. But then of course this is America, where any manner of behavior is condoned."

"Sean, how can you?" Elizabeth whispered.

Sean regarded her levelly. "How could *you?*"

The blood began to pulse in Devroe's temples and he set his jaw. He drew his pistols from his belt and checked them.

"Oh, no," Elizabeth moaned and reached for his guns, but he knocked her hand aside.

"After him, Sean," Devroe said. "It's time that Zebulon Brand learned that he cannot defame a Connaught."

Little Marianne, distressed by the shouting, began to cry, and Devroe said, "Be quiet, child."

As Sean whipped the horses after Zebulon, Elizabeth's face lost all its color; she crushed her daughter to her and sank back into the cushions.

A quarter of a mile ahead, with the rushing wind in his ears, Zebulon galloped on, unaware of the pursuing carriage.

Baal was in a lather when Zebulon pulled up at the construction site. Work had stopped for the day and he saw the slaves lined up in the field kitchen. He caught a glimpse of Eli—a fine young buck; soon it would be time to buy him a mate.

Zebulon checked the map for strategic lots; those that he knew to be swampy or underwater he dismissed out of hand. He turned Baal onto the path that led to the river's edge. Tree stumps and exposed roots made the roadway hazardous, and he allowed the stallion to pick his way.

When Zebulon reached the riverfront, he heard the carriage thundering up behind him, the horses at full gallop. Turning, he saw the carriage sway and lurch, threatening to overturn with every bump as it came straight at him.

Suddenly Zebulon saw Devroe Connaught lean out the carriage window, a pistol in his hand.

"God!" Zebulon swore, and dug his spurs into Baal's flank. The stallion reared and bolted, tail and mane flying. After his instant of fright, Zebulon became exhilarated by the chase. "The fools!" he cried in Baal's ear, "do they think they can catch us?"

Zebulon bent low over the stallion's neck as he hurdled a fallen treetrunk. Just when it seemed that they would shake their pursuers, Baal shied and reared. Caught unprepared, Zebulon was thrown from the saddle and landed in a stand of rushes. The carriage was on him in a moment.

Lying in the mud, Zebulon saw Devroe Connaught leap from the carriage and wade after him. Zebulon got to his feet and discovered he'd wrenched his leg. "I've come without my pistol," he said desperately. Ducking low, he circled the rushes, slogging through the fetid muck that sucked at his feet, the strange swamp smell sharp in his nostrils. If he could outdistance Devroe, get to where Baal was standing . . . But then he saw young Sean Connaught blocking the way, a pistol in his hand. Zebulon turned and backtracked.

He heard a rustle, then saw what had made Baal shy. About ten feet to the left lay a nest of copperheads; disturbed by the trespassers, they coiled and writhed in agitation. With a cry, Zebulon stumbled on, and came face to face with Devroe Connaught, pistols in both hands.

From where he stood, Devroe couldn't see the snakes. But from the rise of the road, Elizabeth saw the writhing mass of vipers. She cried out, "Devroe! Behind you, watch out!" but he paid no attention to her.

"No place left to run," Devroe said to Zebulon.

"Look, Devroe, we can settle this like gentlemen," Zebulon said, his eyes sliding from the pistols to the nest.

Devroe laughed harshly. "Gentlemen? Why, you don't know the meaning of the word. I've sent my seconds to you twice, demanding satisfaction, but each time you've made yourself scarce."

Terrified beyond reason, Zebulon scrambled for a way out. "Think, Devroe! Do you want the blood of another man on your hands?"

"Save your breath for your prayers," Devroe said.

Zebulon raised his hand in a gesture of supplication, then brought it down in a hard chop on Devroe's arm just as he fired. Zebulon felt a searing pain in his shoulder as the ball passed through his flesh. He fell to his knees, which saved his life, for Devroe's second shot whistled over his head. Devroe started to reload.

Gritting his teeth, Zebulon dove for the older man's legs and caught him off balance. The force of the charge knocked Devroe backwards and he fell, landing close to the copperheads. His face twisted in a scream as the snakes attacked, striking again and again. His body jerked convulsively and then he rolled over, his face turned toward the sky ablaze with last light, the fire-reds and oranges turning the waters into a river of flame.

Sean rushed to pull his uncle away, but couldn't get near him. Zebulon lurched toward his horse, blood staining his shirt and running in rivulets down his arm. He hoisted himself into the saddle. He galloped past the carriage where Elizabeth sat, the flaming world reflected in her eyes while little Marianne screamed unendingly, "Mother, what happened? Mother!"

Elizabeth's gaze turned inward to a place that no one would ever reach again. As she watched Zebulon gallop into the flaming horizon she whispered, "The fire has eaten tomorrow."

And then Zebulon was gone, leaving the wreckage of the Connaught family behind him.

Chapter 6

UNEXPECTED BUSINESS dealings kept James Hoban away from the construction site of the American Palace for two days, and during that time Jeremy never gave up searching for a way to escape. But he never got the chance for Blutkopf was always watching him. The young slave Eli had returned to his labors, and outside of a few snatched moments, Jeremy saw little of him.

Late on the third night, Hoban did return and he poked his head into Jeremy's room. "Are you awake, lad? I have some news for you."

To throw Hoban off guard, Jeremy feigned sleep. Tonight he was determined that he would escape.

Jeremy marked the passage of the hours as the moon moved across the sky. Taking his courage in his hands, he climbed out the window and dropped to the ground. A twig snapped and he froze, waiting for the alarm, but he heard nothing. Edging stealthily from the cabin, he got halfway across the clearing when strong hands grabbed him from behind and swept him off his feet.

"Let me go!" he shouted, as he kicked and punched. Blutkopf carried him back to Hoban's cabin and thrust him into the room. Hoban leapt out of bed and lit a candle.

"I knew the little thief would try it," Blutkopf grunted.

Blutkopf had been imported from Westphalia to work on the President's Palace, but not a day passed that he didn't regret leaving the motherland. Now he worked to save enough money for passage back home. "I get the reward for a runaway, yes?" he asked in his heavily accented English.

"I'll see you get what's owed you in the morning," Hoban said.

Blutkopf hesitated, but at a look from Hoban he left. Then Hoban confronted Jeremy. "Why?"

Jeremy knotted his fists. "God didn't mean me to be traded like some dumb animal."

"Come now, will you attack me like you did your brother, and for no reason?" Hoban asked.

"Before God, I had reason," Jeremy said.

Under Hoban's gentle urgings, Jeremy told him the circumstances surrounding his indentureship. Hoban sat listening in his nightshirt, and when Jeremy was finished, he shook his head slowly. "I don't know why it should be so, but since Cain and Abel, brothers have been at each other's throats."

He stood and paced the narrow confines of the room. "An uncomfortable story," he said, "and worse luck that you fell into the hands of Breech. And so I begin to understand . . . it's the yoke of an indentured servant that's making you so rebellious."

Boy and man looked at each other, and the faintest glimmer of respect passed between the two. "Think hard on what I'm about to tell you," Hoban said. "It seems to me that you have two choices, and whatever you decide this night may well determine the course of the rest of your days."

Hoban led Jeremy to the door and pointed to the moonlit clearing. Ground fog swirled and eddied in the preternatural light. When Hoban spoke, he seemed to conjure images out of the mists. "You see, lad, we're building something here meant to stand for the ages. A city built on a scale so grand that it's meant to make men aspire, to transform them from what they are, to what they could be. A city where the eye will rejoice, and the spirit grow. And its crowning glory will be the President's Palace. A house . . . yet more than a house, for it will be the dwelling of the one man elected by all the people. So in the most profound way, it will belong to all of us, to every American. Jeremy, this is something unknown in all the history of the world! An experiment so noble in design, that I cannot help but believe that God wills it. And this house will be its everlasting symbol."

Jeremy heard the emotion in Hoban's voice, but all the

while he was wondering if he dared make a break for freedom. The moon scudded behind the cloud cover . . . the forest lay about fifty yards away . . .

"You can become part of this noble experiment," Hoban continued, "learn a profession that will serve you for the rest of your life. That drawing you sketched of my design—It was good, very good for one so young. Where did you get your training?"

"No place, sir," Jeremy said. "I've been drawing things since I can remember—birds, houses, animals, sometimes people, though they're a little harder to get right."

"I may be able to help you with that," Hoban said. He sighed and rubbed his hands against the chill. "When I was your age, struggling in Ireland, I was just as surly and ill-tempered as you, though doubtless you have more cause. But many people helped me on my path, and so I swore to Saint Joseph, the patron saint of builders, that I would return that gift when I could. Jeremy, it's up to you to make your own destiny come to pass, no matter what your circumstances. Only you can determine if the cup of your life is half empty, or half full."

When Jeremy didn't answer, Hoban said, "Your other choice is to seek your fortune elsewhere, perhaps make good, perhaps fall into the life of a wastrel and vagabond with trust in nothing and no one. In either case, Jeremy Brand, this morning I secured your indentureship papers from Mathias Breech. And whichever path you choose, I give you your freedom."

Hoban went to the cupboard, took out the papers and handed them to him. "I meant to give you these this evening, but you were asleep. Now you and I, as free and honest men, can strike a bargain," Hoban said. "I'll pay you a daily wage of two shillings, six pence, until you've served the remainder of your term. Let's see, you've six more years to go, and by then you will be sixteen; we can come to new terms then. What do you say, lad?"

Jeremy hardly heard him; he stared at the papers in his hand, not daring to believe this was happening. What he'd dreamed of these long months . . . with a strangled cry he bolted from the cabin and rushed into the forest.

Blutkopf started after him, but Hoban yelled, "Let the boy go! He's free!"

Brambles tore at Jeremy's clothes as he ran, the papers clutched in a death grip in his fist, fleeing before Hoban could change his mind, or before he'd waken and find it had been a terrible nightmare. The exposed root of a weeping willow tripped him and he fell, landing in a thornberry bush. He listened for sounds of pursuit, but heard only the thumping of his heart. Perhaps it was the distant baying of a hungry wolf, or the memory of the kindness in Hoban's eyes that made him stop.

"And where would you run to?" he whispered. "Back to Zebulon?" His brother would doubtless try to sell him again. No, he could never trust his brother again.

". . . We're building something here meant to stand for the ages." Jeremy repeated Hoban's words. "A house that will belong to all of us, to every American."

Jeremy picked himself up from the brambles and slowly headed back to the cabin. When he entered, he found Hoban sitting at the trestle table, lost in contemplation.

Jeremy cleared his throat. "Sir, if you'll still have me, I will work for you."

Hoban broke into a smile. "Excellent, excellent. There's so much to do, so much I've planned for tomorrow. But now, both of us had better get a good night's rest. You see, we don't have too much time. The President's Palace and much of Federal City itself must be ready by December 1, 1800. And that's only eight years away!"

Chapter 7

JEREMY BRAND worked for James Hoban as he'd never worked for Mathias Breech, eagerly and with spirit. In a short time, Hoban couldn't imagine how he'd gotten along without the boy, for freedom had allowed Jeremy to follow his natural bent, to work, build, create.

Everything he needed to learn, Jeremy learned on the job, learned the actualities of building, as well as the book theories. After a day's work, he'd spend his evenings in the loft, poring over Hoban's wonderful books of architecture and drawing, reading until his eyes grew heavy with sleep.

He developed his gift for sketching, and could soon render a building as readily as the wildlife that abounded on the shores of the Potowmack. He learned to catch the despair in the eyes of Eli and the other slaves as they hauled materials to the building site, and sometimes, even a glimmer of revolt. He learned to reveal the gluttony in Mathias Breech's jowled face. But most of all, he drew and redrew Rebecca Breech, hoping to capture her mystery. She would often accompany her father to the site of the palace—the Palace in the Forest, the farmers called it—yet whenever Jeremy saw her, he always found his previous drawings lacking, for with each day she grew more radiant in his eyes.

Autumn gave way with a melancholy rush to a winter of biting winds and swirling blizzards. Work on the President's Palace all but ceased. Behind closed doors and before the safety of their fireplaces, the citizens of Georgetown and Alexandria, and even towns as far away as Bladensburg, whispered of the tragedy that had befallen the Connaughts. Elizabeth dressed only in black, never left her bedroom in the plantation house.

Her face remained impassive, as though time had stopped for her on the day of Devroe's death. The house servants drew the curtains before twilight, for if she saw the sunset, she would begin to scream uncontrollably.

The courts acquitted Zebulon of any complicity in Devroe's death, ruling that it had been accidental. Outraged, Sean Connaught made a number of futile attempts on Zebulon's life, and was finally banished from the territory on pain of imprisonment.

On the day he was to sail back to England, Sean and his Aunt Victoria stood on the wharf at Georgetown. The docks bustled with activity, flatboats coming in with building materials for the President's Palace, sailors singing sea chanties as they climbed high into the rigging preparing to unfurl the sails.

"Though I leave here without satisfaction, rest assured that I shall have my revenge," Sean said. "Not only against Zebulon Brand, but against this entire nation of thieves, misfits, and murderers, the outcasts of Europe!"

Victoria heaved a sigh. Her brother's death had devastated her. "If only we could do something to bring *English* justice to this savage land," she said.

"We can."

"What?" she asked, suddenly alert.

Sean hesitated, debating whether or not to say anything. Though he'd taken an oath, his frustration over Zebulon made him indiscreet. Besides, he felt that it would be too cruel to leave his aunt without a ray of hope. "I haven't told you this before, because I don't know if it will come to pass," he said to her. "Even if it does, it will be highly secret. Can I count on you to keep a confidence?"

Sean's solemn tone piqued Victoria's curiosity. She placed her hand on her bosom. "I swear on the memory of my brother."

He glanced around. Satisfied that no one could overhear them, he said quietly, "You know that when I return to England I go immediately into the service of His Majesty's Royal Navy."

She bobbed her head.

"And as we've discussed many times, Great Britain is determined to bring these colonies back into the Empire."

"It's the dream of every rational human being in the

country," she said. "Less than half the population supported the rebellion, and even now most would prefer the benefits and protection that the Empire offers."

"Well, the admiralty has approached me for service in one of their special branches," Sean said. "Intelligence. Gathering information and the like."

"But that sounds so dreadfully dangerous," she said.

"What isn't dangerous these days?" he said. "When I had my first interview they told me I was a prime candidate for this branch because of my family connections in the United States, and because of our unquestioned loyalty to the crown. I didn't commit myself then, but with all that's happened here..." Sean's slate-colored eyes narrowed and his lips thinned, giving his sharp face a feral quality. "If I can do anything to hasten the destruction of this bastard country, put down the seeds of rebellion...England is the bastion of civilization in our world, and we must do anything we can to strengthen it. Do you agree?"

"I would consider it an honor to do what I could for such a cause."

"It may be some years before this operation is put in motion. These complex situations take time. And of course the war with France comes first."

"But of course," she agreed. "When you're ready, Sean, all you need do is command. You can depend on us."

Sean bowed very formally.

"Godspeed," Victoria Connaught called as he mounted the gangplank. She watched the sails billow and catch the breeze; the ship moved out into the Potowmack River. The purposeful wind seemed to fill her with a new resolve. At last God had given her a worthy cause in life, one in which she would not fail.

A dead brother, a sister-in-law gone mad, a frail niece to raise—she could shoulder all these burdens as long as she knew that ultimately the Connaughts, and England, would prevail.

Among the Connaught family the greatest sadness fell on Marianne. With Victoria daily inculcating her poisons into Marianne's mind, her childhood was snatched from her.

"Your mother, God pity her, was a weak sinful woman," Victoria said as she taught her niece petit point. "No, child, you've missed that stitch . . . There, that's better. But you, Marianne, are a Connaught, and must live up to the name. Swear child," she said, and placed Marianne's hand on the family Bible.

"I swear," Marianne whispered.

Each night, Victoria led Marianne in her prayers: "God protect and cherish the soul of Devroe Connaught, brought to an untimely death by the treachery of Zebulon Brand. And we swear by all we hold sacred, that no Connaught shall rest until the Brands and every one of their issue are brought to their knees and destroyed, may they all rot in hell."

Marianne listened, the terrible vows burning their way into her mind, body, and soul.

The snows gave way to spring thaws, and the construction crew slogged through the mud as they resumed work on the palace. The first course of stone was laid, outlining the ground plan, and Jeremy couldn't quite believe its size.

"Why, it will be the grandest building in all the world," he exclaimed.

"Not quite," Hoban said, smiling. "It's small compared to the great English palaces, or to Versailles, but our building will be unique among them, because of its purpose."

As the work progressed, the great and near-great in the government came to inspect the building. The trip from Philadelphia to Federal City had been a long, arduous one, but a new stagecoach run was introduced. It left Philadelphia at eight in the morning, and with frequent changes of horses, arrived in Washington at five the following afternoon, a trip of more than two hundred miles in less than thirty-two hours! Clearly, the new nation was coming of age, and soon there would be little room left for any improvements.

Dapper, handsome Alexander Hamilton came to watch the construction, but never at the same time as the magnetic and dashing Aaron Burr. Arch rivals, the men detested each other, and did what they could to thwart each other's political ambitions.

Jeremy watched in awe one morning as President Washington, accompanied by Thomas Jefferson, came to inspect the progress. Both men were tall, over six foot, and Washington weighed two hundred pounds. Washington, who'd been a surveyor by profession, and Jefferson, an architect in his own right, made many suggestions to Hoban regarding the disposition of the rooms and other features.

Hoban's fair coloring grew even pinker as the men went on. He'd already had to make major, infuriating concessions. His design, based loosely on the Duke of Leinster's house in Dublin, had called for a four-story structure, with wings. But Congress had considered the cost to build such a structure so enormous—$400,000—that it refused to appropriate funds. President Washington had eliminated the fourth story and the wings, and only the central portion was being built. Hoban refused to make any further changes, and with the utmost tact, managed to circumvent the President's and Jefferson's new ideas.

Jeremy was afraid of Washington; he looked so imposing and austere, and rumor had it that he was capable of monumental rages. Some of his foul moods were said to be brought on by the pain caused by his wooden false teeth. One morning Jefferson said to Hoban, "Ask what you will of the President today. He's in a good humor because he's had a new pair of dentures made, highly unusual, cut from the teeth of a hippopotamus."

"Is it true that Washington intends to be crowned king?" Jeremy asked Hoban.

"I don't know what's in his mind. What makes you ask such a thing?" Hoban asked, amused.

"Why, he acts like royalty, with silver buckles on his knee breeches and on his shoes, and his hair all powdered."

But late one afternoon, Jeremy's opinion of Washington changed drastically. The President and Hoban were wandering through the ground floor of the palace; Jeremy trailed behind, jotting notes for the men. Carpenters were notching beams into place to be the supporting members for the various rooms. Bricklayers worked with trowel and mortar, laying the foundations for the fireplaces. The first story was open to the sky and sunlight flooded the skeletal structure.

Washington seemed in a reflective mood, and in a rare

moment, dropped his guarded air. "One wonders at the ways of the Almighty," he said to Hoban. "For if we had lost the war, then this American Palace could never have risen here."

Jeremy studied him, wishing he could capture his expression, something he'd never seen before, and didn't know rightly how to describe. He wanted to blurt out that his father had fought with General Washington at Yorktown, but felt so awed by the man that he couldn't find his voice.

When Washington spoke again, he sounded distant. "The low point of the war came at Christmas Eve, when our army was encamped at Valley Forge. My men were freezing, bleeding, hungry . . . If the British and Hessians had attacked then, we would have been finished.

"Could I demand of my faithful few that they sacrifice any further? Was our fight for freedom merely an illusion? I knew that my men's lives would be forfeit if we fought on that winter. My despair overwhelmed me, and I lay down on the cot that my dear Martha had sent me. I passed into a state—it was not sleep, but more a reverie. I decided that the only sane thing to do was to disband the army, and surrender to the enemy encamped at Trenton. I rose to give those orders, but a great weight pressed down on my chest, holding me immobile. Then a voice from an invisible world called to me, telling me that I must fight on."

Jeremy felt the hackles on the back of his neck rise.

"This voice reminded me that all during my army career, innumerable horses had been shot out from under me, and fully *seventeen* times had bullets passed through my coat and hat. Yet each time, Providence had seen fit to spare me. I had always thought that I'd merely been lucky, but as I lay there I was made to realize that more than luck had been involved. Each time I'd been spared so that I could face the greater challenge ahead. For I was to become the leader of a great nation, a nation destined by fate."

Washington sighed. "I've rarely spoken of these things before. But today, standing here in the bare bones of this palace . . ." he shook his head slowly. "Who can fathom the mysterious ways of the Almighty?

"I rose from the bed, feeling refreshed, all signs of despair gone. I gave orders to prepare the attack against Trenton. After that victory, we fought on—how, I shall never know, for there was little to sustain us save our faith in God. But fight we did . . . and the rest is history."

President Washington, Hoban, and Jeremy stood quietly for a bit, watching the blocks of stone slowly being fitted into place.

As Jeremy grew older, taller in stature, as his voice changed with the onslaught of young manhood, Hoban gave him more and more responsibility: Drawing floorplans, designing decorative details for a room that would be oval in shape, overseeing the rough carpentry. Blistered hands, cut fingers, Jeremy's very strength went into the building, and somehow the building seemed to give that strength back, for as the house grew with the years, strong and sturdy and marked with grace, so did Jeremy Brand grow.

Chapter 8

BY 1795, homes, hotels, and boarding houses were beginning to spring up in Federal City, particularly along the ridge of New Jersey Avenue; it was easier and safer to build on high ground rather than in the flatlands that were apt to flood with each rainstorm or abnormally high tide. As in any burgeoning community, real estate was the compelling topic of conversation.

Zebulon had gambled that the lots surrounding the Capitol Building, now well under construction, would appreciate most in value, a belief also shared by the land syndicate of Greenleaf, Morris, and Nicholson. President Washington had also purchased a number of lots here and was building two rental dwellings. The speculators then raised their prices so high that they scared off the buyers. One by one the various syndicates were forced to declare bankruptcy. Finally, Zebulon had to do the same.

"Why did we ever listen to this fool?" Audubert Villefranche moaned to Mathias Breech. "We are ruined."

Breech lent his voice to the clamor, but Zebulon interrupted. "Oh be quiet, the two of you. Villefranche, you still have most of your wife's jewelry, and you, Mathias, look at your paunch! You're growing fat on the profits from your stoneworks. If anybody should be complaining, it's me."

"What's to be done?" Villefranche cried. "If I do not recoup I will be as destitute as a peasant."

"I've already discovered a way," Zebulon said with his characteristically imperturbable optimism. "Now this city is growing daily, and who's making money hand over fist? Why the slave owners, by renting out their Negroes to the builders.

With just a few hundred pounds I could outfit a ship and be in business again. This time, it would be foolproof."

"*Absolument non!*" Villefranche cried in a near-hysterical scream, while Breech grunted, "It'll be a cold day in hell before I squander more money on you."

But after a week of worrying it, while Zebulon filled their heads with tales of the fortune to be made, they decided to back him. This time, however, his share of the profits was to be only twenty percent, with Breech and Villefranche splitting the rest.

Zebulon sailed for the West Indies and returned with a hold crammed with slaves. They broke even on the first venture and lost money on the second when an outbreak of dengue fever killed most of the human cargo. But a year later, on their third sailing, they showed a tidy profit. Zebulon spent a great deal of his share in the taverns of Georgetown and Alexandria, and on new clothes.

"Spare no expense," he said to the tailor who'd just set up shop on New Jersey Avenue. "The world must know I'm solvent again, for money begets money."

Dressed in his new green mohair jacket cut away severely in the front to reveal his tight breeches, he went calling on Rebecca. He knew that Mathias had gone to the Aquia quarries with the latest batch of slaves.

Rebecca was not quite seventeen, and the promise of her adolescence was eclipsed by the current reality. Her breasts had become fuller and there was a gentle flare to her hips. She was perhaps a touch too tall for a girl, but Zebulon, who'd reached his full growth of six feet, found this delightful. "I don't have to be forever stooping in order to talk to you."

Rebecca was recovering from a recent sadness; engaged to the nephew of the wealthy Tayloe family, the young man had succumbed to Potowmack fever. Distraught at this, for months she entertained the idea of marrying Audubert Villefranche, much to the objections of her father.

"What can you possibly want with that—that limp asparagus?" he demanded.

"Audubert has a title, a cosmopolitan air, and perfect manners. And he wants to take me to Paris," she said. "Besides, you've always wanted me to marry someone with a title." But in the end, none of that could compensate for Villefranche's foppish nature, and he returned to France without her.

"I've plenty of time to marry," Rebecca said to her maid, Letitia. "I can't *wait* for the government to move here. There's sure to be many a bachelor congressman around. Wouldn't that be wonderful, to be the wife of somebody in the government?"

Yet Rebecca was also sensitive enough to realize that something was missing in her life. She'd never been in love—never—and wondered what that might be like.

When Zebulon came into the sitting room she put aside some pamphlets she'd been reading. Her astute glance took in his new clothes, and his freshly shaven face grown even more handsome tanned by the Caribbean sun. "My father isn't home," she said.

"It's not your father I've come for," he said with his delightful off-center grin. "My carriage is outside. Let's ride over to Federal City and see the progress they're making on the President's Palace."

"What a splendid idea," she said. "Letitia," she called, "get my shawl, and yours too. We're going out."

Zebulon's face dropped. "Are you so bound by the ridiculous rules of our antiquated society that you need a chaperone?"

She smiled sweetly. "Of course not. But I know you wouldn't want to do anything to cast the slightest shadow on our reputations, so I'm really doing it for you. Come along, Letitia."

At Federal City, they found the construction site thronged with workmen and sightseers. The tourists were dressed in their best clothes; young or old, rich or poor, free or slave, the thing to do in the district was to check the progress of the President's Palace. Young men would squire their ladies, and though a proper girl was always chaperoned, many a kiss was stolen among the scaffolds that now reached to the level of the second story.

As they walked across the muddied grounds, Rebecca lifted her skirts and Zebulon caught a glimpse of her finely turned ankle and the arched instep in her high-heeled sandals. Rebecca covered her ears against the din: the rasp of wood being sawed, the clang of chisel on stone being dressed to shape, the roar of the brickmakers' kilns and the smiths' forges.

"It looks and sounds like Vulcan's workshop!" she cried over the noise.

The ground floor by now had its ceiling on it. They walked up a short flight of stairs to the main floor, which would contain the rooms of state.

"Everything looks so vast and lonely," she said. Leaning heavily on Zebulon's arm, she picked her way gingerly over the lumber that lay everywhere.

Zebulon looked behind him; Letitia still dogged them.

Then a voice from high up shouted, "Rebecca!"

They turned to see a wiry youth up in the scaffolding. Jeremy Brand clambered down and stood before them, his face alive with pleasure at seeing Rebecca. He'd shot up about five inches these past years and stood just at the height of Zebulon's shoulder. His voice had deepened, peach fuzz sprouted on his face, and at fifteen, he stood poised at that tentative moment between adolescence and young manhood.

"Jeremy, I didn't recognize you behind all that plaster dust on your face," Rebecca said.

The brothers acknowledged each other, but barely. The hurt had gone too deep to be easily forgotten.

"Have you heard the news?" Jeremy asked eagerly. "President Washington's refused to run for a third term."

"That's last week's news," Zebulon said with a deprecatory wave of his hand. "And why should he run again when the newspapers heap such abuse on him? The *Philadelphia Aurora* accusing him of debauching the nation, of wanting to be king, when we all know that he agreed to a second term only at the insistence of Thomas Jefferson. He knew the country would fall apart without him. 'North and South will hang together if they have you to hang on,' Jefferson told him, and he was right."

"In all fairness, Washington has done a good job," Rebecca said, "but he did make some mistakes."

"Like what?" Zebulon demanded. He could never countenance hearing anything but good about his hero.

"Like his handling of the Whiskey Rebellion in Pennsylvania," she said.

"What else could he do? If he didn't force those loutish

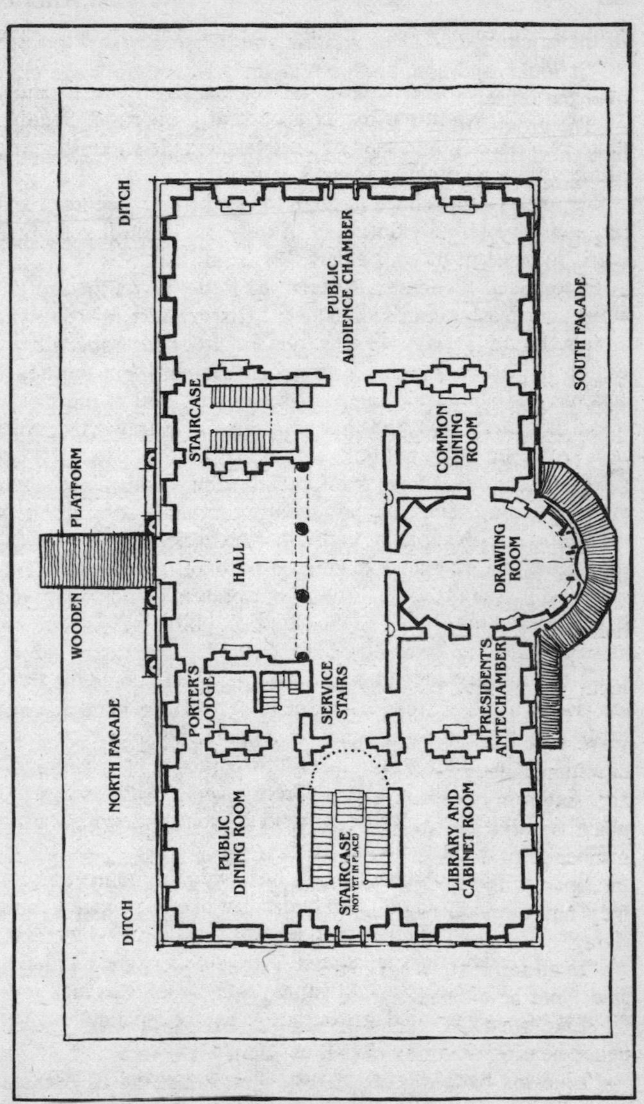

DITCH
PUBLIC AUDIENCE CHAMBER
SOUTH FACADE
STAIRCASE
COMMON DINING ROOM
WOODEN PLATFORM
HALL
DRAWING ROOM
PORTER'S LODGE
SERVICE STAIRS
PRESIDENT'S ANTECHAMBER
NORTH FACADE
PUBLIC DINING ROOM
STAIRCASE (NOT YET IN PLACE)
LIBRARY AND CABINET ROOM
DITCH

FLOOR PLAN

frontiersmen to pay the whiskey tax, the Union could have foundered."

"Oh, nonsense," she said. "He let his favorite, Alexander Hamilton, blow a minor matter all out of proportion. Sending an army of fifteen thousand against farmers? It's like shooting a turkey with an eighteen-pound cannon."

Jeremy's laugh echoed through the grand entrance foyer and Zebulon gave him a painful jab in the ribs. "You'll get worse if you're insolent to your elders," he said.

Encouraged by Jeremy's reaction, Rebecca warmed to the subject of Washington's blunders. "His greatest mistake was signing the Jay Treaty. He sent John Jay to London *specifically* to stop the impressment of American seamen. Yet the treaty says nothing about that, and our sailors are still at the mercy of the British Navy. And that was the final straw that broke the country into two political parties."

"Jefferson would have manipulated such a schism no matter what," Zebulon said. "In spite of all that man's soft talk, he's as ambitious as Napoleon, and will stop at nothing to be President. But that's another matter. How dare the *Aurora* claim that Washington is the cause of all our present difficulties? And that his retirement should be the cause of jubilation? That newspaper and all like it should be blown up!"

"Well, the first amendment does guarantee people the freedom to speak their minds," she said. "And if a man chooses to run for office, then he must be prepared for that."

"I think the saddest thing is that now President Washington will never live in the palace," Jeremy said. "And he was the one responsible for it. Rebecca, who do you think will win the election?"

"Vice-President Adams," she said without a moment's hesitation. "He's a conservative, a Federalist like Washington, and the President's hand-picked choice. Adams has been very careful to paint Jefferson as an atheist, a freethinker, and a radical, and the country's frightened of that. Adams believes in a government run by a monied aristocracy, and since that aristocracy still has the power, the winner will be Adams."

Zebulon's head whirled with what Rebecca was saying. She's always been willful, but this was totally different. "Do you think it seemly for a woman to be so engaged in the political affairs of men?" he asked.

Having heard that response *ad nauseam* from her father, Rebecca flared, "I see no harm in being informed. Surely that's the prerogative of any intelligent person, man or woman."

"But of what use is it?" Zebulon insisted. "Women can't vote and never will. Now come on, Rebecca, leave off this unpleasant topic; it's souring my stomach."

"Would you like a tour of the mansion?" Jeremy asked Rebecca. "I'd be pleased to show you around."

"With everybody lollygagging around like you, no wonder this place is taking so long to build," Zebulon said. "You'd better get back to work." He took Rebecca's hand firmly and led her off.

Jeremy stared after them. Of all the things he envied most about his brother, none compared to the easy manner he had with Rebecca. Just the thought of being able to touch her like that sent shudders through him. He climbed back up the scaffolding and from his vantage point watched them wander about until they disappeared from sight.

Rebecca glanced sideways at Zebulon. "Why so harsh with Jeremy? Sometimes, you seem . . . uncomfortable with him."

Zebulon shrugged with irritation; this outing wasn't turning out at all like he'd planned. "Well, I've spent my life taking care of him, and it's about time he started taking care of himself."

Rebecca thought that was exactly what Jeremy was doing, but said nothing. They poked their heads into a cavernous room; four tall window openings on the far wall and three on each of the shorter walls flooded the long rectangular chamber with light.

"This must be the Public Audience Chamber," Rebecca said. "The one they call the East Room."

Zebulon coughed and said, "This infernal dust has made me parched. Letitia, go and see if you can find us some water." The moment the slave girl went off, Zebulon maneuvered Rebecca into a corner of the room. He put his arm up, preventing her from moving. "It's time you and I had a serious talk."

"About what?" she asked.

"You know the way I feel about you."

"In truth, I don't. Is it different from the way you feel about your tavern wenches? Or is it more like your feelings toward Elizabeth Connaught?"

The blood rose to his face and his dark brown eyes seemed to have a fire behind them. "You have spirit, I'll grant you that. But be careful, lest you go too far."

"Then perhaps I'd better explain myself so that you understand once and for all. I have no intention of becoming another link in your love chain."

"But you don't understand," he said, grabbing both her arms. "I love you."

The suddenness of his declaration startled her. Zebulon had also been surprised and even more confused to discover that he really meant it. He crushed her in his embrace and kissed her full on the mouth. She kept her lips pressed firmly together as he sought to make her yield, and he rubbed his rigid body against hers so she'd know he'd spoken the truth. "That part of us never lies," he whispered.

Fear, revulsion, curiosity—Rebecca was besieged by all these feelings, and then she became aware of Letitia moaning in the background. Rebecca broke free and held Zebulon at arm's length.

Unmindful of Letitia's presence, Zebulon reached for Rebecca again. "Can't you see I love you? Come away with me, right now. I swear I'll make you the happiest woman in the world."

Her eyes became as hard as agates. "Is that the proof of your love then, to treat me like a common trollop?"

"I meant as my wife, of course," he stammered, saying whatever was necessary to win her. "I'll speak to your father as soon as he returns."

"Don't be a fool. He'd never give you his permission. And even if he did, you still wouldn't have mine."

He fell back a step. Then his face softened into a beguiling smile. "I warn you, once I've set my mind to something, I never take no for an answer. Tell me, what must I do to win you?"

"Be honest with me. Don't treat me as just another one of

your intended conquests. And above all, make something of yourself." She crooked her finger at Letitia, who was still holding the dipper, though she'd spilled most of the water. "Letitia, it's time for us to go."

"Yes ma'am!" Letitia exclaimed with a great wave of relief. Mathias Breech had warned her often enough that if she ever let anything happen to Rebecca, he'd hang her.

Later that evening, Rebecca sat before her mirror while Letitia brushed her hair. "Do you like Zebulon?" she asked.

"Yes ma'am."

"Don't say it just to please me," she snapped. "Don't you have a mind of your own?"

"I like him just fine. He's so handsome, and laughing all the time. When he comes into a room, it's like a gust of sea air."

Rebecca stared at herself in the mirror, remembering the strength and insistence of his body pressing against hers. "Letitia," she began absently, "how long have you been married now?"

"Going on three years, Miss Rebecca."

"Did it . . . does it hurt?" she asked in a whisper.

Letitia gripped her shoulders. "Oh, child, no, not if you love the man. Then it's God's finest gift."

But my mother! Rebecca's eyes screamed at her in the mirror.

Letitia saw her terrified look and embraced her. "It's all right, you'll see," she murmured, rocking her back and forth until she finally stopped trembling.

"But . . . but how do you know when you're in love?"

"Don't listen to what Zebulon says. Listen to your heart. It's *that* part that don't ever lie."

Rebecca stood up suddenly. "If you ever tell anybody what we talked about I'll whip you, you hear?"

"Yes ma'am," she said, bowing her head.

"Now get out of here and leave me alone," she ordered.

As Letitia started toward the door Rebecca called, "Wait a minute." She went to the closet and took out a blue-checked gingham dress that Letitia had once admired, and handed it to her. "Take it. I hardly wear it anymore."

Chapter 9

TAKING CARE that Mathias Breech suspected as little as possible, Zebulon began a serious courtship of Rebecca. He squired her to the crude racecourse on Fourteenth Street, and professed his undying love. She professed hers, but would allow him no more than a kiss. At the fox hunt, where they separated from the main party and leapt stone fences, he tried again. The fox got away, and so did she. He'd never run up against this kind of resistance, and that inflamed him all the more. Having her become an *idée fixe,* tormenting his days and sleepless nights. When he sought to sate his desires in the arms of other women, at the moment of completion they all took the face and form of Rebecca Breech.

There were even times when he thought he might truly be falling in love with her.

Late in 1796, Rebecca's predictions came true: John Adams, in a viciously fought campaign, was elected President. But through Alexander Hamilton's miscalculated intervention and a flaw in the electoral process, Adams found himself saddled with his Democratic-Republican opponent, Thomas Jefferson, as Vice-President. It was shortly after their inauguration that Mathias Breech discovered what was going on between Zebulon and his daughter. He fell into a near-apoplectic fit and confronted Rebecca.

"I forbid you ever to see him again!"

Rebecca sat at the small spinning wheel and continued to card the strands of cotton. "Father, I'll have to marry someday."

"That will come soon enough. But not to him, never him. By God, this is what comes of your reading all those pamphlets and books! I'll have no more of that in this house, do you hear? And no more of him."

"I haven't made up my mind about Zebulon, but when I do, I promise you'll be the first to know. In the meantime, I intend to see whomever I want, whenever I want."

Mathias hauled Rebecca to her feet and slapped her. "How dare you speak to me that way? You'll do as I say."

Her hand flew to her cheek but she didn't flinch. This confrontation had been coming for a long time. She knew she had to stand up to her father right now, or else fall into the pattern that had ground her mother into the dust. With as much strength as she could muster, she slapped her father back.

His mouth fell open in shock and he raised his hand. "I'll teach you—"

"If you touch me again, I'll leave this house forever," she whispered. "I swear it on my mother's grave."

A look flashed between them as deadly as one between hunter and prey, parent and child.

His hand remained poised and then gradually it fell. He stormed about the room then, trying to bluster his way out of it, claiming he was doing it for her own good, that Zebulon was a notorious womanizer and cocksman. Rebecca listened to it all, but she knew she'd won. From that moment on, a subtle change took place in the relationship between them, Mathias gradually relinquishing the reins as master of the house, she grasping them in an ever tighter grip.

Having failed to persuade his daughter, Mathias approached Zebulon. "It's come to me that we're fools to deal with the West Indian middlemen," he said. "Why not take a ship directly to Africa, or to the Levant? Slaves are far cheaper there, and our profit margin will be that much greater."

"It means running the French and British blockades, and paying a healthy tribute to the Tripoli pirates," Zebulon said. "But you're right. One such successful voyage could make us all very rich men."

But Zebulon also realized what had really prompted Mathias. "Your father thinks to get me away long enough for you to forget me," he told Rebecca at their last meeting. "But when I come back the richest man in the territory, then we'll see."

Zebulon rented out his slave Eli to Breech and left Baal in Rebecca's care. Rebecca saw him off when he sailed. He demanded some commitment from her. She listened to her heart . . . but it said nothing.

As the building tempo increased on the American Palace, more and more workmen were hired. Their shacks huddled against the low picket fence enclosing the eighteen acres of grounds. James Hoban hired seventeen skilled Scotsmen who were master stone cutters, and an additional ten were employed at the Capitol Building, whose first low courses of stone were just barely visible down the long sightline of Pennsylvania Avenue. High tides came to within twenty-five feet of the roadway, and storms washed across it, leaving fish and eels in their wake.

A stone footpath now paralleled Pennsylvania Avenue from the Palace to the Capitol, and Jeremy would race along its mile-and-a-half length on errands to the Capitol's chief architect, William Thornton. Thornton, a physician by profession, had won the competition to design the building that would house the Senate and the House of Representatives. Jeremy's heart leapt up to see the city rising before his eyes. Livestock grazed in a huge meadow meant one day to be the Mall. Occasionally, a wolf killed a calf or lamb, and during especially harsh winters, the cry of the pack could be heard on the wind.

Then Jeremy would take down the rifle that Hoban kept over the mantelpiece, fill his horn with powder, and set out hunting. A two-hundred-pound bounty of tobacco was paid for every wolf pelt, and he needed the money. He was having daydreams of studying at the small college in Georgetown, and the bounty would help pay for his tuition. Though it was a Catholic school, it did accept non-Catholic students.

One winter eve, Jeremy tracked a wolf to a ravine in Rock Creek. He came within shooting distance and aimed . . . but the gray-blue beast turned and looked at him with its ghostly eyes. There was something magnificent in its stance, a being wedded to the snow-covered forest and the ice-blue rill of the stream . . . Slowly he lowered his rifle. He wanted to capture its life on paper, not kill it.

The spring rains of 1798 were the heaviest in memory,

turning Federal City into a quagmire. The top floor of the President's Palace was without a permanent roof; water soaked through and warped the floorboards and flaked the plaster off the walls. Slaves and laborers alike found it impossible to work and huddled in their shacks against the raw, penetrating weather. During the rainy hours, Jeremy worked on various mechanical projects that intrigued him, including one that involved a rifle.

One stormy twilight Mathias Breech came home from the stoneworks, dismay written all over his face. He shucked off his oilskins and warmed his back by the fire. "Rebecca, I'm afraid I've got some bad news."

Her heart began to race.

"We've just lost a small fortune. The ship I outfitted and sent to the Levant has been captured by the Tripoli pirates."

She half-rose from her chair, then sank back. "And Zebulon?" she whispered.

"Captured also. I've just received word from our government. The Moors are demanding a king's ransom for the release of the ship and crew."

"But we've got to pay it. We can't let them rot in prison. I've mother's jewels."

He shook his head. "It will take far more than that. No, this is a matter for the government. They've already begun negotiations, but it could take years." He shook his head. "I don't know what this world's coming to. Napoleon on the rampage, England and France impressing our seamen, and now these Tripoli pirates holding our men hostage—can things get any worse?"

The weather remained stormy for another day and Rebecca moved through the house like a caged thing. She tried to occupy her mind by sewing, but she pricked her fingers; while canning preserves, she broke the jar. The world was indeed in a volatile state, and the injustice of the XYZ Affair particularly outraged her.

President Adams had sent John Marshall and other ministers to France to negotiate the release of impressed American seamen. But before Tallyrand and his ministers would even discuss the matter, they insisted on a bribe of $250,000. When President Adams disclosed this to the American people, they were so outraged that a rallying cry went up all over the nation, "Millions for defense, but not one cent for tribute!" General Washington was called out of retirement to command the army in the war that seemed imminent with France. But Rebecca knew that a war could seriously jeopardize Zebulon's release from a foreign prison.

The following day the clouds dispersed and birdsong greeted the sun. "Have my horse brought round," Rebecca called to Letitia. "I've got to tell Jeremy about his brother."

"Then you best wait for me," Letitia said. "Your father don't want you going out alone."

"Don't be a ninny! Jeremy's only a child."

"He's 'most seventeen, old enough to father a baby, and that's all I got to say about that."

Rebecca dismissed her and rode to Federal City. When she reached Jeremy's cabin she saw him standing outside, sluicing himself at the pump. He was naked to the waist, and the long lean line of his well-muscled body made her catch her breath. His trousers were soaked through and clung to his thighs and haunches; he might as well have been totally naked. His energy as he sang under the cold buckets of water, his springlike grace all hinted at the promise of the man.

He stopped suddenly when he saw her, grabbed a coarse cloth, and began drying himself. "If I knew you were coming . . . It's been raining for so long—I was begrimed," he stumbled over his words, the fair skin all over his torso flushing with embarrassment.

He led her into the cabin. While he went to a small room to put on dry clothes, she studied the main living area, about twenty by fifteen feet. A hewn stone fireplace dominated one wall. A kettle bubbling with a savory fish soup hung in the fireplace; the crude utensils, most of which he'd fashioned at the forge, hung on the fireplace wall. Jeremy had laid a new floor the year before, wide planks of hard pine. The house had a warm cozy atmosphere and she felt comfortable in it.

"You know that the cabin is mine, don't you?" Jeremy said as he came back into the room.

She smiled agreeably, "No, I didn't."

"When I turned sixteen, James Hoban was kind enough to sell the place to me. He spends most of his spare time in

Georgetown now that he and Susannah Sewell are engaged. I'm paying the house off by giving him a portion of my weekly wage."

"And how much would that be?" she asked, amused by his eagerness to impress her.

"You've no idea how wages have soared since I first began working. Why, a master stone cutter gets two, sometimes three, dollars a day. And journeymen like me can make as much as two dollars a day. Every cent I've earned so far has gone into this place. I know it's hardly what you'd call a mansion . . ."

"Hardly," she agreed. "Tell me, is this the extent of your horizon, then? A small house, earning two dollars a day?"

"Oh, no," he exclaimed. "I'm planning to go to Georgetown College and study mathematics, natural philosophy, and the like, just as soon as the President's Palace is done and I've saved the tuition money. I think it will help me become a better architect."

She moved to a long worktable where a rifle had been disassembled and its components carefully laid out.

"Just an experiment," he said. "You see, Eli Whitney claims that instead of each one of these rifles being made by hand, he can manufacture thousands of them."

"The man who invented the cotton gin?" she asked.

"The same. He's really a genius."

"Can he do it?" she asked.

"I'm not sure. He says he'll use power machinery and cut out jigs so that the parts will be uniform and interchangeable. If he manages it, he'll revolutionize the industry. He's setting up a factory right now in New Haven, Connecticut, to manufacture them for the government."

"New England, again," Rebecca said, annoyed. "Why can't we do something like that here in the South instead of just planting tobacco and cotton?"

"I guess because the good Lord saw fit to give New England cheap water power." His hands moved across the table, touching the gun parts. "Imagine, everything interchangeable. Someday I'm going to invent something like that, I will."

Rebecca made a move to sit and Jeremy hastily brushed the wood shavings from the ladderback chair.

"Jeremy, I've come because I've got some bad news."

When she told him what had happened to Zebulon, he jumped to his feet. "We've got to do something. Raise money somehow . . . I know, I'll sell the house!"

When he calmed down, she told him what her father had said about it being in the hands of the government. Rebecca watched him as he paced the room. Letitia was right, he was no longer a boy. The picture of his near-naked body kept popping into her mind . . . Suddenly feeling uncomfortable and slightly confused, she left.

The seasons flowed one into the other as Jeremy and Rebecca waited anxiously for word of Zebulon. Then in the autumn of 1799, United States emissaries secured the release of Zebulon Brand and other seamen imprisoned by the Barbary pirates. But Zebulon's ship had been lost, and when he returned to Federal City he was destitute.

His meeting with Rebecca was solemn; nothing she could do or say could cheer him. He looked gaunt, his innate happy manner subdued by his imprisonment. "I promised you I'd come home wealthy, and now this," he said.

"No matter, you're here and alive, that's what's important. You'll have plenty of other opportunities to make your mark."

Jeremy offered his brother whatever he had, including living free at his house, but Zebulon refused and moved into quarters in Alexandria. Freedom and Rebecca's support gradually allowed his buoyant nature to resurface. Soon he was saying, "If I'd had one or two cannon aboard, I could have whipped those pirates! Now all I've got left is Baal and my slave Eli. But that's what I started with, and nothing can keep me down for long."

Rebecca couldn't have been more confused about Zebulon. One night while Letitia was turning down the bed, she said to her maid, "I missed him something fierce when he was gone, but now that he's back . . . How do you explain that?"

"You've got a changeable nature, is all," Letitia said, "and that's all I've got to say about that."

Rebecca laughed and playfully threw a slipper at her. Then she became serious. "What if there was somebody that you never took seriously, and then suddenly . . ."

"Who?" Letitia asked.

"Jeremy."

Letitia's eyes opened wide. "Cross your heart and bite your tongue, because that's the devil talking now! You know how they feel about each other."

"But you told me to listen to my heart."

Letitia slapped the pillow hard. "You know more ways of starting trouble than anybody I know. But I tell you this: whatever you decide, you'd best do it quick, because you're getting on to twenty now. Getting married be the best thing that could happen to you. You wouldn't be so nervous all the time and that's all I've got to say about that."

With Zebulon's recovery, he and Rebecca once again resumed their socializing, much to the distress of Mathias Breech. He'd never exactly wished Zebulon dead, but if the Moors could have held him until Rebecca was married to somebody respectable, that would have suited him just fine.

One afternoon, Zebulon and Rebecca were strolling arm in arm along the crushed-stone footpath that paralleled the roadway of Pennsylvania Avenue. Zebulon said, "Why isn't President Adams *forcing* Congress to provide the nation with a strong navy? If we had a fleet in the Mediterranean, the Barbary pirates would never dare to attack us."

"Was it very bad?" she asked, squeezing his arm.

"Worse than any telling of it," he said softly. "Foul dungeons, slop for food, my men . . . abused by the Moors for their own amusement."

"But why? Have they no sense of common decency?"

Zebulon sighed. "You learn much in prison. It's their way of life. For centuries, the people of Algiers, Tripoli, Morocco, and Tunis have lived by their wits, marauding and pillaging all the shipping in the Mediterranean. They grew fat on their piracy. Then when we became a mercantile and shipping nation, the Moors began attacking us. Do you know how much we paid in tribute last year?"

"More than a million dollars," she said. "It's in Adams's report to Congress."

"And that still hasn't assured us safe passage." He kicked a rock in his path. "By God, one day I'll have my revenge on them! I tell you, without Washington at the helm, this country is floundering. Adams is a vain, incompetent fool, and I detest him!"

Rebecca considered that. "I think we're moving into a kind of love and hate relationship with our leaders."

"Love and hate?" he repeated, momentarily thrown off his line of thought. "I don't follow."

"Why, it's easier to deal with a monarch. A king can claim divine right, and the common man is always loath to go against the rule of heaven. Ah, but when the leader is chosen from among mere mortals, then he becomes the repository for all our complaints, real and imagined. Zebulon, I think the truth of the matter is that you yourself want to be President!"

"I'd sooner be king," he snorted. "I don't believe as Jefferson does, in the perfectibility of man. Most men are out for their own ends and the rest be damned. I hold with Hamilton, that the masses are a great beast and, like children, must be guided and taught."

Rebecca bit her lip. She agreed in part with Zebulon, most people were fools. And yet . . . "Since we fought a war for this kind of government—for this way of life, really—don't we owe it to ourselves to give it a chance?"

"We haven't a chance in hell with Adams. Tallyrand insults us in a manner whose only proper response is war, and what is Adams's response? More talk. We toady to the Tripoli pirates until we're made the laughingstock of the world.

"Oh God, why did Washington ever retire?" Zebulon called out to the sky. "If only we could persuade him to run again."

Early in December of 1799, George and Martha Washington visited the President's Palace for a final inspection. Since James Hoban was away on a trip with his new bride, Jeremy escorted the Washingtons on a tour of the mansion.

Martha, less than five feet tall, was more than a foot shorter than her husband. She was plumpish, had white even teeth and gray hair, and boasted a wonderful complexion for a woman in her early sixties. George, at sixty-seven, still looked vigorous. They were outwardly affectionate with each other, and he called her Patsy.

Jeremy pointed out the work in progress. "As you can see,

the permanent slate roof is finally on, and the workmen are scrubbing down the outside sandstone. Then the stone will be whitewashed."

"I rather like the golden tone of the natural stone," Martha said. "I think you should leave it as is."

"But Patsy, look at the color, it isn't even throughout," George said. "Painted white, the palace will stand out from the surrounding buildings, which will all be made of brick. That's how we planned it."

"Perhaps, but you're making a mistake, George. Who wants a white house? You'll have to repaint it every year."

"Tell Hoban to go ahead with the whitewashing," Washington said to Jeremy. "Then have the scaffolding struck as soon as possible. We've less than ten months before the government is scheduled to move here."

The Washingtons appeared delighted with everything they saw, though Jeremy sensed a feeling of regret that they would never live in the palace. Washington was suffering from a severe cold, so they didn't stay long . . .

A few days later, on December 14, Jeremy was struck dumb when news reached Federal City that Washington had suddenly died of pneumonia. The grief throughout the nation was enormous, and President Adams declared a week of mourning.

Zebulon reacted as though he'd lost his own father and galloped at once to Mount Vernon, where thousands of others had come to pay their last respects. The crush around the casket became so great that Martha Washington had to hire special guards to prevent relic hunters from pulling out every hair on Washington's head.

When he returned from Mount Vernon, Zebulon said to Rebecca, "President Adams will never survive this. Washington was his staunchest supporter. Without him, that dour, suspicious New Englander won't be able to rule. The country is headed toward disaster!"

PART TWO

Chapter 10

THE BULLWHIP whirred through the air and cut across Eli's back. Tied fast by his wrists to the whipping post, he shuddered convulsively and rivulets of blood glistened on his ebony back as Blutkopf laid on the stripes.

"Stop at ten," Zebulon called to Blutkopf. He'd ordered twenty lashes for his slave, but changed his mind. "No sense in his not being able to work for days," Zebulon explained to Rebecca, who stood by his side.

A fair-sized crowd had gathered; off to one side stood a group of shackled slaves, forced to witness the punishment. Drawn by some perverse urge, Rebecca had come to the Georgetown square with her father and was now caught somewhere between nausea and excitement. Mathias Breech fortified himself with another tot of rum from his flask. With the passage of the years, his step had become a bit infirm, and his hair grayer, and whiskey flowers blossomed on his cheeks.

Rebecca looked around; only a handful of women were at the whipping, and she felt uncomfortable. Victoria Connaught and her coterie of sycophants were there, but they attended any event in the district, be it a speech, the opening of a new shop, or a public whipping. Victoria had spent the last few years in London overseeing the education of her niece Marianne, and the two had recently returned to the United States.

From a nearby vantage point, Jeremy flinched with each crack of Blutkopf's whip. The injustice of it all infuriated him. He pushed through the crowd and approached Zebulon. The brothers were almost the same height now, with Zebulon perhaps an inch taller and wider in the shoulders and chest. Jeremy put his hand on Zebulon's arm.

"You could stop this if you wanted," he said.

Zebulon pulled free. "He broke the law. If we give them an inch, we encourage rebellion."

In August of that year, a freed Negro named Gabriel had incited a band of slaves to revolt near Richmond. Governor James Monroe had reacted with an iron fist; he called out the militia, quashed the revolt, and hung twenty-five Negroes. But fear swept through the South and new laws were passed: Slaves weren't permitted to gather; three or more constituted a crowd. A strict curfew was enforced; any Negro found in the streets after dark was liable to be shot. In the District of Columbia, the population had risen to 3,200, with 2,464 whites, 623 slaves, and 123 free Negroes. Almost a third of the population was black, a dangerous percentage.

Blutkopf administered the final lash. When Eli's wrists were untied, he slumped to the ground.

"I loathe such violence," Victoria Connaught said, "but the slaves must be taught a lesson. Look what that renegade slave Toussaint L'Ouverture did in Haiti, killed every white man on that isle. And that's exactly what will happen here. We'll be murdered in our beds if they"—her eyes slid to the crumpled form of Eli—"aren't kept in their place."

The timorous ladies surrounding Victoria Connaught bobbed their heads in agreement; then as she swept off, they were pulled along in her wake.

Jeremy helped Eli to his feet. He paid no mind to the angry mutterings from the crowd about a white man helping such a black. He led Eli to the slaves' billet and laved an ointment of aloe on his back. Eli winced and Jeremy said, "It will help your wounds heal faster." He shook his head. "I can't understand why Blutkopf has such an unreasoned hatred of you. What happened this time?"

Eli gradually stopped panting and managed to say, "He found me with four other slaves under the dock. We'd been bartering for some tobacco one of them filched, but Blutkopf accused us of unlawful assembly, though he knew otherwise. He told Zebulon I was the ringleader. Someday, Blutkopf and I," he said grimly, "we'll face each other as equals."

"Keep thinking like that and you will get yourself killed," Jeremy said. He stood up. "I've got to go. There's still another ship to be unloaded down at the dock."

Jeremy mounted his horse and rode to Lear's wharf down near Rock Creek. Despite the gradual silting of the Potowmack, Georgetown was still a bustling port. Three months before in June of 1800, and amidst great fanfare, President Adams had visited Washington City—the capital had fully adopted that name after George Washington's death. Adams wanted to be certain that the city was ready to receive the government. Henry Ingle, a mover who lived on New Jersey Avenue, had gotten the contracts to transport all the federal records from Philadelphia. With the papers came an astonishing number of clerks employed by the government—136 in all—and housing was quickly erected for them. Adams had also inspected the President's Palace and ordered James Hoban to have it completed by December.

Since Congress hadn't appropriated any money for furnishing, Abigail Adams shipped the Adams furniture down from Braintree, Massachusetts, and it had just arrived. Jeremy joined Hoban on the dock and the two men supervised the unloading of the fragile pieces.

"It's too soon," Jeremy said to Hoban. "The palace isn't ready yet. It won't be liveable."

"What else can we do?" Hoban asked. "The law specifically states that the new capital must be ready by the first Monday in December of this year, and that's almost on us."

"I know, and everybody's anxious to meet the date," Jeremy said. "I hear there's a movement afoot to abandon Washington as the capital and stay in Philadelphia."

"That's right. The quicker we're established here, the greater our chances of remaining. So put your back into it, lad."

Hoban had become the busiest architect in Washington. To provide accommodations for the arriving legislators, he'd designed and was building Blodgett's Hotel. Much of his spare time was taken up with the duties and fascinations of a newlywed, and his wife was pregnant. With Hoban so occupied, more and more responsibility fell on Jeremy's shoulders. Hoban was able to divide his time without worry, for Jeremy was dedicated and conscientious to a fault.

The wagons were finally loaded with the furniture and other

household items. Jeremy rode beside one wagon back to the palace. He had it all piled in the center of the entrance hall; he looked around, feeling the pressure of everything yet to be done. The walls weren't completely plastered, cornices and moldings weren't up, and many of the windowpanes were broken; neighborhood ragamuffins used them for target practice, when they weren't scrawling graffiti on the walls.

"Well," he sighed, "let's hope that President Adams has a mellow disposition."

The entire city primped and painted and planted in preparation for the arrival of the government. The *National Intelligencer,* the newspaper that had been founded in October by Samuel Smith, carried daily reports of all the amenities of civilization that President Adams would find in Washington.

Rebecca and Zebulon sat at a table in Tunnecliff's Tavern having afternoon tea and reading the accounts. Zebulon moved his chair closer so that he could revel in the fresh-washed smell of her hair. At twenty, Rebecca was considered one of the most beautiful women in the territory. She'd lost every vestige of girlish plumpness, the well-defined bones in her face complemented her high coloring, and the flush of splendid health radiated from her face and body.

"The paper says the palace is almost ready," she said.

"Everyone's been telling us that for years," Zebulon said. "If my brother remains on that job, it'll be another decade before it's finished."

The palace was flanked by the brick Treasury Building and the partially completed State and War Department Buildings. New Jersey Avénue was dotted with houses, many of them wood frame. The city commissioners frowned on this type of construction, but allowed them for the "lower orders" who couldn't afford brick. Building lots along Pennsylvania Avenue were beginning to sell because the prices had been substantially cut. On the north side of Pennsylvania, a dozen residences had been built, including a turner's shop and a coachmaker's shop. The south side of the avenue, nearest the river, was lined with lumberyards and brickyards; the city commissioners demanded they be moved before the President arrived. A stagecoach, the Royal George, drawn by four cream-colored horses, made regular runs between Washington and Georgetown, carrying commuters to and from work.

Zebulon stretched his long legs, managing to touch Rebecca's. "The other day I heard a stranger ask, 'Where is the city?' He was standing at its very center! Even Abbé Correa da Serra, the minister from Portugal, calls it 'the city of magnificent distances.'"

"Give it time, it must grow into itself," she said, moving her leg away. "Why, we now have seven boarding houses, a tailor, a shoemaker, a printer, a washerwoman, a grocery store, a stationery shop, an itinerant barber, and a drygoods store. What do you think of that?"

Zebulon leaned closer, "I think you're so adorable that I must have you."

She rapped him smartly across the knuckles with her fan. "And how would we live? You're so penniless you can barely afford to stable Baal."

The *National Intelligencer,* eager to apprise its readers of the character of the arriving President, and also to boost its circulation, was running a column about Adams. Rebecca read the sketch aloud. "The son of a shoemaker, Adams was born in Braintree, Massachusetts, in 1735. Let's see, that would make him sixty-five years old."

"There are many who say that Adams should have stuck to his father's profession," Zebulon said, chuckling.

He thought for a moment, lines furrowing his brow, then said, "Rebecca, why is it that whenever we're together, we always seem to get involved with politics? Let's leave off this nonsense. We've so many more important things to talk about."

"Nothing interests me more than how the country is governed," she said. "If you want to be frivolous, there are plenty of other girls who'll accommodate you." Then she continued reading.

"Adams graduated from Harvard, started a law practice, and soon became the state's foremost lawyer. He's a self-made man, aristocratic in his acquired tastes, and one of the foremost firebrands of the American Revolution. Benjamin Franklin had this to say of him, 'Always an honest man, often a great one, but sometimes absolutely mad.'"

"I couldn't agree with old Franklin more," Zebulon said.

"The man *is* mad! Can you imagine Adams thinking he could foist his Alien and Sedition Acts on us? Not being able to speak out against his administration on pain of being imprisoned? He's worse than a tyrant!" Then he leaned back in his chair and burst out laughing.

"What is it?"

"I was thinking of Adams's title!"

Adams had insisted that Congress give him a title, something grander than "Mr. President." Wary of any royalist pretensions, Congress searched carefully for the title that would best suit him; taking cognizance of his short stature and generous paunch, they called him, "His Rotundity."

Rebecca set down her teacup. "And here's this final comment, by none other than Thomas Jefferson. 'Adams is vain, irritable, and a bad calculator of the force and probable effect of the motives which govern men. That is all the ill that can be said of him. . . . He is so amiable, that I pronounce you will love him, if ever you become acquainted with him.'"

"Ha! That was said years ago, in friendlier days," Zebulon barked. "But since this election campaign, all that passes between these two men is vicious slander and character assassination. They've set their newspapers on each other like dogs."

In June of 1800, a reporter named Rind wrote in the *Virginia Federalist,* "I have damning proof of Thomas Jefferson's depravity!" Whispers of an unnatural, unholy love affair flew back and forth, but much of the country thought this was merely electioneering talk.

Then Adams circulated the damning charge that Jefferson was an atheist. Churchmen everywhere demanded that he declare his views on Christianity. Jefferson responded, "I will never court the clergy by offers of compromise. The Episcopalian and Congregationalist churches in particular, still hope to be named as the established church of the United States. And each church knows that if elected, I threaten abortion to their hopes. And they believe rightly. For I have sworn on the altar of God, eternal hostility against every form of tyranny over the mind of man."

"There's nothing like an election to reveal a man's true feelings," Zebulon said.

"The papers claim that if Adams declares war on France

before the election next month, he's virtually assured of a second term," Rebecca said.

"But he won't, even though his own party wants it, because the man's a coward."

"I don't believe that for a moment," she said. "It's Hamilton who wants war with France so that New England can reestablish trade relations with Great Britain. That's a vital necessity for the economy of the North. But I think Adams is putting the good of the country above his own political career. He knows we're unprepared for war."

"I'll wager you this," Zebulon said. "If Adams doesn't give in to Hamilton's demands, then Hamilton will make sure that the Federalist Party turns on him, and he'll lose the election."

"I can't believe Hamilton would be that stupid," she said.

"Well, in a matter of days, we'll know firsthand, when His Rotundity takes up his rule in the President's Palacc."

Chapter 11

ON NOVEMBER second, scant days before the presidential election was to take place, John Adams arrived in Washington, D.C., to take up residence in the President's Palace. A small welcoming committee greeted him and the city commissioners presented him with a basket of fruit sent by Martha Washington.

Looking at the small butterball of a man, Jeremy could well understand why Adams had been nicknamed His Rotundity. But he appeared to be direct and forthright, though his manner was edged with irritability.

After the welcoming ceremonies, James Hoban and Jeremy led the President across a wooden bridge to the main entrance of the palace.

Adams looked down into the water-filled ditch that formed a sort of moat. "What's this?" he demanded.

"We had to leave the ditch open to pump out groundwater when the basement flooded," Hoban said.

"Does it flood often?" Adams asked querulously.

"Oh, no," Jeremy said. "Only at high tide, or if we have a really heavy rainstorm. As soon as the foundation work is completed, then we'll drain the ditch and remove the bridge."

Adams glowered sourly as Jeremy opened the door and led him into the large entrance hall. The President shivered and drew his dark green greatcoat around him. "Eight years in the building, and I still feel drafts everywhere." In his waddling gait he went to one of the tall windows and rattled it.

"Jeremy, make a note to have the windows caulked," Hoban said, trying to control his temper. "Mr. President, I'm not a man to make excuses, but my hands have been tied. If Congress would only appropriate enough funds, we could finish the palace."

"Oh, funds, and more funds," Adams grumbled. "Since this government was formed, the legislature has always been jealous of the chief executive. Congress does whatever it can to thwart me. We must do the best we can. Mrs. Adams will join me in a few days; she isn't well and I'd be obliged if the palace could be made as comfortable as possible for her."

Hoban nodded, then said, "Jeremy Brand has volunteered to stay and show you anything you might need to know. I must return to Georgetown immediately; my wife is about to have her first child."

President Adams gave Hoban leave to go. Then Jeremy led the President through the rooms, explaining various features and functions. "The mansion has twenty-three rooms in all, but only six are ready for use. We haven't yet finished the main staircase to the upper floors, so I'm afraid you'll have to use the servant's staircase until it's built."

Dusk began to filter through the windows, and a gloomy chill filled the empty rooms. Jeremy lit a candelabrum and the men continued their inspection of the house, moving in a halo of light.

Adams stopped, looked all about him and suddenly said, "By the Almighty, I can't believe I'm here! The very first President of the United States to occupy the palace! Well, in this, at least, George Washington will never be able to circumvent me."

Jeremy wondered what Adams meant, but kept his counsel. He led the way into the Oval Room, where he had already installed Adams's desk. Then he lit the fire and the candles, and with the glow and warmth, the room seemed habitable.

"Is there anything else, Mr. President?" he asked.

Adams shook his head.

"Goodnight then, sir," Jeremy said. "We all hope that you and Mrs. Adams will be very happy here." Then he left.

President Adams wandered around the room; he stared out the windows to the dark grounds below. Then he sat at his desk, reflecting on what the future might bring. Where else but in this glorious new nation could the son of a simple shoemaker rise to become President? The thought was staggering to him, and he began to pen his thoughts in a letter to his wife, Abigail. The room lay silent, the only sounds the occasional popping of the fire and the prayerful whisper of his quill as it moved across the notepaper. He concluded the letter with a heartfelt thought, "I pray heaven to bestow the best of blessings on this house, and on all that shall hereafter inhabit it. May none but wise and honest men ever rule under this roof."

The following day Jeremy rode over to Georgetown to Mathias Breech's stoneworks. He ordered some supplies, which Eli loaded onto his wagon, and then lingered, hoping to catch sight of Rebecca. He knew she sometimes came to her father's establishment at this hour and had timed his errand accordingly. But this day she didn't appear.

Disappointed, he left. And then as his wagon creaked along M Street he saw her entering the stationery shop. He hitched the wagon to the post and bounded into the store. She turned as he came up to her and blurted, "Rebecca, will you go to the races with me?"

"I'm sorry, I can't. I've already promised to go with Zebulon."

"Well, there's a company of traveling players coming to Washington. I could get tickets."

"Oh Jeremy, Zebulon invited me to that weeks ago."

He shrugged, not quite able to hide his disappointment. "Always Zebulon," he said.

Feeling awkward and somewhat sorry for him, she cast about for some neutral subject. "And how is President Adams liking his accommodations?"

"Well enough, considering the state things are in." Unwilling to let her go, he repeated what Adams had said about Washington. "Then he said that Washington would never be able to circumvent him as the first President to live in the palace. He sounded almost joyous about that. Why, do you suppose?"

"Really, Jeremy, sometimes you're so naïve I think you must be a fool. It's common knowledge that Adams has always been overshadowed by Washington, even though it was Adams who insisted that Washington be named Commander-in-Chief of the Continental Army."

"I didn't realize that," he said.

"Oh yes, Adams was clever enough to know that was the

way to get the South to join the Revolution. But then Washington eclipsed him. The man of war is always a more natural hero to the people than the theoretician who labors in the background."

He looked at her with admiration. "I swear I never met a woman as smart as you. How do you know so much?"

"It's there for anybody to know if he chooses," she said. But she was flattered that he appreciated her intelligence, which was more than she could say about Zebulon. "Jeremy, I just thought of something. That touring company will be here for a number of performances. Perhaps—"

"Wonderful! I'll get us tickets for the second night."

Abigail Adams joined her husband in Washington on the afternoon of November sixteenth. Accompanying her was their four-year-old granddaughter Susan, a solemn little girl dressed in black.

Jeremy was working high up in the entrance hall and saw Abigail enter. He leaned over the scaffolding, taking measurements for the staircase that would connect the first and second floors. He also took Abigail's measure, for her reputation had preceded her. Martha Washington claimed that Abigail Adams was the smartest woman in America. She appeared thin, almost frail, with sharp features and quick discerning eyes. Her gray hair was crisped in the latest fashion and held in place by a ruffled cap. For the arduous coach trip from Braintree, via New York, Philadelphia, and Baltimore, she'd worn a sensible, sturdy cotton dress.

President Adams embraced his wife warmly. "We were expecting you earlier this day, Madam."

"We got lost on the road between Baltimore and Washington, and thought we would surely have to spend the night in the forest," Abigail said. "But a kindly old Negro gave us directions."

Though delighted to see his granddaughter, Adams also seemed unnerved by her presence. "How is Susan here?" he asked.

"I'll tell you as soon as we're settled," Abigail said. "Any news of the election?"

Adams shook his head. "All the votes have been cast, to

be sure, but it will take several weeks for them to be collected and tallied."

A maid came for Susan and took her to an upstairs bedroom adjoining the one that would be Mrs. Adams's.

Then Jeremy heard President Adams say, "I've just received word from John Quincy on the Continent. His work proceeds splendidly."

Abigail's face beamed with pride. Her eldest son had brought nothing but joy into their lives. He'd already served as minister to the Hague and was now part of the Berlin legation. They had great hopes for him.

Then Adams said tentatively, "And how is Charles?"

Tears came to Abigail's eyes. "I saw him in New York . . . It's why I brought Susan with me. Our son is dying. When I left him, I knew I'd never see him alive again."

A look of dismay crossed Adams's face. "Is there no hope?"

She shook her head. "The doctors say the alcohol poisoning is too far gone. It's corroded his insides entirely. We can only pray that the end will be swift and merciful."

Adams, a man of uncompromising morals even with his own kin, grew red in the face. "I renounce him! King David's Absalom had some ambition and some enterprise! Mine is a mere rake, buck, blood, and beast!" But with his outburst spent, he placed his trembling hand on Abigail's. His voice caught in his throat as he whispered, "Oh, that I might die for him, if that would relieve him of his faults as well as his disease."

For a moment, the two people standing in the entrance hall weren't the President and his lady, but lonely parents grieving for a lost child.

Later that night, as Jeremy tossed in his own bed, he wondered about the difference in the two Adams boys. Charles, dying of alcohol, and John Quincy, already a foreign minister, embarked on a brilliant career. Who could explain why one rose and one fell? He cast his mind to Zebulon and wondered if he would ever enjoy the reputation and favor of his older brother. Zebulon . . . who could embark to the Levant at a moment's notice, romance every tavern wench in Washington, and seemed to be on the verge of winning Rebecca Breech.

Somewhere, there's an opportunity for me, Jeremy thought.

A chance to change my life, my fortune, to be part of some great adventure. Something that will make Rebecca take note of me. He crushed the pillow in his fist. "And when it comes, I'll grab it with both hands!"

Though a semi-invalid, Abigail Adams set herself the task of making a home, taking full responsibility, as she'd done all her married life.

"We should have at least thirty in help to make this mansion work," Abigail said to her tiny staff of servants, "but we'll have to make do. First, we must have wood for the fireplaces. All thirteen must be kept burning to dry out the plaster and dampness, or we'll all come down with rheumatism." Then she threw up her hands. "Though we live in a forest, there's no wood to be had because there's no one to cut or cart it. Further, in all eighteen acres of this property, there isn't one clothesline! Where, may I ask, am I supposed to hang my wash?"

A gang of Negro men carrying lumber tramped into the entrance hall, delivered their load to Jeremy, then left.

"Who are those people?" Abigail asked.

"Why, they're slaves, ma'am," Jeremy said. "They work here."

Her sallow complexion grew even paler. "Slaves? *Here?* How can this be?"

"Well, ma'am, you see, the subcontractors are allowed to use their slaves to help build the palace, and then they charge the government for their time."

"Disgraceful! Building a free society on slave labor."

Jeremy didn't know what to think of that. Having once been an indentured servant, he felt a certain sympathy for the slaves; certainly, he considered Eli a friend. But since slavery was an ingrained way of life in the South, he couldn't conceive of what it would be like without it.

By the end of the day, Jeremy and the rest of the work crew had been run ragged, trying to get the accommodations settled to Abigail's satisfaction. Sometimes she sounded like a common scold, but to her credit, she worked as hard as everybody else, and Jeremy gradually grew to respect her.

• • •

"Are you finding the city to your liking?" he asked one day as he strung an enormous rope line for her across the width of the East Room.

Abigail swept the floor of loose plaster. "The other day I went to Georgetown and found it a dirty little hole and a quagmire. And as to the roads there, we shall make them by frequent passing before winter."

Jeremy swallowed. "Well, I hope that the mansion is now a little more comfortable for you."

"The only room in this entire house that's acceptable is the Oval Room. I fear you architects built this not as a home but to be looked at by strangers and visitors, and will render its occupants an object of ridicule to some, and pity to others."

Jeremy blushed with embarrassment and laughed at the same time. And Abigail Adams even ventured a slight smile.

Jeremy discovered as the days passed, that as irascible as John Adams was in his public life, so was he the devoted parent and husband. He worried constantly that Abigail might overwork herself, and when little Susan came down with the croup, he stayed up with her all night. He and Abigail seemed to have the most supportive marriage, and she engaged in heated discussions with him on the issues of the day. Her contribution to her husband's thoughts and policies were profound. She was his good right arm, her mind was as sharp as his, if not sharper; and further, she could be conciliatory in ways that he could never be.

"If I should lose this election—" Adams began.

"We won't even entertain such a thought," Abigail interrupted.

"—it will be Alexander Hamilton's fault completely," Adams finished. "That Creole bastard will do anything to further his own ambitions. My cabinet members are nothing more than spies for him."

"I've never encountered a man more fiercely ambitious than Hamilton," she agreed.

"His ambitions spring from an oversecretion of his glands, from which he cannot find enough whores to draw it off! Women and war, that's all he wants. Doesn't he realize that going to war with England or France now would court ruin? Every plan I had to increase our navy, denied by Congress;

every plan to enlarge our army, denied by Congress. And those who voted against me were the ones who clamored most vociferously for war. One wonders at the intelligence of the men we elect to Congress."

"Men riven with ambition, and more interested in personal power than in the good of the nation," Abigail agreed.

"From start to finish, my aim was simply to force France to change her policy and accept the United States as a free and equal nation. The only way to do this was to arm our merchant ships, build up our army, and at the same time engage in diplomacy of the most delicate nature. But that diplomacy would be to no avail unless the French realized we were ready and willing to fight for our honor and our independence. And that would have carried the day for the Federalists in this election, had it not been for that degenerate, womanizing bastard."

In an effort to have the Federalists choose Pinckney as their candidate over Adams, Hamilton had circulated a secret letter among party regulars, listing all of Adams's faults. A copy had fallen into the hands of the Democratic-Republicans, and Thomas Jefferson had made great use of it.

"All isn't lost," Abigail said. "I can't believe that the American people will forget all you've done. Didn't Jefferson call you the colossus of the Second Continental Congress? He said that no man did more to make the Declaration of Independence a reality than you."

"Then why did he run against me?" Adams fairly shouted. Then he hung his head in his hands. "There are times in my life, my dear Abigail, when I view myself and my own accomplishments, and I look so much like a small boy in my own eyes, that I think I'm a failure. Monuments and mausoleums will not be built to me."

"John, you must be content with the knowledge that you've always acted out of principle. Now the people must decide . . . and after them, the greatest judge of all, history."

The following day, Abigail called together the entire staff of the President's Palace. "We must get the mansion ready for the first levee," she said. "Jeremy, I count on you especially to see that there's no lumber or mounds of plaster in evidence that day. We still don't know the outcome of the election, but we must assure the people that though our leaders may change, the system will go on. Therefore, the President and I want his levee, the first in our new capital, and in our new home, to be most successful, and we ask your help."

With that, everybody fell to for the grand event.

Chapter 12

REBECCA AND Jeremy were standing in the foyer of Blodgett's Hotel during an intermission of *Julius Caesar*. The traveling players had set up the performance in the hotel's ballroom, and the audience milled about, chatting and very pleased with themselves. Culture was finally coming to Washington.

But Rebecca had other things on her mind. "Do you know in which room the Adams's levee will be?" she asked Jeremy.

"In the upper Oval Room," he said. He was still a little dazed that she'd consented to go out with him; he squirmed, wishing that he hadn't so outgrown his good suit, it was binding him everywhere.

"Describe the room to me," she said. "The furniture, the curtains, the color scheme."

"Why?"

"Never mind why, just describe it."

He'd gotten well into the description when Zebulon pushed his way through the crowd and grabbed his brother's arm. "What are you doing here?" he demanded. "You know she's affianced to me."

Jeremy's eyes flashed from Zebulon to Rebecca. "Is it true?" he asked.

"Absolutely not," she exclaimed. "Zebulon, you presume too much. As long as I haven't declared myself, I'll see whomever I want."

People turned at the raised voices and Zebulon's face twisted with anger. "Oh, in that case, perhaps I'd better forget about the invitation to the President's levee."

She felt her heart wrench. She'd accepted his invitation earlier. She was dying to go; everyone important in Washington society would be there. Now he was obviously using it as a weapon, expecting her to capitulate. She reached out and took Jeremy's arm. "I believe it's time for the final act."

Zebulon's face hardened and he muttered after them, "Take care, Jeremy."

When Rebecca returned home later that night she stormed around her bedroom, alternately crying and venting her anger. "He expects me to come begging to him, but I won't!"

"Yes ma'am," Letitia said, trying to calm her.

"But what am I going to do? I must go to the levee!"

"What about that Jeremy? Couldn't he take you?" Letitia asked.

"Oh, no. He's not going as an invited guest, but as hired help." She went to her father's bedroom and shook him awake. He peered at her, his nightcap askew, and listened to her tale.

"Rebecca, why do you waste your time with those Brand brothers?" he exclaimed. "There's nothing ahead but heartache with either of them."

She became very quiet. "Sometimes I think you're right, yet I can't seem to shake myself of them. It's as if we're in some kind of macabre dance, unable to break free—" She broke off suddenly and said, "Father, you must get me an invitation, you must. If I don't go I'll never be able to show my face in Washington."

"Utter nonsense," Mathias grumbled. "Now go to bed, we'll talk about it in the morning."

The two-mile walk back to Washington from Rebecca's house in Georgetown had exhilarated Jeremy. His step was jaunty; as he passed beneath an oak he leapt up with a cry and swung himself on a low bough.

"She went out with me!" he cried.

He was so preoccupied that when he got back to his cabin he didn't notice the dark form flattened against the side of the house. But as he opened the door, a strong hand clamped on his shoulder and spun him around. He had only a moment to see his brother's twisted face before Zebulon's fist smashed into his jaw. The punch sent him sprawling and he landed on his back, the wind knocked out of him.

"You'll get worse if I ever catch you with her again," Zebulon muttered. Then he started toward the rear of the cabin where he'd tied Baal.

Jeremy struggled to his feet. His head was reeling and one of his teeth felt loose. Then he stumbled after Zebulon, catching him just as he put his foot in the stirrup. He dragged Zebulon off the horse, yelling, "She told you—she'll go out with whomever—"

Caught off balance, Zebulon fell on him and both men toppled to the ground. Spooked, Baal whinnied and began to rear, his flashing hooves kicking up the turf as the men rolled around beneath him.

Jeremy managed to land a punch to his brother's solar plexus, a punishing blow that enraged Zebulon. He was the stronger, more canny fighter, and he scissored Jeremy's waist in a leg lock, then brought his elbow sharply against Jeremy's temple, stunning him.

Zebulon sprang to his feet; before Jeremy could get up he opened his cheek with a left cross and followed it with a right to his nose that made the blood spume. Jeremy fell forward to his knees, furious with himself that he somehow couldn't make his arms and legs do his bidding. Zebulon clenched both his hands and brought them down in a sledgehammer blow on the back of Jeremy's neck.

It paralyzed Jeremy, he couldn't move at all, he could only hear Zebulon cursing him.

"She's mine, I tell you—always has been, always will be. And you're a swine to try to steal her behind my back."

Jeremy managed to croak, "But she said—" then gagged as Zebulon kicked him in the ribs.

"Stay away from her, I'm warning you," Zebulon said. "The next time I'll forget you're my brother!" With that, he sprang on Baal and cantered off.

Jeremy watched him disappear into the darkness, then dragged his way into the cabin. He cleaned up as best he could, tested his tooth . . . He wouldn't lose it. But his rib ached something fierce; cracked probably. Morose with the beating, and with self-doubt—was he trying to steal her away from Zebulon?—he poured himself a stiff shot of whiskey. Then he collapsed on the bed, his head churning with nightmare images of a brother who could always best him.

"I don't care," he groaned. "His fists will turn into pulp before I give her up. But next time, I'll be ready."

The following day, Mathias Breech made inquiries about the Adams's levee and found that all the invitations had been sent out. There wasn't a single one available.

"It's exactly the kind of challenge I like," he told Rebecca, "especially if my girl's happiness is at stake. Go ahead with the fittings for your gown. You'll have the invitation."

Mathias hung around the Capitol Building most of the day, collaring legislators, but without any luck. That evening in the Fountain Tavern he found a congressman from Maryland who wasn't averse to a bribe.

"I'm a Democratic-Republican anyway," he said, pocketing the money. "The levee won't be much good. That Adams sets a very frugal table, like all those dour New Englanders."

When Mathias handed the neatly written invitation to Rebecca she threw her arms around his neck. "You're the only one I can count on."

"See you don't forget that," Mathias said.

For days before the event the Breech household hummed with activity. Letitia applied warm compresses of boiled milk to Rebecca's face, neck, and shoulders, washed her hair with Castile soap and ale, rinsed it in lemon water, and dried it in the sunlight. When Rebecca was finally dressed, Letitia looked at her. "You got to be the most prettiest creature God ever made."

Rebecca pressed her cheek to Letitia's. "Oh, I just know that something wonderful will happen today. I feel it in my blood. Perhaps I'll meet somebody new, or maybe—I don't know, but it's going to be wonderful."

The carriage took her to the President's Palace and she entered and climbed the back stairs to the upper floors. Everybody important in the government had jammed the house—since November seventeenth, Congress had been in session in Washington. From local society there came the Van Nesses, the Tayloes, and Victoria Connaught glittering with gold and diamond jewelry. She had in tow a thin, frightened-looking thirteen-year-old, her niece, Marianne Connaught.

The President was receiving in the upper Oval Room, and Rebecca entered a chamber wonderfully furnished with mahogany chairs and sofas upholstered in red damask, with window curtains and swags of the same fabric. Primed by Jeremy's description of the room, Rebecca had chosen her gown accordingly; in her saffron-yellow satin dress, with her titian hair hanging loose to her shoulders, she moved through the red room like a flickering candle flame.

President Adams stood at the head of the receiving line, wearing a suit of black velvet with white silk stockings, silver knee and shoe buckles, white waistcoat, and gloves. The two patches of frizzled hair sticking out from the sides of his shining head were powdered white; that and his round face and aquiline nose gave him somewhat the appearance of a bald snowy owl.

He noticed Rebecca staring at his hair and said with a wry smile, "My opponent, Mr. Jefferson, insists that straight hair is more democratic than curled, but I think curled hair is just as republican."

Emulating the courtly behavior established by George Washington, Adams didn't shake hands on greeting, but bowed from the waist. Rebecca curtsied low, exposing a fair amount of her glorious bosom to the eager assembly.

Abigail Adams wore a lace headdress that framed her crisped hair, a rope of fine pearls around her neck, and high-heeled shoes with black silk stockings.

"What an exquisite gown," Rebecca said, admiring Abigail's gunmetal-gray dress. "Such workmanship could only have come from the Continent."

"Paris, my dear," Abigail said. "The French monarchs may have lost their heads, but the world gained dressmakers."

Rebecca looked at her inquisitively and Abigail explained, "With the French Revolution, hundreds of seamstresses who'd labored at Versailles suddenly found themselves out of work. In order to live, they opened their own shops, and gowns once reserved for queens and countesses found their way to the bourgeoisie, and then to other countries. That's how France hopes to establish the finest dressmaking industry in all the world. I hear the same is true of their culinary arts, and for like reason."

Abigail left to greet some newcomers, and then Rebecca

saw Jeremy enter, freshly scrubbed, though his face looked a little swollen. He was with a man wearing the uniform of a U.S. Navy captain. When he spotted Rebecca, Jeremy came directly to her.

"May I introduce Captain Tingey?" he said.

Rebecca chatted amiably with the old salt. "Which is your ship?" she asked. "The *Constitution*? The *Constellation*?"

"Nay, I'm afraid I'm a landlocked captain."

"You see, President Adams has finally wrestled enough money from Congress to build a Navy Yard right here in Washington, and he's put Captain Tingey in charge," Jeremy explained. "If we're ever in a war, the Navy Yard would be vital to the defense of Washington."

Then the moment Rebecca had been anticipating arrived; Zebulon appeared in the doorway of the Oval Room. In his navy velvet jacket, skin-hugging breeches, and white ruffled shirt, she thought he cut a dashing figure.

Zebulon had planned to ignore Rebecca at the levee, but when he saw her standing with his brother and looking so radiant, his resolve evaporated. Much as he hated to admit it, the passion he'd always had for her had turned into a commanding love. "And after all the women I've bedded," he thought aloud, "she's hoist me by my own petard."

Zebulon's greeting was so gay that nothing might have happened between them. After complimenting her extravagantly, he said, "I noticed you talking to Abigail Adams. Now there's a woman not after my liking. She's got a meddlesome barbed tongue. Already they're calling her Mrs. President, a title which I think she rather likes. Have you heard? She's advocating that women get out more in the world."

"Well, perhaps she's right," Rebecca said.

"Your rightful place is in the home, bearing children," Zebulon said, with his crooked half-smile that intimated so much more than his words. "Isn't that what the good Lord intended since Eden?"

"You fall back on scripture when it pleases you," Rebecca said with an equally gay smile. "If only the commandments weren't so sorely lacking in your daily life."

Zebulon colored with her meaning. "Say what you will,

there's little you can do that would offend me."

Rebecca turned to Jeremy. "And what do you say?"

All at once his tongue felt lashed and tied. "I think . . . that a woman's place is wherever she chooses to make it."

"What tripe!" Zebulon barked.

Jeremy felt a surge of anger and clenched his fists, ready to fight it out right here. "Well, what about Queen Elizabeth, or Cleopatra? How much poorer the world would be if they'd been content to stay at home and churn butter."

"Fool, those women inherited their thrones," Zebulon said. His half-playful jab landed harder than he'd intended and Jeremy fell back a step. His body tensed, but Rebecca stepped between them, her eyes flashing from one to the other. Something had happened between them. A fight? . . . How strange that two men with the same father should look so different. Jeremy's eyes were wideset and of the clearest blue, the bones in his face were craggy, his jawline squared, and his nose straight, narrowing to a thin bridge. A hank of thick blond hair kept falling over his forehead and he brushed it out of his eyes. Zebulon was just a bit taller than his brother, a bit wider in the shoulders. His hair was so black that in some lights it had a bluish sheen. Heavy eyebrows and thick black lashes framed his deep brown, magnetic eyes. Yet something about his violent good looks was redolent with an unwholesome quality. He had the look of a man given to sybaritic excesses and deep dark urgings.

But it was Jeremy who'd surprised her with what he'd said. For somewhere in Rebecca's regimented life, made up of pinching corsets and boned stays, she yearned to break free. She wanted so much more than the lives of the women she saw around her, so much more than the fate of her mother. And yet nobody seemed to understand her need.

With the fireplace roaring, the crowded room became unpleasantly warm. Rebecca, Zebulon, and Jeremy walked outside and wandered through the palace.

"As soon as Congress appropriates the money, we'll be able to finish all the rooms," Jeremy said, his tensions somewhat eased.

"That may be never," Rebecca said with a twinkle. "Congress is jealous that the President has his own house while they're forced to sleep three and four to a bed at Blodgett's Hotel."

"Well, as they've said since time immemorial," Zebulon said on a rising note, "politics makes strange bedfellows."

They moved on to the Public Audience Room, and Rebecca, startled by what she saw, exclaimed, "What in heaven's name is happening here?"

Jeremy sighed. "The East Room was designed to be the grandest room in the mansion, where all important state functions would be held. But as you can see, Mrs. Adams uses it as a laundry room to dry her clothes."

The presidential linen, sheets, pillowcases, and underclothes hung from the clotheslines criss-crossing the vast chamber.

Back in the Oval Room, wine and cakes were served, and the normal gossip flowed. As the levee progressed, Abigail Adams and Victoria Connaught became engaged in a lively discussion about the state of the Union. Rebecca gravitated toward the two women, delighted that Victoria seemed to have met her match.

"We must all work for the abolition of slavery," Abigail was saying.

"But the slaves are my private property, bought and paid for," Victoria exclaimed. "Who will reimburse me? Anyway, these Negroes are little more than savages."

"Such a thought is surely anathema to a good Christian," Abigail said. "True, they must be educated to our ways, but the only way to improve the lot of *everybody,* white and Negro, is by compulsory education, starting with the young."

Victoria's wattles vibrated as she shook her head vigorously. "Am I to be responsible for everybody? As the Bible says, 'The poor shall never be out of the land.' If anybody wants to learn, then let him earn it."

"Compulsory education through a fair tax system," Abigail insisted. "And what's more, we must have the vote for women. I think it a sin that half our population is relegated to the role of chattel by their men. A married woman can't own or will property, she can't sit on a jury, nor can she sue for redress. And she cannot vote. That too is slavery."

Rebecca listened, her blood surging with these ideas. She'd

never been able to articulate them for herself, but hearing them now . . . Except in the domestic and social skills, her own formal education had been sorely lacking. Yet she could add more accurately than her father, read better than Zebulon. But she was a woman, and so much in the world was denied her.

"Forgive me for interrupting," Rebecca said to the ladies. "But Mrs. Adams, what you're saying sounds so sensible. Imagine what an enormous pool of skills might be tapped under such a system! Why, everybody in the nation would benefit."

"Exactly, my dear," Abigail said, appraising her sharply. "It's a cause worthy of a crusade. If men won't lead, then women must."

"It sounds like work for a virago," Victoria Connaught said, and retreated to the punchbowl, hauling Marianne along after her.

"Do you really think that one day women will have the right to vote?" Rebecca asked.

Abigail shrugged her frail shoulders. "Sometimes the battle seems so endless. But I do know that we'll never achieve it unless we fight for it."

"But how is such a thing possible?"

"Not all men are misguided. Some states have already given women the vote, but we must make it a *national* policy." She let out a long, weary sigh. "My own experience is that women themselves must be enlightened, most times mere lassitude keeps them in bondage." Then she reached out and gripped Rebecca's hand with her long slender fingers. "It may take ten years, fifty, or even a hundred, but I believe in the women of this nation. One day they'll claim their God-given rights as equals."

Rebecca's head was spinning, as if she'd just inhaled the clearest mountain air. Then Abigail Adams relaxed and smiled at her. "Here I am filling your head with my ramblings when you're probably more interested in the young men here."

Rebecca looked across the room to where Zebulon was flirting with one of the Tayloe heiresses. "I've always wanted much more than marriage, though if you pressed me, I doubt I could tell you what."

"How well I know your feelings, my dear," Abigail Adams said. "But marriage needn't be the end to any other dreams.

I raised four children, ran the family farm in Braintree, coped with illness and long years of loneliness while Mr. Adams was away serving our country. But I considered his absences badges of my honor. And yet in spite of all that, I still managed to write articles about what I believed, and even managed to get them published. If only to let the world know that a woman too could have a mind."

"Oh, yes," Rebecca responded eagerly.

"Unless one speaks out, nothing will change. And you daren't leave that task to others, for your own voice must be heard also. And in that groundswell, my dear, perhaps one day we'll be able to abolish slavery in its every form."

"I promise I will," Rebecca said, feeling as though she was taking some holy vow.

With an encouraging smile, Abigail Adams walked off.

Rebecca stared after the frail, extraordinary woman. "I will do something with my life," she whispered fiercely, "I will." And then it suddenly came to her, an insight so deep it was almost too painful to bear. This is why I came here today, she thought. Not to flirt, or to gossip, or even to meet somebody new. But to discover myself.

Chapter 13

SEVERAL DAYS later, great sadness overwhelmed the Adamses in the President's Palace. The popular vote had finally been counted, and the legislators cast their ballots in the Electoral College. Adams received 65 votes; Thomas Jefferson and Aaron Burr each received 73 votes, thus tying for the presidency.

Adams was devastated and Jeremy learned to walk softly in his presence. His narrow margin of just three votes in his first election, plus his loss in the second, convinced him that all along the nation had misunderstood his intentions.

One winter morning, Jeremy was helping Adams crate up his books in the library. Adams looked so morose that Jeremy said, "Sir, I just wanted you to know that it's been a privilege working for you."

Adams tried to be gracious but his hurt was patent. "Washington set the precedent of serving for two terms, and the electorate should have done the same for me."

Jeremy shifted uncomfortably on the library ladder, not knowing what to say. "Well sir, no man's served his country better than you. The Continental Congress, our War for Independence—"

Adams stamped his foot, "The history of our Revolution will be a continued lie from one end to the other. The essence of the whole will be that Benjamin Franklin's electrical rod smote the earth, and out sprang George Washington!"

Jeremy burst out laughing in spite of himself, and Adams continued, "You worked here when Washington inspected the palace, didn't you? Then doubtless he's told you the story of his revelation that Christmas Eve at Valley Forge? Ah, I see by your expression that he did. Believe me, young man, it's a tale oft told and oft embellished by our esteemed Washington. But far be it from me to deny a man his revelations."

During his final weeks in power, Adams sought to preserve his political point of view and named to the bench twenty-three judges with strong Federalist sympathies. Of all these midnight appointments, the one that was to have the farthest-reaching consequences was that of John Marshall as Chief Justice of the Supreme Court. Like Adams, John Marshall was an avid champion of a strong federal government.

In her sitting room in her Georgetown house, Rebecca watched the winter snows swirl and eddy on the northern winds. Spinning, sewing, canning, candle-dipping—she had no patience for these boring household tasks. Taking her courage in her hands, she went to her desk and tried to write an article. She chose as her subject, the first levee in the President's Palace, and penned it somewhat in the style of the society columnist of the *National Intelligencer*. In a moment of caution she thought, no point in it being rejected just because I'm a woman, and signed it with a male pseudonym, Rebel Thorne. She sent it off to the newspaper, using general delivery at the Post Office as a return address.

For days she waited anxiously for a reply and was crushed when the piece was rejected. Girding her loins, she tried another essay, this time somewhat parroting Abigail Adams's views about compulsory public education. Another rejection, but there was also a short note from the publisher saying that though Abigail Adams was no longer newsworthy, the author of the article showed considerable insight and ability. Encouraged, Rebecca searched for the one cause that would engage her, something so pressing that the newspaper wouldn't dare reject it.

With the tie vote for the presidency between Aaron Burr and Thomas Jefferson unresolved, a grave problem developed for the nation. The capital buzzed with rumors that the ballots had been tampered with, and with Aaron Burr's reputation for being a party hack wedded to New York's political machine, the Sons of St. Tammany, those rumors could easily be true.

Though Jefferson had won the popular vote by a large margin, the system was such that the two highest vote-getters in the Electoral College became President and Vice-President respectively. But with both men deadlocked at 73 votes apiece, the election was thrown into the House of Representatives.

Rebecca thought this might be the news she'd been searching for and made ready to go to the Capitol to witness the voting.

Zebulon happened to be in the Breech house discussing outfitting another slave ship with her father. When he discovered her plans he objected. "It's not safe for you to go alone. There's a mob of unruly people there, ready to riot over the slightest incident." He insisted that he accompany her, and for once, Mathias Breech didn't resist.

A crowd had indeed gathered at the Capitol, and Rebecca and Zebulon had to fight for seats in the chamber of the House of Representatives.

"The election being thrown into the House is a fierce blow to Jefferson's chances," Rebecca said. "We have a lame-duck Congress, mostly Federalists, and they're all highly antagonistic to him."

"Jefferson doesn't deserve to win," he said, turning around and punching a drunk who was bellowing in their ears. "The man is a milksop. When the time came for him to take up arms in the Revolution, he retired to Virginia!"

"Not every man is suited to fight," she said. "And by God, he did win this popular vote. Isn't that more an expression of the will of the people than these politicians making shadowy deals in back rooms?"

Rebecca listened intently as the bitter debates on the floor of the House continued. She took to coming to the Capitol every day with Letitia; she eavesdropped on some Congressmen, talked with others, and came away convinced that here was an issue burning to be heard. Late one night she set pen to paper.

"Our founding fathers never dreamed that the voting system they devised might one day disenfranchise the rightful winner of an election. Clearly, as the popular vote proves, Thomas Jefferson is the choice of the people. Just as clearly, Aaron Burr, who was presented to the voters as Jefferson's Vice-President, should remain precisely that.

"But then why do the Federalists seek to deny Jefferson his

due, and elevate Burr in his stead? Are they fearful that Jeffersonian democracy will oust these privileged few from their sinecures? Can it be that they realize the power-hungry Burr will be more easily manipulated than Jefferson? Particularly if Burr owes the Federalists his soul for having gained him the highest office in the land.

"Burr is the leader of the Society of the Sons of St. Tammany, a powerful mercantile organization with strong economic ties to New York and New England." Here Rebecca digressed for a moment and threw in a bit of information she thought might amuse the reader. "Tammany, as many of you will recall, was an Indian Chief friendly to the first white settlers in this country. In appreciation, and perhaps facetiously, the settlers conferred sainthood on him, and the New York political machine took Tammany's name.

"Every decent American calls on Aaron Burr to resist this dastardly Federalist attempt to thwart the democratic process. But if Burr should prove to be without conscience, then it will be time for Alexander Hamilton, the leader of that party, to prove to the nation that he can respond to the will of the people. We call upon you, Alexander Hamilton, to support Jefferson. In your hands lies justice."

This time, Rebecca's article was snapped up by the *National Intelligencer*. She barely had time to celebrate her good fortune before the piece was reprinted in newspapers in Baltimore, Philadelphia, and New York. The immediacy of the writing, the sense that the reader was overhearing political deals being made in smoky back rooms, made it an instant success.

Send more posthaste! the newspaper's editor wrote frantically to Rebel Thorne, and Rebecca complied. She wrote a detailed biography of Aaron Burr, his reputation as a rake, his undeniable charm with women, and the bastard children he'd fathered. "And what of his tender age?" she wrote. "Dare we entrust the government to a man who at forty-two is apparently still more interested in sowing his wild oats than in governing? In a moment of crisis would we find him at his desk, or in some libertine's bed?"

When this article appeared, the Federalists thundered, "Who is this damned Rebel Thorne?" They were pinked to the quick by the rapier thrusts of this journalist. Word was that Aaron

Burr was so incensed that he swore he'd challenge this Thorne to a duel as soon as they met.

The circulation of the *National Intelligencer* shot up and the editor clamored for more articles. Rebecca had never experienced such a feeling of excitement. She was doing something worthy, and it fulfilled her as nothing else had ever done.

Believing it only fair to show both sides of the question, she responded with an account of Alexander Hamilton's life. She wrote of his beginnings as the bastard son of a Scotsman in the West Indies, and the accident of foreign birth which forever denied him the presidency. She painted a portrait of the dazzling personality that had made him a favorite of George Washington's, and which had enabled him to marry the Schuyler heiress of New York's society.

She gave a brief history of why Hamilton disliked Jefferson. "When Jefferson succeeded Benjamin Franklin as minister to France, he actively aided and abetted their revolution. This enraged Hamilton, who believes that the masses are a 'great beast.' Hamilton is convinced that Jefferson's ideas of equality and of a democracy of the people is a dangerous thing for the United States."

Then she held a candle up to Hamilton's darker side, the affairs he'd confessed to with prostitutes and other women of low orders. "His arrogance and political manipulations have made him the power behind the throne, and earned him the name, 'Kingmaker.' But for what purpose did thousands die in our Revolution if not to free us from those who would foist kings on us? Hamilton, the nation beseeches you, repent your royalist ways, clasp truth, honor, and justice to your bosom. Repudiate Burr!"

The mixture of insinuation, scandal, and an almost evangelical patriotism was so potent that whenever Rebel Thorne's name appeared in the *National Intelligencer*, that edition was immediately sold out.

"Who is Rebel Thorne?" became the question in the shops, in the drawing rooms, and in the halls of Congress. Was it Thomas Jefferson himself, cleverly playing the baiting game? The consensus was that the style was too young, too reckless, and far too racy to be Jefferson. "Rebel Thorne writes with a pen dipped in the venom of a viper," said the Federalists, while the Democratic-Republicans proclaimed him a voice of truth. Sensing a good commercial twist, the *National Intelligencer* ran an ad calling for the author to reveal himself.

Only one other person knew Thorne's identity, Letitia, and that knowledge sat uneasily with her. "Never knew a body to cause so much commotion as you," she said. "I'm telling you, no good can come of it."

"I suppose you're right," Rebecca said. "What's the good of all this if I can't tell anybody it's me? Well, then, let's go down to the newspaper and tell them."

Letitia rolled her eyes but accompanied her mistress to the newspaper's offices at Pennsylvania Avenue and Seventh Street. Rebecca presented herself to the owner, Samuel Smith, known as Silky Milky Smith because of his smooth ways.

"Would you like a subscription?" he asked.

She shook her head. "I've come in answer to your ad. I'm Rebel Thorne."

He lit up a cheroot and blew the smoke at the ceiling. "My dear young lady, I don't have time for these silly jokes. I'm a very busy man. You're the fourth person to claim that."

She reached into her reticule and placed the originals of all her articles on his desk. Silky Milky's eyes bulged as he riffled through them. "Who gave you these, your father? Brother?" When he finally realized that she had indeed written them, he mopped his perspiring brow. "By the merciful Lord, what are we going to do about this?"

"To begin with, I trust you'll pay me for my labors. As yet, I haven't received a dime. Then I expect you'll explain to your subscribers just who I am."

He stabbed out his cheroot with a nervous gesture. "Let me be frank Miss Thorne—Miss Breech. I'd like very much to continue to publish what you write."

"I would like that too," she said, smiling.

"But readers are apt to be peculiar. When it comes to politics and the important issues, they take a male's voice far more seriously."

"It occurs to me that readers' attitudes are no more peculiar than editors'," she said with a burst of courage.

"Now see here, Miss Breech, there's absolutely no reason to be testy." He was accustomed to a diffident manner in his women and wasn't about to countenance her behavior. "Grant me that I know this business better than you. Women do well writing society columns, or helpful household hints, but in the political arena, you won't be taken seriously. As a man, however, Rebel Thorne can have a promising career."

Torn between resentment at his attitude, and the sneaking suspicion that he might be right, Rebecca said, "I find this altogether distressing. Perhaps it would be wiser for me to deal with another newspaper."

Silky Milky was suddenly all concern. Solicitously he poured Rebecca a glass of water. "No need for that," he said. "One of the reasons I was anxious to meet you was to tell you that we're going to pay you our top rate. A penny a word," he said, and gave her a lavish smile.

"Well, that's very kind of you," she said, returning a smile in the same coin. "I was thinking more in terms of three cents a word."

"Out of the question," he said, knocking over a tray of type in his haste to get up. "Not even our chief editor, Joseph Gales, gets more than two cents a word."

"Oh, how unfortunate. I just had my heart set on three. Well, I guess I'll just have to take my new article about Thomas Jefferson elsewhere. Come along, Letitia."

Rebecca got to the door and Silky Milky Smith called out, "All right, three. But no one must know. And no one must ever know that you're Rebel Thorne."

"I give you my word," she said.

Once outside, Letitia fanned herself furiously. "Lord be my witness, I was near to fainting in that man's office."

Rebecca let out a huge sigh of relief. "Me too, if you must know."

"Miss Rebecca, you got more nerve than *anybody*. Going to get you in trouble someday."

"Well, no matter what their excuses, they're not giving me the recognition I deserve. So I ought to get some other sort of compensation, shouldn't I?"

"I don't hardly understand those high words, Miss Rebecca. I only knows that you got a very hard mind in that soft body of yours. That means trouble, sure as fish swim. And that's all I got to say on that matter."

• • •

During this period, Rebecca went back to the Capitol every day and spent long hours there. By now, twenty ballots had been taken, but there'd been no shifting in anybody's position, and the election remained unresolved.

The tension in Washington mounted. Congress declared that failing the election of a President, they would appoint Chief Justice Marshall as interim President until a totally new election could be held.

Jefferson, usually a mild-mannered man of compromise, was outraged at this turn and rose to the challenge. After all, he'd won the majority vote, and led Burr eight states to six, with Maryland and Vermont evenly divided. Jefferson declared openly and firmly, "If Congress appoints the newly confirmed Chief Justice Marshall as President, within that day the middle states will arm themselves and march on Washington!"

The Federalists cried out at that, accusing Jefferson of agitating for civil war. Jefferson rejoined, "I will call a new convention to reorganize the government, amend the Constitution, and this time make it a document even more radical."

The voting became so intense that to break the tie, all-night sessions were held in the Capitol Building. The delegates slept in chairs or on the floor, complaining bitterly about the snowy, cold weather. Outside, the crowd gathered until they were a thousand, then two thousand strong. Rebecca didn't know where she was getting the strength from, but along with Letitia, she too kept the all-night vigils.

At one point Letitia left her seat and Jeremy Brand slipped in beside Rebecca. She looked at him in dazed surprise. "I'd no idea you were interested in this," she said.

"Who occupies the President's Palace is very important—not only to the nation, but to me personally, since I'll be working for the man."

"And whom do you prefer?"

"Jefferson, without question. To my mind, he's more the statesman. But even if I didn't prefer him, the presidency should be his because more people voted for him."

Rebecca nodded absently. After a bit, her heavy-lidded eyes closed and she fell asleep against his shoulder. Jeremy put his arm around her, thinking that happiness would be to cradle her so every night. "I love you," he whispered, daring to say while she slept what he'd never dared while she was awake.

Rebecca wakened to find the voting still dragging on. Soon thirty ballots had been cast, with no resolution. "Look over there," she gasped. She and Jeremy watched Joseph Nicholson of Maryland carried into the chamber on a stretcher. Though he was delirious and suffering from a high fever, he'd come through the raging snowstorm so that he could cast his ballot. His hand trembled so badly that his wife had to steady it for him to write his name.

"We're at a crucial point in the history of our country," Rebecca said to Jeremy. "Unless this is resolved, and soon, we'll have a civil war on our hands."

"And unless you get some sleep, you're going to collapse," he said, lifting her in his arms.

She fought against him weakly until he put her down. "I must see this to its end."

And then Alexander Hamilton once more made his power felt. As much as he mistrusted Jefferson, Hamilton absolutely loathed Aaron Burr. He was convinced that if Burr was elected he would usurp the powers of the presidency and seize control of the government just as Napoleon had done in France. Hamilton therefore let it be known to the Federalists that he preferred Jefferson as the lesser of the two evils.

On February 11, 1801, exactly three weeks before the date set for the inauguration of the new President—whoever he might be—the thirty-sixth ballot was cast. Matthew Lyon of Vermont cast the tie-breaking vote, and a weary Rebecca sobbed with relief when Thomas Jefferson became the third President of the United States.

Chapter 14

ON MARCH 4, 1801, the first Inauguration Day to be held in Washington, a company of artillerymen and riflemen paraded in front of Conrad and McMunn's boarding house, where Jefferson was staying.

Rebecca and Zebulon, along with everybody else in the district, had come to see the ceremony. When Jeremy saw them, he edged closer until Rebecca waved for him to join them, much to Zebulon's annoyance. Rebecca started at the roar of cannon coming from a fortress near the river's mouth.

"This is the first time we'll have a Democratic-Republican in the President's Palace," Jeremy said. "Already Jefferson's said that he wants it to be called the President's *House*."

"A small sop to throw to the masses! It's yet another example of Jefferson's deceit," Zebulon said. "Never was a man more an aristocrat. His estates are grand, and he owns as many slaves as Washington did. How paradoxical for him to claim that all men are created equal, and yet to own slaves."

"You own slaves," Jeremy challenged him.

"Of course, but I don't believe that men are created equal. Some are born to rule, others to serve, and if God hadn't willed it so, then it wouldn't be. The Negro is lazy and shiftless, and wants only to be taken care of."

"You mean like Eli?" Jeremy said hotly. Eli had run away again, and it had taken months before he was caught and returned.

Zebulon shook his head at Jeremy. "Never in all my days have I met anybody as contrary as you." Then he turned his back on him and said to Rebecca, "What do you think of Adams not staying for the inauguration? What a breach of manners!"

"I know he sent a note to Jefferson claiming family problems," Jeremy cut in. "After all, his son Charles did die."

Rebecca shook her head. "The truth is that Adams couldn't bear Jefferson's moment of triumph. He believed that the entire campaign was a vicious act against him, rigged by Jefferson and Hamilton. I doubt if Adams will ever forgive either of them."

"Here he comes," Jeremy said, as Jefferson came out of the boarding house.

Cannon salutes thundered throughout the city as Jefferson, flanked by Chief Justice John Marshall and Vice-President-elect Aaron Burr, started walking to the Capitol along muddy, rutted Pennsylvania Avenue.

"Does he intend to walk the entire way?" Rebecca asked, as they followed.

Jeremy nodded eagerly. "Walking is truer to his belief of how a real democratic President should act."

"Will you look at his clothes?" she said, aghast.

Jefferson wore a blue coat, gray hair waistcoat, red under-waistcoat, green velveteen breeches, and gray yarn stockings. Though his rag-tag clothes were purposely designed to contrast with the aristocratic deportment of Washington and Adams, they couldn't hide his own patrician qualities. At fifty-seven, he strode along like a man half that age. He was six foot and lean of body; his tousled shoulder-length gray hair still revealed traces of the sandy red mane he'd had when he'd drafted the Declaration of Independence twenty-five years before.

Jefferson walked with two men he loathed, the consummate Federalist Marshall, who happened to be his cousin, and wily Aaron Burr, burning with political ambitions of his own.

The crowd reached the Capitol; only the right wing, the Senate, was completed. Perhaps a thousand people crowded into the chamber to witness the transfer of power. Chief Justice Marshall administered the oath and Jeremy strained to hear Jefferson's response:

"I do solemnly swear that I will faithfully execute the office of President of the United States, and will to the best of my ability preserve, protect, and defend the Constitution of the United States."

With these thirty-five fateful words, the power of the office passed peacefully from one American to his elected successor. Jeremy found this a thrilling thought and whispered to Rebecca, "One day you'll tell your grandchildren that you saw the first inauguration ever held in Washington."

I'll be telling more than my grandchildren, she thought, forming an idea in her head for a new article.

Jefferson began his inauguration speech in a soft, nearly inaudible voice. "We are all Republicans . . . we are all Federalists," he began, and the chamber immediately fell silent at Jefferson's attempt at reconciling the nation after the venomous campaign.

Zebulon casually put his arm around Rebecca's waist, but she paid no attention, for a thought had suddenly occurred to her. No woman would ever take that oath of office! The patent unfairness made her tremble. Politics was a man's game in this man's world, and by accident of birth, she was destined to play a secondary role in all things. "I won't have it!" she whispered fiercely.

Mistaking the cause of her vehemence, Zebulon hastily withdrew his arm.

Jefferson droned on, "We wish a wise and frugal government which shall restrain men from injuring one another, and shall leave them otherwise free to regulate their own pursuits of industry and improvement, and shall not take from the mouth of labor, the bread it has earned."

Jeremy's face was transfigured with hope. "That's the man's greatness," he murmured to Rebecca. "He makes me feel that we can build a great nation, not in some distant future, but right here, right now."

After the inaugural ceremonies, Jefferson and his party returned to Conrad and McMunn's, and the rest of the crowd slowly drifted away. Rebecca's eyes filled with tears, in part from the raw smarting March wind, but also because of the upsetting thought she'd had.

At home, Rebecca's restlessness grew. Letitia brought her a hot toddy. "Make you sleep better," she said.

She took a long swallow, feeling the warmth suffuse through her body. "You know, Letitia, I never really understood grasping women before. But after all, what choice did Lucrezia Borgia have except the poisoned cup?"

"Who?"

"And Madame Pompadour? She was forced to be a courtesan to get what she wanted."

"Who?"

"But that way of life's disappeared," she said as she drained the drink. "I've got to face facts. Whatever I get out of life, it will have to be through a man."

"Been telling you that for years."

"And so I'd better be very careful about whom I choose. Somebody industrious."

"That Zebulon, he'd sail around the world for you."

"I believe he would. But you know, Jeremy's just as hard a worker. I need somebody who's as bright as I am, somebody who'll put me foremost in his life." Her head reeled slightly with the effects of the toddy. "Oh, Letitia, which one?" she whispered, her voice edged with despair.

One of the first things that Jefferson did on moving into the American Palace was to investigate the possibility of installing a new kind of water closet. The raw sewage ran from an open pipe onto the grounds, making the approaches to the mansion distinctly unpleasant. Jefferson also officially ordered that the mansion be called the President's House, so determined was he to wipe out any vestige of the Old-World aristocracy.

For that reason, he gave the area in front of the home to the city, deeming it too large and pretentious for a front lawn. It quickly became known as President's Square, though there was a movement afoot to call it Lafayette Park.

Acting on orders from Jefferson, Jeremy worked to improve the vista from the President's House to the Potowmack, though Jefferson lamented the fact that so many glorious trees had to be cut down. In the weeks that followed, a measure of privacy was achieved by the erection of large earthmounds to the east and west of the grounds, which shielded the house somewhat from the ever-growing number of the curious. The acreage was surrounded by a simple rail fence with occasional stiles to keep out the cattle, but the people were allowed to roam about freely, including in the mansion. The workers' shacks were slowly being removed from the area, but Jeremy's cabin fortunately lay outside the boundary, so it was left standing.

Jefferson, possessed of boundless energy, and with very set ideas of his own, immediately wanted to change the American Palace to his own liking, and he summoned James Hoban for a conference.

"I don't like the sound of this," Hoban said to Jeremy as he prepared to meet the President. "I've had trouble with Jefferson from the very start of construction, what with his wanting changes and all."

Jeremy waited impatiently while Hoban and the President were closeted in the library for more than two hours. When Hoban finally emerged, his face was bright pink and his eyes were wide with anger.

"What happened?" Jeremy asked, feeling his stomach sink.

"Handed in my resignation is what," Hoban exclaimed. He rattled and slammed drawers as he packed his T-square and triangles, and his set of compasses and drawing pens. "The man wants to tear the palace apart, change the façade, add wings, and make it so different from what I designed that I want no part of it!"

"But can't you talk to him, reason it out?" he asked.

"He's the President, and there's no reasoning with that."

Jeremy's shoulders slumped. "Well, I guess I'd better pack my things too. I've been with you so long, I don't think I could work for anybody else."

Hoban caught his arm. "Aye, that's a fine sentiment and I appreciate your loyalty. But there's no reason to worry about me, lad. I've plenty to do what with repairing Blodgett's Hotel and overseeing all the other buildings I'm putting up in Washington. Besides, I told the President that you'd probably stay on. And I'm asking you to, Jeremy. After all, you're the only one in this place who knows where everything is. And you've got to protect our interests, see they don't ruin things too badly."

"Well, I'll have to sleep on that," Jeremy said.

But before the afternoon ended, President Jefferson called Jeremy into his office and personally asked him to stay. Jefferson's manner was so gentle and ingratiating that Jeremy immediately said yes, and felt a great sense of relief for his decision. He did love this house.

Within the week, Jefferson had hired another architect,

Benjamin Latrobe, and Jeremy breathed easier, for he'd met Latrobe and gotten on reasonably well with him.

Latrobe, an Englishman who'd recently come to the United States, was a confirmed Grecophile in his architectural preferences, whereas Jefferson preferred the Roman style. The two men planned to alter most of the rooms radically.

But we've only just gotten the place livable, Jeremy thought with a groan, as he listened to them.

"The entrance hall is all stomach," Jefferson said, "and large enough for an emperor, the Pope, and the Grand Lama."

But much to Jeremy's relief, Jefferson and Latrobe were stopped dead when Congress refused to appropriate any funds. Some changes were made: the flaking walls were replastered, the windows reglazed and secured against drafts.

Jefferson's wife, Martha, had died many years before, and so Jefferson's daughter sometimes acted as his hostess. But since she was married with a family of her own, the role of hostess was gladly assumed by Dolley Madison, the indefatigable wife of James Madison, Jefferson's secretary of state.

Dolley took an instant liking to Jeremy, but then she liked almost everybody. She was a buxom tallish woman, and with such a gay, irrepressible manner that Jeremy couldn't resist her.

But one woman in Washington disliked Dolley intensely—Victoria Connaught. She spent her days sharpening her knives for Dolley, for she would brook no competition in her role as social arbiter of Washington. And then came the day when Victoria locked horns with the President himself.

Early in his administration, Jefferson announced the abolition of the levee. When the news reached the ladies of Washington, via the *National Intelligencer,* the enraged flock converged on the President's House one morning, led by Victoria Connaught. Sensing a newsworthy event, Rebecca had also come. She was more intrigued by the confrontation than by this female silliness. The women crowded into the entrance hall, disrupting the work being done there by Jeremy and his construction crew.

"The President isn't in," Jeremy told Victoria.

"We'll wait," she said determinedly. Then she turned to the women, "Why the weekly levee is our prerogative! Are we to be made mere country outcasts by this man who should know better? Or perhaps it's because he has something to hide?"

Rebecca saw the knowing looks pass between some of the women. Victoria Connaught's unearthed something, she thought.

They waited until Jefferson arrived; he'd just finished his usual morning ride on his favorite mount, Wildair. He'd done away with the ostentation of coach and six and went everywhere on horseback. He greeted the ladies with all the charm of a Virginia aristocrat, led them to the Green Room, which was outfitted with table and chairs, and ordered his chef, Monsieur Julien, to send up tea and cakes from the kitchen.

Jefferson listened patiently as Victoria Connaught pressed her case for the levee. "It's traditional," she insisted. "George Washington held them in Philadelphia, and Adams continued them right in this very mansion. How else are we to know our leaders? How else are they to know our will?"

"Why, by election, madam," Jefferson said gently.

Most of the ladies in the group felt predisposed toward Jefferson, but none as much as Rebecca. She studied him intently. He was handsome, with a wide, firm-set mouth. His gray eyes sometimes appeared to be a light blue, and his broad brow hinted at the massive intelligence that had made him a mathematician, scientist, city planner, architect, linguist, and writer. She knew that he'd been devastated by the death of his wife, and had sworn a deathbed vow never to remarry. His grief had been so great that he'd burned every picture, likeness, letter, and personal memento of their life together. If I could have one wish . . . it would be to make Jefferson forget his vow, Rebecca thought. To be married to such a brilliant man, and be the First Lady of the United States, was a thought too heady to bear.

But Victoria Connaught wasn't taken in by his looks or manner. Friends of hers who lived near Monticello had written her disquieting rumors about Jefferson. A reporter named Callander had been rooting around, and what he'd uncovered was so awesome that Victoria didn't dare repeat it until she was absolutely certain. She had, however, anonymously alerted certain Washington and Georgetown newspapers.

"My dear ladies," Jefferson began, "surely you must realize that levees are a carry-over from the old world, and what we are trying to do here is create a new one. Levees are a waste of time; they sap our energies and prevent us from doing work more appropriate to the well being of the nation. But I'll tell you what I'll do."

He stood up and slowly walked back and forth in front of the women. "We shall announce two grand functions, one every New Year's Day, which will be an open house for all to come and celebrate the New Year. And the second will be a pelle melle on the Fourth of July to celebrate our independence. And with all the hoopla and fireworks that President Adams once recommended." He stopped before Victoria Connaught and smiled at her. "Further, I'll be available to any of you, at any time."

A babble of agreeable comment came from the ladies, and Rebecca saw how completely he'd disarmed them. She looked at Victoria Connaught, but that worthy's lips remained pinched, much like a weasel about to ferret out some choice piece of information.

What can Victoria possibly know? Rebecca wondered. And is it something that would interest Rebel Thorne? She began to read everything she could about Jefferson—his early life, his years as a minister in France, his home and life in Monticello, the slaves he owned. As casually as she could without creating suspicion, she talked to many senators and congressmen from Virginia. A rumor from one, a suspicion from another, something left unsaid by a third, all pointed in a direction so chilling that Rebecca didn't dare believe what she'd begun to piece together.

"This is one thing I'll never write about," she said to Letitia.

"What?" Letitia asked breathlessly.

"If it's true, it could bring about the impeachment of the President, maybe even bring down the government."

Chapter 15

ZEBULON BARGED into the Breech house in Georgetown. "Mathias!" he shouted.

Rebecca and her father came running downstairs. "What is it?" Rebecca asked.

"Have you heard the news? Tripoli has just declared war on the United States!"

"By God, how did this happen?" Mathias asked.

Zebulon slapped his riding crop against his leg. "When President Jefferson refused their demands to pay more tribute, the Moors declared war."

Mathias's hand trembled as he poured them a round of port. Outside, the trees stirred lazily in the mid-May weather, dappling the sitting room with soft light. "Thank the Lord you hadn't put out to sea yet," Mathias said to Zebulon. "But what does this mean for us?"

"It means we daren't sail yet. At least until this is resolved one way or another. Every American ship in the Mediterranean is now fair game for the Moors."

"But surely President Jefferson won't allow that," Rebecca said.

"What's his choice?" Zebulon asked. "The first thing he did when he took office was to cut the Navy's budget. We have no fleet of any size to send against them."

"Well, then, the dangers must be made apparent to the President and to the people," Rebecca said. "He must—"

Before she could finish, Zebulon and her father fell into a heated argument about their best course: should they sail to the West Indies again, or lay in port in the hopes that the hostilities would soon be resolved?

Rebecca excused herself and went to her room. She locked the door and sat at her writing desk.

"War," she wrote, "a subject every sane man loathes. Yet in this instance, war has been declared on us by the barbarous Tripoli pirates. For years these bloodthirsties have raped and plundered our shipping. American seamen have languished and died in their prisons. All this despite the king's ransom we've paid.

"President Jefferson was entirely right when he refused to bow to their further demands. But he was also entirely wrong when he followed the advice of his frugal-minded secretary of the treasury, Albert Gallatin, and drastically cut the budget of our Navy. For the Navy is our first line of defense!

"If ever we are to be taken seriously by the nations of the world, then we must not allow ourselves to be intimidated by criminals. If ever there was a time once again to raise the cry, 'Millions for defense but not one cent for tribute!' surely this is that moment.

"In this light, every responsible American entreats the President to review his position about our defenses. We all know that Jefferson doesn't believe in a standing army, but champions a civilian militia that will presumably appear in case of invasion, defeat the enemy, and then disband and return to their homes. But are we willing to risk the safety of our entire nation on such a presumption? Isn't it naïve to assume that such an untrained militia would be a match for the dreaded war machines of either Wellington or Napoleon? Reason cries out for an adequate army and navy, and we urge Jefferson to move posthaste to rebuild that which he's torn asunder. Only then will Americans be able to hold their heads high, only then will our people be able to sleep peacefully in their beds."

She wrote at a furious pace. It came from the depths of her beliefs, and when she'd finished she was so exhausted that she flung herself on the bed and fell fast asleep.

The *National Intelligencer* printed the article twice within the same week. With the nation now at war, everybody talked about it; legislators quoted the article on the floor of Congress. Jefferson claimed that with the war, he'd already instituted plans to revitalize the Navy, but there were many who felt that Rebel Thorne's call to arms had had a profound effect.

"How strange," Rebecca said to Letitia. "The world listens when Rebel Thorne speaks, but if I were to say the same things in the company of men, I'd be branded a fool."

"Will you escort me to the President's pelle melle on the Fourth of July?" Rebecca asked Jeremy.

He slapped his thigh, "Damn, I can't! I promised Dolley Madison I'd help her prepare for the party."

"Oh, Dolley this and Dolley that! Ever since she's moved here, that's all I hear from you," she said. "Never mind, Zebulon's asked me anyway." She walked away briskly.

Jeremy ran after her, trying in every way he could to make it right, but Rebecca refused to listen.

The Fourth promised to be the hottest day of the year, and Rebecca wore a cool white organdy dress with small white bows on the sleeves and bodice. Zebulon sported a new tan French coat cut so severely in the front that the entire front of his tattersall vest showed. His leather souvac boots had scalloped edges, and tassels hung from them.

At the President's House, Jeremy followed Dolley Madison around wherever she went, helping her to set up chairs and tables on the lawn, seeing there was enough ice for the punchbowls, getting the fireworks ready for the twilight display. The guests started arriving at noon, and the Marine Band played spiritedly in the entrance hall. Throngs of people came to the pelle melle, not only to celebrate Independence Day, but also to see what changes had been made in the mansion in the past four months.

The President chose the Blue Room to receive his guests; he purposely abandoned the formal courtly bow so favored by Adams and Washington, and instead shook hands with every man, woman, and child. "The pressing of the flesh signifies that we are all equal," he said.

Victoria Connaught couldn't believe that she was made to wait on the receiving line with the mere commoners—"titles confer no precedence," Jefferson said—and almost swooned when the man had the temerity to pump her hand. "Well, with the news I've just received, he'll think twice about touching a lady's hand," she said to her niece Marianne.

"Yes, Aunt Victoria," Marianne murmured. At fourteen,

Marianne still hadn't lost her frightened look. Each passing year brought a more startling resemblance to her mother, not only physically, but in temperament. A child yearning to laugh, yearning for girlhood pleasures, she had had her natural exuberance crushed under her aunt's domination.

Dolley greeted the guests in the drawing room. She was wearing a pale jonquil gown, and in deference to the stultifying heat, only one ostrich plume in her hair, which was cut short in the new French bob called "La Guillotine." The plunging neckline of the gown displayed a fair amount of Dolley's fashionably pink cleavage. Earlier, she'd wet the fabric of the dress so that it would cling more revealingly. When Rebecca and Zebulon entered, Dolley noticed a look of distress across Jeremy's face. When the couple moved off to the punchbowl, she questioned him.

"You have the look of a hound dog."

"Everytime I see them together . . ." He shrugged.

"Is she somebody you love?"

"Yes, but so does everybody else in Washington."

"What are you going to do about it?"

"What can I do? You've seen for yourself how she favors my brother."

"I've seen nothing of the sort. Oh, you men are so certain of everything, and yet you understand nothing. I saw the way she looked at you."

"You did?" he said, his face brightening.

"Why not find out for yourself? If her answer is no, would that make you any more miserable than you are now?"

"You're right," he said resolutely. "I will talk to her, find out once and for all which one of us she prefers."

At a momentary pause in the greetings, Dolley surreptitiously reached into a tiny silver box, took a pinch of the contents between her thumb and forefinger, and sniffed. A look of indefinable pleasure crossed her face, her eyes glazed, and then she sneezed.

Just then, Victoria and Marianne Connaught entered the drawing room. "Well, there we have it finally," Victoria said. "She snuffs! Look how stained her fingers are. What a disgusting habit. But then, what can one expect in this den of Democrats?"

Jeremy looked at Marianne. She was far too pale and thin to be attractive, but she seemed so out of place that he felt a stab of compassion. "You're Marianne Connaught, aren't you? I understand you've been away in London. Well, welcome back."

Marianne broke into a smile that made her look almost pretty. Her eyes came to life; she was about to speak when Victoria grasped her arm and forcibly drew her away.

"Don't you know that he's a Brand?" she hissed, and Marianne seemed to visibly shrivel.

Then Victoria approached Dolley and tapped her fan on her arm. "My dear Mrs. Madison, President Jefferson said you might be persuaded to take us on a tour of the palace. Would you be good enough?"

Standing nearby, Margaret Bayard Smith furiously took notes for her society column in the *National Intelligencer*.

"Why, I'd be delighted," Dolley said. "After all, this house does belong to all of us." She emphasized the word *house* but Victoria seemed not to notice. "Let's begin at the beginning." Taking Jeremy's arm, she led Victoria and the group of ladies who'd joined her to the entrance hall. "Mind what you say," Dolley whispered to Jeremy. "That Victoria Connaught has a curdled disposition and a tongue to match."

Rebecca and Zebulon also drifted to the group and when everybody had gathered, Dolley said, "Twenty-eight mahogany chairs with hair-cloth covers are arranged around the walls for your comfort if any of you should be fatigued. The floor is covered with a green-painted baize rug, and on the walls you will notice the globe lamp, four girandoles, eight brackets, and of course the eight fire buckets."

Next she led them to the Oval Room where the ladies cooed over the elegant Brussels carpet. "The chairs and sofa are done in blue and gold. Glass lusters and girandoles are on the walls, and there we have the Gilbert Stuart portrait of George Washington."

Victoria Connaught cleared her throat. "Madame Jumel, who is an acquaintance of mine from New York, boasts that she is the only woman in the world to have slept with both George Washington *and* Napoleon Bonaparte."

"And right over here we have President Jefferson's library,"

Dolley said hastily. "As you may know, the President is much interested in languages and is conversant in four. His library is considered among the finest in America."

But Victoria Connaught and her claque weren't to be put off so easily. "Is what Madame Jumel claims true?" "We thought Washington was a man of impeccable morals, and now this?"

Rebecca held her breath, waiting to see how Dolley would answer. She wasn't immune from scandal herself. It was common knowledge that she'd had a serious liaison with Aaron Burr in Philadelphia after her first husband, Payne Todd, had died of the plague in 1793. She'd even named Burr as guardian to her son Payne Todd, Jr. But Dolley soon recognized that Burr was interested primarily in his own political career, and when Burr introduced her to James Madison, and he professed his intentions, she sought advice from her friends. Martha Washington told her that she and George were not opposed to such a marriage, even though Madison was seventeen years older than Dolley.

Once more, questions were raised about Madame Jumel, and Dolley turned to Victoria Connaught, her ostrich plume quivering in agitation. "Whatever transpired between Jumel and our late great President is surely their own business. As for Napoleon, I have no knowledge of his tastes and suggest you ask him yourself."

Believing the matter closed, Dolley swept to the next room. Victoria Connaught's lips turned bloodless. "Did you hear her? She insulted me," she muttered to Marianne. "We'll see who has the last word in this matter!"

"As you can see, the East Room is a catch-all for the President's things," Dolley said.

In one corner lay the remains of a 1,600-pound cheese sent by the citizens of Cheshire, Massachusetts, for his inauguration. There were also thirty-four black-and-gold chairs used for special occasions, kettles for washing glasses, Indian paintings on buffalo hides, baskets, pottery, and Indian sculpture.

"Jefferson was brought up on the frontier by his father, who was a colonel, and he has a profound interest in all things Indian," Dolley said. "Of all our Presidents, he best understands and sympathizes with the plight of the red man, who's constantly being pushed farther and farther west."

"Is that why we've seen so many savages wandering around the President's Palace today?" Victoria Connaught asked. "Well, I suppose it's understandable, seeing how Jefferson does manifest an inordinate interest in . . . half-breeds."

The blood crept up Dolley's neck and colored her face. With an effort of will, she curbed her tongue. Rebecca's eyes flashed from one woman to the other, waiting for that final moment of confrontation. She tried to think of something that would stop Victoria, but she knew it was hopeless. Such devastating news, particularly about a man always in the public eye, could never be kept secret for long.

Dolley led the group up the staircase to the second floor. The upper Oval Room still sported Abigail Adams's red damask furniture. In the President's bedroom stood eight crimson-and-gold chairs. "Jefferson uses them when he conducts informal conferences with his cabinet advisors," Dolley said. Dimity draperies hung on his bed and on the windows. On the walls were portraits of Washington, Adams, and Jefferson.

"And here is something of which the President is especially proud," Dolley said as she opened a closet door.

"What is it?" Victoria asked, poking her head in.

"A clothing machine," Dolley said. "It works on this revolving rack. Jefferson designed it, and this young man here, Jeremy Brand, built it for him. Jeremy, would you explain how it works?"

"The clothes hang on an elliptical rack," he said, "but only a portion of the rack is visible, as you can see. The rest of the rack fits into this well which is built into the closet. The clothes are arranged by season, and whenever the President wants a particular garment, he revolves the rack to that place."

"Cunning," Victoria Connaught said. "But then your President has always been cunning. Now tell us, Mrs. Madison, which room belongs to Sally Hemings?"

Dolley's usually benign face hardened into a mask of hauteur. It's out at last, Rebecca thought.

"Who is Sally Hemings?" one of the women asked, confused.

"Who is Sally Hemings indeed!" Victoria Connaught exclaimed. "Why she is Jefferson's slave, his concubine, and the mother of his five bastard children!"

The shock rippled through the group, setting up cries of "No! It can't be!" "Consorting with a slave?" "He'd never dare!"

"I assure you, it's perfectly true," Victoria said. "This Sally Hemings is the daughter of Jefferson's deceased father-in-law, by Betty Hemings, a slave of his own. As such, Sally is the half-sister of Jefferson's wife, Martha, to whom he'd sworn such undying faithfulness."

"Ladies, the tour is over," Dolley said coldly, and herded the women out of the room and down the stairs. She looked so distressed that Rebecca linked arms with her. Dolley smiled wanly at this gesture of support.

Victoria kept up her rapid-fire detailing of the affair. "For years, Jefferson masked his degenerate desires, leading us to believe he was a saint. But sin and corruption will out! Sally was maid to Jefferson's youngest daughter, Maria, and when Maria joined her father in France, Sally accompanied her. But once Jefferson cast his covetous eye on Sally, he had to have her—and have her he did, though she was only fourteen years old!"

Another chorus of shocked Nos! reverberated among the women.

"He trained her to his nefarious ways in Paris—such a wicked city anyway—then brought her back to Monticello, where they continued their affair, and in the past decade this mulatto slave has borne him five illegitimate children. If we needed further proof, one of these little bastards is named after Jefferson's best friend: James Madison Hemings!"

One woman sagged into a swoon. Dolley looked like she was ready to kill, yet she couldn't deny the accusations, since she was the one who'd suggested that the child be named James Madison.

Victoria Connaught finished in a rageful triumph, "And it is to this sinning hypocrite that you Americans have entrusted your destiny!"

Within hours, news of the scandal reached every household in Washington, and the itinerant barber soon spread the gossip as far as Alexandria and Bladensburg. Then the *Baltimore Sun* clarioned it, and everybody took sides, as might be expected, along party lines.

Energized by the turmoil, and desiring all the information she could get, Rebecca made a special trip to see Jeremy. She caught him just as he was leaving work at the President's House.

"What do you think of what's happened?" she asked with a concerned air. "Is it true?"

He hunched his shoulders. "I don't know."

"Oh, really, you needn't be so loyal! You're in that house every single day. You know what's going on."

Jeremy had promised himself that he wouldn't be a party to any of the scandalmongering, but he'd never been able to deny Rebecca anything. "I know that members of Jefferson's cabinet, including James Madison, have pressed him to reply to the charges. But Jefferson's refused, on the grounds that he won't lend them dignity."

"Or perhaps it's his way of avoiding the whole issue," Rebecca said.

"If it is true, then Jefferson's managed to keep it a secret from everybody in Washington, I mean up to now. Of course, he never brought Sally Hemings here, so who can say?"

"Are you sure? You've never seen her or the children?"

"Never. I would surely know that."

Rebecca looked into his brilliant blue eyes, framed by the thick dark-blond lashes. "And do you agree with what Jefferson's done? Consorting with a slave, a mulatto?"

"I can't put myself in his shoes," he said.

"But could you ever do such a thing?" she persisted. Suddenly it seemed very important to her to know his mind.

He shook his head slowly. "To be involved with a half-breed? Such a thing never crossed my mind. I want no slave, I want an equal." He reached out impulsively and took her hands. "To speak the truth, you're the only one who commands my heart."

She pulled away from him. "I've never seen it to fail. You men will say anything to get what you want."

"That's not true. I've never had the courage to speak my mind before because . . . well, because of Zebulon. But then Dolley said—Oh, what's the use of trying to explain? I only know that I love you. I want to marry you."

She hadn't expected this, and she was taken aback. "But

how? You're still a journeyman. It will take you years before you can earn a decent living as an architect."

"Does that matter if two people love each other?"

She thought about that very carefully. "It matters to me. Marriage is difficult enough without loading it with insurmountable troubles. Jeremy, love dies with trouble."

"Is your answer no, then?" he asked with a sinking heart.

"My answer is that I can't marry, I *won't* marry anybody, until I believe in my heart that it has a chance."

He took courage from her saying she wouldn't marry anybody—which meant Zebulon also.

"What else do you know of this Sally Hemings affair?" Rebecca asked.

"Just that it's taken a serious turn. I hear congressmen—Federalists and Democrats alike—are talking about the ramifications."

"Like what?" she asked.

"Well, the President is living in sin, outside the law. That is, if it's true," he added quickly. "This could be the perfect opportunity for Chief Justice Marshall to start a move to have Jefferson impeached. Lord knows he hates him enough."

"Oh, Marshall won't do that," she said. "And certainly not on that issue."

"Why not?"

"Oh, come now," she exclaimed. "All of you men very well know that Chief Justice Marshall has a slave concubine of his own. And so do most of the other southern legislators."

Jeremy blushed furiously and lowered his eyes.

Then Rebecca said quietly, "You know, we're all brought up to believe that this nation was conceived in liberty. How many times have I heard Jefferson say that this democracy is the realization of the greatest spiritual quest that mankind has ever had . . . a dream of equality for all men under the law. And yet why should any of us believe that if a man can . . . ?" Her unfinished question hung on the wind.

"No," she whispered, "have no fear, President Jefferson won't be impeached. Sally Hemings is only a slave . . . and a woman."

Chapter 16

SHORTLY AFTER Jefferson was inaugurated, a young man named Meriwether Lewis became his secretary and moved into the President's House. Jefferson had had a number of male secretaries, usually young, boisterous, and irreverent, chosen for just those qualities. Meriwether Lewis was no exception.

When Lewis had settled in, President Jefferson took him and Jeremy into the East Room. Hoban had designed the room to be used for the grandest state functions, but each day saw more and more of Jefferson's paraphernalia stored there.

"Can you partition this room so that Meriwether can use half for an office, and I can use the other half for my purposes?" Jefferson asked Jeremy.

Jeremy looked around at the space, wondering how that might best be accomplished. "I think it can be done sir, but it would probably be best to ask Mr. Latrobe."

"I've already expressed my wishes to him," Jefferson said. "In truth, he didn't seem pleased, but for the moment, this will suit my purposes." Jefferson spoke in his low, calm voice, and though one might have to strain to hear him, his authority was never questioned.

Within a week Jeremy had the partitions up. "This room hasn't fared too well under our Presidents," Jeremy said laughingly to Meriwether Lewis as he helped him set up his desk and cabinets. "First Abigail Adams hung her laundry here, and now this."

Meriwether laughed also. A highly intelligent determined young man, he was full of raw energy, and he and Jeremy soon became friends. Meriwether was busy from first light until dusk, handling Jefferson's prodigious correspondence. But he seemed to fret under the confinement of the four walls, and in the months that passed, Jeremy would often see him staring out the window, the way one might look from behind prison bars.

Jeremy continued to work in the other half of the East Room, building shelves and cabinets. Ranged around the walls were specimens of flora and fauna from all over the United States. As befit the president of the American Philosophical Society, Jefferson had a passion for all things new under the sun. Many of his inventions were also stored here, including his polygraph machine, a device that wrote two identical letters at once, and his "plough of least resistance," a farm implement he'd invented which won first prize at a scientific exhibition in France. Stacks of books lay everywhere; they hadn't yet been catalogued and added to his library.

One Saturday evening in the winter of 1802, Jeremy rode over to Tunnecliff's Hotel on Capitol Hill to hoist a few mugs of ale, see if there was any mischief brewing, and if there wasn't, maybe start some himself. In the tavern, he found a lot of hard-drinking congressmen arguing about whether Napoleon might indeed conquer all of Europe. By threat and intimidation, Napoleon had just acquired the vast Louisiana Territory from Spain, and so France was now considered a dangerous threat to the United States. One senator declared, "If Napoleon manages to establish a military base in New Orleans, he would then move to conquer the entire North American continent."

The more salacious of the legislators were discussing the scandal of Jefferson's liaison with Sally Hemings. A great deal more information had been revealed since the reporter Callander's definitive exposé in September of 1802. Though Callander had been somewhat discredited because of accusations against him of sodomy and libel, and was now dead of drowning, the scandal still haunted Jefferson.

"The President is still sleeping with this mulatto slave. That's why he spends so much time in Monticello. But he won't free her, or their children," said one lawmaker.

"He fooled us all," said another. "For all his high flown talk of life, liberty, equality, he was still dipping his wick in Sable Sally."

Jeremy wanted to smash their faces, but then he'd have had to beat up everybody in Washington, because they were all whispering. Then Jeremy saw Meriwether Lewis sitting at a far table, glaring at the gossips. Jeremy joined him.

"They're worse than women, and not worth Jefferson's spit," he said to Jeremy.

Meriwether had gotten to the tavern earlier, and had already consumed a fair amount of ale. "Innkeeper, a drink for my friend here!"

"Are we celebrating?" Jeremy asked.

"We are," Meriwether said, clapping him on the shoulder. "Exactly what, I'm not at liberty to say. But when the news is known, believe me, it will be a cause for the entire nation to celebrate!"

Jeremy pressed him for more details, but Meriwether shook his head. "On this matter I'm sworn to secrecy by the President himself!"

Two ladies of the evening approached them, and though Jeremy had half a mind to buy them a drink, Meriwether would have none of them. "They're painted, expensive, and doubtless diseased. Better leave them to their own kind, those congressmen." Then he challenged Jeremy to a game of darts. But Lewis was so erratic in his aim that the innkeeper begged them to desist, "lest I lose some of my customers."

After a few more rounds, Jeremy and Meriwether left Tunnecliff's, and on the way out, Lewis managed to dump a mug of ale on the head of one of the congressmen. Riding back to the President's House, Meriwether broke into song, and Jeremy lustily joined in singing "Hail Columbia!"

> O'er vast Columbia's varied clime,
> Her cities, forests, shores, and dales,
> In shining majesty sublime
> Immortal liberty prevails

Dogs started to howl, but this only made the two young men sing louder in the cold, brilliant starlit night:

> Rejoice! Columbia's sons, rejoice!
> To tyrants never bend the knee

But join with heart and soul and voice
For Jefferson and liberty!

By the time they reached the fence surrounding the President's House, Meriwether had fallen asleep in the saddle. Jeremy led him through the gate, across the lawn, and over the wooden causeway to the entrance. But the doorkeeper, Etienne Le Maire, had already closed the mansion for the night and Meriwether couldn't find his key.

"No need to worry," he yawned, and curled up on the doorstep.

Jeremy tried to rouse him but couldn't; finally he hefted Meriwether's dead weight onto his shoulder and carried him back to his cabin. He put him in the spare room, then lay down on his own pallet and soon fell asleep.

The following morning, Jeremy woke with a pounding headache. He found Meriwether already up, sitting at the table and looking through Jeremy's portfolio of drawings.

"I hope you don't mind," he said, barely looking at Jeremy. "But these caught my eye and so intrigued me that I had to see them all. They are yours, aren't they?"

Jeremy nodded. "Something I do in my spare time."

Meriwether went through the folio again, and when he'd finished, he said quietly. "They're good. Very good indeed."

"Well, then, take your pick," he said. "Choose whichever you want."

"I will, and thank you," he said. "And will ask another favor of you. May I borrow them some evening? I promise I'll return them without harm."

"Done," Jeremy said.

The two men went to church later that morning. It was in a meeting house, for the Protestants in the district had as yet no formal place of worship in the new capital. President Jefferson was conspicuously absent, and many members of the congregation commented on it, reviving all the old accusations that Jefferson was an atheist.

Meriwether glowered through their remarks. "Never was a man born more in tune with God and his works than our President. But these hypocrites only pay lip service on Sundays."

After the services, the men stepped out into the crisp air.

"My head needs clearing," Meriwether said. "I've a mind to go hunting, bring back some venison for the table. Will you join me?"

Jeremy agreed, and they gathered their hunting equipment and set out into the hills of Maryland. The air burned in Jeremy's nostrils and the tips of his ears and nose quickly froze. The horses plodded slowly through the snowdrifts and the men dismounted. Meriwether strode off at a fast pace, as though testing Jeremy's stamina. They followed the cloven-hoofed track of deer, then lost it; a wild turkey fled into the bush before either man could draw a bead.

"The countryside is getting so built up that game is scarce. No wonder men constantly head west," Meriwether said.

Jeremy nodded absently.

Meriwether looked at him closely. "You seem miles away, and have been for some weeks."

Jeremy shrugged. "I suppose I am. I must come to some decision, and soon. Shall I go to the academy in Georgetown? Do I continue working in the President's House? What? It all seems so . . . tame."

"Is there no great adventure that calls to you?" Meriwether asked tentatively.

"I've often thought of getting away from Washington. And Rebecca Breech—that one will torment me to death."

"Ah yes, the girl in your drawings. I've seen her in the city. God must have been working very hard the day he fashioned that one. And she's the object of your heart?"

"Mine and everybody else's," Jeremy said with a desultory shrug. He scooped up a handful of snow, crushed it into a ball, and threw it at an evergreen, hitting the trunk squarely.

"Can you shoot as well as you throw?" Meriwether asked.

Jeremy took his rifle from the saddle holder. He pointed to a pinecone hanging from a branch, then fired, neatly nipping the cone off.

Meriwether's voice grew alive with excitement. "Suppose I told you there was an adventure brewing, one so important that anyone who participated in it would be famous. I don't mean just for our time, I mean for the ages."

Jeremy turned and looked at him. "What is it?"

"I can't tell you now. But when the time is right, I promise you'll be the first to know."

"Whatever this adventure is, you think I might be part of it? But how? I'm an ordinary laborer."

"Ah, man, you're far more than that. Why, you can draw a deer so that I see it sniffing at a salt lick. Your birds take wing from the page. Your drawing of that Negro slave—why, there's insurrection burning in that man's eyes. And you've shown me the heart and soul of Rebecca Breech."

Meriwether increased his pace so that he walked abreast of Jeremy. "There's only one thing I haven't seen. The portraits you've done of yourself—they're almost wooden, with no spirit."

Jeremy nodded. "It's true, sometimes I think I must be a stranger to myself."

Meriwether considered that and then said quietly, "Then you must discover yourself. Find out what it is you really want."

Jeremy mulled this over. How did Meriwether know this about him? Was it because he was having similar problems of his own? And what was the great adventure that would make everybody famous? That question remained the most intriguing of all.

Chapter 17

REBECCA MOVED uneasily through Jeremy's house, not at all relishing the unpleasant task ahead of her. Since she'd last been here, Jeremy had added two large rooms to the cabin, a bedroom and a studio where he worked. Both had brick fireplaces; winter weather in Washington could be mean.

"You said the place was too small for you," Jeremy said. "So everything I've earned has gone into building these rooms."

"And you've done a wonderful job," she said. Everything he was saying was making it that much more difficult. She didn't have the heart to tell him she'd decided to accept the engagement ring Zebulon had pressed on her, and waited for the right moment to ease into it.

As she wandered around the studio she spied the portfolio on his worktable and started for it, but he sprang into her path.

"Don't, please," he said.

"Nonsense," she laughed. "Are you ashamed of your work?"

"No, but what's there might not please you."

She brushed his hand aside, opened the folio and was stunned with what she saw. There she was, captured in sepia tones, in chalk, watercolors, drawings of her when she'd been a teenager and as she'd grown through the years, on her horse, running along the paths, in her black bonnet and veil when her mother died, and another at eighteen when her father presented her to Georgetown society, all the freshness and hope in her face shining from the portrait. He'd made her more beautiful than she was, and it grieved her that she would never look that way except in his eyes.

Tears filled her eyes and she turned away.

He knelt by her side and took her hands. "I've offended

you, and I never meant to do that, I swear it."

She rushed from the cabin, mounted her horse, and was away before he could follow. She galloped through the fields, taking the fences with superb leaps, feeling one with the beast beneath her. The wind was in her ears, tossing her hair as she fled before the force of his love. For he must love her, to have done so much through the years, and with such devotion. She reached her house, tossed the reins to the stable boy, fled to her room, and locked herself in.

For two days she would let no one near her, and ate next to nothing. She fed herself on the memories of the portraits. She tossed and turned with the problem confronting her. Zebulon—he would rise in the world; it was merely a question of time before he found the proper route. If she married him, sooner or later she'd live in a fine house, know the right people, have all the things she'd dreamed of since she'd been a child. But Jeremy . . . what did he have to offer except his love? He might become a painter, but excepting Gilbert Stuart and John Trumbull, artists in this country starved.

Endlessly she worried the problem. Letitia hovered outside the door, pleading to be let in. In the small hours of the second night, Rebecca realized what she must do. I must take the devotion of Jeremy, and to it, add the ambition of Zebulon. That way she'd have the best of both worlds. One man who loved her to distraction, whom she could always count on, and one who'd rise in the world and give her the kind of life she needed.

If she married Zebulon . . . oh, he'd remain faithful for a while. She knew in the secret recesses of her being that Zebulon loved her—but only because he couldn't have her. Once he'd conquered her, would he lose interest, as he had with all the others?

A week later, she returned to Jeremy's house and found him preparing dinner. The smell of a stew simmering in the kettle made her stomach knot, though she couldn't tell if it was from hunger, or from distaste at the common odors she remembered from her childhood.

He stood up. Then his face broke into a grin and he swept her in his arms. "You do love me, I can see it!" he shouted.

She pushed him away. "It's too soon for love. Love is

something that must be nurtured, that must grow; love comes with two people building, sharing, making their lives together. The rest is all nonsense. If you love me, then do something with your life. You're wasted here; other men get the credit for the work you do."

"If you love me, then I can do anything."

"Like what?" she asked.

He shrugged. "I haven't thought of it fully. First my schooling. I have almost enough money saved. Then James Hoban suggested that I go to England and study with one of the painting masters."

She set her face and said nothing.

"What would you have me do?" he asked.

"My father is almost ready to retire. His stoneworks, the merchant ships he charters, provide us with a good living. You could make something better of it. Soon there'll be a great city rising here, I *feel* it! If you were supplying the stone for all these fine government buildings and the private houses, why, we would be assured of a future."

He sat down at the table, still and contemplative. "It would mean giving up everything I've dreamed of."

"And have you not dreamed of me?" she asked quietly.

She moved toward him and he buried his face against her breast, murmuring endearments. When he reached for her she backed away. "There's time enough for that when you've made up your mind."

She didn't tell him that she was about to put Zebulon to a similar test.

Rebecca spent all afternoon getting ready for the Smiths' reception, scrubbing her face with rosewater and olive soap, being laced into a waist cincher a size smaller than the human body could endure. Over this she'd put on a pale blue moiré gown artfully cut to accentuate her nipped waist and expose a good deal of her breasts and shoulders. Around her neck she wore a circlet of small diamond chips, appropriate to an unmarried maiden of twenty-four. Disdaining the current fashion, she hadn't frizzed her hair with curling irons, but twisted it into a love knot and let it hang over one shoulder.

Zebulon came into the house and stopped dead in his tracks when he saw her.

"We'll be late," he said, holding her matching moiré cloak for her. As he slipped it over her shoulders he caught the scent so unmistakably hers, of steeped cloves mixed with cinnamon, subtly heightened with the essence of carnation. He knew he would carry the memory of that smell to the grave.

"I'd bite you if I dared," he whispered in her ear so that her hovering father wouldn't hear. "Bite you until all your flesh knew the imprint of my teeth and lips."

Rebecca shrugged with feigned annoyance, but deny it as she might, she felt a thrill course up her back and end in a buzzing in her ears. Every fiber in her being yearned for completion. But first she had to be sure which of the Brand brothers she'd choose.

Zebulon's carriage took them from Georgetown along Pennsylvania Avenue to the Samuel Smith residence in the heart of Washington. In the three years since Silky Milky Smith had founded the *National Intelligencer,* it had become the District's leading newspaper. It's meteoric rise was due in part to the articles of Rebel Thorne, whose ringing commentary always appeared in time of national crisis, and to the gossipy society column written by Sam Smith's wife, Margaret Bayard Smith. The Connaughts and their comings and goings to Europe dominated the column, and the Tayloes were mentioned in practically every issue, whether for their racehorses, their plantation in Virginia, or their new town house. Called the Octagon House because of its unusual shape, it had been built by William Thornton on the corner of New York Avenue and Eighteenth Street and was the grandest private residence in all Washington. Stephen Decatur, the dashing young naval lieutenant, found his way into thc *Intelligencer*'s pages whenever he was in Washington, and so did the District's leading banker, General John Van Ness. This afternoon, the Smiths were hosting a buffet dinner to raise money to complete the new Episcopal Christ Church on Capitol Hill. Everyone of note had been invited, and though President Jefferson had sent his regrets, Margaret Bayard Smith, one of Washington's most prominent hostesses, had been hinting all week that her drawing room would be graced by surprise mystery guests.

When Rebecca and Zebulon entered the drawing room, conversation stopped. Not only were they an extraordinary-looking couple, but in her new hairstyle and gown, she looked as if she might have stepped from another world, another time.

Introductions and greetings went around the room: Mr. and Mrs. James Hoban were there, she pregnant again; Captain Tingey of the Navy Yard kissed Rebecca's hand, as did Commodore Joshua Barney, a wicked old salt rumored to have had an interlude with Marie Antoinette; and Stephen Decatur made a great fuss over her.

"How nice to see you," Rebecca said, "I thought you were still at sea."

"Just recently returned," Decatur said.

"And with good news, I hope."

"Not as good as we'd like. The Tripoli pirates are far stronger than we thought."

Decatur looked the part of the hero. Dark, almost swarthy in complexion, with piercing black eyes and an aquiline nose, he boasted Dutch, French, English, and Irish blood in his veins. He came to the sea naturally—his grandfather, Stephen Decatur I, had been a lieutenant in the French Navy, and his father, also Stephen, had been a privateer captain during the War for Independence.

When he'd been appointed first lieutenant in 1801 and sailed on the frigate *Essex* to fight the Tripoli pirates, he told his crew, "We are now about to depart on an expedition which may terminate in our sudden deaths, our perpetual slavery, or our immortal glory." Some time later, while the ship was docked in Malta, Decatur seconded a midshipman in a duel with the Maltese governor's secretary. The secretary was killed and the governor put up a fearful row. Both officers were shipped back to the United States; as punishment, the midshipman was promoted to lieutenant and Decatur was given command of a beautiful new brig, *Argus*, carrying sixteen guns. The ship now lay in the Navy Yard, being outfitted to rejoin the American squadron in the Mediterranean. Dueling was recognized as a fact of life for headstrong seamen; for every three officers lost because of enemy action, two were lost as a result of duels.

More guests crowded into the house, and Rebecca took it all in avidly. With the exception of Zebulon, none of the men were tradespeople. They were cotton or tobacco planters with hordes of slaves; doctors and lawyers; congressmen, senators, and judges. She regarded them, men puffed with their own importance and discussing world affairs as if their paltry efforts were the cause of the earth's turning. She shrugged with annoyance as she experienced an edge of . . . what? Being slightly out of place? Outclassed?

Suddenly Zebulon's hand tightened on her arm; all the blood had drained from his face. His eyes were riveted on a group of people who'd just entered the room. Rebecca followed his gaze and saw Victoria Connaught and her timorous niece, Marianne. They were escorted by a tall gentleman; Rebecca thought she recognized something familiar about him. With his square shoulders and ramrod spine, he appeared to be standing at attention at all times. His thinning blond hair made him appear older than his age, about twenty-seven or twenty-eight, Rebecca estimated. His austere look was further accentuated by flat gunmetal-gray eyes, and by his starched white-and-gold uniform, that of a lieutenant in the English Navy.

And then she recognized him and involuntarily gripped Zebulon's hand. "My God," she whispered, "I never expected to see him again in my life. What is Sean Connaught doing here?"

Chapter 18

REBECCA FELT Zebulon's hands grow cold and clammy. "Would you prefer it if we left?" she asked.

"Of course not!" he exclaimed. "If he says so much as one word, I'll give him a sound thrashing." And then in a brazen move typical of him, he downed his drink and led Rebecca to where the Connaughts were standing, chatting with the Smiths.

The greetings were stiff and formal; Sean refused to shake hands. Marianne Connaught's eyes flashed from Sean to Zebulon to Rebecca. Along with the thumping of her heart, Marianne felt a distinct nausea at the hatred that even now flowed between these people. She remembered her childhood prayers, her aunt's admonition never to forget what the Brands had done—murdered her father, driven her mother mad. And she herself was hopelessly entrapped in the hatred, unable to break free.

Sean Connaught's eyes bored into Zebulon's until he turned away. Sean was hardly the impulsive seventeen-year-old youth who'd been forced to leave the country for threatening Zebulon's life. In the past decade he'd been thoroughly trained in the Intelligence Branch of His Majesty's Royal Navy. Possessing a formidable memory and a total lack of fear, he'd risen fast in the ranks.

He'd volunteered for this assignment, and because of his American contacts, had been sent to Washington to test the pulse of the Jefferson administration. Jefferson, a known Francophile, might easily align himself with Napoleon; therefore the more information the British had, the better. Sean's presence had aroused no suspicion, for he'd come on the pretext of carrying a conciliatory message from his government concerning the impressment of American seamen, an issue that

Jefferson and the rest of the country were eager to settle.

Sean's wife stood by his side, a bloodless creature with an anemic complexion, watery eyes, nondescript brown hair, and a heavy, raspy cough aggravated by the miasmic humidity of the Potowmack basin. She hung on her husband's every word as he continued the tale he'd been telling when interrupted by Zebulon.

"The ceremony of presenting my credentials to the President has left a lasting, and if I may say so, a most painful, memory. I naturally appeared in my official uniform, since I was representing Great Britain. But imagine my consternation when Jefferson entered the Cabinet Room in total disarray. His pantaloons, coat, and underclothes were utterly slovenly, and he was wearing bedroom slippers! I don't doubt that the entire exercise was intended as an insult, not to me personally, perhaps, but to the sovereign I represent. Really, what boorish manners!"

Outraged by Sean's patronizing manner, Rebecca moved closer to him. She saw him eye her appraisingly, a look she'd seen too often before to mistake, as though she might be a commodity in a shop. This infuriated her all the more. "My first formal introduction to the President was quite different," she said. "I found him in the East Room, drawing plans for several new additions to the President's House. I confess my time with him was of short duration, but he couldn't have been more charming. And to have spoken to the man who drew up the Declaration of Independence was an honor I shall never forget. That to me is a far greater gauge of a man's value than the kind of shoes he happens to be wearing."

A corner of Sean's mouth twitched; he'd never been able to countenance any kind of reprimand, particularly not from a colonial, and a woman at that. His back became even more rigid, and he said, "If forced to, one might dismiss his dress as an unpleasant aberration, but that, coupled with his . . . ah, questionable liaisons, makes one wonder about the man's sanity."

Victoria Connaught's face beamed approval, but Rebecca wasn't about to let him have the last word.

"It's obvious that you don't understand the genius of Jefferson."

"Genius?" Victoria said with a laugh.

"No less a description will do," Rebecca said. "I don't need to tally his prodigious accomplishments; they speak for themselves. Yet all you talk about is his 'questionable alliance.' And what of it? Are all you gentlemen here so innocent that you can cast the first stone? Or must we forever deal in hypocricies?"

An audible gasp rose from the ladies, and teaspoons rattled in their cups. "Five bastard mulatto children," Victoria blurted. "A contamination of the body and the blood."

Rebecca hunched her shoulders irritably. "I don't know the intimate details, and further, I don't care. I leave that to the gossipmongers amongst us. But if they've had five children and he's given this slave shelter under his roof, that's more than many a man here would do."

Victoria turned to her niece. "Marianne, leave the room at once!" She herded the teenager to the door.

Stephen Decatur leapt into the awkward situation. "I say Connaught, couldn't we persuade our navies to join forces against the Tripoli pirates? The entire world would benefit if we could crush these Moors and free the Mediterranean once and for all."

Rebecca, the bit firmly in her teeth, said, "Perhaps England doesn't find it to her advantage to join forces with us. As long as only American ships are stopped, then she's free to continue her lucrative monopolistic trade with the Levant."

Sean Connaught blushed to the roots of his rapidly receding hairline. "Madam, such a statement is slanderous to my government."

Zebulon wished that Rebecca wouldn't pursue this line; enough animosity existed already. He gulped down his drink, then turned to Decatur. "We must beard the followers of Mohammed in their own den. When they imprisoned me and my crew, they promised us our freedom if we would convert to Islam—taking the turban, as our sailors call it."

"But surely our good Christian men wouldn't convert to a heathen religion," James Hoban said.

"The Moors have a way with their nefarious practices," Zebulon said. "And if a man's spent years in a foul dungeon, with little hope of being rescued because of his country's impotence, can one blame him if he converts? At least then he's no longer in prison. And there have been instances of other barbarisms. The Arabs follow the covenant of Abraham, and those men who haven't been—well, it's far too indelicate a subject to discuss in front of the ladies."

A pall settled over the room. Then Decatur said, "There's glory to be gained for all men of good heart who'd fight these devils." For a moment, Zebulon felt a rush of zeal to revenge himself on those criminals who'd held him hostage.

A short time later, when Rebecca and Zebulon were about to leave, Sean Connaught drew Zebulon aside. "You and I have unfinished business. Your insult to my family cannot go unpunished . . . My seconds will call on you in the morning. The choice of weapons is yours." With that, Sean turned on his heel and left.

"What did he want?" Rebecca asked.

"Oh, some silliness." Zebulon would say no more. But his mind was working . . . Pistols? Swords? With which of the two would Sean be less accomplished? He had a nagging fear that Sean could handle both equally well.

On the way home, Rebecca sat staring at the darkened road that stretched before them, then suddenly she burst into tears.

"What is it?" Zebulon asked, putting his arm around her shoulder. The shock of Sean's appearance and the alcohol he'd consumed had left him feeling slightly intoxicated.

"I made a perfect fool of myself," she sobbed. "I know I did. And I'll never be invited back to the Smiths' again. But I don't care! Who does Sean Connaught think he is, making fun of Jefferson? If any of us wanted, couldn't we have poked fun at mad King George? They're miserable, haughty people, and I hate them all! What's more, I'm glad we won the war. I wish we'd go to war with them again, just to teach them a lesson!"

She broke into sobs once more, and Zebulon laughed aloud at her spirit. He put her head on his shoulder; by the time they got back to Georgetown, she'd cried herself out. But her cheeks remained flushed and her eyes feverish with pent-up emotion.

No one was at home, neither her father, nor Letitia, nor the stableboy when they reached the carriage house, and Zebulon had to unhitch Baal himself.

"I wonder where everybody can be?" Rebecca asked, piqued by this new inconvenience. "The stableboy must be about; he's left the lantern burning near the stall."

Zebulon gazed at her, overwhelmed by her beauty. If he had only one wish it would be for the Lord to give him words to describe how he felt. How he would cherish, worship her . . . all the women he'd known were nothing compared to her; she was the one for whom he'd been created.

He caught her arm and whirled her into the carriagehouse, desperate to tell her all this, to tell her what he planned for them. Every part of his life up to this moment had been a waste, but now he would put that all behind him.

But Rebecca knew only that he'd laid sudden hands on her, was forcing her into the deserted carriagehouse, and she slapped him hard across the face. When he tried to speak, she slapped him again, and all the endearments on his tongue vanished with the blow.

A sardonic grin spread across his face along with a flash of unreasoned anger. He caught her arms. "You fight, because deep within you're afraid to admit how much you want this."

She shrank back at the truth in his words, all the while searching desperately for a weapon, anything to hold him at bay. "Zebulon, you're drunk. Think of what you're doing!" When he persisted she cried, "Not this way, I'd sooner die first!"

Her fingers scrabbled behind her and she felt the shaft of a pitchfork. She brought it around suddenly and managed to jab him in the thigh.

With a cry of pain, he knocked the pitchfork from her hands and tumbled her onto the haystack. His body pressed down against hers, his hands moved along her thighs, rousing her to a state where she thought she must give in, must know this elusive love that had tormented her all these years. He caught her hand and pressed it to his groin, and she reacted as if burned. She might have loved him, with tenderness; he could have released the raging flood of desire in her. But because the Lord had not given him words, because only his hands spoke, she fought him.

"My father will kill you," she gasped as he tore at her gown.

"Your father is an old man," he muttered, his mouth pressed against her neck. "You've need of a new protector. All those years you tantalized me, invited me with a glance, only to repel me when I dared touch you. All those years . . . But now it's just you and me."

She screamed, and he clapped his hand over her mouth.

"It will hurt only for a moment," he murmured, "and then, I promise, you shall know paradise."

Then she saw the lantern hanging on the beam. Flinging her arms back, which he took for abandon, she chivvied her way closer to the beam. With a swift motion, she grabbed the lantern and cracked him on the side of the head. The glass chimney broke and the flaming oil spilled onto the straw. The flames caught the hem of her gown and she screamed as the fire seared her legs.

"Oh my God!" he cried. He beat at the flames with his bare hands. The horses in the stall smelled the fire and began pounding their hooves against the planking, their shrill whinnying adding to the confusion.

The smoke curled upward, thick and acrid, and the two of them coughed and gasped for breath. All about them bales of hay caught fire, cutting off their escape. Suddenly the flames leapt to the hayloft, turning the carriagehouse into an inferno.

Zebulon darted his head in every direction. If he didn't move quickly . . . He lifted Rebecca in his arms and ran through the fire to the front door, barely making it outside.

The alarm had been raised and citizens came running from all directions, setting up a bucket brigade against the common enemy. If the fire spread, it could easily wipe out all of Georgetown. In the carriagehouse, flames shot through the roof. The trapped horses gave one last pathetic whinny and then were silent.

Zebulon set Rebecca down. She stared at the carriagehouse and then turned to him, seeing the fire reflected in his wide dark eyes. Her hands moved over her torn gown and petticoats.

"My father will kill you," she whispered.

This time, he knew she was right. And if Mathias didn't, then he still had to contend with Sean Connaught. Suddenly it all became too much for him—the threats, her hatred—and he mounted Baal and galloped off.

He rode straight to Stephen Decatur's house. Once there he signed up with him, and within a short time had set sail for the Mediterranean.

Chapter 19

SOME WEEKS later, Jeremy sat in his workroom struggling over a portrait of Zebulon. He studied it, then crumpled the paper and threw it into the fire. He watched the edges turn brown and then flare into a puff of flame. Rebecca had been confined to her bed, but thank the Lord, the burns on her legs were healing. What had happened had left Jeremy with a residue of anger at his brother, and curiously enough, against Rebecca also. What was she doing with him in the first place?

He answered the rap on the door and Meriwether Lewis strode into the room. They shook hands warmly, then Jeremy poured them both mugs of hard cider. Lewis drained his in a gulp and refilled his glass.

"You've been away for a while," Jeremy said.

Meriwether nodded. "Studying celestial navigation with Andrew Ellicott in Lancaster, Pennsylvania. Then off to Philadelphia for some quick instruction in the rudiments of medicine from Dr. Benjamin Rush. And then to Harper's Ferry, to requisition supplies from the Army arsenal there." Meriwether set his mug down with a bang. "Do you remember when I told you about the chance of a great adventure?"

"I've thought of little else," Jeremy said. "But for the life of me, haven't figured out what it might be."

"Suppose I let President Jefferson explain it to you." He handed Jeremy an invitation written in beautiful flowing script.

Jeremy read aloud, "President Jefferson invites you to dinner—" He broke off. "Is this some kind of joke?"

"None, I assure you. But you must promise me this. If you do accept the invitation, you must swear yourself to secrecy. Agreed?"

Jeremy didn't know what to say. It was one thing to work in the President's House, even to pass the time of day with Jefferson when he chose, but to dine with him? A man considered among the greatest in the nation? What would he say? Was he getting himself into something he couldn't handle? Caught between the realization that the invitation was a great honor, and the fear that he might make an imbecile of himself, Jeremy threw up his hands. "All right, I accept."

"Good!" Meriwether said. He took the Bible that lay near Jeremy's bedside and put his hand on it. "Do you swear to remain silent about all you'll hear?"

"I swear," Jeremy said. "But why all this secrecy?"

"Never mind. You'll see at dinner tonight," Meriwether said with a grin. He strode out the door, leaving Jeremy so excited he could scarcely think straight.

Dinner was being served in the Green Room, where the six-piece oval table had been set. Jeremy, hands clutched tightly in his lap, looked at the other guests. A beaming Dolley Madison sat on the President's right, resplendent in a silk gown of citron color, her macquillage artfully applied. Next to her huddled her adoring husband, the diminutive James Madison. Madison, acknowledged as the most astute political theoretician the nation had produced, and the "father of the Constitution," was Jefferson's secretary of state.

Meriwether Lewis, in his uniform of captain of the U.S. Army, sat across from the President, and next to Lewis, Captain Tingey of the Navy Yard.

Jefferson preferred to dine at a round table; that way there could be no argument about protocol or precedence. Even so, Jeremy had heard there were times when it hadn't worked, for certain wives of ministers had pushed and shoved their way to grab the chair next to the President.

"This dinner is like a family gathering," Jeremy commented to Meriwether. "Except that Vice-President Burr is missing. Come to think of it, I haven't seen him in some weeks. Is he off on a mission?"

Meriwether shook his head. "Burr is out of favor. In fact, Jefferson never really trusted him, particularly after the tie vote that threw the election into the House of Representatives. Now

Burr realizes he'll never gain the presidency through Jefferson—Jefferson's grooming Madison as his successor—so Burr plans to run for governor of New York State, and gain the presidency that way."

"Can he do it?" Jeremy asked.

"Burr is very strong with the St. Tammany political machine, but he'll have to contend with Hamilton, and you know how he hates Burr."

Jefferson looked across the table at Jeremy and raised his wine glass. "I've just this day received news that I'm sure will interest you. Our fleet has been sighted near the Azores and will soon enter the Mediterranean to engage the Tripoli pirates. I know your brother is on one of the vessels of Commodore Preble's squadron. I drink to their safety."

Jeremy felt the Madeira wine catch in his throat; in his gut he experienced a twinge of envy that Zebulon was halfway around the world, about to cover himself in glory. If he came back a hero, Rebecca might easily forgive him.

Despite the scanty appropriations from Congress, Jefferson had managed to furnish the President's House in a style somewhat befitting its purpose. He'd brought a great deal of his own furniture from Monticello; being a man of habit, having his own familiar things about him made him feel easier. A green-painted canvas rug lay on the floor. A Hepplewhite sideboard with knife cases stood against one wall, and there were also glass cases for silver and plate. Fifteen gold-and-black Louis XVI chairs were ranged around the room, and chintz curtains hung at the windows.

The house staff numbered fifteen, which included eleven slaves, though once in the dining room, the guests were never conscious of the help. For the President had invented a device he called "the Lazy Susan," a revolving tray that circled through a cut in the wall and allowed the servants to load the food in the adjoining room and deliver it to the diners without interrupting any conversations. Foreign diplomats, always sensitive to the possibility of spies, were delighted with this. A dumbwaiter had also been built so that wine and food could be sent up from the kitchen, where his chef, Monsieur Julian, concocted the culinary masterpieces which had once enchanted the crowned heads of France.

"Say what you will, the French do make extraordinary chefs," Dolley Madison said.

Jefferson nodded. "When I served as minister to France, one of the enchantments was the food. A battery of a hundred and sixty chefs cooked for the court at Versailles. With the coming of the French Revolution, these masters suddenly found themselves out of work. Many of them opened restaurants in Paris, and it's why that city is fast becoming known for its food. Many other chefs, like our Monsieur Julian, were delighted to take positions in foreign countries."

Jeremy picked a feather from his plate, a memento from Jefferson's pet mockingbird; it flew freely about the dining room and was fed while perched on the President's shoulder.

Dinner included fried eggs, fried beef, a roasted turkey, ducks shot in the nearby flats, rounds of beef, and the dish that Jefferson had brought back from Europe, macaroni. Six wines were served, including a rich Hungarian and an even richer Tokay.

"This is a far cry from the boiled beef and the frosty smiles that graced the frugal Adams table," Jeremy said to Meriwether. "But then, Adams knew he was a lame-duck President. That couldn't have given him much cause for gaiety."

"Do you know that Jefferson is paying for all the food served in the President's House out of his own pocket?" Meriwether said in an aside to Jeremy.

He shook his head, surprised. "I didn't know that."

"It's true," Meriwether said. "And though it's fast draining his own personal monies, he's determined that the food served here will equal or surpass any in Europe."

Dessert came, a treat that Jeremy and most of America had never experienced—ice cream wrapped in warm pastry. He could have eaten a dozen helpings.

Jeremy turned his attention to the President, who was talking about the new regime in France. "Napoleon thought he could reestablish French dominance in North America, for much of the Mississippi River region is hunted by French trappers, and New Orleans and Quebec have allegiances to France. But for such a conquest, Napoleon had to have an advance base of operations; he sent his brother-in-law, General Leclerc, and an army of forty thousand men to Hispaniola in the West Indies.

"But Napoleon reckoned without Toussaint L'Ouverture and his Negro army. They fought the French to a standstill, then fever took over and wiped out practically all the French forces. Occupied as he was with his war with England, Napoleon could risk no further losses, so he's given up the dream of reconquering the New World. And that finally presented us with a solution to the problem of New Orleans. Come with me." Jefferson rose and led the gathering into the Cabinet Room.

A long center table heaped with clusters of papers and gardening tools dominated the Cabinet Room. Maps covered the walls. Jefferson tapped the map of America. "New Orleans . . . the port right at the mouth of the Mississippi is vital to our settlers west of the Alleghenies. A few years ago, fifty flatboats a year might come down the Mississippi; this year more than five hundred will dock at New Orleans. From there, the settlers can ship their produce to the eastern seaboard, or to European markets."

"The river traffic will grow heavier as the country grows," Meriwether said.

Jefferson nodded. "As you know, many congressmen have been agitating for war with France, so that we can seize the port. But such a war would last at least seven years, cost us a hundred thousand lives, and add millions to the national debt. Not to mention the terrible demoralization that war superinduces on the human mind. Better to *purchase* New Orleans than to go to war over it."

"Hear, hear," James Madison said, for it had fallen to him to keep the congressional warmongers in check.

Jefferson continued, "Knowing that Napoleon needed money to finance his battle with Great Britain, I sent our ambassadors to France to negotiate the purchase of the port."

Working in the President's House had made Jeremy privy to some of the circumstances surrounding that mission. Ambassador Livingston had arrived in France in December of 1802. Livingston warned the French that their occupation of New Orleans, which had been ceded to them by Spain, would force the United States into an alliance with Great Britain. France could avoid that by selling us New Orleans. Livingston's mission was made somewhat difficult by the fact that he could not speak French—nor hear it, for he was practically stone

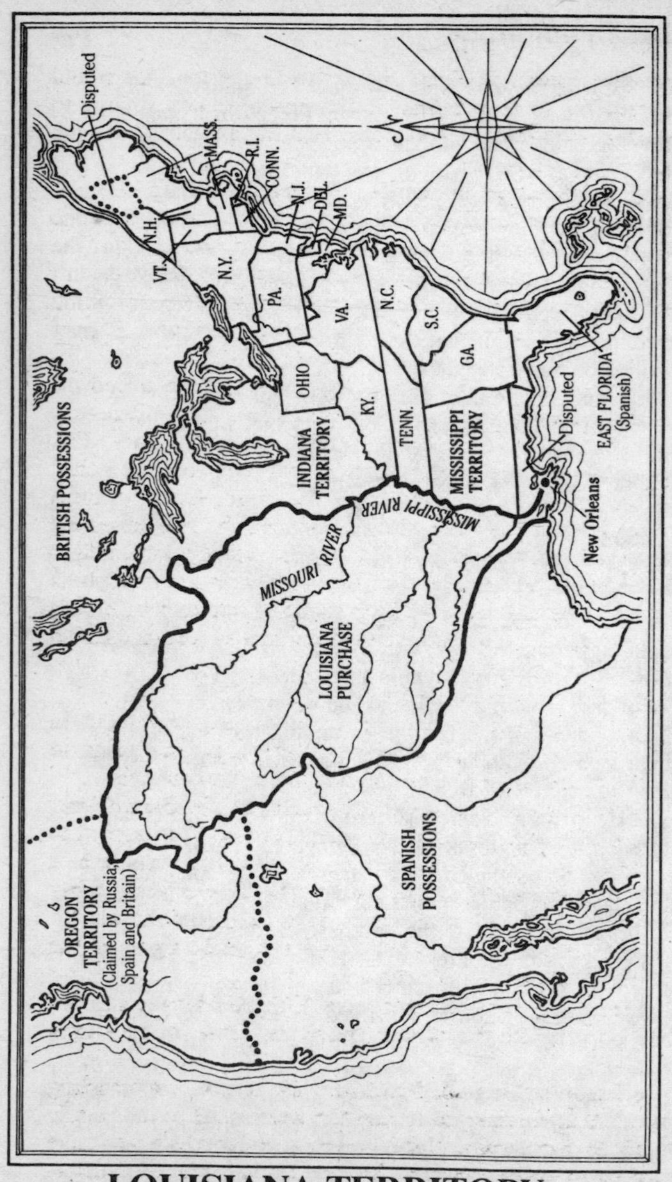

LOUISIANA TERRITORY

deaf. The French wouldn't say yes to Livingston, nor would they say no. In desperation, Jefferson sent James Monroe to Paris to revitalize the negotiations. That was as much as Jeremy knew about the matter.

Jefferson rubbed his hands, obviously relishing his tale. "Monroe so badgered Tallyrand about New Orleans that one day the French minister said, 'What would you give for the entire territory of Louisiana?' Monroe was shaken; we hadn't even planned for such a contingency. But he said, 'Four million dollars.' 'Not enough!' Tallyrand answered. 'Think it over tonight and then come and see me tomorrow.'"

Jefferson could not contain his excitement. He traced the enormous area on the map. "We've struck a bargain whereby we'll pay France fifteen million dollars for the territory. This includes a bit more than eleven million in six-percent notes, and the rest in the assumption of the claims of our citizens against France. For fifteen million dollars, we've doubled the size of our country, gained what we think may be in the neighborhood of two hundred fifty million acres, at a cost of about four cents an acre. And without shedding one drop of blood! We have enough land to last for the thousandth and thousandth generation of our children!"

A palpable thrill swept the room.

"We expect the treaty to be consummated very soon. In anticipation, Captain Lewis has already begun his plans to explore the territory. Captain, if you'd be good enough . . ."

Meriwether stepped forward to the map. "William Clark, under whom I've served in the Ohio Territory, has agreed to co-captain this expedition with me. I chose him because he's the best frontiersman in the country. He'll train about thirty men—all tough, all unmarried—in a camp just outside St. Louis. When our corps is fully hardened to the rigors of the trip, we'll embark on our mission."

"When do you expect that to be?" Captain Tingey asked.

"I hope before this winter, but at the latest, in the spring of 1804."

Jefferson nodded and then said in his soft but commanding voice, "You are charged to find the water route to the Pacific Ocean, to discover that Northwest Passage for which men have searched for three centuries. You are further charged to determine the boundaries of the Louisiana Purchase as set forth in our treaty with France, and to establish the claims of the United States. The territory from the western slopes of the Rocky Mountains to the Pacific Ocean is claimed by England, Spain, and Russia, so when you set foot there, tread softly, for they'll try to stop you. What you discover will give future generations knowledge of the West, its rivers, mountains, the Indian tribes that dwell there, its flora, fauna, and natural wealth. Our scientists in Philadelphia and elsewhere in the nation anxiously await whatever specimens you bring back." He paused and then said quietly, "There are other reasons for this expedition, profound reasons which may one day affect the destiny of this nation . . . but on this I can say no more, for they're little more than dreams, and must remain dreams until the appropriate time."

Everybody talked at once; Captain Tingey told Meriwether that he would give him whatever shipyard supplies he needed. Jefferson said, "Mrs. Madison, would you be good enough to help raise funds and provisions for this expedition? As usual, Congress has been niggardly with their appropriations. Try to remember things like needles, thread, and other items that a man might not think of but which are absolutely essential."

"I will see to it immediately, and enlist all the ladies in the district," Dolley said.

Then the President turned to Jeremy. "You may wonder why you've been asked here this evening."

Jefferson reached for a sheaf of drawings and held them up one by one for the assembly to see. "These were done by the hand of Jeremy Brand." Jeremy turned pink under the praise heaped on him by the company. Jefferson continued, "Captain Lewis believes that it will serve his mission if he has somebody along who can draw."

"Since this territory's never been explored by an American," Meriwether said, "we've no idea of who and what we'll see. New animals perhaps, plants and rocks, and certainly new Indian tribes. Our plan is to send back as many specimens as possible, but in those instances where we cannot, drawings will have to suffice. Now William Clark can draw passably well, but it would be better to have two men along who can."

Jeremy felt his body going numb, not daring to hope.

Then President Jefferson looked at him. "Would you be willing to undertake this journey? It's unknown, uncharted territory, and will doubtless present many dangers. You'd serve under Captain Lewis, and we can probably arrange a temporary commission in the Army, which would expire when you returned. What do you say?"

Jeremy was so overcome that he picked Dolley Madison up and whirled her around. "Yes!" he cried, "Yes!"

Chapter 20

"NO!" REBECCA shouted. "You can't go!"

Jeremy jerked back, stung. He'd gone to her house to tell her the news, fully expecting that she'd be thrilled. Instead, he'd encountered this.

Rebecca's taffeta skirts whispered angrily as she paced the drawing room. She'd dismissed the maids—no point in them overhearing anything; the gossip would be all over Georgetown in the morning. Her father was out at his favorite haunt in the Union Tavern and wouldn't be home till closing.

She whirled on Jeremy, her eyes glinting as hard as gemstones. "You said you'd make something of yourself. You promised."

"But this is the opportunity of a lifetime, something every man in the territory would trade his soul for. And they've chosen me."

Tears filled her eyes. He'd never seen her cry before, and it cut him to the quick. When he reached for her, she didn't resist. He held her close, feeling her warmth, and he kissed the tears from her face. "Don't cry, please."

She looked at him, her huge hazel eyes pleading. "Then you mustn't leave. Oh, Jeremy, I have such a dreadful feeling. If you go, I know I'll lose you forever."

"I've loved you since I was a boy, loved you through countless nights of dreaming. You'll never lose me."

"But you could be gone for years. And what of the danger? Going into the unknown like some mad fool? I couldn't bear it if you died."

He embraced her again. "I'm going on this journey for you,

for us. Meriwether says that everyone who takes part in it will be famous."

She broke away and adjusted her bodice. "Captain Lewis says that to lure you away from me. Let him go with his soldiers."

He gazed at her, torn between her obvious concern and his own promise. "I've already told Jefferson I'd go," he said quietly.

With a strangled cry she came at him, beating him with her fists, that he could do this, cut her out of his life in one merciless motion. Here was the world of the man again and she was helpless in the face of it.

She'd suffered terribly as a consequence of Zebulon's attack—from the burns, of course, which had taken many weeks to heal, but more from the injury to her pride and spirit. What a terrible feeling to be forced to do something, and be too weak to prevent it. Zebulon had accused her of leading him on; was he right? she wondered. And then he had disappeared. In a way, that made it simpler for her because only Jeremy was left. But now she was in danger of losing him, too. The thought that she might somehow be at fault made her strike out even harder at Jeremy.

He grabbed her shoulders; try as she might to break free, he held her immobile. She stopped struggling, and gradually his hold relaxed. She looked deep into his eyes, her glance telling him better than words ever could.

He leaned down and brushed his mouth against hers, tentatively at first, and when she responded, he kissed her harder, until her lips parted and he was in the warm wonder of her. He lost any sense of time and place, knew only that the woman of his dreams stood before him, willing, loving him as he loved her.

They moved to the settee and his hands roamed over her body, feeling the firmness of her breasts. His fingers moved with an instinct of their own, loosening her clothes and gently easing them off of her until she lay before him, a long-limbed alabaster goddess, so beautiful that his breath caught. He lay down beside her, and with gentle endearments tried to win, through love, what Zebulon had lost through force.

But she would allow him to go so far, and no further. When

he persisted, she caught his wrist. "That," she whispered, "must wait for the marriage bed."

For what seemed like hours she held him at bay, until he thought he must go mad. Once she had to lace her fingers through his hair and pull his head away. Finally, the torment became too much and he fell away from her. The shame of lying naked with him, being devoured by his eyes, was nothing compared to the triumph that beat hugely in her chest.

So . . . this was what the poets had sung of through the ages. She sensed by her inflamed nipples and lips that there was a great deal more to this than she had ever expected, wondrous and fulfilling. But there'd be time enough for that when matters were settled.

She sat up, drawing her gown about her. "Quickly. My father will be home as soon as the tavern closes."

Jeremy slowly ran his fingers down her brow, her nose, and then traced the outline of her lips. "I love you."

"Then you must speak to my father tomorrow, tell him you're willing to work for him. I'll talk to him also. As soon as we're married, I know he'll make you a partner. He's never refused me anything I wanted."

Jeremy got dressed slowly, his head ringing with the plans she continued to make for them. He felt the way a snared animal must feel.

"We'll marry immediately, of course," he interrupted her. "But we'll have to keep it a secret for a bit. You see, Meriwether's only recruiting single men. He thinks a married man might be too worried about his wife and children to be able to serve without being afraid." He gripped her in his arms. "At least we'll have two or three weeks before I leave."

She reacted as though he'd slapped her. But before they could get into a further argument, they heard a carriage roll up.

"That will be Father," she said, quickly turning up the lamps, and straightening the folds of her dress.

Mathias Breech stumbled into the house, bellowing a song. He gawked at the sight of Jeremy. "What's he doing here?" He glanced around suspiciously, then a mighty hiccough rocked him. "Well, no need to worry about that one, my girl can take care of herself, eh? Rebecca, everybody at the tavern was singing this new song about Jefferson and his mulatto:

Of all the damsels on the green
On mountain or in valley
A lass so luscious ne'er was seen,
As Monticellan Sally
Yankee Doodle, who's the noodle,
What wife were half so handy,
To breed a flock of slaves for stock,
A blackamoor's the dandy!"

Mathias Breech finished on a burst of raucous laughter. "Our esteemed Jefferson puts on plenty of airs. But in the dark, he's like all men; he can't do without his little honey pot!"

Jeremy clenched his fists. He wanted to smash Breech's face, but he controlled his temper for Rebecca's sake.

Mathias Breech struggled out of his coat, then fell onto the settee, his bloated stomach sticking up in the air. Rebecca tried to rouse him but in short order his snoring filled the room. The way she felt, she'd have gladly strangled both her father and Jeremy. She dug her fingers into Jeremy's arm. "It's no use talking to him now. We'll tell him tomorrow."

She was convinced that Jeremy would change his mind about the expedition. Now that she'd declared her love, revealed things sacred only to the marriage bed, how could he refuse her?

But the following day Jeremy didn't appear. She fretted, imagined that he'd taken ill, had been in an accident, or worse, was dead. She sent Letitia to the President's House to inquire. When the maid returned and reported, "Jeremy is just fine," Rebecca threw a glass at the terrified girl.

Swallowing her pride, Rebecca rode to Jeremy's house the following evening. She found him sharpening his knives on a honing stone; his guns and other equipment were neatly stacked in a corner.

"What are you doing?" she demanded, not daring to believe what she saw.

"Packing," he said quietly.

She tried to reason with him, but he kept repeating, "I've given my word to the President of the United States."

"And what of your word to me?" she flared.

"Rebecca, you don't understand. This is an adventure that calls out to my soul. If I don't go I'll spend the rest of my days regretting it."

"You sound like some addled schoolboy," she exclaimed. She used every argument she could think of, but Jeremy refused to budge. With a final, exasperated cry, she slammed out of the house.

For days, Rebecca alternately wept and went into tearing rages. She grew edgy and thin, and the servants stayed out of her way. She felt betrayed and could do nothing about it. She cursed her position in life, cursed Jefferson and Jeremy in the same breath, and cursed the fate that had made her fall in love with him.

One afternoon, a footman called at the Breech residence and delivered an invitation from Dolley Madison. "It's to a 'colored bead party,'" Rebecca said to Letitia. "What in the world is that?"

"I don't know. But why don't you go? Mrs. Madison, she likes you, and going to one of her fancy parties might just shake you out of your miseries."

In no mood for such frivolities, Rebecca tore the card up. But as the hours passed, she reconsidered. "After all, Letitia, I've closeted myself for days, and that hasn't solved anything."

"Already ironed your dress for you, it's all laid out in your room, and you're going, and that's all I've got to say about that matter."

At the Connaught estate in the hills above Washington, Victoria showed Dolley's invitation to Sean. "What can be on that woman's mind? How can she have the temerity to invite me to one of her silly parties?"

Sean held the invitation to his teeth and whistled, thinking. "Where's Marianne?" he asked.

"In the sewing room with her mother, the poor demented woman," Victoria said. "Doing their infernal needlework."

"I'd like to see her," Sean said, and Victoria ordered the

butler to bring her niece to them. Minutes later, Marianne came into the room. Sean smiled at her; he had a tender spot in his heart for this tentative creature; she looked so nondescript. He showed her the invitation, then said, "I want both of you to go to Mrs. Madison's party."

"But why?" Victoria exclaimed. "I demand to know why. I refuse to be insulted by that woman again for no good reason."

Sean straightened to his full height. "Madam, you're my aunt, and as such I respect you. But I'm unaccustomed to responding to anybody's demands, save those of my king and country."

Flustered, Victoria said, "I didn't mean it that way, of course . . . I apologize; I meant only—"

Sean cut her off with a gesture, and Marianne took courage that somebody in the family had finally stood up to her aunt. Sean said, "I've just received word from my government by packet boat. The acquisition of the Louisiana Territory by the United States is counter to England's best interest."

"But then why didn't England contest it in the first place?" Marianne asked.

Sean's smile was slightly condescending. "At the moment, it's important not to antagonize America, lest she enter the war on Napoleon's side. But there is a master plan. We *allowed* the United States to purchase the territory, but once France is conquered and has no further claims in this continent, it will be much simpler for us to wrest the territory from the Americans, particularly the vital port of New Orleans."

"But how clever of England to have structured it so!" Victoria exclaimed.

Sean nodded. "In fact, with the permission of our king and parliament, English banks have loaned the United States the money to pay for the purchase, and at a very healthy interest rate. Once the United States has repaid the loan and the interest, we invade and conquer Louisiana. That way, we shall get back both the money and the land!"

Victoria hugged herself with delight at the sheer justice of it all.

"And that's why you must both go to Dolley's party," Sean told them. "You see, we hadn't expected Jefferson to send out this expedition so quickly. You must find out everything possible about these men, especially their route. If during their long journey they should somehow be . . . intercepted, should disappear . . ."

"I'll get my cloak," Victoria said and left the room.

Sean took Marianne's cold, delicate hands in his. "Cousin, how old are you?"

"Sixteen, almost," she said.

"Marianne, I count on you in this," he said. "Our aunt means well, but she is . . . past her prime."

She was so overcome with the kindness he was showing her that she felt on the verge of tears. "I'll do everything I can," she murmured.

When Rebecca swept into the drawing room of the Madisons' house on F Street, she heard a gaggle of women gossiping and almost left, particularly when she saw Victoria and Marianne Connaught. Rebecca didn't usually enjoy the company of females; with the exception of Abigail Adams, she'd never met a woman she thought her equal in intelligence.

But before she could escape, Dolley beckoned her in. Dolley, bedecked in a buff-colored gown and coq feathers in her beige turban, said, "I was just explaining why I'd thrown this colored bead party."

As Dolley went on, Rebecca listened intently, not only because of her own personal involvement, but because she suddenly suspected that this might well be a subject for Rebel Thorne's pen.

". . . And so very soon, our men will depart on this expedition to explore the Louisiana Territory," Dolley said. "They must have certain necessary things if they're to survive. My dear ladies, it's been left to us to gather materials, things like leather for shoes, buckskin for clothing. But most of all we must have colored beads."

"Colored beads?" Victoria repeated incredulously. "What ever for?"

"I'm told that the Indians in the western lands use them for barter," Dolley said. She didn't much like having Victoria here, but if she excluded everybody who'd spread rumors about Jefferson and Sally Hemings, her drawing room would have been empty. Further, she knew that Victoria owned a blue beaded shawl she'd bought in London, and hoped to get her to donate it.

Everybody in the room was soon talking about the Louisiana Purchase and the riches that would flow into the nation's coffers. "They say the Chinese will pay an emperor's ransom for the skins of the sea otter." . . . "Beaver hats have become all the rage on the continent." . . . But always the conversation returned to the men who'd been chosen for this dangerous task.

"My husband *pleaded* with Meriwether Lewis to be taken along on this expedition," one matron said, "but the captain refused. It's a very great honor to be asked."

"Without question, they'll all go down in history," Dolley said.

Have I been a fool? Rebecca wondered.

"Oh, Mrs. Madison, it sounds so wonderful," Victoria said. "Pray by which roads and rivers will these men go?"

The coq feathers in Dolley's turban waved first one way then the other as she shook her head. "Of roads and rivers I have no knowledge. I leave such details to the men."

Marianne smiled sweetly. "I have a beaded bag that I can donate to the cause, and Aunt Victoria has this wonderful shawl."

"Oh that would be a blessing," Dolley said.

Then Marianne said, "I've heard rumors that Captain Lewis is going to Pittsburgh."

"To purchase some equipment, a keelboat and the like. But beyond that I know nothing," Dolley said.

Victoria Connaught waggled her finger at her. "You, who have the ear of President Jefferson, to say nothing of your own husband? A likely tale."

Dolley laughed engagingly but said nothing more. She did know the general route, but to protect the lives of the men, Jefferson had sworn her and all the others to secrecy. It was entirely conceivable that the English, the Russians, or the Spanish, all of whom had strong interests in this land, might try to ambush the men.

After attending several of these "colored bead parties," Rebecca's viewpoint began to change until she'd done a complete about-face.

"If the mission is successful, and Jeremy does come back a hero," she told her father, "then he could do anything he wanted to—go into business, even politics."

Mathias Breech made a face. "The thought that you're even considering marrying any of those Brands makes me dyspeptic. Look what Zebulon did to you! And now this one, making you promises and then leaving. Have you no sense?"

Rebecca paid no attention. "I hear that the journey is so dangerous, through unknown, hostile territory, that they might never come back. Should I marry him now?" she wondered aloud.

"Suppose he doesn't come back?" Mathias said. "You'd be a widow. Better wait."

Later that night, Rebecca sat before her mirror, brushing her hair, which seemed aflame in the glow of the oil lamp. Jeremy, Zebulon, Jeremy, she counted with each brush stroke. She paused at Zebulon . . . She knew it was only a matter of time before the American fleet would engage the Tripoli pirates. A chill coursed along her body, and she was surprised to discover that though she detested what he'd tried to do to her, some deep secret part of her applauded his audacity.

She stared at the pinpoints of light flickering in her eyes. How strange that the physical contact she'd scorned these many years now seemed so attractive. In her girlhood, the brutal relationship between her father and mother had frightened her, and perhaps that was the reason she'd delayed marrying for so long. But Jeremy's tenderness, and his own innocence had dispelled her fear. Jeremy . . . Yes, she did love him. And now all she yearned for was for him to return home safely, so that her life might begin.

PART THREE

Chapter 21

"THIS IS a disaster of the greatest magnitude," Commodore Preble said as he paced the low-beamed captain's quarters aboard the U.S.S. *Constitution,* anchored in the Mediterranean. "It may mean the end of our entire expedition against the Moors, damn them!"

Preble was an irascible New Englander who'd seen naval service in the Revolutionary War. His "boys," as he called his squadron leaders, were all under thirty, and from the middle or southern states. Preble's squadron had consisted of the frigates *Constitution* and *Philadelphia,* each with forty-four guns; the *Argus,* eighteen guns; the *Siren, Nautilus,* and *Vixen,* each sixteen guns; and the *Enterprise,* which had the shallowest draft, with fourteen cannon.

Commodore Preble paused before the seaman slumped in the chair. Patches of sunburned skin were peeling from his shoulders and back; his hair was matted with salt, his lips cracked from days adrift. He'd been picked up by the sloop *Siren,* then transferred to the *Constitution.* After hearing the seaman's terrible news, Preble had called all his squadron officers together. Seated around the table were Lieutenant Charles Stewart of the *Siren,* and Lieutenant Decatur, in command of the sloop *Enterprise.*

Preble handed the rescued seaman a glass of water and a lemon and salt, and he drank greedily. "Would you repeat your name and ship," Preble asked.

"Zebulon Brand, of the frigate *Philadelphia,*" he whispered.

"When you're able, tell my men what happened, and don't leave out a detail," Preble said.

Zebulon felt the eyes of the officers on him. Of the more than three hundred men aboard the *Philadelphia,* he'd been the only one to escape. He would have to tell his story with care.

And the whole expedition had begun so gloriously! When Preble joined the U.S. squadron already cruising the Mediterranean, he found that Morocco, heretofore neutral, was on the verge of joining Tripoli in her war against the United States. Preble's response was to mass his squadron and salute the Moroccans with twenty-one-gun salvos. Seeing the strength of the Americans, the Moroccans quickly saw the wisdom in remaining neutral, and Preble was then able to direct his attention to Tripoli.

Zebulon studied Commodore Preble, trying to find some clue to the man's nature, for he held the key to his own future. Preble had a long aquiline nose and a receding hairline, with the remaining strands of hair brushed forward in bangs. His dark hair was shot with white and his sideburns grew below the tips of his ears.

"In compliance with your orders, sir," Zebulon said, "the *Philadelphia* was cruising the waters around Tripoli, harassing the Moorish shipping. On the last day of October, at nine in the morning, the lookout in the crow's nest spotted a sail on the horizon.

"Captain Bainbridge immediately gave chase to a ship about five leagues westward of Tripoli. The ship hoisted Tripolitan colors, and we opened fire and continued firing until eleven-thirty that morning. We were in seven fathoms of water, but finding that our fire couldn't prevent the enemy ship from seeking refuge in Tripoli's harbor, we gave up the pursuit."

Zebulon took another swallow of water. Decatur fidgeted impatiently. "Get on with it, man."

"We were sailing off, when suddenly we ran onto a shoal not laid down on any of the maps."

"How far would you estimate from the town of Tripoli?" Decatur asked.

"About four, maybe five miles," Zebulon said. "Captain Bainbridge immediately ordered a boat lowered to sound; I was in command of it.

"I found that the greatest depth of water was astern, and told Captain Bainbridge. In order to back her off, all sails were then laid back and the top-gallant sails loosened. Three anchors were thrown from the bows; and the water pumped in the holds, in an attempt to rock us free. But it did no good. Then Captain Bainbridge had to make a decision. Our forty-four guns were the heaviest items aboard."

"Good God, no!" Decatur exclaimed.

Zebulon hung his head. "At the time, it seemed the best plan: cast them overboard, and thus free the vessel from the reef. I'd seen the keel scraping against the reef. Each time the captain jettisoned some heavy piece of equipment, I dove down to check the progress; the ship seemed to be freeing itself. The captain then ordered all the guns thrown overboard, save for a few abaft.

"But all efforts to free ourselves proved of no avail. The captain even attempted to lighten her forward by cutting away her foremast. And then what we'd all feared happened—the wind dropped and the canvas fell slack. We were becalmed.

"We lay thus, when the lookout in the crow's nest shouted, 'Boats approaching!' From my place in the water, I could see my comrades aboard the *Philadelphia* spring for the firearms that the captain broke out. If only we hadn't jettisoned our cannon!" Zebulon groaned. "We could have blasted those pirates out of the water."

"They wouldn't have approached unless you had thrown them overboard," Preble said dryly.

"Though there was no wind, the Moorish boats had galley slaves chained to the oars, perhaps fifty in each vessel, rowing in unison to the drumbeat, propelling their long boats at incredible speeds and circling us at will. More boats appeared until the water seemed alive with them.

"The gunboats, a cannon in each prow, bore down on us, with trumpets sounding, cymbals clashing, and loud cries to Allah to help them slay the unbelievers. For almost four hours we managed to fight them off, while they raked our decks with grape and chain, killing some of our best seamen. All the boats converged on us now, and for the first time we knew the fear of losing our vessel. They could shoot at us at will, and as long as the Lord kept his saving wind from us, we were doomed.

"The leader of the Moorish vessels shouted to Captain Bainbridge that if we struck our colors, we would be treated fairly, held for ransom, and released when it was paid. But if we resisted further, no quarter would be given; our bodies would be hacked to bits and fed to the jackals. What could Captain Bainbridge do except strike our colors?" Zebulon asked glumly.

"I'll tell you what he could have done," Decatur exclaimed. "He could have set fire to the *Philadelphia* to keep it from falling into enemy hands!"

"There were three hundred and fifteen seamen aboard, and twenty-two officers," Zebulon said softly.

"And in protecting them, he's jeopardized the lives of every man in our squadron! For if the Bashaw refits the vessel, she will mount as many guns as the *Constitution,* and will play havoc with us. Our expedition could go down in ignominious defeat. Can you imagine what the French and English would make of that? Never again will they take us seriously, and we'll have to toady to them." Decatur was so angry that he could barely control himself. He turned to Zebulon. "How is it that you managed to escape?"

Zebulon clenched his hands. "The Lord must have been looking kindly at me. When the attack started, all the men in our sounding boat climbed back aboard the *Philadelphia.* Only Seaman Johnston and I remained, diving every so often to see if the vessel was freeing herself from the reef. Johnston and I kept close to the hull of the *Philadelphia,* so we were never spied by the Moors. When they finally boarded her, it had gotten dark, and we swam away. We found a hatch cover that had been thrown overboard, and paddling with our hands, managed during the night to get a fair distance from the *Philadelphia.* We drifted on the currents, and in the morning a strong breeze came up. Due to the changing winds, we saw that the Moors had managed to free the *Philadelphia* from the reef. Now she's anchored close to shore, under the protective guns of the Bashaw's castle."

"God damn it to hell!" Decatur exclaimed.

"What happened to Seaman Johnston?" Preble asked.

"Died of exposure, sir," Zebulon murmured. "I said a few words over his body and commended him to the sea."

Zebulon took a deep breath. He'd gotten through that all right, he could tell by the way the officers reacted. He'd rehearsed the story so often in his mind that he almost believed that was the way it had happened . . . He and Johnston had drifted for four days. Their attempts to catch fish came to naught. They grew weaker, finally lacking the strength to move. Zebulon knew they'd die unless they had some food and water. A gull, believing them dead, landed on the hatch cover. With the last of his strength, Johnston lunged at it, managing to seize its wing, but he toppled off the raft into the water. Johnston broke the bird's neck, then threw it onto the hatch cover. Then he tried to climb back on, but was too weak.

Zebulon reached for the gull, feeling its plumpness, not hearing Johnston's cries, growing weaker as the hatch cover drifted from him. By the time Zebulon tried to paddle to him, Johnston had disappeared into the deep.

He plucked the bird, gutted it, and gnawed at the raw flesh. For two more days he drifted, growing more delirious. There were times when he dreamed of the Connaughts, saw Devroe writhing in a tangle of snakes, and heard Elizabeth's insane screams. Other times he'd see Rebecca's face limned against the burning carriagehouse. That vision troubled him most, for he knew that he would always love her. He vowed that if he lived, he would make it up to her. And it was with that prayer on his lips that he was sighted by the *Siren* and taken to the *Constitution*.

The winter winds swept across the Mediterranean, and the vessels ploughed through the seas, searching for the enemy. The bilge gas in the holds grew fierce, and some of the men were taken down with fever. Then sea worms bored holes through the planks, which had to be augured and rebunged.

But the difficulties of sailing in foreign waters were nothing compared to the mood among the squadron commanders. They were certain that the *Philadelphia* was being rearmed, and in a matter of weeks would sail out to fight against them. On the fourteenth of December, Commodore Preble sailed from Malta in company with the *Enterprise,* under the command of Lieutenant Decatur. The ships cruised along the Tripolitan coastline, and on the twenty-third of December, Decatur captured an enemy ketch, the sixty-ton *Mastico,* recently out of Tripoli.

Decatur renamed the vessel the *Intrepid*. "We have been asking for some sign from Providence," he said. "This is it!"

Lieutenant Decatur came aboard the *Constitution* to confer with Commodore Preble. He asked that Seaman Zebulon Brand be brought to the captain's quarters.

Decatur unrolled a map of the Tripoli harbor, showing the reefs and shoals that protected the seaward entrance to the port. "Mr. Brand, would you be good enough to show us the general position of the *Philadelphia*?"

Zebulon studied the map. "The *Philadelphia* ran aground here," he said, pointing to a spot about four miles north of Tripoli. "After the Moors freed her, she was taken right into the harbor. She lies under the protective guns of the Bashaw's castle and the harbor emplacements."

"Thank you," Decatur said. "Now Yusuf Caramanli, the Bashaw, has refused to ransom our prisoners and is puffed with pride over the capture of the *Philadelphia*. He knows that when he replaces her forty-four cannon, she will equal the firepower of the *Constitution*, and could destroy our entire squadron."

Decatur said softly, "Gentlemen, as terrible as the thought is, we have no other alternative. The *Philadelphia* must be destroyed before she can be used against us."

Silence blanketed the captain's quarters, the only sound the creaking of the ship as she rolled with the swells. "The reefs and shoals make a direct approach into the harbor impossible," Decatur said. "But our pilot, the Sicilian Catalano, has agreed to guide us into the port on a zigzag course."

Decatur traced the intended course. "Catalano swears he knows these waters; he's been a pilot for the Tripoli harbor for years."

"What if he's leading you into a trap?" Preble asked. "There are a hundred and fifteen guns in that harbor, and they'll all be trained on you."

"That's a possibility," Decatur said. "But what are our alternatives? Now this is my plan. We sail into the harbor aboard the *Intrepid*—the captured *Mastico*—with as many men as can be crammed into her hold. On deck, there will be a half dozen officers, dressed in the costumes of these Moors. The *Mastico* has the lines of an enemy vessel, and so they will believe that we're one of them." He held up a red flag emblazoned with the crescent moon and a lone star. "And we will also be flying the enemy flag."

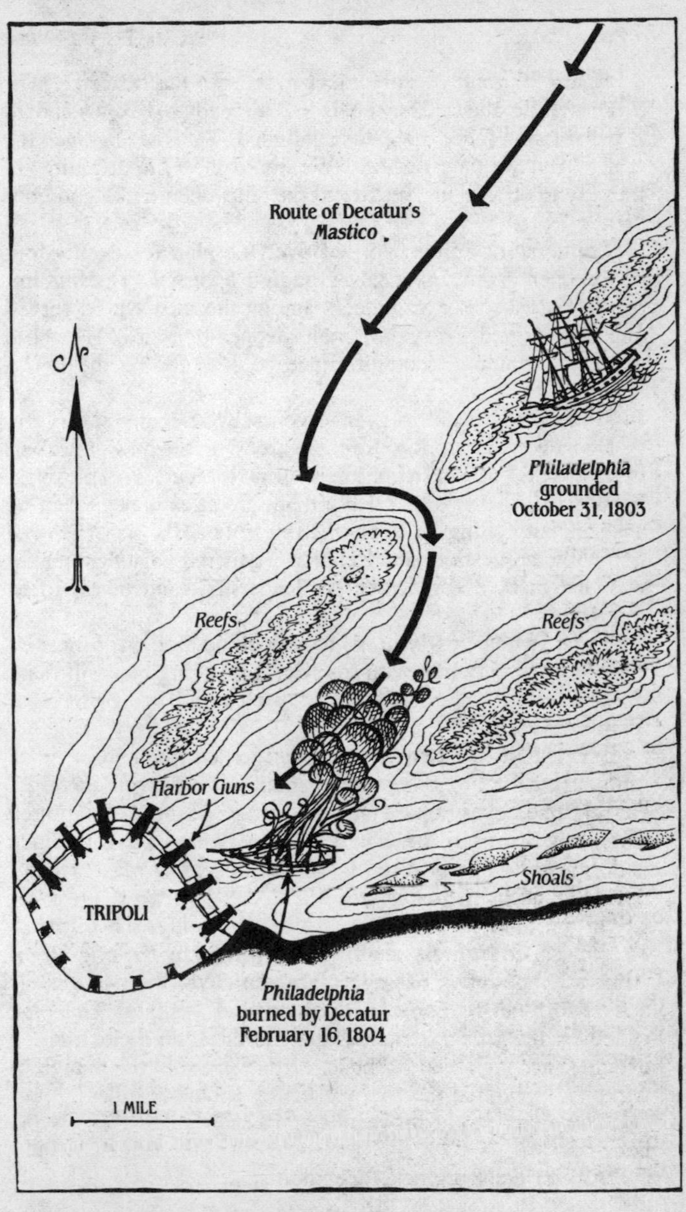

Route of Decatur's
Mastico
Philadelphia
grounded
October 31, 1803
Reefs
Reefs
Harbor Guns
Shoals
TRIPOLI
Philadelphia
burned by Decatur
February 16, 1804
1 MILE

A low murmur of agreement rose from the officers. "The *Siren* will lie outside the shoals and be ready to take us aboard if our mission fails," Decatur continued. Then he slammed the table. "But we dare not fail! We board the *Philadelphia,* kill those who oppose us, set fire to the ship, then make good our escape."

Commodore Preble worried over the plan for twenty-four hours, then finally gave his grudging approval. Decatur immediately asked for volunteers among the men who'd served under him, and every last man stepped forward. He chose seventy, including Zebulon, since he'd served on the *Philadelphia*.

"I know you want to avenge yourself," Decatur said.

Decatur set to work to train the crew: men who were expert in boarding, others who knew how to handle explosives. Zebulon had never seen such a man, sweet as honey when he wished, but cutting as steel when need be. His men followed him without question, and Zebulon wondered what that quality was that marked some men for leadership, and others to be followers.

As he swung slowly in his hammock he thought, I must do something worthwhile with my life! Something that will mark me above other men. It's the only chance I'll ever have of winning Rebecca.

Every night for two weeks, Decatur led his men in mock raids, using the *Constitution* as a stand-in for the *Philadelphia*. He rehearsed every phase of the operation; since the captured ketch rode lower in the water than the *Philadelphia,* the men had to learn to board from high in the rigging. At last Decatur decided that his men were ready.

On the third of February, a bleak cold day, the *Intrepid-Mastico* sailed from Syracuse, accompanied by the brig *Siren*. After a tempestuous passage of fifteen days, the two vessels arrived off the harbor of Tripoli toward twilight. The plan called for the *Mastico* to enter the harbor at ten o'clock in the evening, accompanied by boats of the *Siren,* but a change of wind had separated the two vessels by about six miles.

"The delay might prove fatal," Decatur said. "What's the hour now?"

"Almost eight o'clock," Zebulon said.

"We must go it alone then," Decatur said, and ordered on full sail.

A skeleton crew, dressed in the costumes of the Moors, and with their faces blackened, manned the sails. Belowdecks, armed to the teeth, hid the seventy volunteers, ready to avenge the honor of every American sailor who'd ever been humiliated by these pirates.

"There she lies," Zebulon whispered, pointing to the dim outline of the *Philadelphia*'s hull. She lay within half a gunshot of the principal shore batteries. Behind her rose the city's walls and the Bashaw's castle, and above them the slender minarets of the mosques. Decatur had timed their arrival so there would be no moon, and they were running without lights.

On the starboard of the *Philadelphia,* Zebulon made out the masts of two Tripolitan cruisers. "They're within two cable lengths, I'd say," he told Decatur. "And there are a number of other boats within half a gunshot."

Decatur took the telescope from him and scanned the *Philadelphia*. "It looks like they've already replaced her guns. She's ready for battle."

"Then we're just in time," Zebulon said. Whatever his original qualms about coming on this venture, they'd long since disappeared. His blood pounded through his body, and he knew he was ready to fight . . . and to kill.

Because the wind was light, it took Decatur three hours to sail the final three miles to the *Philadelphia*. When they came within two hundred yards of her, they were challenged by the Moors.

"Stand fast and anchor, or we'll blow you out of the water!"

Having foreseen such a challenge, Decatur turned to the Sicilian pilot. "Catalano, tell them we've lost all our anchors."

"This is the *Mastico,*" Catalano shouted in Arabic. He repeated Decatur's message and told them they were disabled and limping back to port.

The Moors guarding the *Philadelphia* had no way of knowing that the *Mastico* had fallen into American hands. And what they saw on deck were men in Arab dress; in the darkness, they couldn't see that their faces had been disguised with pitch and burnt cork.

Decatur maneuvered his ship to within fifty yards of the

Philadelphia, when suddenly the wind dropped.

"Dear God, please," Zebulon prayed. "Just a bit more wind and we'll be alongside."

Decatur and his men held their breaths, for the Moors on board the *Philadelphia* had crowded to the rail, watching the *Mastico* drift toward them.

"We're close enough now," Decatur said. "Secure a rope to the chains of the *Philadelphia!*"

Zebulon ran forward and threw a line around the anchor chain, and the *Mastico* warped alongside.

"Boarders away!" Decatur shouted, and swung from the rigging to the *Philadelphia*'s deck.

Not until then did the Tripolitans realize they'd been duped; without any of their own officers aboard, their confusion was great. Decatur was quickly followed by Midshipman Morris and Zebulon.

A precious minute elapsed before the Americans hidden in the *Mastico*'s hold could scramble out, climb their own rigging, and then swing over to board the *Philadelphia*. During that minute, which seemed like an eternity, Decatur, Morris, and Zebulon fought off the hordes of Moors that charged them, scimitars raised, their bloodcurdling cries alerting the other Tripolitan ships to the danger.

The Moors preferred this kind of hand-to-hand fighting; for centuries they had terrified travelers with their no-quarter tactics. They also outnumbered Decatur's men about three to one. But the Moors hadn't reckoned with the wild lieutenant and his equally wild crew.

Fighting back to back with Decatur, Zebulon held off two Moors, and then with a lunge, thrust his sword into one pirate's chest. The other came at him but Zebulon ducked aside nimbly and the scimitar cut into the wood railing. Before he could retrieve his weapon, Zebulon jabbed his knife into the man's stomach and he fell in a heap.

By then the other boarders were swinging onto the *Philadelphia,* forcing the Moors back. They crowded together on the quarterdeck, trying to fight, but they were no match for the fury of Decatur and his crew. Ten minutes later, Decatur cried, "The *Philadelphia* is ours!"

But the onshore batteries were now aware of the deception,

and the harbor guns were trained on the ship. Alongside, pirates on the other Tripolitan vessels tried to board the *Philadelphia* but were driven off.

"Lay the fuses!" Decatur called, and the men who had practiced so diligently for three weeks set about their task. They opened casks of powder and ran lines of it along the decks to where the munitions were stored. Then they threw lighted torches into the holds. The flames leapt into the air, catching the canvas that was wrapped around the booms and spars.

"Look there!" Zebulon shouted to Decatur. "There are more boats coming out of the harbor."

"Light the munition fuses!" Decatur shouted.

Torches were held to the powder and the fire sped along the line. Then came a fearful explosion as the munitions caught. Flames shot toward the *Mastico,* almost setting her on fire.

"Boarders away!" Decatur shouted. The sailors retreated, swarming back onto the *Mastico*. Zebulon released the rope holding them to the anchor line of the *Philadelphia*. "Jump, jump!" he shouted to Decatur as the ships began to drift apart.

Decatur waited for the last minute before leaping from the rigging. As he did, a series of explosions rocked the abandoned, burning ship.

The flames lit up the harbor. The guns from the castle and the shore batteries began to bombard them, and Decatur shouted, "Fire at will!" With their small complement of cannon they fired at the pursuing boats.

Sailing with skill and daring, Decatur maneuvered the *Mastico* in the rising light breeze until she was out of range of the Moors, and then joined the *Siren,* which lay just outside the shoals.

A quick count was made of all hands. "None killed, sir," Zebulon reported, "and only four wounded."

In the distance, the sinking *Philadelphia* was a fiery pyre, her flames leaping hundreds of feet into the air and casting a glow on the city of Tripoli.

"And that shall be the fate of their city also," Decatur said. "They shall know once and for all that the strong arm of America can reach anywhere in the world and chastise those who would humiliate us!"

No one experienced greater joy over the victory than Zebulon. "I swore I'd repay them for all their unreasoned cruelty," he said to Decatur. "But this is only the beginning. I won't be satisfied until every last one of them begs for mercy."

"You may get that chance sooner than you think," Decatur said. "We plan to keep up our offensive at sea, naturally, but I understand that an effort will be made to mount a land campaign as well."

Charged with elation, Zebulon blurted, "If a land offensive does come to pass, I'll be among the first to volunteer."

Chapter 22

JEREMY DUG his long ash pole into the river bottom, and with his muscles bulging, toed the cleated footway running around the gunwales of the keelboat; step by step, he pushed hard, bow to stern. The other men of the Corps of Discovery did the same, as they poled the boat up the Missouri. A platoon of men tramped along the bank of the river lined with willow and aspen, pulling the two ropes attached to the boat's prow. Scannon, the Newfoundland dog that Lewis had purchased in Pittsburgh for twenty dollars, barked at a deer on shore.

After months of preparations, training, and drill overseen by William Clark, Meriwether Lewis's co-captain, the corps had set out from Wood River Camp on the fourteenth of May, stopped briefly in St. Charles, a few miles north of St. Louis, and were now well into the wilderness of the Missouri, making about fifteen miles a day. The work was exhausting; violent storms, brutal heat, sandbars, crumbling riverbanks, dysentery, boils, ticks, snakes, and mosquitoes plagued the men, but an intense camaraderie began to develop among them. No one had ever done what they were attempting, and that knowledge bound them together. At every bend in the river, Jeremy was overwhelmed by each new vista of this wondrous, endless land.

"There's a breeze coming up," Pierre Cruzatte shouted. The French riverman hired for his expertise stood at the stern, steering with an eight-foot rudder. The men scrambled to raise the sail on the forty-foot-high mast, with its twenty-foot crossbeam. The wind caught the square canvas and the keelboat surged upriver, giving the men a chance to catch their breath.

Jeremy rested a bit; gradually, the ache in his arms and shoulders subsided. Then he took his pad and began to sketch the boat. Fifty-five feet long and twelve wide, with twenty-two oars at the prow. Two blunderbusses were mounted on the sides, and a small swivel cannon was mounted on the forward deck. A small fortress-type cabin had been built amidships, with an inside clearance of six feet.

An upended tree rushed toward them on the spring-swollen currents, and George Shannon, the seventeen-year-old lookout in the prow, shouted, "Sawyer on the port side!" Cruzatte squinted his one good eye, and deftly steered the boat away from the danger.

The boat drew only two feet of water when empty, but it drew four when fully loaded with the tons of equipment: bales of clothing, food, ammunition, and goods to trade with the Indians. In fact, they'd been so overloaded that Captain Lewis had had to acquire two pirogues, one white and one red, and the two of them followed along downstream.

Jeremy chuckled as he remembered Meriwether's request to Congress concerning his expenses. Congress hadn't balked at appropriating the $2,500 for the journey, but they would have had different feelings if they'd known that Meriwether, acting with President Jefferson's approval, had secretly requisitioned $60,000 worth of equipment and food from the United States Army arsenals.

After a backbreaking day's labor, the men would camp, Cruzatte would break out his fiddle, and they'd dance around the campfire. Jeremy's graphite stick caught the abandon as the men played as hard as they worked. Nobody loved to dance more than Ben York, William Clark's gigantic Negro slave. He wore a brilliant red-orange kerchief around his head, and a loop earring dangled from his ear. Ben's mother had been a slave in the Clark family, and from boyhood on, York had served as Clark's personal bodyservant. Enormously strong, though a little paunchy, he towed the boat with the others during the day, and at night served as cook and orderly to the two captains.

But most of all, Jeremy liked to sketch the leaders of the expedition. Meriwether had turned twenty-nine, and a new resolve shone in his intense blue eyes. But his face belied his name, and sometimes Jeremy would catch him with the strangest expression, as though the melancholy man suffered from sickness of the spirit.

William Clark, on the other hand, was rough and garrulous, and beloved by all for his fairness and general good humor. At thirty-three, Clark stood over six feet tall, had blue eyes and a thatch of thick red hair. His freckled face burned under the warming sun, and he wore a tricorn hat to protect himself. Good-natured as he was, he could also be a stern taskmaster; when Private Collins refused to carry out a direct order, Clark gave him fifty lashes for insubordination.

As far as Jeremy knew, never in the history of any military expedition had a command been shared; he wondered at the temperaments of these two men which made that possible. Both were woodsmen, both had served on the frontier, though Clark was a better riverman. He usually stayed with the boats, while Lewis reconnoitered on shore, collecting specimens or hunting. Only Jeremy knew that the War Department had refused to honor the agreement that Lewis had made with Clark about sharing the command; instead of granting Clark the rank of captain, they'd only commissioned him a lieutenant. Lewis had been outraged when the news reached them at Wood River Camp, and insisted that the other men not be told; he shared his command with Clark as they'd agreed.

But Lewis, through the force of his personality, was the actual commander; he'd dreamed of this exploration all his adult life. Jeremy came to believe that this great adventure gave his friend the will and reason to live.

They celebrated the Fourth of July with a gunshot over the bow and an extra gill of whiskey per man. Days and miles blended into each other. As the keelboat progressed upriver, the summer sun burned a hole in the sky.

When Jeremy thought he had no more strength, he'd set his mind thinking of Rebecca, of home, and what would happen when he returned to Washington. In those reveries, he found hidden reserves of energy.

At dusk, when they made camp, swarms of gnats and mosquitoes made life miserable. Exhausted as he might be, Jeremy sketched the day's events, a bluff they passed, the deer, wolf, and other wildlife that watched their passage. President Jefferson had charged them to record as much as they might see, and the land paraded its wealth for them.

What fascinated Jeremy most was the subtle changes in the

men. From a raw group of volunteers, Lewis and Clark were slowly forging the Corps of Discovery into a superb team. Jeremy had his own opinion of the men: Next to the two captains, the guide Drouillard, called Drewyer, was proving himself indispensable. He was the son of a French father and a Shawnee mother, and his instincts in the wild were infallible. By mutual consent, Ordway, the first sergeant, took command if Lewis and Clark were both engaged in scouting, hunting, or exploratory trips. The Field brothers, rough and ready Kentuckians, and John Colter had become expert hunters.

Not that there weren't serious breaches of discipline; Moses Reed and the French waterman, La Liberté, deserted. Drewyer and a party went to hunt them down. La Liberté escaped, but Moses Reed was captured; he was sentenced to run the gauntlet four times while the men lashed him with switches. He was drummed out of the corps, and given only menial tasks to perform; Lewis planned to send him back to St. Louis with the keel boat when the river grew too narrow for the boat to proceed.

One blistering day in August, Sergeant Floyd collapsed at his station. He'd taken sick earlier in July, but had appeared to recover. From the anguished look on his face, Jeremy knew it was serious. Meriwether ministered to him, trying every remedy that Dr. Benjamin Rush had taught him in Philadelphia, but nothing helped.

"Plainly, some vital organ has ruptured in his stomach," Captain Lewis told the men.

"I'm going away," Sergeant Floyd whispered to Clark. "I want you to write a letter for me."

Clark composed the letter while Jeremy did a final sketch of Floyd so that his family would have a keepsake. He died the following morning and the solemn band of men buried him atop a bluff. Many of Floyd's comrades wept unashamedly, for he'd been a decent and just man. After paying full military honors to their fallen brother, they continued on their journey.

On September fifth, while out on a scouting expedition with Meriwether, Jeremy spied an animal bounding across the plain. It stopped at the river's edge and drank, its nose touching its water twin. "What is it?" he asked excitedly. "I've never seen anything like it before."

"Quiet, lad," Lewis cautioned him. "I must bag one of these creatures and send it back to President Jefferson." He began to stalk the animal, but suddenly it lifted its nose to the message on the wind and bounded away.

"Did you see that?" Lewis exclaimed. "It moved across that ridge more like a low-flying bird than a four-footed animal." Writing in his journal later that night, Lewis named the animal *antelope*.

With the passage of August, they came into buffalo country, and Jeremy's pencil never stopped. The herds were vast, stretching to the horizon line in the treeless prairie. The buffalo were huge, bigger than oxen, with great humped shoulders and shaggy heads. Though they looked fierce, they were docile and easy to kill. The men ate heartily, as much as seven pounds of buffalo meat per man.

As they approached the domain of the Teton Sioux, the corps became tense. From St. Louis on, all the trappers had warned Lewis and Clark about this tribe. "The Sioux have closed the upper Missouri to all traffic from below, terrorizing traders, exacting tribute, killing indiscriminately," Clark said. Every night he posted extra sentries; all the men took their turns.

One night Jeremy patrolled the perimeter of the camp. He watched the embers of the campfire fly skyward, seeming to join the millions of stars in the heavens. An owl hooted, bristling the hair on his neck; then came the sudden beat of wings and the hapless cry of a rabbit caught in the taloned death-grip. Jeremy clutched his rifle. Life and death here moved in their own inexorable rhythms, and with the warlike Sioux hard upon them . . .

A rustle in the bush made him whirl. But it was only Meriwether, inspecting the sentries.

"What will we do if the Sioux don't let us pass?" Jeremy asked.

Meriwether's blue eyes narrowed. "Our instructions from President Jefferson are specific: 'If a superior force should be arrayed against your passage, and inflexibly determined to arrest it, then you must decline its further pursuit and return.'"

The moon swung from behind the cloud cover and the meandering river glowed with phosphorescent traces of light. Meriwether said, "On the other hand, we are the representatives of our government west of the Mississippi, and so we cannot allow ourselves to be intimidated. Someday soon, Americans will settle this land. The Indians must know that though we come in peace, we won't give in to their tactics of terror."

Autumn gradually colored the terrain, the grasslands had lost their lush green look, and the prairie seemed withered and sere. Antelope and buffalo had fed all summer for the hard season ahead, and even the wolves, constantly circling the herds, looked sleek and glossy.

At the end of September, the voyagers reached the land of the Teton Sioux, and Meriwether posted a twenty-four-hour guard. He scouted the river ahead in case they should have to make a run for it. Though dotted with sandbars, it appeared navigable.

Jeremy nudged Drewyer and pointed to plumes of smoke rising above the plain. "What are those?"

"Signal fires," Drewyer said tersely, and continued to hone his hunting knife. "The Sioux have been watching us all this while. They're calling in their braves and allied tribes for council. And perhaps for war."

Chapter 23

EARLY THE next day the corps came to the mouth of the Bad River and saw the first Sioux villages. The captains broke out their dress uniforms—brass-buttoned navy-blue coats trimmed with red, buff-colored trousers, and calf-length leather boots. The men donned their parade uniforms.

By midmorning, several hundred prancing, spear-waving Sioux had gathered along the riverbank.

"More braves will be arriving all the time," Drewyer told Lewis. "They'll make a great show of strength to force us to give in to their demands."

"Make sure your rifles are ready," Lewis told the men. Then he ordered the swivel cannon loaded with sixteen musket balls—all it could hold—and the blunderbusses loaded with chain and shot.

An hour later, the grand chief of the Sioux, Black Buffalo, arrived in full regalia, accompanied by two lesser chiefs, Buffalo Medicine and The Partisan.

Drewyer nudged Jeremy. "The Partisan is said to be the worst villain on the river."

Jeremy drank in the scene, sketching quickly and surreptitiously. He thought these Sioux ugly and ill-made, their arms and legs far too short for their torsos. Their heads were shaved, except for one fall of hair worn in a plait. The chiefs wore buffalo robes laced with porcupine quills that rustled when they walked. Their bodies and faces were painted in odd geometric designs.

Each of the three chiefs had bodyguards; these men were dressed differently than the other braves. "These men are the chiefs' protectors," Drewyer told Lewis. "They consider it a point of honor to die for them."

Jeremy's pencil flashed across his sketchbook. Each of the chiefs' aides wore three raven skins fixed on the small of his back so that the tails stuck out horizontally. Another raven skin had been split in half and was tied around the head, with its beak sticking out from the wearer's forehead. One of these aides, a burly brave named Wawzinggo, elbowed his way to Jeremy and grabbed for his sketchbook. Jeremy yanked it back. Wawzinggo's eyes narrowed covetously as he stared at Jeremy's thatch of long, sun-bleached blond hair.

Around noontime, Captain Clark ordered the American flag raised. The corps presented arms and paraded smartly. The chiefs and about thirty other Sioux sat down to parlay.

Then Lewis delivered his standard speech.

"The French and Spanish and English no longer own the territory. They've been replaced by a Great White Father who lives in Washington, and he wishes for nothing better than peace and friendship with all the tribes."

Jeremy could tell it was going badly; the Sioux just sat and glowered.

Hoping to save the day, Captain Clark handed out the presents. To Black Buffalo, the great chief, he gave an American flag, a large bronze medal of Jefferson, and a laced uniform with a cocked hat. The Partisan and each of the other chiefs received a smaller medal, a blanket, garters, tobacco, leggings, and knives. With a hawking spit The Partisan let it be known that he was not pleased with his presents, and Wawzinggo seconded his chief's displeasure.

With the entire Sioux tribe looking on from the riverbank, Lewis and Clark escorted the chiefs aboard the keelboat. Lewis showed them the mysteries of the compass, the telescope, and the magnet, and the Indians grunted and agreed that all these things were very powerful medicine.

"And wouldn't they like to get their hands on these things," Jeremy whispered to Cruzatte, who blinked his good eye in agreement.

But of all the white man's magic, nothing impressed the Sioux more than the air gun, powered by a sphere of compressed air. They couldn't figure out how it could shoot so many times without need of powder and without reloading.

"Look at it, you devils," Drewyer muttered. "It can gun down forty men at a clip, and that's something you thieves can respect."

As a special treat, Captain Lewis dispensed a quarter of a cup of whiskey to each Indian. Jeremy flinched as The Partisan's blood-curdling shout rent the air, then the chief began lurching around the boat.

"Never have I seen anybody get so drunk so fast on so little," Jeremy said to Cruzatte.

"That one, he only feigns drunkenness," Cruzatte said in a low voice. "He thinks that's the way to hide his rascally intentions."

When The Partisan and Wawzinggo began to tear at the bales holding the supplies, Lewis ordered all the Indians off the keelboat. With great difficulty, Captain Clark and a half-dozen men including Jeremy herded the Sioux into the white pirogue and rowed them ashore.

As Clark's boat approached shore, three braves waded into the river and grabbed the cable. The chiefs got off, but Wawzinggo jumped from his seat, shoved Jeremy aside, and grabbed the mast, clinging to it ferociously.

Clark and the Indians began arguing on shore. The Partisan became very insolent: "The white men are stingy with their presents!" He lurched against Captain Clark, swearing he would not allow them to go on.

Clark colored to the roots of his red hair. "We are not squaws, but warriors!"

"I too have warriors," The Partisan shouted, and scores of braves crowded forward.

On board the keelboat, Captain Lewis saw this sudden turn of events, and even as he gave the order, twelve of the most determined men jumped into the red pirogue and rowed furiously to join Clark.

Seeing the reinforcements coming, The Partisan became outraged and began shoving Captain Clark. "By God, I've had enough of this!" Clark shouted, and drew his sword. At this signal, all the corpsmen cocked their rifles. The Indians strung their bows.

"Aim at the three chiefs," Clark ordered, and Black Buffalo,

The Partisan and Buffalo Medicine found themselves staring down the barrels of more than a dozen Harper's Ferry rifles.

"Get that damned Indian off the mast," Clark ordered. Jeremy, who stood closest to Wawzinggo, moved toward him.

Wawzinggo let go of the mast long enough to smash Jeremy in the face and then grab the pole again. Jeremy recovered and threw himself at the grinning brave, who clung to the mast with the tenacity of a bear. With all his strength, Jeremy punched him in the kidneys.

Yowling with pain, the raven-bedecked brave let go of the mast. He doubled into a crouch and faced Jeremy, murder in his eyes. The two men feinted for an opening aboard the rocking pirogue. The rest of the tribe and the corpsmen watched them, knowing the fate of the expedition could hinge on this man-to-man battle.

They caught each other in a bearhug. Wawzinggo, the stronger and more canny of the two, gradually forced Jeremy's head back, all the while trying to peck out his eyes with the raven's beak attached to his forehead.

Sweat and blood broke out on Jeremy's face as the beak slashed him. He knew he was losing; if his head was forced back any farther his neck would snap. Then from a bygone time came the enraging memory of another fight . . . of Zebulon ambushing him, beating him. With a desperate move he twisted free from Wawzinggo's grasp and smashed his head into the brave's face. The Indian reeled backwards, blood gushing from his nose, and Jeremy's punch knocked him into the river.

"Good lad!" Clark exclaimed.

The braves started forward, their bows fully drawn, but Black Buffalo, realizing he would be the first killed, stayed them. The braves hauled Wawzinggo out of the river and he slunk off. Gradually, the tension eased.

"Everybody into the pirogues," Captain Clark ordered. They hadn't rowed more than a few yards when Black Buffalo and Buffalo Medicine waded after them. They demanded to spend the night aboard the keelboat. Since the captains wanted to promote good relations with the Indians, both Lewis and Clark agreed, though grudgingly.

Night fell, and from the keelboat, the men could see the scores of Indian campfires along the riverbanks.

"They outnumber us by about ten to one," Jeremy said, and turned to Drewyer, sitting beside him. "I don't feel easy with those chiefs aboard. Why do you think they wanted to sleep here?"

Drewyer scratched his beard. "If they're like other Indians, then they want to absorb the magic of the white man. They believe some of the boat's power will pass to them." Then he said, "Jeremy, a warning. Watch out for Wawzinggo. You've made him look bad in the eyes of his chief, and nothing will satisfy him except your scalp."

Jeremy swallowed and rubbed the stiffness in his neck. Around dawn, he dozed off briefly and then wakened with Drewyer's warning ringing in his head. The entire corps couldn't have been more surprised when the Sioux did an apparent about-face and acted with great hospitality. Arranging a feast, they carried Lewis and Clark into their village on white buffalo skins, an honor reserved for only the greatest chieftains. Buffalo steaks, beaver tail, roast dog—they feasted on it all.

Then the Sioux proudly showed off their latest trophies of war, squaws and boys taken prisoner in a battle with the Omahas thirteen days earlier. The Partisan boasted that they'd destroyed forty lodges, massacred seventy-five men, and taken forty-eight prisoners.

Then, accompanied by drums, the braves did their war dance, brandishing their lances, which were decorated with scalps. Jeremy counted sixty-five of them. If only there were some way to read these savages' minds! he thought. Then an idea came to him, and he scooted over to Meriwether. "Sir, perhaps if we could talk to the Omahas, they might be able to tell us something about the Sioux's intentions."

"Cruzatte speaks a little Omaha, but the chiefs will never let us do it," Lewis said.

Jeremy thought for a moment. "Tell The Partisan that I'll draw a picture of his captives, so that he'll have proof of his victory for all time to come."

"By God, that just might do it," Lewis said. He called Drewyer, and the scout explained it to The Partisan, who eagerly agreed.

Jeremy grabbed Cruzatte and they went to the pens where the Omahas were being kept prisoner. While Jeremy went through the motions of drawing them, Cruzatte talked to as many captives as he could. "The prisoners all say the same thing," Cruzatte whispered to Jeremy. "The Sioux mean to lull us into a false sense of security, and then kill us."

They hurried back to Lewis and Clark, and reported what they'd learned. "We'll let them believe we suspect nothing," Lewis said. "They're the vilest miscreants on the river, because everybody's always given in to them. It is time to stop that."

With two sleepless nights behind them, the captains ended the festivities early. This time, The Partisan and another chief asked to spend the night aboard the keelboat, and Lewis once more agreed. While Clark was ferrying them out, an inexperienced corpsman at the tiller swept the pirogue full force into the keelboat, snapping the anchor chain.

"The keelboat is adrift!" Clark shouted.

The sudden shout alarmed the Indians; within moments hundreds appeared on the banks. It took some minutes before Clark managed to tie up the keelboat, and the only spot he could do it was under an overhanging bank. The swift appearance of the Sioux, all armed, convinced the captains that the Indians intended to massacre them.

Half the crew stood sentry duty ashore that night, and those on the boat had no sleep either. Tied as they were to the bank, they were dangerously exposed. All night long, the braves whooped and hollered, probing for an opportunity to strike.

Jeremy stood watch near the stern of the boat, which protruded somewhat into the river. The moon swung higher, marking the passage of the hours. He didn't see the brave slip into the river and swim underwater toward the keelboat. The warrior reached the huge wooden rudder and began to hack away at it with his tomahawk. Scannon, Meriwether's Newfoundland, began to bark furiously.

"Captain!" Jeremy cried, "they're trying to cripple the rudder!" If the rudder was damaged, they'd be at the Sioux's mercy.

Meriwether leaned over the side, but the hull prevented him from getting a clear shot at the Indian.

Jeremy flung off his jacket and dove into the river, coming up close to the brave. And then he recognized Wawzinggo. He grunted and came at Jeremy, swinging his tomahawk. Jeremy dove to avoid the blow, and it glanced off his shoulder.

Underwater, he grabbed Wawzinggo's legs and pulled him down. The two men struggled in the swift currents. Other Indians tried to swim to Wawzinggo's aid, but a few well-placed rifle shots from Drewyer and the Field brothers drove them back.

Wawzinggo writhed under Jeremy's grip and fought to the surface. As they broke water, Jeremy took a deep breath, then pulled Wawzinggo down again. The warrior panicked and struggled to get away, splashing frantically toward shore. When Jeremy saw he was no longer a threat, he let him go.

Strong hands reached down into the water and pulled Jeremy aboard. All through the dark hours, the corps fought off the Indian efforts to seize the boat. At the same time, they had to keep a close guard on The Partisan and the other chief.

"I was never so happy to see daybreak in my life," Jeremy said to Drewyer.

"It's not over yet," Drewyer said ominously, and pointed to the shore. There the entire Teton Sioux nation had congregated.

Black Buffalo and his aide rowed out to the keelboat and came aboard.

"We're moving upriver now," Captain Lewis told him.

Black Buffalo grunted, and made mean, cutting signs. "They say they won't allow us to go," Drewyer said.

"The hell!" Lewis exclaimed. "Get all the Indians off the boat!" Suddenly, three braves grabbed the cable, preventing them from casting off.

Enraged, Lewis cocked his rifle, ready to fight it out this very minute.

Captain Clark, usually more phlegmatic than Lewis, was now just as angry. He pointed a blunderbuss at the chief. "You have told us that you are a great man, have great influence. Show us you have influence by taking the rope from your men and letting us go without coming to hostilities."

Black Buffalo, again seeing all the rifles aimed at him and the swivel cannon pointed at his lodges, jerked the cable line held by his braves and handed it to the bowsman.

"Cast off!" Lewis shouted, and the keelboat and the two pirogues swung into the deep channel. The canvas caught the wind, and the Corps of Discovery sailed on.

Chapter 24

ON OCTOBER 29, the corps reached the territory of the Mandan Indians. They found the Mandans to be a highly intelligent tribe; along with the Minnetarees and the Amahanis, they constituted the largest concentration of Indians in the entire west, some 4,400 people living in five villages. Having now traveled about 1,600 miles from St. Louis, and with the weather turning bitter cold, the captains decided to winter with the Mandans.

After much reconnoitering, Lewis and Clark chose a site on the north shore of the Missouri, and fell to constructing a fort.

"We've a lad here who helped build the President's House in Washington," Lewis said, clapping Jeremy on the shoulder. "Let's see if you can't do something of the like for us."

Jeremy designed a simple structure, a triangular affair with two rows of log huts forming an angle where they joined each other, each row containing four rooms. The third side was a stockaded fence which would be opened at sunrise and shut tight at sunset.

By November 20, the fort was nearly finished and the corps could move in. "And not a moment too soon," Jeremy said. The winds howled from the north, bringing swirling snowstorms; the river froze solid, a flash of icy blue against the snow-white landscape. By December 12, the temperature had dropped to 32 degrees below zero. Never in his life had Jeremy been this cold.

Word spread in the territory that the white men worked strong medicine, and the Mandans began bringing their sick to the fort. Lewis and Clark worked hard and willingly to cure the frostbitten toes and fingers and the cases of pleurisy; their good deeds soon solidified their friendship with the Indians.

Then one evening, the fort buzzed with news about Ben York. He'd gone on a buffalo hunt with Clark, and had come back with his toes and penis frostbitten.

"Let's hope it isn't serious," Drewyer said with a grin. "Otherwise, there'll be a lot of disappointed squaws."

Ben York had proved to be a sensation among the Indians. Braves brought their wives to him to be serviced, hoping to preserve in their tribe some memento of this genial giant. York was out of commission for a bit, and among the Mandans, the year became known as "The Winter of Black-Man-Froze-His-Thing."

The days passed quickly for Jeremy; the men were always at something, whether it be hunting, or repairing the equipment, or hollowing out treetrunks to make six canoes. The river had become too shallow for the keelboat and it would be sent back to St. Louis in the spring. In his spare time, Jeremy filled page after page of his sketchbook with drawings of Indian dress, customs, and artifacts.

"Jeremy, save those drawings," Lewis said. "When we return to civilization you must have it published. Not only will it be valuable for scientists, but it could make your fortune."

Jeremy colored with embarrassment, but the idea made him work with even greater vigor.

The men celebrated Christmas Day with singing and dancing. But they were getting restless in the close quarters, and late one afternoon, Cruzatte took his fiddle, and along with Shannon, Drewyer, and a half-dozen other men went to the main lodge of the Mandans to entertain them. Jeremy went along.

From the outside, the log lodges looked like gigantic beehives, standing twelve to fifteen feet high. Jeremy had to stoop to get into the entry. An eight-foot passageway, with buffalo hides at either end, led to a giant inner domed space. As his eyes grew accustomed to the gloom, Jeremy saw that the lodge measured some fifty feet across. Horses and dogs lived inside with the families.

A fire blazed in the center of the floor, the smoke curling up through a narrow opening at the top of the mound. Though the thermometer registered twenty degrees below zero outside, it was pleasant inside. No drafts, Jeremy thought. Abigail Adams would be pleased.

A large tripod held a cooking pot into which a squaw diced pumpkin, corn, beans, and chokeberries, to make the Mandans' favorite dish, pemmican. After the meal, the men smoked a pipe with the Indians. Then Cruzatte struck up his fiddle, Shannon beat the tambourine, and Drewyer tooted his horn, sending the men into a spirited square dance, with much shouting, clapping, and leaping. The Indians, some of whom had traveled far to see these white men, watched in amazement.

Ben York stood up and danced a jig, and the braves marveled that a man so huge could move so nimbly. When York finished, one chief came over to him, wet his finger and tried to rub the black away.

York, who loved the attention, said to Drewyer, "Tell them that I was a wild animal and that Captain Clark captured me and trained me!" When the children came closer to stare at him, he threw back his head and roared. Shrieking, they fled, only to sneak back as soon as he turned.

The Indians stripped York of his buckskin jacket, poking and pushing him to see what stuff he was made of. "Well, Captain Clark told us to be nice to the Indians," York said with a grin, and took a willing squaw to a dark place.

One by one the men were approached by the women, and went off. A young maiden came to Jeremy and opened her robe. She was naked underneath, and Jeremy felt his blood quicken. It would be wonderful to share the warmth of this woman, to thaw the months of loneliness, to smooth the jagged dreams he'd had. He reached to touch her, but his hand stopped short of her glistening skin. He could have gotten past the smell of rancid bear grease on her braids, could have forgotten not understanding her language, but he could not forget the vow he'd made to Rebecca.

Jeremy left the warm lodge. Trudging through a new snowfall, he made his way back to the fort and found Meriwether Lewis poring over his journal. Captain Clark was off visiting another Indian lodge, for he had a prodigious appetite for "the young ladies," as he called them.

Not once during the entire trip had Jeremy been aware of

Lewis consorting with the Indians as the other men did. He wondered if he too had taken some kind of vow. Or perhaps such carnal thoughts were not in this man's nature; he was consumed only by one objective, to cross the continent and find the water route to the Pacific.

One lowering gray day, a French trapper named Toussaint Charbonneau arrived at the fort. He'd lived for years among the Minnetarees, and had three Indian wives. One of them was a young pregnant girl, a sixteen-year-old Shoshone named Sacajawea. Her tribe lived far west near the Shining Mountains; they had been raided by the Minnetarees and Sacajawea had been captured. She lived among the Minnetarees for years until Charbonneau won her in a game of cards and took her to wife.

Charbonneau, a cocky blowhard, applied to Lewis for a job as guide and interpreter. "I travel this river many times," he said in his pidgin French-English. "I take you anywhere you want to go."

Lewis hired him. But then Charbonneau insisted that he not be given guard duty with the others, and that he be free to leave the expedition whenever he wanted. Lewis fired him. After sulking for a few days, Charbonneau came crawling back and pleaded to be hired again. Lewis relented, and Charbonneau and Sacajawea moved into the fort.

For some reason Jeremy couldn't fathom, he took an intense interest in the young Indian girl. She didn't act like the other squaws. Her demeanor was reserved, and though she was big with child, she did her chores without complaint. Her expression was inquisitive, her features chiseled, her eyes bright and penetrating. Though she couldn't yet speak English—she and Shannon began teaching each other words in their own tongues—she managed to convey her meaning with hand signs and her facile expressions. She told Jeremy that among her own Shoshone tribe, her family had been very powerful. He took that with a grain of salt, but still, Jeremy liked her and did a drawing showing her in full pregnancy.

She hid her face in her hands and blushed.

"Sixteen years old and owned by that old goat Charbonneau, who does nothing but mistreat her," Jeremy complained to Drewyer.

"Well, lad, you're not going to change the custom of thousands of years. Among Indians, women are chattel. It's her lot in life, and if she's not making a fuss about it, why should you?"

But having been mistreated in his own youth, Jeremy felt for the girl, and often helped her with heavy work—hauling water, and skinning antelope or buffalo, though in the latter tasks, she was much more adept than he.

On February 12, a bitter cold day, Sacajawea came to her time. "It's going to be a difficult birth," Lewis said. "She's still a child herself, and I'm afraid that the baby is big."

Throughout the day, Sacajawea labored and tried not to scream. Lewis feared that if she continued to suffer this way, she might weaken and die. One of the French trappers told Lewis about an ancient Mandan remedy. "If Sacajawea is given a potion made from the rattles of a rattlesnake, she will bring forth the child more easily."

Lewis, at his wit's end, decided to try anything. He broke off two rattles from a snake he'd killed months earlier, and had planned to send back to President Jefferson. He ground up the rattles, mixed the powder with water, then gave the potion to Sacajawea.

Ten minutes later she gave birth.

"Coincidence," Lewis insisted. He and Clark went in to see how Sacajawea was doing; she had the baby wrapped in a swaddling blanket supplied by the U.S. Army.

"Pompy," she said weakly, pointing to the child.

Lewis turned to Charbonneau. "What does she mean? Is that the name she wants to give her son?"

Charbonneau shook his head. "I think *pompy* is the Shoshone word for *firstborn*. I name him Jean Baptiste."

"Pompy, I like that," Clark said, and squeezed Sacajawea's hand. He'd grown very fond of the young girl. From that day on, everybody called the child Pomp.

As Lewis and Clark gathered information they realized that the journey over the mountains might be impossible without horses. "The Shoshones are known for their horses; that's why the Minnetarees raid them," Clark said. "If Sacajawea went with us, maybe she could intercede with her people, arrange for horses."

"You're mad!" Lewis exclaimed. "This is a military expedition."

"Precisely, and that's how the hostiles will see us. But when a woman travels with a company of men, the Indians always take that as a sign of peace."

Lewis shook his head. "But she's sixteen, and with an infant. How could she manage?"

"Ah, that one," Charbonneau said, "she can do anything." He was anxious for her to come along, to tend to his needs. "She can show you the way to the Great Falls of the Missouri. That is where she was captured."

"Is this true?" Clark asked her, and she nodded. They argued for several more weeks. Meriwether Lewis didn't like Sacajawea very much; perhaps he felt left out because of all the attention Clark paid her. Finally, because of Clark's insistence, Lewis relented and allowed the girl to come along.

By the end of March the river had thawed sufficiently for the boats to be riding free, and on Sunday, April 7, the Corps of Discovery made ready to leave Fort Mandan. Everybody seemed in good health, except for an occasional venereal complaint.

The keelboat that had afforded them protection with its swivel gun and blunderbusses was being sent back to St. Louis, manned by six soldiers under the command of Corporal Warfington. The precious cargo included a live prairie dog, a sharp-tailed grouse, and four magpies. In other boxes lay the horns of a bighorn sheep and a wapiti, the skins and skeletons of antelope, jackrabbit, badger, and coyote, most of them unknown to science. Another casc hcld sixty-seven specimens of earth samples, salts, and minerals, and sixty pressed specimens of plants.

"Mark me," Lewis said to Jeremy. "When we get back to Washington, we'll find all of this stored in the East Room!"

The two men laughed, and then Lewis shouted, "Cast off!" The sails of the two pirogues were raised, and the men shoved off in the six dugouts they'd made. "Columbus may have had better sailing ships," Lewis said joyously, "but we take just as much pride in ours."

The prow of the boats pushed upriver, into the unknown.

Chapter 25

THE MISSOURI cut through the high plain. The river remained difficult to navigate: sometimes the men had to wade in icy water up to their chests, dragging the pirogues against the swift current; other times the banks would crumble, threatening to bury the boats and their occupants. On a good day they might manage as much as twenty-five miles, but a realistic average was more like fifteen.

"No white man has ever seen such a profusion of game," Meriwether Lewis said to Jeremy as they marveled at the vast herds of buffalo and antelope. The curious beasts stared at the boats, sometimes following them. On April 29, Meriwether and a scouting party which included Jeremy encountered their first grizzly bear; it was half grown, and Lewis easily dispatched the beast. But it led the corps into a false sense of security.

On May 14, the men in the two rear canoes discovered a large bear in open ground about three paces from the riverbank. Since the corps planned to camp nearby and didn't want such a dangerous beast around, six men went out to dispatch it. With Drewyer leading the way, they crawled through the tall grass to within forty paces of the bear, an excellent range for their Harper's Ferry rifles.

Jeremy studied the grizzly. The coat, a thick buff-blond, had a ridge of longer fur extending from its head to its withers. The bear was mauling the carcass of a buffalo, and the claws on its front paws measured at least five inches long.

Suddenly the animal sensed something amiss and growled, revealing teeth more than two inches long. The bear looked so massive—over eight feet tall, at least six hundred pounds—that the rifle in Jeremy's hand suddenly seemed puny.

Drewyer signaled that four men were to fire simultaneously; the other two were to hold their fire. The men fired and each of their bullets found its mark, two of the bullets clearly passing through the bear's lungs. In that instant, the monster rose, his yellow teeth bared. Drewyer and Jeremy, who'd reserved their fire, aimed and pulled the triggers as the bear charged them. Jeremy's bullet hit him, and Drewyer's broke the bear's shoulder. But that didn't stop him.

"Separate!" Drewyer shouted.

The men plunged into the tall grasses. Incredible, Jeremy thought as he ran, that an animal of that bulk could move so fast. And with six bullets in him!

The four men who'd fired the first round had reloaded, and they fired at the animal again. The muzzle flashes directed the bear to these men, and the beast overtook them on a bluff. The bear got so close to two men that they were forced to jump off the twenty-foot-high bluff into the river.

The grizzly hesitated only a moment, then plunged into the river after them. The animal got within a few feet of the slowest swimmer when Drewyer, on shore, took careful aim and fired. The bullet went through the bear's brain, killing him.

The men looked at each other, breathing in jerky, panicked gasps. When they hauled the grizzly onshore and butchered him, they found that at least eight bullets had passed through him.

"I'd count it too soon if I ever saw a grizzly again," Jeremy said, and the sentiment was echoed by the others.

Fearful that the bear might have a mate, the men proceeded on. Usually, one of the captains stayed with the boats, but this time they both happened to be ashore. Drewyer had gotten back into the white pirogue where he served as helmsman. But being a little shaky from the encounter with the bear, he relinquished the tiller to Charbonneau.

In the boat were Sacajawea with her infant Pomp, in a cradleboard on her back, Jeremy, Drewyer, Cruzatte, and most of the medicines, books, and other indispensable items.

Jeremy listened to Charbonneau humming a little French ditty, obviously very pleased with himself. But then a sudden squall came out of nowhere and struck the sail, turning the boat sideways.

"Put her into the wind!" Jeremy shouted, but the fuddled Charbonneau turned the wrong way and the sail luffed. As the wind snatched the brace of the square sail from Jeremy's hands, the pirogue turned on her side, pitching him into the water.

"God have mercy on our souls," Charbonneau cried, clutching his head with his hands and leaving the tiller untended.

Cruzatte stood up and pointed his gun at Charbonneau. "Grab that tiller or I'll put a bullet through your head!"

Blubbering, Charbonneau finally responded and the men managed to right the swamped boat. Sacajawea, with the baby still on her back, reached out and pulled Jeremy aboard. Then she swam into the river to retrieve floating papers and other things.

"Never again do I want to spend a day like this," Jeremy said, as he dried his clothes by the campfire.

The men talked about what a treasure they had in Sacajawea, and even Meriwether Lewis, who'd had little to do with her up to now, remarked about her fortitude.

In the days ahead, the river became very rapid. High, rugged bluffs bordered the banks. One day they passed the remains of a herd of buffalo that had been stampeded over a cliff. Sacajawea told them that this was a favorite Indian method of killing the game.

Jeremy gazed about in wonder, for they had moved into a land more awesome than anything he'd ever seen. The river cut through white sandstone cliffs that rose perpendicularly as high as three hundred feet. Rain and wind had sculpted the bluffs into fantastic forms, and huge boulders balanced precariously on tall stone pillars. At night, with an ethereal moon reflected in the river, Jeremy thought the place haunting.

During those nights, he began to dream, wild flights of imagination, ending always with a young maiden who would call to him across eons of time, a twin of his soul. Though he could never quite make out her face, he knew in his heart that it wasn't Rebecca Breech, and this saddened and confused him.

On June 2, by Captain Clark's reckoning, the Corps of Discovery had traveled 2,508 miles from their embarkation point. That day, they came to a bewildering fork in the river, one branch going southwest, the other to the north. All the men, including Drewyer and Cruzatte, thought the northern branch would lead them to the headwaters of the Missouri, but Sacajawea said the Great Falls lay to the south. Lewis set out to reconnoiter the southern fork, taking Drewyer and Jeremy with him.

Days later, the men were hiking along the precipitous cliffs when they heard a distant roaring.

"Is it thunder?" Jeremy asked, looking to the sky full of billowing sunlit clouds.

"Far more important than thunder!" Lewis cried, and broke into a run. Neither Jeremy nor Drewyer could keep up with him. Then Jeremy realized that the roaring sound was too tremendous to be anything less than the Great Falls of the Missouri.

The water thundered off a huge cliff, sending up a fine mist through which undulating rainbows played. "If only President Jefferson could see this!" Lewis shouted.

Investigating further, the men discovered there was a series of five falls, which dropped the riverbed about four hundred feet. "No other way," Lewis said. "We'll have to portage around the falls." They proceeded back to the main party.

The boats and all the tons of equipment would have to be carried over the hilly terrain to a point above the falls. During the preparation for the portage, Sacajawea became violently ill. Lewis diagnosed her ailment as a serious menses blockage, and treated her as best he could with purges, bleeding, and doses of laudanum and opium, but she grew progressively worse and fell into a delirium.

"She may die," Lewis told the others. "And what will we do then? Pomp is no more than six months old, and still needs his mother's milk. How can we cross the continent with a motherless child?"

"And we counted on her to intercede with the Shoshones for horses," Clark said. He stared at the formidable range of mountains that blocked their path; beyond them rose another range, and then another, seeming to stretch to infinity. "We'll never be able to make the climb without horses."

All night long Sacajawea hovered near death, and with her, the hopes for the success of the expedition.

The following morning, Jeremy said to Meriwether, "Once when I was a boy, and given up for dead with swamp fever,

I remember my father made me drink water from a nearby sulphur spring. Captain, a few miles back, we passed such a spring."

Lewis looked at Sacajawea. If he did nothing she would die; but water from the sulphur springs might even hasten her death. That was the risk he had to take. He nodded at Jeremy, who raced to the springs and brought back a leather canteen full of the foul-smelling water.

Lewis fed Sacajawea pint after pint of the mineral water. At first she didn't respond. But the next day she gradually improved, and after several days her own youth and recuperative powers came to the fore and she recovered.

Knowing that they couldn't carry all their equipment, the captains cached everything they didn't need, including the larger and heavier of the pirogues. They felled cottonwood trees, and cut sections of the trunk to make wheels to haul the boats and their gear over the seventeen-mile portage. For an axle, they used the mast of the cached pirogue.

They began their trek at dawn of June 21, and within hours their feet were cut and sore from the prickly pears growing everywhere. That night, Sacajawea sewed double soles onto all their moccasins, but by the next evening, they too were worn through. They pushed, hauled, and dragged the equipment, stumbling and falling, and getting up again. When the wind came up, Jeremy called out, "Why not raise the sail?" They did, but the going remained treacherous. The wheels broke, and the forest rang with the thwack of axes as they felled more trees to make new ones. The men were so exhausted that if they stopped for a momentary break, they instantly fell asleep.

But inch by inch they hauled the boats and equipment until they reached a point above the falls where they could set out on the river again. On July 19, they rowed through a spectacular gorge, with cliffs rising to a height of twelve hundred feet. Trees bearded the mountainside, and the current ran swift and clear. "I'll call this place the Gates of the Mountains," Lewis said.

Sacajawea told them they would soon approach the three forks of the Missouri, and several hours later they did. Lewis named these three branches the Madison, the Gallatin, and the Jefferson.

"This is the high valley where my people live," Sacajawea told them.

"We must find the Shoshones and barter for horses," Lewis said. "Unless we get across the mountains before the September snows, we'll be stranded here." He gazed at the snow-covered peaks, and realized that the dream of finding a northwest river route across the continent was a myth. To cross the Shining Mountains, as Sacajawea called them, would take weeks, perhaps months.

After several more days of struggling up the twisting Jefferson River, the men became hopeless with exhaustion. Game had become very scarce, and many a night they went to bed famished. Then one day Sacajawea rushed to Captain Clark and pointed to a huge rock promontory rising in the high plain. "That is Beaverhead rock," she said excitedly.

Captain Clark studied the rock. "By God, it does look like a beaver's head!"

"Not far from here is where I was captured when the Minnetarees raided my tribe."

Lewis and his small band went on repeated expeditions trying to locate the Shoshones. On August 11, they spotted an Indian on horseback coming toward them. When they got within a mile of each other, Lewis made the sign of friendship, throwing a blanket up in the air three times, as though spreading it on the ground to powwow. He kept calling out "Ta-ba-bone" which meant "white man" in Shoshone. But the Indian, mistaking his intentions, galloped off.

Bitterly disappointed, Lewis continued on, following the Indian trail through a narrow valley between high mountains. Jeremy thought the land magnificent, with stunning cliffs and scudding clouds snagged by the mountain peaks. But what good was all the beauty when they were lost, and slowly starving to death?

As they climbed into the Lemhi Pass, Meriwether said, "I think we're coming to the continental divide." Beyond that point the rivers would begin to flow westward rather than to the east.

Night found them camped on a windswept bluff, the air sharp and growing colder with darkness. Luckily, Drewyer had shot a beaver and was cooking it, the tail being a special delicacy. Jeremy picked prickly spines from his feet. "What day is this?"

Meriwether showed Jeremy the page in his journal. "Saturday, the 11th of August, 1805." He began to read what he'd written, "We begin to feel considerable anxiety with respect to the Shoshone Indians. If we do not find them or some other nation who have horses, I fear the successful issue of our voyage will be very doubtful. . . . We are now several hundred miles within the bosom of this wild and mountainous country . . . however, I still hope for the best. . . ."

They bedded down near the fire. "What are you thinking of, lad?" Meriwether asked.

"Oh, Washington, I guess. Wondering what's going on there, and who has my job in the President's House."

"No need to worry about that. Jefferson promised you'd have it back as soon as we returned."

"If we ever do," Jeremy said.

"Are you sorry you came?"

"Oh God, no!" he exclaimed, raising himself on an elbow. "This has been the most glorious time in my life. I wouldn't have traded it for anything."

"I'm glad," Meriwether said. "I feel the same. My only disappointment is that we've failed the President, and our people."

"We've done the best we can, and even better," Jeremy said. "But I can't believe that the good Lord allowed us to go this far, only to thwart us. From the very first moment you mentioned this trip, there's been something—I don't know—*destined* about it."

"Well, I've felt that way all my life," Meriwether murmured.

In the half-light of the dying fire, Jeremy thought he saw tears glinting in Meriwether's eyes. He reached out and gripped his friend's arm. Then Jeremy gradually dropped off to sleep, lulled by the spirit of the mountains and the plaintive, sighing winds.

Chapter 26

THE FOLLOWING day the advance party started out again. They traveled through a steep ravine that blocked everything from sight, and suddenly stumbled on three Indian women. The older woman cried out; the youngest, about eleven, clutched at the old woman's skirts; but the third, a girl about sixteen years old, stared at the men, the look in her eyes that of a startled woods creature. The blood rushed to Jeremy's head and he felt his limbs go weak with the recognition—she had the face and form of the girl in his dreams.

She bounded away, her lithe form moving with the wind. Jeremy called out, "Wait! We mean no harm." He threw down his gun, but she'd already disappeared into the tall grass.

The old woman and the eleven-year-old, seeing that they couldn't escape, bowed their heads, resigning themselves to their deaths. Lewis raised up the woman, repeating the word "Ta-ba-bone." Jeremy rolled up his sleeve trying to show the women that his skin was white, but he was deeply tanned.

"Tell her to call the one who ran away," Lewis said to Drewyer. "Otherwise she may alarm other Indians."

Drewyer relayed his message in sign language and the woman called after the girl. In a few moments she returned, tentative, still ready to flee. She gazed at the strangers, her eyes lingering on Jeremy's hair and beard, bleached almost white by the sun. Lewis gave the women gifts of beads and other trinkets. Impulsively, Jeremy gave her his hunting knife.

Jeremy couldn't take his eyes off the young girl. Because she had paler skin than most in her tribe, she was called White Doe. Her black hair hung in two long braids; her eyes, dark and luminous, looked slanted because her cheekbones were so pronounced. She moved with such grace that in her presence Jeremy felt awkward, and waves of heat and cold sweat swept over him.

They all set out for the Shoshone camp, and had walked about two miles when suddenly sixty braves on swift horses came charging down on them. The horses had no saddles; the braves controlled their mounts with their legs.

"We're in for it now," Jeremy said, and began waving the small American flag with its fifteen stars.

But White Doe ran a few paces before the men and raised her arms. She told the chief that these were white men, and they came in peace. She showed them the gifts that they'd given her.

All sixty braves dismounted, and embraced the three men, repeating "Ah-hi-e, ah-hi-e!" Drewyer said to Lewis, "I know enough to know that means, 'I am much pleased, I am much rejoiced.'" All sixty braves hugged the white men, leaving a great deal of their paint and grease on them.

In camp, the Shoshones acted friendly, but the friendliness was edged with suspicion; they thought that the white men might be allied with their enemies, the Blackfeet. It took all of Lewis's skill to persuade the chief, Cameahwaite, to send a party of braves back with him over the mountains.

"The rest of my men are there struggling with our equipment," Meriwether told the chief. "Unless we find them, they may die."

Finally, Cameahwaite agreed and sent out a band of braves with Meriwether Lewis. White Doe and a number of other squaws accompanied them. After they'd camped one night, Jeremy moved to White Doe, who was sitting near the campfire. Haltingly, he tried to explain that he'd dreamed of somebody like her for many weeks. At first she didn't comprehend, but finally, through some preternatural sensitivity, she began to intuit what he meant. She didn't seem unduly surprised, for such things weren't foreign to the Shoshones. They believed that spirits resided in each living thing, and that past, present, and future were all one, part of the great rhythm of life.

Jeremy had never met anyone as extraordinary as this girl. Her face reflected every emotion, sad at the sight of his thorn-torn feet, then tense at the growl of a nearby puma, and joyous when they managed to understand each other. They exchanged words in English and Shoshone. "You, me," he taught her. "Happy."

Meriwether, marking Jeremy's interest, said to him, "Don't get too many ideas, lad. These Shoshones aren't as generous with their women as other tribes."

Drewyer nodded. "They've a strict code, and White Doe is also the niece of Cameahwaite. I don't think the chief would take kindly to his kin bedding down with a white man."

Jeremy's ears burned, annoyed that his friends would even think such a thing. He wrapped himself in a blanket and tried to sleep. The dream returned, more powerful than before. He woke at intervals during the night, to glance at White Doe, to realize that the dream and the reality were one.

At last, Captain Lewis and the Shoshones intercepted Captain Clark and the rest of the corps. Sacajawea dashed toward the Shoshones, sucking her fingers to indicate that as a child she'd been suckled by that tribe.

Lewis and Clark called for Sacajawea to interpret for them. She sat down and was beginning the complex method—Lewis talked to Labiche, who translated into French for Charbonneau, who then translated into Minnetaree for Sacajawea, who then translated into Shoshone. Chief Cameahwaite's response required the same complex routing.

We'll all grow old here, Jeremy was thinking, when suddenly Sacajawea broke off in the middle of her speech, stared at Cameahwaite, and ran to him. She threw her blanket over his head and embraced him, weeping without restraint.

"What is it? What's happening?" Lewis asked.

Finally they determined that Cameahwaite was none other than Sacajawea's brother. During the years after her capture, Cameahwaite had risen in the tribe and become chief.

"It's a coincidence too complicated to comprehend," Clark said, shaking his head. "But how lucky for us that we brought her along."

After a great deal more tears, Sacajawea explained the mission of the white men to her brother.

"The Great White Father, who lives in a far-off land called Washington, sent us to make peace with all the tribes, so that we may all live as brothers," Lewis said to Cameahwaite. He explained their need for horses and offered to barter for them.

Cameahwaite considered the request, and then agreed to help them, for they had brought back his sister, whom he'd given up for dead.

While the chief went back to his village to get the horses, the captains decided not to waste time. Clark, with a party of eleven men, would set out to search for the Salmon River, rumored to be on the other side of the continental divide, and determine if that waterway was navigable. Lewis remained in the camp they named Camp Fortunate. A number of Indian women stayed with the Lewis party, and Jeremy was overjoyed that White Doe chose to remain.

The following evening, Jeremy saw Meriwether staring solemnly into the campfire. "Why so sad, captain?" he asked.

Lewis shrugged. "Today is my thirty-first birthday."

"But that should be a time for rejoicing," Jeremy said, and was about to rouse the men for a celebration.

Lewis seized his arm in a strong grip. "I'm in no mood. I look back at the years and regret all the indolent hours I've wasted."

"You? Why, there would be no expedition at all if it hadn't been for you."

Lewis stood up abruptly and kneaded his fist into his palm. "From now on I will live only for mankind, as heretofore I've lived only for myself."

A long moment passed between the two men. Then Meriwether said, "I've seen you looking at that girl. Just remember where your responsibilities lie; you're not a free man until the expedition is over."

"Captain, there's nothing to worry about," Jeremy said. But try as he might to deny it, he'd been irresistibly drawn to White Doe. He'd tried to control himself, tried to find resolve in the vow he'd made to Rebecca Breech. But the long months, the thousands of miles, and Rebecca's own vacillating attitude through the years made his vow seem only a distant echo on the wind.

The men spent a backbreaking day loading the pirogue with rocks and sinking it in the river. "This way it will be hidden from Indians or wild animals, and we can retrieve it on our return journey," Meriwether said to Jeremy.

At twilight, Jeremy hiked to a nearby mountain pool. The Shoshones believed the pool had curative powers because it was fed by hidden thermal springs. Jeremy laid his rifle on the bank, stripped off his buckskins, and waded into the pool. The water crept up to his calves, thighs, and loins, and he reveled in the warmth that gradually eased the ache out of his muscles and blistered feet. He found a ledge against the rock face of the pool and dove from it, swimming and splashing about, feeling his doubts wash away.

White Doe, who was upstream drawing water for camp, heard him bellowing a boyhood song, and she peered through the foliage. She watched his strong tanned body glide through the water, and then she realized that he was naked. She dropped her eyes, and then peeked again. How beautiful he was, with eyes the color of the sky, and hair the color of the sun at high noon. But then she froze, something was stirring in the bush.

A scream was on her lips when she saw the huge silver-tipped grizzly make his way toward the pond. But sense returned to White Doe, and she remained silent. She was downwind, and so it wouldn't catch her scent. If Jeremy stayed perfectly still in the water, the nearsighted beast might not see him. He would drink his fill, then leave.

But then Jeremy spotted the grizzly. Arms and legs working furiously, he swam for shore and his gun. Seeing the commotion in the water, the grizzly stood on his hind legs, measuring at least seven feet tall. A rumbling came from deep within its throat, and he bared his fangs.

Jeremy scrambled ashore and grabbed his rifle. Dear God, make my aim true, he prayed. He fired, and his bullet tore into the grizzly's chest. The beast roared at the pain and fell to all fours. Jeremy worked furiously to reload, but before he could manage it, the grizzly charged him.

Then suddenly he heard screaming. He looked up and saw White Doe running toward the bear. She hurled a rock at the grizzly and the monster turned at this new attack. The distraction was long enough for Jeremy to dive back into the pool and make his way toward the ledge.

"White Doe, follow me!" he shouted.

Her escape cut off, White Doe ran into the pool. The grizzly plunged in after her. Jeremy swam to White Doe, hoisted her onto the ledge, and then climbed up himself. They flattened themselves against the rock face as the bear's murderous claws hooked onto the ledge.

Jeremy shouted for help, but he knew they were too far from camp to be heard. He had an oblique realization that he was naked, but there was no time for that now. The bear had gotten both front paws onto the rock, its hunched back legs clawing for purchase. Jeremy hurled a large rock; the grizzly shook it off as though it was a walnut.

Then White Doe unsheathed her knife and stabbed at the bear's paw. The grizzly screamed but when she stabbed again, it let go and fell back into the pool. Again and again the bear tried to climb up, but they fought him off.

Finally, the gunshot wound Jeremy had inflicted began to weaken the grizzly, and with blood running from his chest and paws, it swam for shore and slunk into the forest.

"Thank God, I think we've driven him off," Jeremy said.

Then White Doe began to tremble. Jeremy held her, whispering reassuring words, only to discover that he was trembling also. Gently, he eased her down on the moss-covered ledge. They lay quietly for a bit and she offered no resistance when he removed her buckskin tunic and skirt.

He caught his breath as he gazed at her tawny beauty. Her breasts were firm, with small rosettes around her nipples. Her stomach felt flat, and he ran his fingers over her satiny skin, gently stroking her jutting hipbones. Her dark hair clung to the stalk of her neck, and as he bent to kiss her, tears started from her eyes and rolled down her cheeks.

"Don't cry, please don't. I wouldn't hurt you for the world. I'll stop."

But she shook her head and clutched his hand. "Happy," she whispered.

They made love while dusk stole over the land and the first stars appeared. Then at last, when their bodies could bear no more preparation, he eased into her. She cried out in pain, but that soon gave way to a sensation so thrilling that she could barely stand it, and this spurred him on and the rhythm of their love was the rhythm of being.

In all the wonder and harmony, Jeremy realized he was tied to this woman forever. Hers was the face he'd dreamed of, hers the body he'd made love to in the nightly wanderings of his soul.

When they'd finally exhausted the strength of their passion, and all that was left was gentle endearments, they lay back. White Doe stared up at the stars and ran her hands over her stomach. She was certain that she'd conceived, and told him so. He chuckled at the idea, but she seemed so convinced, that finally he listened to her.

"Our son, the child that you and I have fashioned, will be greater than either of us. He will have the strength of a bear, the healing powers of water. He will be the bravest of warriors and a chief among chiefs."

Jeremy could barely make out what she was saying. He knew only that he'd given her his heart, he wanted no other. In the deepest part of his being, he sensed that he'd received a gift beyond value. What he'd known with Rebecca, he understood now to have been infatuation. But White Doe had given him his first, his only experience of love.

Chapter 27

JEREMY AND White Doe made their way back to camp.

"We were about to send out a search party!" Meriwether yelled at them.

Jeremy recounted the tale about the bear while Meriwether saw to their cuts and bruises.

Later, Jeremy whispered to White Doe, "I'll tell Chief Cameahwaite about us just as soon as he gets back."

She shook her head violently. "He will be angry. He might refuse to give you horses. Sacajawea told me how important this journey is for you, and if you could not go on because of me, you would only hate me."

Jeremy argued with her, but in addition to being gentle as a spring rain, she was also stubborn. She said she would never see him again if he told the chief. Finally, Jeremy gave in.

"We have two weeks, then," he said. "Two weeks before we begin the trek through the mountains."

"I will come with you?" White Doe asked tentatively. "If my cousin Sacajawea travels with the white men, then . . ."

"That's a thought," Jeremy said, his hope springing. But he knew in his gut that Meriwether would never agree. Captain Clark had worked long and hard to convince Lewis to let Sacajawea travel with them. Another woman? Meriwether would surely draw the line at that.

For the next two weeks, Jeremy and White Doe contrived to meet at all hours. He'd finish his assigned work with zest, and then be off. "Hunting," he'd say to anybody who'd ask, and the gods smiled at him, always allowing him to catch something to show for his labors. White Doe would be waiting for him in the forest. They made love day after day, night after night, as if they only had that one moment left in their lives.

And then one day that moment finally came.

"Darling, we leave day after tomorrow," Jeremy told her. "I'll talk to the captain tonight, convince him that you must come along with us."

But when Jeremy broached the subject with Meriwether, he reacted with fury. "You took an oath to complete this mission. If you fail to do that, I'll have no alternative but to have you court-martialed like the other deserters."

Jeremy stood to his full height. "Captain, I gave you my word and I'll stand on it. I have no intention of deserting."

"Good, then we'll say no more of it."

Jeremy cleared his throat. "But there is something else. Captain, I want to marry her."

"What?" Lewis exploded. "Jeremy, for God's sake, she's an Indian. Think, man! How will she fit into your world?"

"We'll make our own world," he said resolutely. "You see, I've got to marry her. She tells me she's conceived."

"Don't be a fool! How can she know that? You've only known her two weeks."

"Indians know these things," he said stubbornly. "But that doesn't matter. If she is going to have a child, I don't want it being born a bastard."

"Jeremy, practically every one of our men has fathered a child on this expedition. And if that's happened to you, then why not take it in your stride?"

Jeremy shook his head vehemently. "You don't understand. I love her. You've a right to perform a marriage ceremony, don't you?"

Lewis shrugged. "In the absence of a minister, performing such ceremonies might lie within my jurisdiction. Though I must say this is something I never expected to encounter."

"Nor I, Captain," Jeremy said, smiling.

Positive that this was some sort of aberration, and that it would soon pass, Lewis agreed to marry them. If he didn't go through the motions, he was afraid that Jeremy might do something drastic, and he needed him along to document the rest of the journey. But to make sure the other men didn't find out—they might demand the same destructive things for themselves—he insisted on a secret ceremony.

That was just as well, for Jeremy didn't want White Doe exposed to the jibing of the men. He took Meriwether and White Doe to a secluded glen where cathedral pines reached for the sky. White Doe wore a white doeskin dress which she'd made for her wedding day. She wove a garland of wildflowers and laced it through her hair.

Jeremy handed Meriwether the Bible that Dolley Madison had given him as a going-away present. Meriwether read a few words from Genesis, and then from the Song of Solomon. A lone deer and her fawn were the only witnesses.

When Meriwether said, "Do you take this woman . . ." Jeremy murmured, "I do," and slipped a ring on her finger made of plaited buffalo hair. Meriwether then repeated the question to White Doe. When Jeremy nudged her, she crossed her hands over her heart, signifying that she clasped him to her bosom forever.

Seeing the look in the two young people's eyes, Meriwether realized for the first time the extent of their love. "A word of warning, lad. If you're really this serious about the girl, then make sure you formalize the marriage as soon as you can. Though when that will be, God only knows."

With Meriwether's permission, Jeremy and White Doe spent their last night together. They lay on the mossy ground, making love, sleeping lightly, then waking to find themselves locked within each other. If Jeremy could have had one wish, it would be for this night to never end. But finally dawn broke over the mountains, a wondrous purple haze that lightened to a pale pink with the rising sun. They woke to the song of birds and made love one last time.

Then White Doe packed up her doeskin wedding dress and put on her ordinary buckskin clothes. They walked back to camp through the dew-diamonded grass.

"I'll come back for you, I swear," Jeremy said. "As soon as the expedition's over, I'll come back."

"If you do not, then I will come to you," she said. "Fort Mandan, St. Louis, Washington," she said, repeating the words he'd told her over and over again. In her mind, she'd imprinted the map he'd drawn for her, showing the way back to his land. She'd struggled desperately to understand, but the idea was so strange . . . of great stone lodges, and one palace, built of blocks of stone, tall as the trees, where the Great White Father lived. Sacajawea too had heard these stories, and so she knew them to be true.

The time came to depart, and the men completed their last-minute packing. Captain Clark had bartered with Cameahwaite for twenty-eight horses and one mule, and Chief Toby and his son agreed to guide them through the little-known mountain passes.

On August 30, the thirty-two men of the Corps of Discovery and their Indian guides set out on the final leg of their journey.

"Look sharp now, men," Meriwether said. "We're heading into territory no longer claimed by the United States, so this might prove to be the most hazardous part of our journey."

When the horses filed out of the campsite, White Doe stood as still as a sentinel. Jeremy turned and waved, his heart so heavy with a sudden sense of foreboding that it was all he could do to keep from galloping back to her.

"I will come back," he swore under his breath. "I will."

Chapter 28

THE MEN climbed high into the Bitterroot Range, following the Lolo trail, which hugged the high ridge.

"According to my calculations we've already reached a height of more than six thousand feet," Captain Clark said.

"First time in my life I've been above the clouds," Jeremy said, staring down at the thick cover that concealed the valleys. Some of the men became lightheaded with the altitude and had to stop. Several times during the day, a cold wet snow fell, making the narrow winding trail even more treacherous.

"Nothing up to now has been as murderous as this," Jeremy said to Drewyer. "The portage around the Great Falls was bad, true; but this could mean our lives."

The tall, taciturn hunter nodded. "I don't know how many days it will take for us to get through this."

The mountain ranges were herringboned far into the distance. The path dipped and curved into the dense forest. Sometimes they would break free long enough to see the range ahead of them blurred into a deep purple; the farthest mountains were a pale blue where they joined the clouded sky. They plodded on, ever mindful that a blizzard or avalanche could wipe them off the face of the earth.

Jeremy gave in to the slow rocking motion of his horse. He couldn't pass a wildflower without thinking, 'That would look pretty in White Doe's hair,' couldn't pass a stream or glen without being reminded of some spot where they'd made love.

Drewyer went out on repeated hunting trips but couldn't find game anywhere. He saw some bighorn sheep but they eluded him, scrambling from crag to crag. One night they had to kill a colt in order to feed the men. They called their camping spot Colt Killed Creek.

They came to a trail along a cliff face so sheer that several of the horses slipped and went crashing down the hill. The rugged terrain closed in on them, harsh, mysterious in the swirling fog. They melted snow for drinking water. A day later they killed another colt for food. Chief Toby and his son decided that the trail was far too hazardous in this weather, and one night they quietly slipped from camp and went back to their own people.

Monday, the sixteenth of September, proved to be the worst day in the Bitterroot Range. It began to snow shortly after midnight, and by morning it was a full-fledged storm. To stay in one place meant certain death by freezing, so they renewed their march. The horses stumbled and fell on the jagged rocks beneath the snow; some bolted when they were spooked by a small avalanche. The storm continued until three that afternoon, and then it became so dark that they couldn't see farther than two hundred yards.

"If we go on it could mean disaster," Lewis shouted. Dispirited, they camped near a small stream.

Captain Clark rubbed his arms and elbows, trying to work out the pain from his rheumatism. "I'm colder and wetter than I've ever been in my life," he grumbled. There wasn't a man in the corps who couldn't say the same thing.

For the first time since they'd left St. Louis in the spring of 1804, the morale of the men appeared to be sinking. The following day, Clark went ahead with six men to hunt for food for the main party. If they killed any more horses, they wouldn't have enough transportation through the mountains. Lewis and the main force plodded on through the drifting snow, pushing themselves to their limits.

Jeremy came up to help Lewis raise a horse that had fallen. "What do you think, Captain?" he asked, seeing his breath freeze as he spoke.

"If we don't get out of the Bitterroots soon, it's possible that we'll just die from starvation or the cold. So keep moving!"

Then on September 19, with very little strength left, they saw a broad fertile valley to the southwest. Lewis peered through his telescope. "I make it out to be about sixty miles distant, but at least we know there's a way out of this labyrinth." It took them another three days to reach the Weippe Prairie. They descended from the mountains into the high plain. There they came upon Captain Clark's band, who'd just made contact with the Indian tribe who lived here, the Nez Percé.

The Nez Percé were highly civilized Indians, so called because they pierced their noses and wore decorative items there. Two chiefs of the tribe, Twisted Hair and Tetaharsky, treated the corps with the utmost hospitality, offering all they had in the way of food, which consisted mainly of dried salmon. Starving as they were, the men ate too much and too quickly, and every one of them came down with miserable cases of dysentery.

"It's from the dried salmon, probably," Lewis told the men as he ministered to them, though ill himself.

But the salmon had come from the Columbia River, and Chief Twisted Hair's village was only a few miles from one of that river's tributaries, the Clearwater. Weakened though they were, the men immediately fell to work, chopping down huge ponderosa pines to make canoes. Tetaharsky showed them how to hollow out the trunks using small fires, which proved to be much easier than axing out the centers.

By October 5, the men had finished five canoes. They branded their remaining horses and left them with the Nez Percé to keep until they would return. With Chief Twisted Hair and Tetaharsky as guides, they set out with the five dugouts on the Clearwater River. Now the current was with them and they traveled rapidly, reaching the confluence with the Snake River on October 10.

The hunters still could not locate any game, but occasionally the party came across Indian villages and were able to buy dogs, which they killed and cooked. Scannon, Lewis's Newfoundland, seemed to take a very dim view of this, for on the nights when the men dined on dog, he conspicuously absented himself from the campfires.

Continuing along the Snake River, they approached a series of rapids that looked unnavigable. But Drewyer insisted that they could be shot, and Cruzatte, the other experienced riverman, agreed. The men shoved the canoes into the boiling waters that dashed against the precipitous cliffs lining the banks. They used long poplar poles to keep from crashing into the cliffs, or to pole away from the boulders as they shot the rapids. Jeremy was in a dugout with Sacajawea, Charbonneau, and Lewis; Drewyer was at the helm. Charbonneau was totally useless, his face white, his lips trembling in prayer. Sacajawea had Pomp securely lashed in the cradleboard tied to her back.

"Mon dieu!" Charbonneau screamed as the canoe hit a rock and capsized, throwing the occupants out. Struggling in the swift currents, the men managed to right the canoe and drag it ashore. Making sure to keep Pomp's head above the waves, Sacajawea, an accomplished swimmer, swam after the equipment, retrieving a sextant and Jeremy's portfolio of drawings.

They built a campfire and hunkered around it, drying themselves out. Jeremy had wrapped his drawings in waterproof material, and so they weren't too badly damaged. He thanked Sacajawea profusely.

"I'd have saved it for you anyway," she said, keeping her head down so no one could hear her. "But now we are related also. White Doe told me."

Jeremy reflected on that. Since Sacajawea and White Doe were cousins, they were indeed related, if only by marriage. Well, he couldn't think of a finer person to call kin than this Indian woman.

In his sleep that night Jeremy tossed and turned, missing White Doe as if a limb had been taken from him. In the dark hours, her shade would come and lie with him. Once, he thought briefly of Rebecca Breech, how she might have reacted with the grizzly, or worked for this expedition the way Sacajawea did, and he smiled with the idea. He knew now that he could never have made Rebecca happy. She was a woman who wanted the world, and he could never have given it to her. Embarking on this expedition had been the greatest blessing of his life, for it had brought him White Doe. And then a strange new feeling crept into his reveries, a sense that White Doe might be in danger.

He talked about it to Sacajawea, who believed implicitly in dreams; but she couldn't fathom the meaning.

"Winter will be upon us before we reach the Pacific Ocean," Captain Clark said. They were deep within the gorge of the

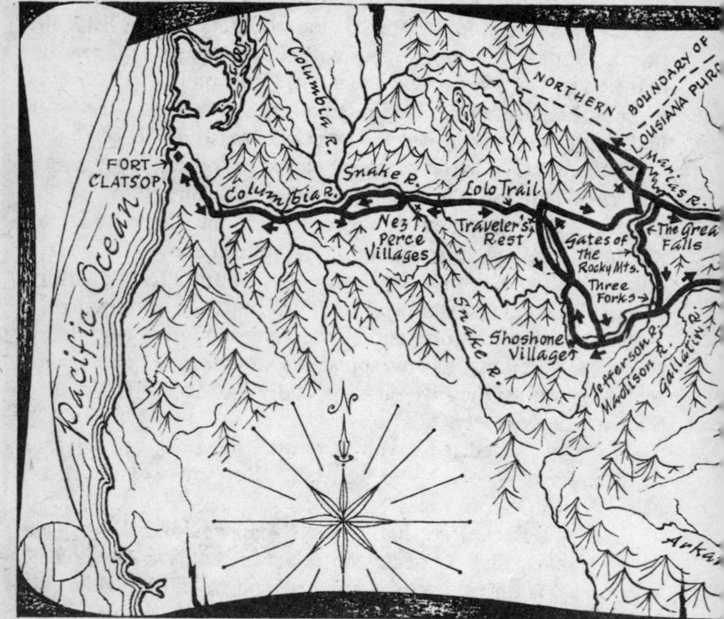

THE LEWIS AND

Columbia River, and the place was oppressive. Gloom hung from the trees clinging to the sides of the hills. It rained constantly, and nobody had any dry clothing left.

The river opened up shortly thereafter, but still it rained. The closer they got to the mouth of the Columbia, the more they were beset by unfriendly Indians. "Anything that isn't nailed down, these devils are apt to steal," Drewyer said as he slapped the hand of a Kwakiutl squaw. She had come to camp to sell her body to the men, and in the meantime had filched a can of flour.

The Indians of the Columbia Basin had been perverted by their contact with the white traders who plied their wares up and down the northwest coast. They were a dirty, unkempt lot, and full of venereal diseases. After making camp near one such village, the corps was attacked by a plague of fleas and had

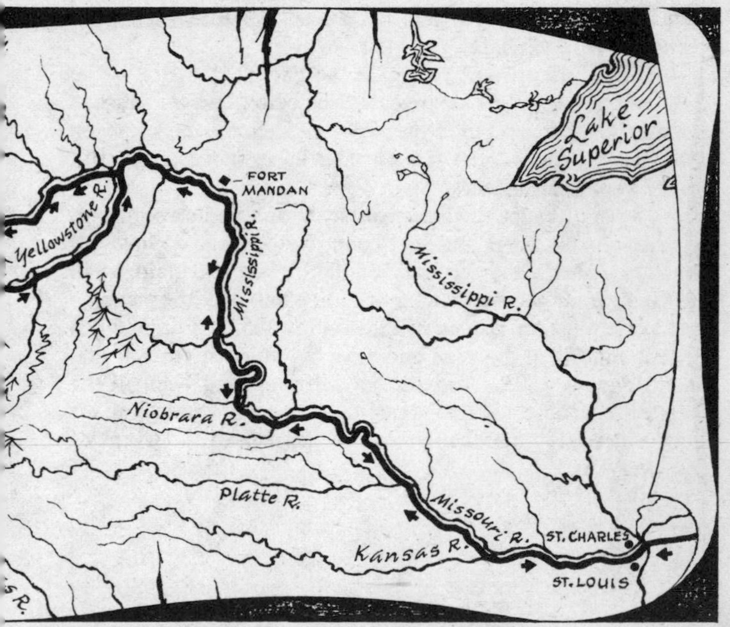

CLARK JOURNEY

to squirm out of their clothes and travel naked.

From the time they'd left the western slopes of the Shining Mountains, and all during their sojourn along the Clearwater, Snake, and Columbia Rivers, the corps had been traveling through territory not owned, or even claimed, by the United States. Consequently, they were in effect trespassers, for this land was hotly contested by the English, Spanish, and Russians, each desperate to claim the fabulously rich territory.

In early November, Sacajawea put her hand into the river while they were canoeing and cried out excitedly. The tidal currents indicated that they must be nearing the mouth of the Columbia River. Sacajawea sniffed the air and said, "Salt."

Then on November 10, straining to see through the fog and rain, the Corps of Northwest Discovery spied the mighty Pacific Ocean. In the twenty months since they'd left St. Louis, they'd traveled more than 4,100 miles, through terrain as difficult as man had ever traversed, and under constant threat from the elements, wild animals, and Indians.

And now they stood gazing at the Pacific, the first white men ever to cross the continent. Thunderous waves crashed against the cliffs, spuming the water high. Some men stopped and danced a jig, others fell on their knees and prayed, still others wept unashamedly.

As Jeremy watched the ocean swell and come rolling in, he knew in his heart that his country, the United States of America, would never be satisfied until it had laid claim to all the land, from sea to shining sea. For this was the nation's destiny. It must have been in President Jefferson's mind when he first conceived the plan and gave the order to embark that fateful day in 1803. And though Jefferson had been in the President's House all this time, the force and energy of his spirit had always marched alongside the men of the Corps of Discovery.

Chapter 29

LIVING QUARTERS had to be built for the winter, so the men felled the huge cedar and fir trees that grew near their campsite. They built a fort they named Fort Clatsop, after a local Indian tribe that had been friendly to them. The post consisted of two parallel buildings each fifty feet long, and connected on each end by a high picketed stockade. Entrance was through a gate at the south end. The men's quarters on the west side consisted of three rooms, each about sixteen feet square, each with a fireplace in the center, an absolute necessity in this damp, foul weather. On the east side, across the forty-eight-foot-by-twenty-foot parade ground, were the captains' quarters.

Meriwether insisted on building the fort away from the Indian settlements, believing most of the natives untrustworthy. "They might turn on us at any moment."

But the distance didn't stop an old wily squaw whom the men called the "Old Bawd" from coming to the fort with her retinue of girls and bartering their favors for whatever wasn't locked away. With thirty warm-blooded men, the corps soon depleted their supplies.

Jeremy thought these natives the strangest he'd ever seen. They were true flatheads, their heads having been strapped between boards at birth and permanently flattened. With White Doe ever in his thoughts, he didn't find it difficult to resist the blandishments of the "Old Bawd."

The months dragged, it rained every single day, and some of the men got "enfluenzy." To keep occupied, Jeremy worked diligently on his sketchbook, filling in those drawings which he'd only indicated. He did a reasonable likeness of White Doe in her wedding dress, and when he showed it to Sacajawea, it brought tears to her eyes. But his nightmares about White Doe persisted; always she faced some kind of mortal danger, always he struggled to reach her, but before he could determine the outcome, he'd waken.

Lewis and Clark spent the long rainy days completing their journals, detailing every aspect of their trip, and cataloguing the specimens they'd collected. Knowing that their journals were sure to be read by President Jefferson, by scientists, and perhaps by the entire nation, they were careful with their entries. The minor difficulties amongst the men, the horseplay and practical jokes, the commonplace sexual encounters with the various Indian tribes, all these they considered too frivolous, expunging them from the journals.

Thinking ahead to the day when the Corps of Discovery might reach the Pacific Coast, President Jefferson had dispatched certain American merchant vessels to the Pacific Northwest, to pick up the men when they reached the sea. If a ship did appear, they were to embark, to sail around the Cape of Good Hope and thence to Washington. Such a sea voyage might take months, but it was considerably safer than retracing their route across the continent. Jeremy knew it might mean he'd never see White Doe again, and every day he prayed that a ship wouldn't appear. His prayers were apparently answered. Actually, the *Lydia,* commanded by Captain Hill, had anchored off the mouth of the Columbia River, but the Flatheads withheld that information, thinking to rob the corpsmen if not kill them outright.

Just when Jeremy gave up hope of spring ever arriving, one day the sun shone brighter, the winds warmed, and presumptuous wildflowers poked their heads above the earth. The corps made ready for the return journey.

On March 23, 1806, the canoes were loaded and launched and the expedition made its way back up the Columbia River. They reached the Nez Percé tribe the first week in May, and retrieved the horses they'd left with Chief Twisted Hair the previous autumn. On horseback, they began the climb over the Rockies, and on June 15 reached the western entry of the Lolo Pass in the Bitterroot Range. Dogtooth violet, columbine, wild roses, and bluebells honeyed the air, but winter still held the mountains in its stormy grip. By the twenty-first of June, they knew they'd never find the trail under the heavy fall of snow, and so they had to go back down the mountain. They waited impatiently for warmer weather and finally managed to cross early in July. The closer they got to Shoshone country, the more anxious Jeremy became. Sacajawea tried to calm him, tried to reason with him, but he was beyond reason.

The morning of July 3 found the corps at Traveler's Rest, a camp they'd made the preceding autumn. Here the expedition split in two: Lewis and eight men headed north to explore the farthest reaches of the Marias River and determine if it watered an area rumored to be rich in fur-bearing animals. Clark led the main party to the pirogues they had cached the year before, and then proceeded down to the three forks of the Missouri—the Gallatin, Madison, and Jefferson. The captains planned to rendezvous at the junction of the Yellowstone and Missouri Rivers.

Though Meriwether wanted Jeremy to accompany him, Jeremy respectfully requested permission to go with Clark's group; on their route, they were more likely to run into the Shoshones. In the days that followed, Jeremy kept a sharp eye out for any sign of the tribe's presence. And then on the morning they reached Three Forks, he spied a column of smoke. He begged Clark for permission to search for the Shoshones. Clark, knowing how much it meant to him, allowed him to go off, though first extracting his promise to return, no matter what.

Jeremy searched for two days, growing more desperate with every hour, and then on the evening of the third day, he found the village. The tepees were pitched on the edge of a buffalo-grazing land, and the Shoshones looked well fed.

Cameahwaite acted surprised to see a white man again, but when he recognized Jeremy, he became bitter.

Employing the sign language he'd learned from Drewyer these past two years, and the smattering of Shoshone he'd picked up, Jeremy told Cameahwaite he'd come for White Doe.

A scowl contorted Cameahwaite's bony face. "She no longer lives among us," he said.

Jeremy's heart dropped. After a long parlay, he learned that when spring had come, then early summer, and he hadn't returned, White Doe had gone off with a party of French trappers.

"She promised to give them everything she owned if they would take her with them to the Mandan villages," Cameahwaite said.

"And you let her go? A lone girl?" Jeremy demanded.

Cameahwaite glowered at him. He did not like this soldier, but he admired his bravery. "White Doe brought dishonor on our family. She was promised to a brave of our tribe from the time she was a child. When this brave found out that she was pregnant—"

"Pregnant? Oh, my God!"

"And by a white man, the brave refused to have her. Nor would she have him; she threatened to kill herself if forced to marry him."

"Of course she did," Jeremy exploded. "She's married to me!"

An uncertain look flickered in Cameahwaite's eyes. "She told us you had taken her to wife, but none in the tribe believed her, thinking she said it only to hide her shame."

"God damn!" Jeremy cursed. "And now she's out there in the wilderness, traveling with some strangers?"

"And with a child," Cameahwaite said solemnly, "barely two moons."

With a child . . . the words pounded in Jeremy's brain. His son. He ran for his horse, leapt into the saddle, and galloped back in the direction of the corps, reaching them in one day. He explained the predicament to Captain Clark and pleaded for permission to go after White Doe.

"How far do you think you'd get, alone in hostile territory and with thousands of miles to cover?" Clark demanded. "Use your head, man! We're going to Fort Mandan anyway, and with us you'll get there in one piece."

When he'd calmed down, Jeremy realized that what Clark said made sense. The following day they were en route again, canoeing down the Yellowstone. They reached the junction with the Missouri where they were to meet Captain Lewis, but he wasn't there. Leaving signals for Lewis should he come along, they continued downriver. By August 8, they still hadn't contacted Lewis and by now, Clark was convinced that Lewis was behind, not ahead of them. If he was alive at all.

Then on August 12 a great shout went up from Clark's scouts when they spotted Lewis's band coming downriver. They were in a pirogue they'd unearthed from their old cache. Meriwether was lying on his stomach in the bottom of the boat.

Lewis had a hair-raising tale to tell. Exploring the Marias, his band had come upon a party of Blackfeet, the most ferocious warriors on the entire continent. "The Blackfeet professing friendship, we camped with them," he said. "We had little choice, for they outnumbered us, and we feared that a larger party was close by. Then near dawn, I woke to find them trying to steal our rifles. Reuben Fields knifed one warrior, and I shot another, though before he died he sent a bullet whistling through my hair." Believing that the entire Blackfeet nation would pursue them, Lewis and his men had ridden, hell bent for leather, and had reached the river.

To complicate matters further, one afternoon when Lewis and the nearsighted Cruzatte had gone hunting, Cruzatte mistook Lewis for an elk and shot him in the rump. The bullet passed through both buttocks. The wounds still caused him great pain, and when Clark attempted to dress them, he passed out.

The river ran swiftly and the men made great time, covering in an hour what had taken them a day when they'd hauled the boats upstream. But for Jeremy, they couldn't travel fast enough.

Chapter 30

ON AUGUST 14, the weary men of the Corps of Discovery arrived at the territory of the Mandans. With Meriwether's permission, Jeremy immediately went to all the Indian villages, searching for White Doe. At one village, an old squaw told him, "Yes, a Shoshone woman arrived here one moon ago."

Springing with hope, Jeremy searched every lodge and found her at last. When he saw her, his heart contracted into a tight fist. She was lying on a pallet and she looked dreadful. She turned and stared at him in the gloom, then blinked, as though she might be dreaming.

"Yes, it's me," he whispered, kneeling beside her. He lifted her and crushed her close, rocking her back and forth, growing even more frightened when he felt how thin she was. Both of them were crying, then smiling, only to start crying again. He tried to feed her some oxtail soup, but she could only manage a few swallows.

She told him that when her pregnancy became obvious, her people had turned on her and she'd withered before their anger. Her delivery had been difficult, and it left her very weak. Then when he hadn't returned in the spring as he'd promised, she'd gone to find him. It was too soon after the birth of the child, and the arduous journey had sapped her remaining strength. "But we are together now," she whispered. "Happy."

A squaw brought the child to Jeremy and he gazed at it in wonder. It had the same dark hair as she did, and the same high cheekbones. And when the babe opened its eyes, Jeremy stared, for they were the brightest blue, lighter even than his own.

"He's a fine-looking boy," he said with a trace of wonder.

"Aii," White Doe wailed. "Everything I have done is wrong. I hoped to give you a brave warrior to hunt for you in your old years, but this child is a girl."

He looked at the tiny form. Did he feel this . . . anger because she was a girl? he wondered. No, he thought, it's because the child is responsible for White Doe's illness.

Jeremy took White Doe to where Lewis and Clark had camped. Meriwether, still sick himself, tried to treat her, but after he'd tried all his remedies, she still grew weaker. He shook his head sadly, "I'm afraid she's too far gone."

"I don't believe that. I won't," Jeremy said resolutely. "Captain, I want to take her to St. Louis with us. The doctors there will be able to help her. Captain, please. Otherwise she'll die!"

Meriwether pondered that. He and Clark had tried to persuade the chiefs of the Mandans to accompany them to Washington, there to meet with the Great White Father. Most of them refused, but finally, Chief She-he-ke agreed to go, providing he could take along his wife, some relatives, and all their children. If they were accompanying the corps, could he refuse White Doe?

Jeremy spoke to Chief She-he-ke, promising him his rifle if his women would look after White Doe on the journey.

The chief agreed, but said, "The papoose is too young to make such a journey."

"She'll make it," Jeremy said resolutely. "She's got Brand blood in her veins."

When Captain Clark found out about Jeremy's child, he clapped him on the back. "What's the little girl's name?"

"My wife named her Rainbow, because of her eyes," he said.

"Well, that's fine among Indians, but you'll be living in Washington. There aren't many young girls there named Rainbow. She'll have a hard enough time as it is, if you get my meaning."

Jeremy nodded. "You're probably right, Captain."

Clark stroked his red beard. "Now let's see, Sacajawea named her baby Pomp, because that meant firstborn in Shoshone. And from what you tell me, your little girl is related to Pomp, so why not call her . . . Circumstance? Now there's a good Puritan name."

Jeremy smiled at the idea. Pomp and Circumstance. If he remembered the books James Hoban had lent him, it was right out of Shakespeare. He chucked his daughter under the chin and she smiled at him. "Circumstance it is then, Circumstance Brand."

Captain Clark had grown so fond of Pomp that he wanted to raise the child as his own, and asked Sacajawea and Charbonneau to come live with him in St. Louis. But Charbonneau, a man of some influence among the Indians, knew that he wouldn't have any among the whites, and so he refused. Though Sacajawea wanted to go, she chose to remain with her husband. The day of parting was sad, and as they left, the men gave three rousing cheers for the woman who'd helped guide them on their journey.

After traveling many more days on the Missouri, the corps finally approached the little town of St. Charles, a few miles north of St. Louis. The quiet of the pleasant Sunday afternoon was shattered as the corpsmen fired volley after volley in the air. The startled townspeople rushed to the river and stared at the boats in disbelief. Not having heard from the expedition in more than a year, everybody assumed they were dead, their bones bleaching somewhere in the wilds of the continent. And yet these bearded, bronzed, trail-hardened men who waved and shouted at them were no ghosts. They'd been gone two years, four months, and eight days, had traveled more than eight thousand miles, and now they were back among the living!

Pandemonium broke out all through St. Charles, and a great celebration was held. While the men drank and ate their fill, Jeremy carried White Doe to the local healer, a man versed in the uses of healing herbs. But the practitioner shook his head. "There's nothing I can do."

Jeremy held on tightly to White Doe, as though holding her would keep death at bay. If he could have given his own life for hers he would, so desperately did he love her. That she should be cut down before her life had begun was unbearable to him. He sat with her all night, praying, promising God anything if only he would let her live. When she weakened further, he was even willing to make a pact with the devil if that would save her.

The baby lying in her wooden cradle whimpered, and Jeremy glared at her, terrible thoughts in his mind. White Doe moaned, and her eyelids flickered. She stared at him for a long time, trying to find the strength to speak. Finally, she managed to whisper, "My heart, we have made something, a life that will be greater than our own. The child has taken the very best in our bodies and souls, and will fashion it into something new and wondrous."

"Hush, don't tire yourself," Jeremy said, wiping the tears from his eyes.

White Doe swallowed and shook her head wearily. "I must speak. This child is my future. As long as you love her, then you love part of me. As long as she lives, I live." As she spoke, each word burned away more of her feeble strength, until she lay heaving for breath. "Do not mourn for me too long, for that is not the way of life, and life is what you must choose for our daughter. I ask only one thing . . . If you should find someone to warm your lodge, then I pray you choose one that may like the child. She is so good, she never cries. And her eyes, so like the sky, see and accept everything."

Jeremy nodded his head, barely able to see her face through his swimming eyes. He bent closer, trying to hear her last words.

She raised her arms and crossed them on Jeremy's chest, as she had done on their wedding day. "I love you," she whispered. Then her dark eyes, which had reflected all the sadness and joy of her life, turned blank and unseeing as her life slipped away.

He sat with her for hours, and in his grief, terrible thoughts snaked into his mind . . . that she was only asleep . . . that she would waken and they'd make love again. And then when she grew cold to his touch, other, morbid thoughts overcame him. That since he was responsible for her death, he deserved the same fate.

Only when Circumstance stirred was he pried back from this dark torment. He picked up the child, and, cradling her in his arms, returned to the world of the living.

PART FOUR

Chapter 31

THE CARRIAGE bumped along the rutted roadway of Pennsylvania Avenue, the line of newly planted poplar trees casting intermittent shadows on Rebecca Breech's face. President Jefferson had planted the trees, but they were somewhat sparse. Rebecca fidgeted in the carriage; she was having serious doubts about the dinner. She knew that Zebulon would be there—he'd probably requested her presence—and only the presidential invitation had persuaded her to attend.

Zebulon had returned to the United States a great hero. For all practical purposes, the Tripoli Wars had been won through the heroism and enterprise of the United States Navy and Marines. Despite Zebulon's newfound glory, Rebecca still hadn't forgiven him. How long ago had the fire been—two years? three? "A lifetime," she murmured to herself. How wonderful if this dinner were being given in Jeremy's honor . . . but there'd been no word from the expedition in two years, and everybody said that even Jefferson had given up hope for the men.

The carriage rolled past the new gateposts, on which stood two open-winged eagles; a Negro footman grabbed the horse's reins, and another liveried servant helped Rebecca out of the carriage. Self-proclaimed man of the people or not, Jefferson certainly doesn't lack for servants or slaves, Rebecca thought, as she arranged the folds of her green silk taffeta gown.

The brisk autumn air felt heady after the beastly hot summer that had just passed; she and everybody who could afford to had fled Washington's malarial climate for their summer homes, or the watering spas in Virginia. This year there'd hardly been any autumn; the foliage had changed within a week, and now Washington looked barren.

Much the way I feel, Rebecca thought, as she climbed the stairs. Every morning when she looked in the mirror, she saw tiny lines radiating from her eyes. Pearl makeup and rouge, applied as Dolley Madison had taught her, helped hold off the ravages. But soon not even makeup would help. My Lord, I'm twenty-seven years old! she thought with a twinge of fright. Almost beyond the marrying age.

With Jeremy gone she'd thrown herself into writing with a vengeance. God knew there was enough happening in the nation. Ohio had joined the Union as the seventeenth state, and Rebel Thorne applauded the fact that slavery was forbidden there.

The growing battle between Chief Justice John Marshall and President Jefferson intrigued her. "In his ruling in 'Marbury versus Madison,' Justice Marshall can clearly be interpreted to mean that the Supreme Court has the power and the duty to set aside any law or act of Congress or the President's which the high court deems unconstitutional. With this bold step he's placed the Supreme Court above the office of the presidency. How long will Jefferson allow this? Each man would have the other's head!"

Rebecca's pent-up energies found full expression in a series of attacks against Aaron Burr. When he ran for governor of New York, Thorne warned the nation that this was part of a plan of the New England Federalists, "the Essex Junto," to secede from the Union. When Burr lost that election he blamed Hamilton, and challenged him to a duel. On July 11, 1804, he killed him, and an outraged Thorne cried out, "How can a man who's under indictment in New York and New Jersey continue to serve as Vice-President of the United States? Burr must be brought to justice, lest highly placed men make a mockery of the law!"

Rebecca's passions flowed into her pen, and this somewhat calmed her. Not that she hadn't had suitors, some wealthy, some socially prominent. But she refused them all. Love lay dormant in a cloistered part of her being, and in all her years only Jeremy's touch had wakened it. She felt her skin flush with the memory, and when she entered the main hall of the President's House, a glow of vitality radiated from her.

President Jefferson greeted her with a smile. Always an

admirer of beauty, he commented on how well she was looking.

She flushed all the more, and then Jefferson introduced her to a tall, distinguished-looking man with something of a perpetual scowl on his face. "This is William Eaton."

"Honored to make your acquaintance, sir," she said, "and my heartiest congratulations on your victory against the Moors."

Eaton bowed, then they moved into the Oval Room where the other guests were chatting and sipping wine. Rebecca curtsied to the older women, wives of preachers and cabinet members, and of course, Dolley Madison. Rebecca couldn't quite hide her shock at Dolley's outfit. She wore a clinging beige silk gown with a scooped neckline that exposed the greater part of her breasts, of which Dolley boasted a sufficiency, if not an overabundance.

Dolley said gaily to Rebecca, "Don't you love this new style? It's called Empire, and it's the rage in Paris. Its success in the United States is already assured, for preachers in Boston, Philadelphia, and New York are thundering against it from their pulpits." Dolley also wore her omnipresent turban, with a few loose curls peeking from beneath its folds. The attached ostrich plumes waved gaily as she led Rebecca around, introducing her particularly to the unattached men. Dolley hadn't lost her touch as both matchmaker and Jefferson's indispensable hostess.

Compared to Dolley, James Madison looked diminished to the point of being unobtrusive. But what he lacked in physical presence, he more than made up in his intellectual capabilities. As Jefferson's secretary of state, Madison had performed brilliantly. The two men, lifelong friends, acted almost as each other's alter egos, and it was no secret that Jefferson was grooming him as his successor to the presidency.

From the corner of her eye, Rebecca saw Zebulon standing near the window. A barrage of impressions assaulted her, leaving her weak and near fainting . . . rough hands that roused her body despite her will . . . the whinnying of dying horses above the roar of the flames. She clutched at the chair for support, thinking, I loathe him! But gradually her heart stopped racing and in a moment of clarity she realized that she didn't hate him, quite the contrary. Something dark and elemental in her responded to him, sought to attract him, and at the same time fought to hold him at bay. But why? she wanted to scream aloud, and instead regarded him intently.

He limped slightly when he moved, the result of a flesh wound in the thigh, and he sported a saber slash across his cheek that gave his face character and made him seem even handsomer. He was chatting with a tall, slim young woman whose back was to Rebecca.

When Zebulon saw her, he blanched. He'd prepared for this meeting, but despite that, he looked undone, and barely managed to stammer his greeting.

"I believe you know Marianne Connaught," he said to Rebecca.

Rebecca nodded. Marianne wore a decorous high-necked white peau de soie gown embroidered with seed pearls at the neck and wrists. Rebecca had never seen anything quite like it. "It's an enchanting gown," she said. "Is it a family heirloom?"

Marianne laughed, showing perfect white teeth. Her violet eyes sparkled, and Rebecca was struck with how much Marianne resembled her poor mother.

"I've just returned from London, and this is the latest fashion there. You see, France and England are at war not only on land and sea, but in fashion also." Marianne spoke with the ease of an heiress. The shy little girl had grown into a young lady of wit, accomplishment, and demure beauty.

"And how did you find London?" Rebecca asked. She felt a pang of envy that this scrawny creature, with no breast or hips to speak of, should be heir to the vast Connaught fortune and name.

"London is a source of constant delight," Marianne said. "The Court of St. James's has no equal. The theater is the finest in all the world; Congreve, Sheridan, and Wycherly point their finger at the flaws and foibles of humanity. Alas, when I see our productions here, how ragged they seem in comparison."

Rebecca seethed under the slights disguised with such airiness. "Were you visiting family?" she asked.

Marianne nodded. "Do you remember my cousin Sean?"

Rebecca tapped her chin with her fan. "That overly tall young man with the receding hairline?"

Zebulon, trying to make light of what might become an awkward situation, said with a laugh, "Rebecca, how could you forget the young hothead who threatened to kill me?"

If Marianne was upset by the memory of her father's death and her mother's subsequent madness, she betrayed no sign. Her laugh floated across the room, so melodious that people turned to smile at the contagion of her mood. Only Rebecca knew that Marianne had been cut to the quick.

"You needn't fear my cousin, Mr. Brand. Sean Connaught has far more important things to attend to these days. He's recently been made a captain in His Majesty's Navy, and has acquitted himself with great distinction serving with Lord Nelson. We shall beat Napoleon, you'll see."

Two latecomers entered the room and Rebecca exclaimed, "Is there to be no end to surprises this day?"

Aaron Burr came in with a slight dark-haired young woman whom Rebecca recognized as his daughter, Theodosia.

"I didn't think I'd ever see the day when Aaron Burr was welcomed here," Rebecca said.

"They say that Jefferson invites him as a way of keeping track of him," Marianne said.

Really, the man leads a charmed life, Rebecca thought. When he was finally brought to trial for the murder of Alexander Hamilton, he'd defended himself with such brilliance that he was acquitted, though his guilt was undeniable.

"I cannot countenance it," Rebecca said. "Who can believe in the rule of law when such an injustice can take place?"

"Come, Rebecca," Zebulon said. "The men dueled according to the code of gentlemen, and Burr exacted his due."

Marianne gave him a look as though to remind him of Sean's challenge, and Zebulon flushed.

Rebecca said, "Burr killed a man. Doesn't that mean anything anymore?"

Zebulon's eyes fastened on Theodosia as he said quietly, "There are some insults that merit death."

Rebecca knew that Hamilton had made it a practice to thwart Burr at every turn, first in the presidency, then in the governorship of New York. But his final insult had centered on Theodosia. What exactly that was, Rebecca didn't know, for those who did, claimed the information was too heinous to repeat. Dolley circled over from the buffet table and joined them.

"Theodosia is considered the most accomplished woman in America," Dolley confided to them. "She speaks six languages fluently, is versed in the philosophies of the ancient masters, and plays the pianoforte with concert skill. In the art of conversation, she has no equal among those of her own sex."

And she might have been your stepdaughter, Rebecca thought, recalling Dolley's affair with Burr. Rebecca had never liked Theodosia; she thought her an invention of her father's, and as such, a puppet and far too full of herself.

The butler, Etienne Le Maire, opening the doors to the State Dining Room, said, "Dinner is served."

Jefferson led Dolley into the gold-colored room, and James Madison graciously extended his arm to Rebecca, who towered over him. Jefferson preferred dining in the smaller Green Room, but this night the party was too large.

The dinner was sumptuous. "I believe that cooking is an art—a minor one to be sure, but an art nevertheless," Jefferson said. Wine accompanied every course, and the conversation grew animated, if not gay. Jefferson's hair had turned almost white, but he still had the florid complexion of a redhead. His gray-blue eyes were lively and intelligent, yet a weariness had veiled their brightness. Being President had proved emotionally exhausting. When the Sally Hemings scandal broke, Jefferson had taken a dreadful beating in the Federalist papers throughout the nation. He refused to answer their charges; consequently, when he spent long periods away at Monticello, the gossip started all over again. Though he pretended to be immune, the barbs hurt him sorely, and he looked forward to retiring at the end of his second term.

Jefferson tapped his wine glass for attention and looked at Zebulon. "Mr. Brand, along with Stephen Decatur, Commodore Preble, and our other gallant seamen, we've been aware of your valor. Perhaps you'd be kind enough to tell us about the final phases of the Tripolitan War."

All eyes focused on Zebulon, but he nodded in William

Eaton's direction. "I'm sure the commander of that expedition can recount it far better than I."

Jefferson smiled benignly at Eaton. "We've heard Mr. Eaton's version. It would be refreshing to hear another."

Jefferson's slight was marked, and intentional. When Eaton had returned from the Mediterranean, he'd presented Congress with a bill for $10,000 for his additional expenses. Many congressmen and the President felt his demands were exorbitant, and refused to pay them. Jefferson looked inquiringly at Zebulon. He reached for his wineglass, gulped the heady Madeira, then began.

"After we'd managed to burn the *Philadelphia,* Commodore Preble tried to conquer the city of Tripoli. Five times we attacked with all the firepower we could muster. But the fortress guarding the harbor withstood all our pounding. And then we heard of William Eaton and his plan."

President Jefferson interrupted quickly, "For those at table who don't know, our Connecticut-born legislator proposed to Congress in 1804 that Tripoli's hostile Bashaw, Yusuf Caramanli, be replaced by his exiled brother, Hamet. Hamet, by virtue of his seniority, claimed the throne. If the United States would aid him, then Hamet would make a separate peace with us, and end the piratical wars."

Eaton could barely contain his anger. The President was deliberately stealing his thunder, and he could do nothing to stop it.

Jefferson nodded at Zebulon, who took over the telling of the tale. "With the blessings of our government, Eaton went to the mid-East, and found Hamet in Egypt. He took him to Alexandria and there recruited a force of about three hundred and seventy men."

"Paid out of my own pocket," Eaton put in quickly.

"They were an unlikely lot," Zebulon continued, "and included Greek mercenaries, Arab camel drivers, and the like. But we were fortunate in enlisting the services of seven United States Marines under the command of Lieutenant Presley Neville O'Bannon."

"If you were with Commander Preble," Rebecca interjected, "how did you manage then to serve with Eaton?"

"I volunteered as part of the Marine detachment sent to act

as liaison with the sea forces. We were planning a two-pronged attack, from land and sea. Eaton marched us six hundred miles across the desert—now I know what hell must be like. It took us more than a month, but finally we reached the town of Derna, on the seacoast, the Bashaw's capital."

Zebulon had another swallow of wine to ease his parched throat. "Last year, on April 6, 1805, a day that shall forever live in the hearts of the Marine Corps, we attacked Derna. The liaison worked, and we were supported by gunfire from three American ships in the harbor. We took the Moors completely by surprise, and were able to capture the citadel without losing a man. The moment the inhabitants saw that Hamet was with us, they swore allegiance to him, and victory was ours."

Zebulon stood up and showed the sword he wore at his side. "This Mameluke saber is a replica of one that Hamet gave Eaton. I understand the Marine Corps plans to have its officers wear such a facsimile for all time. We taught those pirates that the arm of the United States is not so short that we cannot strike our enemies wherever we want!"

A chorus of congratulations greeted Zebulon's tale, and he glowed under the praise. He stole a glance at Rebecca, and she too seemed slightly more disposed toward him.

Zebulon unbuckled his sword and handed the Tunisian saber to President Jefferson. "A small memento of our victory."

Jefferson smiled, then handed the sword to Dolley. "Here you are, my dear. You never know when you may need it."

"I shall keep it by my side constantly," Dolley said, to the amusement of the company.

Marianne Connaught said, "Would that we could teach the French fleet those same lessons. Sailing from London, we were stopped and harassed no less than three times by their men-of-war."

"Ah, but surely our difficulties on the high seas are compounded tenfold by the British," Rebecca said.

Knowing that such a line of conversation could only lead to hostility, Jefferson adroitly changed the subject. "Zebulon, I believe you have a brother who is also serving the nation with Meriwether Lewis and his Corps of Discovery."

"I'd planned to ask you about them this evening. Have you received any word?"

Jefferson shook his head. "The last news we had was when the keelboat returned to St. Louis from Fort Mandan. That was eighteen months ago. Since then, nothing."

Jefferson spoke so softly that he could hardly be heard, and Rebecca leaned forward intently. "According to my instructions, Captain Lewis was to have sent back another small detachment of men when he reached the Yellowstone River. For whatever reason, these men never appeared. Then ships were sent to the Pacific Northwest, but they saw no sign of the expedition either."

Zebulon asked the question on everybody's lips. "Do you think our men are dead?"

Jefferson sighed deeply. "I pray nightly for their safe return." When Zebulon tried to press him for more information, the President refused to commit himself and rose, signaling that dinner was over.

As an after-dinner divertisement, the party listened to an Italian band perform the music of William Linley, "An Air From Othello." Jefferson had recently imported the musicians from Italy, for he couldn't bear to hear any music murdered by inexperienced American musicians.

"Would the ladies here play a favorite of mine?" Jefferson asked. "Johann Christian Bach's Second Sonata, Opus Eighteen."

The piece for harpsichord required four hands, and naturally Theodosia volunteered. "I will be delighted to assist," Rebecca said, and moved to the instrument. From the first note struck, Rebecca realized that Theodosia meant to show her up, playing with dazzling virtuosity, her fingers flashing across the keyboard. Rebecca's heart raced faster than her hands. She knew she could never catch up to the vixen, but then her anger surfaced, and she pushed aside all thoughts save that her honor was at stake. She played with abandon, chasing after Theodosia's figurations, until the women ended on a resounding note.

The applause was generous, then Rebecca saw Aaron Burr lean to Zebulon and William Eaton; he said something and the two men nodded. Theodosia went back to her chair, but Rebecca remained at the harpsichord, and without being asked, began to play and sing "Psalm 100."

Make a joyful noise unto the Lord . . .

Her clear soprano rang true, she closed her eyes, her fingers finding the keys, her voice reaching for impossible notes, all of which she somehow achieved. Dimly, she was aware that she was at the crest of her powers. The audience sat entranced, moved by her feeling and verve, and with her final phrases,

For the Lord is good, his mercy is everlasting,
And his truth endureth to all generations!

the room broke into resounding applause. The men crowded around her. So much for Theodosia, she thought, and for Marianne Connaught!

When the guests began to leave, Zebulon insinuated himself next to Rebecca. "May I see you home?" he asked.

"I don't think that would be wise," she said. As she turned to leave he blocked her path.

"Rebecca, you and I have known each other for a lifetime. Am I to suffer forever for one wrong? Even a priest offers absolution to a sinner; can you as a decent human being do less?" And so saying, began to hum a bar of the psalm, "The Lord is good, his mercy is everlasting."

She smiled at his impudence and allowed him to see her to her carriage, which had driven up the curved path to the north entrance. When he climbed in beside her it was too late to resist without creating a scene. Besides, with her driver up front, she wasn't too frightened.

Zebulon leaned out of the window and called to his slave, "Eli, follow me with my horse."

As the carriage began to roll, they settled back, watching the haze of twilight steal over the land. Rebecca felt the power and energy emanating from him . . . so different from Jeremy's gentle presence.

Zebulon cleared his throat. "I need to talk to you about . . . what happened." She didn't respond, and he went on. "Rebecca, I was young, inflamed by you, and if that be a crime, then I admit my guilt, as I've been guilty all my life where you're concerned. I love you, it's as simple as that. There's never been another woman who could command those words from me. But enough. I didn't mean to burden you with the past. You see, my years of fighting the Moor have given me another perspective, one more in keeping with my true nature."

She looked at him in the growing darkness, seeing the long sweep of his lashes. What had happened . . . true, it was years ago. And if the truth be known, the experience had not been without its . . . stimulations. Sometimes she wished she had the morals of a loose woman. God knows Washington was full of them, now that so many congressmen were away from their families for long periods of time. But she'd never been able to break the constraints of her society, even though she knew those constraints to be stupid and unreasonable.

Taking her silence for a small victory, Zebulon said earnestly, "I'm afraid I'll have to do something to declare Jeremy dead."

Her audible gasp made the driver turn, but she motioned that she was all right. "How can you say such a thing?" she demanded. "Something's happened; they've lost their way; the weather's delayed them—anything, but not dead."

"You saw Jefferson's concern," Zebulon said. "He practically admitted there was no hope. Maybe they perished in an Indian massacre, maybe they were swept over a mountainside. But if they were alive, we would have heard long ago." He paused, and then murmured, "There were times when Jeremy and I didn't get along. Many times. We're both headstrong, both willful . . . and we both loved the same woman."

She looked at him and seeing tears in his eyes, reached out and tentatively touched his arm. They continued the ride to her Georgetown house in silence. When they said goodnight at the door, he asked if he could see her again. She said no, but in a manner that gave him some hope.

"You'll see," he said to Eli, as he mounted Baal. "Within a week, she'll be dining with me. We're tied together, she and I, for better or worse. I don't know why the Lord cursed me with a love only for her, but he did." He sighed, then said, "Now follow me close by, Eli, and don't get lost in the dark, because if you're found alone on the streets, you're liable to be shot."

"Where are we going?" Eli asked, climbing on his mule.

"To Blodgett's Hotel. To meet with Aaron Burr, and hear what new schemes activate his fertile brain. Unless I miss my guess, they'll be monumental."

Chapter 32

"I MAY be gone for an hour or more, so wait for me here," Zebulon said. Eli didn't answer and Zebulon said sharply, "Did you hear me?"

"Yes, sir," he muttered.

Zebulon shook his head. Really, the man was incorrigible; Eli's manner hadn't improved one whit in the three years he'd been away. He'd have to do something to tame his spirit—a diet of bread and water, or maybe the lash.

Zebulon strode into Blodgett's Great Hotel. The building on Eighth Street, designed by James Hoban, bore a striking resemblance to the President's Mansion. Because of the dearth of housing in the capital, congressmen used the hotel as a boarding house while the legislature was in session, the conservative Federalists living in the right wing, and the Democratic-Republicans occupying the left. They soon became known as the right-wing and left-wing parties.

Zebulon bounded up the stairs to the top floor, searching for the room number Aaron Burr had given him. As he walked along the corridor he saw a door open. A girl slipped out and hurried down the servant's staircase. Zebulon loped to the staircase and caught a glimpse of her as she descended. This was no serving wench; her cloak couldn't quite hide the white peau de soie silk gown encrusted with seed pearls.

"Why the old rake!" Zebulon chuckled. "Imagine Burr having an affair with Marianne Connaught!" He knocked on Burr's door and, when he was admitted, was surprised to see Theodosia sitting on the settee. Her presence certainly precluded any sexual assignations. Clearly, something else was going on between Burr and Marianne Connaught.

Theodosia exchanged some pleasantries with Zebulon and then left. Shortly thereafter, William Eaton arrived. The slight he'd suffered at Jefferson's dinner had put him in a foul mood. Burr listened to Eaton's vociferous complaints about the President, commiserating with him, and artfully inciting him all the more. Burr poured them a round of brandy. Zebulon thought Burr nervous and agitated, and he downed two snifters in quick succession—very unusual, for he rarely drank. He went to the window and looked out at the darkened capital. In the distance, candlelight shone in the windows of the President's House.

"By rights, that mansion should be mine this very minute. And it would have been, had I given the Federalists the sign when Jefferson and I tied for the election. I didn't, because I thought Jefferson would treat me fairly, as I had treated him. I was forty-four then; at the end of Jefferson's second term I would have been fifty-two, the perfect age for the Presidency. But from the day we were sworn in to office, he let it be known that James Madison, that pale stunted cipher, would be his successor. He never could forgive me for having won as many votes as he, and so had to destroy me."

William Eaton, far more interested in his own complaints, fretted, but Zebulon listened intently. He'd never heard this side of the tale before, and in Burr's skillful hands, it was made to sound plausible.

Burr set his brandy snifter down and rubbed his earlobe, a mannerism he'd perfected while a trial lawyer. "I knew I had to find another route to the presidency, so I ran for the governor of New York State. The Sons of St. Tammany supported my candidacy, but here too I was opposed, and by none other than Alexander Hamilton, my *bête noire*. He called in every political debt ever owed him, enlisted the aid of the mighty Livingstons and the Clintons, spent a great deal of his wife's vast Schuyler fortune, all to stop me. Gentlemen, I have the dubious distinction of being the only person who ever brought Hamilton and Jefferson together!"

Eaton and Zebulon laughed uneasily, not quite understanding what Burr was driving at. Surely he hadn't asked them here to bemoan past history.

"It's clear that you had to challenge Hamilton to a duel," Zebulon said. "Any gentleman can see that."

Burr turned from the window; his face looked pinched, and his lips were white. "I could have forgiven Hamilton anything. After all, we had served in the Revolutionary War together, we'd argued many a court case together, and we both wanted what was best for the Union." He paused for a moment, the trace of a smile on his lips. "And we both had the reputation for being profligate, though our tastes in women were hardly the same. He preferred—how shall I say it, the lower classes, prostitutes, the scum of the earth. Only a mind sunk so low could have thought up the heinous lies he spread everywhere. How could I not kill him, after he accused me of having slept with my own daughter?"

In the stillness of the room, Burr stared at his hands, as though seeing the dueling pistol . . . His eyes turned inward to the field in Weehawken, New Jersey, where he'd aimed his pistol at Hamilton's heart, and fired. With that one shot, he'd snuffed out the life of one of the most brilliant minds in America, and forever forfeited his own chance to become President.

Zebulon touched the sleeve of Burr's velvet coat. "Are you all right?" he asked.

Burr passed his hand before his eyes and nodded. "I asked Jefferson for a post—ambassador, or perhaps the governorship of one of our western territories. Do you know what he had the temerity to tell me? That I'd lost the public's confidence, and he would do nothing to help me. Imagine! That from the coward who turned tail and ran from the fighting in our own Revolution. That from a man who seduced a fourteen-year-old mulatto slave and still sires bastard children with her."

Burr's shoulders slumped and suddenly he looked much older than his fifty years. He became aware of Zebulon's intense gaze, and with an effort of will, Burr straightened his shoulders and a beguiling smile lit his face.

"But we're not here to examine old wounds. No, this evening we look to the future. I've asked you here because I believe you to be men with interests and ideologies similar to mine. While our legislators waffled over the debacle of the Tripoli pirates, you took matters into your own hands, and rendered the nation a great service."

"Would that Jefferson felt the same," Eaton grumbled. "The

government refuses to reimburse me. For years, we paid millions in tribute and saw our seamen held for ransom. Ten thousand dollars seems a small enough price to pay for regaining our honor. Yet Congress balks. Where is justice in all this?"

Burr said cautiously, "There are times when strong men must make their own justice." Zebulon and Eaton shot each other a glance.

"Gentlemen, in the past months I've traveled extensively, ranging as far west as the Ohio Valley, and south to New Orleans, and I've encountered nothing but discontent for our policies. Our frontiersmen feel that this eastern government has no concept of their special needs. Everywhere, men talk of establishing a new nation, whose borders would be from the Appalachian Mountains to the Mississippi River."

Zebulon started, but Burr plunged ahead. "Captain George Morgan of Pittsburgh is with us. Blennerhassett has agreed to give us his island fortress in the Ohio River as a staging point. When we raft downriver and reach Tennessee, we'll be joined by Andrew Jackson. Yes, I see the surprise on your faces, but even Jackson is convinced that with a few hundred men, we could take the port of New Orleans."

Burr stopped for breath, and he blotted the sweat on his forehead with a handkerchief. Eaton worried a mole on his cheek. "Mr. Burr, in some quarters, what you've just said could be construed as treason."

"That's the argument the British leveled at us when we fought our own war for freedom," Burr said.

"But General Wilkenson is the commander of the American armies in the west," Eaton said. "Surely he'll defend his territory."

Burr trembled with excitement. "Gentlemen, General Wilkenson is with us! In fact, he first presented this plan to me. And it encompasses far more than I've already told you."

Eaton looked dubious. Burr reached into his pocket, took out a letter, and spread it on the table. Zebulon and Eaton leaned forward to read it. The letter was indeed from Wilkenson. He urged Burr to make haste to carry out their plan. He ended by saying he was ready to march the moment Burr was.

Zebulon sat back hard in his chair. What had seemed like

madness at the outset of the conversation suddenly looked like it could become a reality. George Morgan, Andrew Jackson, James Wilkenson—three powerful military men, with large followings among the tough frontiersmen. Couple that with Blennerhassett's enormous wealth, and Burr's charismatic leadership . . . it might just work. It could bring him position and wealth . . . and make him that much more attractive to Rebecca.

Burr said, "We won't stop with the secession of the western states, but move on to our main objective, Mexico! That country is ripe for the plucking. With five hundred good soldiers, that country will be ours in three weeks."

"How could such a thing be done?" Eaton asked, intrigued. "It's tantamount to declaring war on Spain."

"Exactly," Burr said. "I have assurances from the British ambassador, Merry, that a move to oust the Spaniards from Mexico and their holdings on this continent would be looked on with great favor by England. In fact, the British will give us naval support. Covered by their guns, we land at Vera Cruz, and within the month, sit on the throne in Mexico City. Gentlemen, I am talking about an empire, our own empire!"

Eaton stood up and shook his head slowly. "I have little stomach for this," he said. "True, the government hasn't yet reimbursed me, but—"

"For that, Jefferson should be shot and his body dumped in the Potomac," Burr exclaimed. "In fact," he said, his mind heady with the brandy, "with a few hundred good men, we could take Washington this very night!"

Eaton, made exceedingly uncomfortable by the conversation, told Burr he would think about his plan and then left.

Burr spent the remainder of the evening outlining his plan to Zebulon. As he listened, Zebulon grew convinced that the plan would succeed, if only by virtue of its very audacity.

"And what would be my role in all this?" he asked.

"I need somebody to galvanize my men into a fighting unit. When we're joined by Andrew Jackson and General Wilkenson, I personally guarantee that you shall have the highest rank after them."

Zebulon's head spun with the possibilities. But other pressing matters concerned him. "I've just returned from three years overseas. There's a young woman in Washington . . ."

"Ah yes, Rebecca Breech," Burr said. "It was my pleasure once to escort her home after a dinner at Ambassador Merry's. I've met many beautiful women in my life, but that one . . . There's more than beauty there; I sense a magnificent passion."

As always when somebody praised Rebecca, Zebulon felt an uneasy mixture of pride and jealousy, especially from a man of Burr's reputation. He said, "I mean to press my suit with her, so you understand why I cannot leave Washington."

"All right then," Burr said. "Stay in Washington, and be my eyes and ears here. Alert me if anything is suspected, or if the political climate changes. You can also help raise funds. There are many legislators from the western states who would be overjoyed if we succeeded."

"How much money do you need?"

"As much as possible. Money will buy mercenaries—and guns for our own frontiersmen," he added hastily. "Those who contribute five thousand dollars or more are assured of the governorship of a Mexican province."

"I can raise that," Zebulon said. "There's the back pay due me, and my property, and my brother's house." Zebulon knew that wasn't enough by far, but he was also counting on Mathias Breech's solid wealth; surely he'd give Rebecca a fine dowry.

"Well then, shall we seal this bargain with another drink?" Burr poured two more glasses of brandy.

Zebulon raised his glass. "Will you call yourself Emperor?" he asked, grinning.

"It has a nicer ring to it than President, don't you think? Who knows, perhaps Jefferson did me a favor after all. But, let's conquer the land first; the titles can come at our leisure." He tossed back his drink. "It will be absolutely imperative that I know the political situation as it changes in Washington, and in Europe. You will send your dispatches to me by special courier, and in code."

"And how will I contact this courier?" he asked.

"His name is Sisley Urquhart."

"The servant of the Connaughts?" Zebulon asked.

"The same."

"Coming here this evening, I saw Marianne Connaught leave your room. Is she involved in this?"

"It's no secret that the Connaughts are Tories. They think to use me and my plan to divert the United States and prevent her from going to war with Great Britain while she battles Napoleon. Well, it is we who shall use the Connaughts. They know a great many important Englishmen who can help us."

Burr clapped Zebulon on the shoulder. "Our plan is fool-proof, and the course laid. Within a year, we will have gained an empire! An empire man, can you understand that? I drink to your health, Governor Zebulon Brand."

Vitalized by his new prospects, Zebulon began to seriously court Rebecca. He sent Eli with an invitation for her to accompany him to a party at the Tayloes' Octagon House. When Rebecca heard that the levee was to be the social event of the autumn season, she accepted.

Thereafter, she and Zebulon were seen everywhere, at the concerts given in the President's Mansion; at the racetrack, where the entire Congress went, having recessed for the racing season; at the theater. The young nation was hungry for heroes; Zebulon was feted and lionized, and soon Rebecca began to take a degree of pride in him. But Zebulon's appetites were far too lusty to be satisfied with mere praise from a woman. If Rebecca couldn't give him his due, well, there were others. A slave would probably be the safest and he cast about for one.

The coastline of the Chesapeake Bay area was sparsely settled and too vast to be adequately patrolled by the authorities, and so here Zebulon set up a receiving station for the boatloads of refugees fleeing the terror in the West Indics.

The Haitian general, Jean Jacques Dessalines, had ordered death for every Frenchman on that island, and Zebulon was able to make a killing smuggling in the poor French planters who'd escaped. Along with such a cargo, Zebulon bought a slave girl, a young mulatto beauty named Tanzy. Until Rebecca made up her mind, he thought, Tanzy would help the idle hours pass quickly.

Tanzy had been the prize concubine of a white slave trader; he'd been so jealous that he forbade her to have contact with any other man. Then she became pregnant by her master, and gave birth to a child whose skin was jet black. In vain, she pleaded that her own father had been that color; her master accused her of sleeping with another slave, and dashed the baby's brains out. Twice Tanzy had tried to kill him, and finally he realized it made better sense to sell her than risk being murdered in his bed. Zebulon had bought her cheaply.

He took her to Alexandria and locked her in the slave quarters. When he saw Eli looking at her, he warned him, "If you so much as lay a hand on her, I'll make a capon out of you." Zebulon had an appointment with Rebecca, so the slave would have to wait.

After a titillating evening, Zebulon returned, planning to work out his passions on Tanzy. When he unlocked her door, she stepped from behind the door and tried to brain him with a stool. It caught him a glancing blow on the head, but he yanked her down to the floor. She kicked and scratched. He put his arm across her windpipe. When she gagged for breath, he released the pressure, and when she began to fight, applied it again.

"Do you get my meaning?" he asked with a grin, and systematically ripped off her clothes. Her skin, the color of maple syrup, was as sweet to his lips. She writhed under him and called out to all her gods.

"None of them are here in Washington," he said, laughing.

When he'd weakened her sufficiently, he entered her, and the warm mellow tightness of her body was a revelation. She regained her strength and tried to fight him off again, but the more she fought, the more inflamed he became. When he climaxed, he rolled off her with a groan. The moment her arms were free, she came at him again, her teeth struggling to reach his jugular. Zebulon's blow knocked her senseless.

Seeing her lying there, helpless, he became aroused again and took her once more, amazed at the wild abandon this nubile tawny girl created in his blood. Not since the youthful days of his affair with Elizabeth Connaught had he known this kind of sex, and he pounded out his desires until they were both raw with his excesses.

When she regained consciousness she whispered, "You'd best kill me, or I'll kill you."

He grinned at her, paying no attention to her at all. But what did make him anxious was Rebecca. The moment she agreed to marry him, he'd have to sell Tanzy. But meanwhile, some wanton dark side of himself had surfaced with this creature, a bestial streak that frightened even him. But it was something he could not deny.

After several more meetings with Zebulon and others in Washington, Aaron Burr departed for the west, there to contact Morgan in Pittsburgh, Blennerhassett in the Ohio territory, Jackson in Tennessee, and finally Wilkenson in New Orleans. Within that month, Zebulon sent his first message off to Burr, reporting how Jefferson had managed to avoid the call for war against Great Britain.

And then came the day when Zebulon felt that time and temptation had been mixed in proper proportions, and he asked Rebecca to marry him.

She wouldn't say yes, she wouldn't say no. But this time, Zebulon wouldn't settle for that.

"Whatever your fantasies about Jeremy, you know in your heart that he's never coming back. I propose that we wait one more month. If Jeremy doesn't return by then, you must accept me."

"And if I refuse those terms?" she asked.

"Rebecca, I love you. I've loved you since you were a young girl, I love you now. If you don't realize that by now, you never will. I'm getting on, well past thirty—time for me to settle down and make a mark for myself. Time for me to found a dynasty."

She laughed at that, but he remained serious. "Great things are in the wind. I can't divulge them now, but if they work out, and there's every reason to believe they will, I'll be a very powerful man in . . . in North America. And you would lead a life beyond your wildest expectations."

She could tell by his manner that he believed what he was saying, and that quickened her interest.

"If you refuse me, then I'll have to press my suit elsewhere," he said. "I need a woman by my side, a mother to my children, someone I can trust, count on, share my dreams. Rebecca, I need you."

At this sign of resolve in him, Rebecca felt a surge of desire. She tried to imagine what her days would be like without this constant suitor. She too yearned desperately for children; the longer she waited, the more dangerous it became. She lowered her eyes and murmured, "All right, one month from today."

With a cry, Zebulon embraced her. Then he toasted her with a glass of wine. "To you, my darling Rebecca, and to me, and to the House of Brand. May the Fates and the good Lord bless this House, and may it rise to its rightful place in the nation!"

Two weeks later, President Jefferson sent an ecstatic message to Congress and the nation. News had reached him that Captain Meriwether Lewis and his Corps of Discovery had returned to St. Louis, and they would be in Washington before the end of the year!

Chapter 33

MERIWETHER LEWIS, Jeremy Brand, and other men from the Corps of Discovery returned to Washington a few days before the end of 1806. In the celebration that followed, the citizens went wild. Everybody who could walk turned out to parade along Pennsylvania Avenue with the men. Bands played, children waved flags, and dogs barked after the marchers. Chief She-he-ke, his squaws, and their children accompanied the men, and the spectators gawked at the Indians' feathered headdresses, painted faces, and ceremonial buffalo robes. The fearful-looking savages were proof of the success of Lewis's harrowing mission.

The corps marched directly to the Executive Mansion, where they were to be honored by President Jefferson. He greeted them in the entrance hall along with select members of Congress and a sampling of the capital's society. Zebulon Brand was conspicuously absent. His exploits in the Mediterranean had dimmed beside this new excitement; Rebecca's attitude had also changed. Frustrated beyond reason, Zebulon found release for his anger in his slave, Tanzy.

As the men of the Corps of Discovery crowded into the entrance hall, Rebecca searched their faces. Her heart sank when she didn't see Jeremy. And then relief flooded through her when she finally recognized him. But he was so changed! His buckskin clothes had been patched and patched again, and were worn to a glistening patina. His features . . . more distinct, hardened into a toughness that she found at once threatening and attractive. His skin, tanned to a hue almost that of an Indian, and his hair sun-bleached to a color near white.

Other women besides Rebecca eyed Jeremy with interest,

notably Marianne Connaught. "He's attractive, don't you think?" she asked her great Aunt Victoria, standing beside her.

"He's a Brand," Victoria Connaught said.

Marianne gauged him; he'd always acted decently toward her. But her aunt was right, none of that could matter to her, not with her father dead, and her mother lying tormented in a mad corner of her world.

Rebecca fretted through the ceremonies. Jefferson spoke softly, but she did catch some fleeting snatches, including the statement that each man was to receive four hundred acres of land for his heroic service to the nation.

Finally Jefferson finished; the crowd milled for a bit, then dispersed. Those invited for dinner made their way to the State Dining Room. The moment Rebecca had waited for these three long years was upon her, for Jeremy came striding toward her. The urge to rush into his arms overwhelmed her, but he seemed so remote, so strange. Then she realized that something terrible had happened to him. It flickered in his eyes, sounded in the cadence of his step, transmitted itself through his touch as he took her arm and led her in to dinner.

During dinner, Jefferson questioned Lewis endlessly about the trip, and when Lewis grew weary, the President pressed Jeremy for additional details. "Captain Lewis tells me you've recorded the journey in sketches. I look forward to seeing them."

"Thank you, sir," Jeremy said. "I've a few revisions yet to make."

"I've asked a panel of scientists in Philadelphia to correlate all the information that the corps collected," President Jefferson said. "They tell me it may take as long as ten years to evaluate it all. Jeremy, I'm sure that your drawings will be invaluable."

"Sir, since the nation paid for the journey, I feel that these drawings are the property of all the people," Jeremy said. "They're at your disposal."

Rebecca couldn't get over the change in Jeremy. Something about the way he responded, the quiet confidence in his voice, clearly marked him as the equal of any man.

As dinner progressed, Rebecca noticed that Jeremy grew increasingly uncomfortable with his chair and with the cutlery. Once she caught him tearing apart the game hen with his hands, and part of her bridled at his loss of ordinary manners, while yet another part thrilled at the primitive force that had been unleashed in him.

She caught him looking at her with such intensity that she felt he was trying to read her heart. She wanted to tear off her clothes, rush at him, discover the same freedom he had gained on his own voyage of discovery. He had crossed the continent and returned, and she knew that until the day he died, the conquest of the country would set him apart from other men. At that moment, Rebecca decided she would give herself to him that night.

With that as the prospect, the dinner seemed interminable. When at last they were ready to leave Jeremy said to her, "I must talk to you. It would be simpler if we went to my house."

Her blood quickened, and she hardly felt the bitter chill of the frosty evening. A light snow began to fall, covering all the debris on the President's lawn, and making the grounds look serene.

"A new year, a new beginning," Rebecca said, pressing his arm. Her shoes were caked with snow and the hem of her gown soaking wet when they reached his cabin, but she didn't mind. Inside, he lit the candles, and started a fire in the hearth. A crackling warmth suffused the room, and the snowflakes drifting past the window made it wondrous. "I could stay here forever," she sighed.

They stared at the flames. He still seemed remote, and she took his hand and pressed it to her heart. "If you knew how much I missed you, how I prayed for your return . . ."

As gently as possible, he tried to tell her what happened. It took some time before she got the meaning, but when he said, "And then we were married," she jerked her hands away from him.

Then she shook her head and a short laugh escaped her. No, she hadn't heard him right, or something had happened to his mind on the trip; yes, that was it! But she would nurse him back to health.

"Rebecca, the last thing in the world I want is to hurt you, but you must know the truth. Otherwise, I'd only compound our misery."

She took deep breaths, fighting her rising hysteria. "But

how could you be married? How could such a thing happen in the wilderness?"

"Captain Lewis performed the ceremony, reading to us from the Bible."

"How could a heathen know what any of it meant?" she asked, struggling to keep her voice level. If she showed any emotion at all, she would have either fainted or killed him. "And is your . . . bride one of those swarthy women with Chief She-he-ke?"

He shook his head and his eyes clouded with pain. "White Doe died before we reached St. Louis."

Her heart sprang up.

He stared at the floor, his face expressionless. "Her delivery had been very difficult, and she weakened further and died."

Her hope evaporated as his words registered in her pounding temples. "And what of the baby?" she asked.

"She's with one of the Indian women, who's her wet nurse, though I'm told she'll be weaned very soon. I'm bringing her home tomorrow. Rebecca, she's a wonderful little girl, so good, never cries. I was hoping you'd like her. I'd want that more than anything in the world."

Rebecca scarcely heard him. What she'd yearned for so desperately for herself . . . Some savage had usurped that joy. "You must realize how much of a shock this is to me," she murmured. "It's something I'll have to think about." Then like a sleepwalker, she gathered her belongings and left.

Riding home in her carriage, Rebecca managed to control herself; it wouldn't do to go to pieces in front of the servants; they were all just waiting for some sign of weakness in their masters. But when she reached the safety of her room, she burst into tears. She cried from the depths of her being, she cried for love lost, and when she thought she had no more tears left, she cried for her betrayal.

"It's so unfair," she sobbed into her pillow. Had she acted as he, she would have been branded a whore, or worse. But because he was a man, the world looked the other way. Why, look at the President, with his mulatto mistress! But could she have ever taken a slave for a lover? Never! She wanted to scream her rage at this hypocritical duplicity and did, and it brought Letitia running. She hurled a vase at her and Letitia ran for Mathias Breech.

He lumbered up the steps and hurried to her. When he tried to comfort her, she beat her fists against his chest. He was a man, too, part of the breed that had so humiliated her. When she'd exhausted herself, Mathias put his arm around her shoulder. "Tell me," he said.

Mathias Breech had grown almost bald; two lone bushy locks of hair belled out just above his ears, bordering a pink scalp. His drinking and philandering had been slowed somewhat by a minor stroke, and fearful of dying before he saw her properly cared for, he'd become cautious. He left the heavy work to the slaves. Supplying stone for the President's Mansion, and then later for the public buildings, had made Breech moderately wealthy, and if the Lord called him, he knew Rebecca would be left well-off. But he wanted happiness for her as well.

When she told him what happened, his face turned so red that she feared he might have another fit. That roused her from her own miseries.

Gradually, Breech's heart stopped palpitating. "You have a number of choices," he grunted. "The most sensible is to forget the lout. He's never been worth your salt, but then you were never very sensible."

Rebecca managed a smile and Breech continued, "His Indian trollop is dead, so we don't have to worry about her."

"But the child," she said, on the verge of tears again.

"Suppose the child wasn't a problem either?" Breech said, then outlined a plan that brought a glimmer of hope to Rebecca's tear-swollen eyes. "Suppose Jeremy agreed to that, would you marry him then?" he asked.

She watched a petal fall from a rose in the bud vase. Then she exclaimed, "I'll never forgive him, never!"

"Ah, then it's clear you do love him," Mathias said softly. "Let me tell you something about men. They may graze in other pastures, but they'll always return to the place where the grass is sweeter."

"But suppose Jeremy won't do as I ask?"

"Of course he will! The man has mooned over you for more than ten years!"

Somewhat heartened by her father's advice, the following day Rebecca rode over to Jeremy's house. The snow had stopped, and now the midday sun sparkled off the fields of white. She found Jeremy cleaning out the accumulation of three years of dust and cobwebs. She caught sight of a small cradle. Rebecca moved toward it and couldn't help staring at the baby. The child's complexion was lighter than she'd expected, and she had the strangest almond-shaped blue eyes, even lighter than Jeremy's. For an impossible moment she thought of rearing the child as her own. Trembling, she bent to pick her up, but the baby, reacting to her distress, began to cry. Rebecca hastily put her back in the cradle.

The child is right, she thought. I'd never be able to forgive her being the product of another love; there'd never be any peace between us.

Eyes welling, she turned to Jeremy. "I love you," she whispered, and having uttered those impossible words, found the courage to go on. "Whatever you've done, that's past. My concern is the future. I want to spend my life with you, I want to bear your children." She began to cry again, the tears streaming down her cheeks.

He moved to comfort her, but she stayed him. "You must let me finish, or I'll never find the courage again, and then the rest of our lives will be tormented."

The violent attraction he'd always had for her surfaced again, strong and hard. White Doe's death had almost destroyed him, but now here was his old love, offering him life again.

"Jeremy, what I'm about to say may sound harsh, and it tears me apart to say it, but I must, for our happiness. This child, a product of a mixed love, a half-breed—can't you see how difficult it would be for her in Washington? Look at President Jefferson. He can't bring his own half-breed children to Washington, but must hide them at Monticello."

He started to interrupt, but she put her finger on his lips. "Let me finish, you must, it's our life I'm talking about. Every time we went anywhere, wherever we chose to live, this child would be a constant reminder of the past. And what would happen when we had our own children? Jeremy, she's an *Indian*. Can't you see? She must go back to her own people. You tell me that Chief She-he-ke is returning to the Mandan territory in the spring. Then let him take her with him. Jeremy, I beg you, do this for the child's sake, as well as our own."

Jeremy's jaw set. "I can't send her back into the wilderness."

Her disappointment was plain, but she hurried on with her alternate plan. "Well, then, I know of a wonderful orphanage in Philadelphia, run by Quakers."

She hurried on, explaining it all with her sweet reasonableness. Jeremy couldn't find the words to stop her. Somewhere in the back of his mind, he'd hoped that she might embrace Circumstance . . . rear her as part of their own family. And he remembered White Doe's last words.

Not hearing any objections from him, Rebecca became convinced that she'd won the day. "Oh, darling, you can't imagine how happy we're going to be. All the love I've stored within me, waiting for you—I can't tell you." She threw her arms around him, but he moved away from her.

"Rebecca, you must listen to me before you say another word. This child is part of me, perhaps the best part. How can you ask me to deny my own flesh and blood? Whatever sins I've committed, she's innocent in all this, and I won't make her suffer."

Rebecca's eyes opened wide. She started to speak, but gagged and went into a violent fit of coughing. When he tried to help her, she pushed him away, and stumbled out into the snow. She fell into a bank, and the icy-burning sensation was akin to the pain in her breast.

She mounted her horse, whipped him fiercely, and galloped through the drifts, racing she knew not where, but away from this shame that coursed through her body. For the sake of a half-breed bastard, he'd denied her.

She didn't return home until hours later. Her father and the servants were beside themselves when they saw her, white-faced, her clothes bedraggled.

"You'll catch your death!" Mathias Breech scolded her.

"No, not mine," she whispered, "not mine."

For the next several days, Rebecca rode to within sight of Jeremy's cabin; from a vantage point behind a copse of trees, she stood watching, waiting. Neither cold nor dampness deterred her, for she burned with the fires of revenge. Several days later, she saw Jeremy leave the house. He was taking the child to James Hoban, who already had three children of his own and another on the way.

She waited until Jeremy had ridden out of sight, then approached the house. She had no idea what she was going to do, but she had to do something to appease her rage.

She tried the door, found it unlatched, and stepped inside. The room looked neat and spare again. The cradle lay in the corner, and she kicked it as she went around the room, searching for something, anything, on which to vent her spleen. She would have torn his clothes to shreds, but he only owned the buckskin garments on his back. The embers of a fire glowed in the screened hearth, scenting the house with a fresh pine smell. Her eyes narrowed. If she could have set fire to the cabin and gotten away with it . . . but since Washington was a tinderbox of wooden houses, such an action might well land her in jail.

She rummaged through an old wooden chest, only some worn linen, then searched the sideboard; pewter utensils, a few wooden plates he'd carved. Nothing, she could find nothing of real value. And then she saw his backpack. Fingers trembling, she untied the securing laces and took out half a dozen sketchbooks, the very books she'd given him before he'd embarked on the journey. She riffled through the pages, and fantastic drawings assaulted her eyes, of birds and strange beasts unknown to her, of perilous mountains, rushing rivers, and thundering cataracts. Strange faces peered at her, painted with frightening designs, some with rings through their noses, others with shaven heads. And then she saw the drawings of a young Indian girl; many of the sketches were laughing, others were reflective, and with the secret knowledge of her sex, she knew that this was the tramp who'd borne him the bastard.

She bolted the door from the inside so that she wouldn't be interrupted, then went to the fireplace and worked the bellows, fanning the embers into a flame. She added more wood until the fire was blazing.

"He can't do this to me," she repeated in bitter litany as she stared at the roaring fire, the sketchbooks clutched in her hands.

When Jeremy returned home about an hour later he found Rebecca sitting in front of the fire. At first he thought she'd had a change of heart and had come to see the baby, but then he saw his sketchbooks and guessed her intent.

She glared at him, her eyes blazing with reflected firelight. "I would have burned them if I could . . . but I couldn't be as cruel as you."

She stood up and swept past him, the pain in her eyes so visible that he didn't try to stop her. The thought that he'd caused her such suffering—somebody he'd once loved—was crushing.

Rebecca went straight to Zebulon's house in Alexandria. "Where is Mr. Brand?" she asked Eli.

Eli looked distracted and then said, "Why, I don't know . . . uh, maybe's in the barn."

"Find him and tell him I'm here."

"Ma'am, he said not to be disturbed."

She stamped her foot on the broad-planked hardwood floor. "Did you hear me? Get him, or I'll go myself."

Eli trotted off to the slave quarters and hesitantly knocked on the door of a cabin. "Mr. Brand, Mr. Brand."

"Eli, I'll have your hide for this!" a muffled voice called.

"It's Miss Breech. If you don't come out, she'll be coming to get you herself."

Eli heard a round of curses and moments later Zebulon came out of the shack buttoning his trousers. Through the half-open door, Eli caught sight of Tanzy, her hands tied to the bedposts.

"Untie her," Zebulon said. "And not a word to anybody, or I'll hang you."

Zebulon strode off. Eli went into the cabin and untied Tanzy. When her hands were free she grasped the coverlet and hid her nakedness. Then she started to weep softly.

"It's all right," Eli murmured. "It's not your fault. We're theirs to use as they want. But it won't always be this way, I swear." He held her until she stopped sobbing, then helped her dress.

Zebulon found Rebecca in the drawing room. When he grasped her hand, he thought she was burning with fever. Her eyes also looked strangely unfocused, and feverish.

"Yes," she said.

With a cry of joy, he lifted her in the air.

"But it must be today, right now," she said breathlessly. "I won't be denied another moment of happiness."

"All right, we'll find a minister somewhere—"

She shook her head. "Oh, he'll only want us to delay it—church service, family, all that nonsense. Look, I know the Supreme Court is in session in the Capitol. Chief Justice Marshall is an acquaintance. I know he'll do this for me."

Zebulon threw on his greatcoat, took along the wedding ring that had belonged to his mother, and off they went to the Capitol. They found the justices in their quarters in the basement, a cold room with sweat-beaded walls and a window below ground level. Their business done for the day, the men had shucked off their black robes, and were relaxing with a bottle of Madeira.

"Ah, Rebecca, come in," Marshall said, and offered them a glass of wine. "On wet days it gets so damp down here that we must warm the innards with the blood of the grape. Have you heard the news from the west?" he asked.

Zebulon shook his head.

"They say Aaron Burr is planning an insurrection against this country. Colonel Morgan of Pittsburgh, reported to be one of Burr's co-conspirators, wrote to President Jefferson and confessed all."

Zebulon's half-smile remained frozen on his face. His mind raced, trying to determine how serious this might be, and whether or not he could be implicated. He started to question Marshall further, but Rebecca interrupted him. Ordinarily, she would have been fascinated by this inside information, but at the moment she had more pressing things on her mind.

She said to Marshall, "Zebulon and I have come here to ask a great favor of you. We want to be married, right here, right now, and by you."

Taken by surprise, Marshall said, "But this is highly irregular. No wedding party? No guests? No one to give the bride away?"

"Could there be a more illustrious wedding party than one made up of the justices of the Supreme Court?" she asked, lavishing a smile on each of them in turn. In the back of her mind she knew she must do this right now, this very minute, or else she'd lose her nerve. "True, we might have gone to our minister," she went on, "but what better way to reinforce the doctrine of separation of church and state than by having a civil ceremony, and performed by you?"

The justices all laughed at that. Rebecca linked her arm

through Marshall's. "Gentlemen, I beseech you, as defenders of the weaker sex, please say you'll do me this honor."

"By the Almighty, why not?" Marshall exclaimed, and the other justices concurred, two of them agreeing to act as witnesses. "Considering the caliber of the officiating judges, I'd say that this marriage will last for the ages," Marshall said.

She heard the words ". . . love, honor, and obey . . . till death do us part . . ." and they echoed down and down through the windswept void of her being. And then it was done.

Amid thc general laughter and the congratulations, all the justices demanded the right to kiss the bride. Then Rebecca and Zebulon walked out of the basement chambers, man and wife.

Zebulon was still overwhelmed by this sudden turn—something must have happened between her and Jeremy—but he knew better than to question her. She was his at last!

They went for an impromptu wedding dinner at Tunnecliff's Tavern, and Rebecca sent a stablehand to fetch her father. Mathias arrived within the hour, shocked and out of sorts. He found the newlyweds in a large booth, and being expansive in the libation of the wine.

"It's unseemly, Rebecca," Mathias grumbled as he bulled his way into their booth. "You're my only child. I had counted on a big wedding. Now what will people say?"

She filled his wineglass to the brim. "Father, you may give your party whenever you like, but tonight, no recriminations, no long faces, only happiness for all of us." Her voice dropped to a murmur, "Oh, father, *please*."

He compressed his lips, then impulsively leaned over and hugged her. His eyes filled with tears as he said, "You're my darling, and your well-being is all I've ever wanted." Then he turned to Zebulon, "See you make her happy, or you'll have me to answer to!"

"Yes, Poppa," Zebulon said dutifully, and they bellowed with laughter.

When the other patrons learned that the couple had just been married, the wine flowed, the fiddles struck up, and the entire inn joined in the rollicking celebration. Rebecca danced longer, laughed harder than anybody else, and everyone remarked that she'd never looked more radiant.

That night, Zebulon waited for Rebecca to come to bed.

She entered the darkened room, holding a candle before her. She'd put on a white cotton eyelit shift, and her hair hung loose around her shoulders. Watching her in the halo of flickering light, Zebulon thought he'd never seen anybody more beautiful in his life.

He loved her as he'd never loved another, giving his heart and soul to this woman he'd sought for so many years. He discovered a gentleness in himself that not even he knew had existed.

Rebecca bore it all dutifully, fulfilling her marital obligations to the letter.

In the dark hours, after Zebulon had finally spent himself and lay asleep, she gazed out the window at the moonlit night. She had chosen her course, and she would live with it. She would give him children, and she would be the best mother and wife in the territory.

But she could never love him. That corner of her heart she'd reserved for Jeremy, and with that no longer a possibility, she ruled love out of her life.

"It's not so terrible," she whispered to the night-filled well of the room. "There are other things that can compensate, and I shall have them all."

And so on her wedding night, Rebecca Breech Brand determined that she would become the grandest woman in all Washington, and to that end she would direct all her energies. For her, Jeremy was dead. And as she stared out the window, the waning moon dissolved in her welling eyes.

Chapter 34

ZEBULON AND Mathias Breech soon revitalized their shipping ventures. On the wharf at Georgetown, a number of slaves Zebulon had brought in from the West Indies were put on the auction block. All the states north of Maryland had already abolished slavery, though New York and New Jersey were phasing it out gradually. But the South still clung to the system. The law prohibited the importation of new slaves, but cheap labor was still vital to the plantation owners. So Zebulon passed around a few small bribes and the authorities judged that these slaves were native-born, and therefore able to be sold.

The damp March winds swept in off the river, and the slaves huddled under their wraps. Jeremy had come to the auction, hoping to find somebody who could take care of Circumstance. He saw Zebulon for the first time since his return, and shook his hand warmly. "I hear you've done yourself proud in the Tripoli Wars. Congratulations. And, of course, on your marriage."

"Thank you," Zebulon said with a gracious smile. "Well, Jeremy, we both pursued her, but the best man won."

"I wish you both nothing but joy," he said. "And I hope that we can all—"

"Excuse me," Zebulon interrupted, "but the auction's about to begin." Motioning to Eli, who was assisting him, Zebulon left.

Jeremy stared after his brother. He'd clearly been uncomfortable. "But then, so was I," he murmured aloud. The marriage had saddened him in a way he hadn't expected, and there were times when he still experienced twinges of envy. Lord, he thought, is there never to be any peace between the three of us?

Then a beautiful dark-haired girl wrapped in a maroon cloak spoke to him, "Hello. We met at the President's reception for you and Meriwether Lewis. I'm Marianne Connaught."

"But of course," he exclaimed. He was quite taken with her fragile, wide-eyed looks. At eighteen, she'd grown from a nondescript, timid adolescent to a young woman of subtle beauty. Scrambling for something to say, Jeremy blurted, "I trust your mother is well," and immediately regretted his gaffe.

"No better or worse," Marianne said softly. "Her fingers never stop with her needlepoint, and though her hair grows grayer, her face remains unlined, like a child's."

He touched her arm impulsively. "I'm truly sorry."

"It's no matter," she said with a tiny shrug. "It's something we've learned to bear." She'd said it matter-of-factly, but her trembling hands belied her calm, for Marianne felt her mother's madness to the core of her being.

"Ah, here come the slaves," she said. "I'm hoping to find a new maid."

Zebulon herded the colored people onto the block; he went down the line one by one, pointing out strong teeth, sturdy shoulders, child-bearing hips. The bidding was sluggish, the only highlight coming when Dolley Madison bought a slave girl named Sukie. Dolley announced to the crowd that Sukie would be freed after five years' service.

Then Zebulon came to his prize. "We have before us a rare beauty, a woman with fire in all parts of her body," he said, winking at the men. With a deft motion, he flicked off the blanket covering Tanzy, exposing her nakedness. A murmur rippled through the crowd as they stared at the satiny skin, the perfectly shaped long limbs, the flat stomach and small pointed breasts.

Zebulon played his riding crop over her body. "For this one, I don't have to make pretty speeches; you all have eyes. But I assure you, the merchandise is even better than it looks."

The men laughed appreciatively. Shackled as she was, Tanzy couldn't protest, but her eyes smoldered with a hatred that could have consumed everybody at the auction. Eli cringed at the indignity done to Tanzy. He prayed she would be bought by a decent master. In the months Zebulon had owned her, Eli had spent sleepless nights thinking of her.

The bidding began and quickly ran high. Jeremy had watched Tanzy with interest. Fortunately, he had two and a half years' back pay, and was richer than he'd ever been in his life. The bidding soon reached three hundred dollars. Zebulon fumed; in ordinary times, Tanzy would have brought between seven and nine hundred dollars. But what with the British and French blockades and Jefferson's embargoes on both those nations, the country was in the grip of a severe depression.

Jeremy called out, "Three hundred and twenty-five!"

"Do I hear more?" Zebulon shouted. But everybody else had dropped out. If he could have denied Jeremy the sale he would have, but the law demanded otherwise.

Jeremy paid Zebulon, then threw the cloak back over Tanzy. Eli managed to whisper to her as they passed, "This is a good man, don't do anything foolish."

Jeremy took her back to his cabin. When he closed the door, he saw her glance about the room.

"You have nothing to fear," he said. "I didn't buy you for my own pleasure, but to take care of my child." He picked up Circumstance; she looked at him sleepily, then dozed off again. He smiled at Tanzy. "I couldn't really afford you; it took most of the money I had. But there was something about your defiant look that made me remember what happened to me many years ago."

Then he told her about James Hoban and his gift. "Now it's time for me to pass that gift along. If you stay with me for the time it would have taken you to earn as much money—let's see, about five years—then you can have your freedom."

Tanzy said nothing, waiting for the trick. But Jeremy wrote out a Bill of Freedom and handed it to her. "When the time's up, we'll take it to the Hall of Records and register it."

Tanzy stared at the paper in her hand. Then Circumstance stirred in her crib. Jeremy picked her up and brought her to Tanzy. She gazed at the babe, torn with the memories of her own child. She reached out and took Circumstance from Jeremy, and in the same motion, gave her heart to the little girl.

With the approval of Congress, President Jefferson appointed Meriwether Lewis governor of the Missouri Territory. When he saw Meriwether off on his journey, Jeremy had serious misgivings about his friend. Ever since their return, he'd been in an agitated state. "What's troubling you?" Jeremy asked.

Meriwether shrugged. "With the dream gained, and only the commonplaces of the world surrounding us, there's not much to look forward to."

Jeremy reflected on that and realized how lucky he was to have Circumstance, for though his own moods were still troubled, the child was a lifeline for him.

With Tanzy to care for Circumstance, the days took on a less harried rhythm for Jeremy and he decided he would enroll part-time in the college in Georgetown. He used the last of his mustering-out pay for the first semester's tuition. He was older than most students and therefore felt uncomfortable at first, but he was also far more motivated, and with all that he already knew, advanced rapidly in his studies. It kept him from surrendering to his abject loneliness.

Jeremy also spoke to President Jefferson and received permission to resume working on the President's House. His small salary just enabled him to squeak by. The mansion was still in a constant state of building and repair. In Benjamin Latrobe, Jefferson had found an architect in tune with his own philosophic bent, and the two men labored long and lovingly on plans for the north and south porticos. They were also adding two long low colonnaded structures on either side of the mansion to house servants, staff, stables, woodshed, icehouse, and privies.

It was no secret that Jefferson disliked the mansion. He thought it pretentious and far too large to be the dwelling of a man elected by the people. He would have preferred a gem the size of Monticello, or the original plan he'd submitted for the mansion under the pseudonym A-Z. However, he was stuck with the house, so he tried to shape it to his own philosophic concepts, but he met with fierce resistance from Congress.

"The people demand grandeur," they insisted. "This is America's Palace!"

One day, Jeremy was replacing some warped floorboards in the President's bedroom when Jefferson came in. "My entire tenure in this place has been a splendid misery," he said.

Jeremy laughed, but he personally had never felt that way.

Working here again was like returning to an old friend; the very walls seemed to welcome him. Here he felt safe, here he felt part of life again. And in truth, engrossed as he was with his studies and with his labors in the mansion, he gradually eased himself from his bitter mood. Occasionally, he even found himself laughing at an antic of Circumstance's, or at some piece of tomfoolery going on at the mansion.

During the day, gawking sightseers wandered in and out, stealing so many souvenirs that finally Jefferson ordered all the good things locked away for safekeeping. Jeremy might be working to repair a leak in the attic, only to see a tourist's tall beaver hat poke its way up the staircase.

Jefferson had sworn that he'd be available to anybody at any time, and had kept his promise. Some officials, including former President John Adams, commented sourly, "Jefferson's entire term of office is turning into one long levee."

There was never enough money for repairs; Congress simply refused to appropriate the funds. As usual, congressional rhetoric dealt in idiocies and hyperbole. But now Jeremy detected something else. Drastic changes were frowned on because the house was slowly becoming a symbol to the American people. True, it was the President's House, but it was also the second home of every man, woman, and child in the United States.

But some vital reconstruction had to be done if the mansion was to survive. Latrobe had discovered that because of the tremendous weight of the slate roof, the walls were being pushed out and they would soon topple. Jeremy joined the work gang replacing the slate roof with one made of sheet iron.

The city had also changed dramatically, and during the first months of his return, Jeremy tried to assimilate it all. Even the spelling of the river was different—now Potomac, simplified from the original Indian. Felled trees gave the land a naked look, and Washington seemed to be growing and declining at the same time. The main streets and grand avenues were dotted with fine Federal-style homes, but in the Hamburg district, where the German immigrants lived, and around the periphery of the President's House, workmen and their families still lived in squalor.

Most of Washington's social functions were held before nightfall. Oil lamps had been erected outside of a few government buildings, but otherwise the streets were dark. Anybody roaming around at night was apt to be a prostitute, or somebody in search of one. Jeremy was amazed at the flourishing business that had grown up in this oldest profession. Legislators were away from home for long periods of time, and the demands of government made relaxing at night an absolute necessity, so wine, women, and song had become an integral part of the city's life.

Appropriations for government buildings remained capricious. Congress funded less for government buildings per year than they did for the President's salary, which was still fixed at $25,000. Yet the principal employer was now the government, and the main work, construction.

"Captain Tingey told me that workers at the Navy Yard are being paid a dollar eighty-one a day," Jeremy told Tanzy. "It's astounding!"

She shrugged; money never had much meaning for her. She planted her own vegetable garden, sewed her own clothes, gathered eggs from the chickens they kept. With this gentle, generous man and the bewitching baby, Tanzy was slowly forgetting her own heartache. She tried to quash any gossip about her and Jeremy. Any slave woman was considered fair game for her master, and with her youth and beauty, everybody believed she served Jeremy in ways other than the kitchen. Yet it wasn't so; in the months she'd been with him, never once had he made a demand.

She didn't know what she would have done if he had. The desires of her own youth burned within her; she still yearned for the arms of a man—but of a man she could love. Eli . . . he had a kind manner, but he was Zebulon's slave. And so Tanzy buried all her love in Circumstance.

The child was quick, intelligent, spoke at an early age, never gave her any trouble. There was almost something unnatural about it, and Tanzy, raised on the voodoo and witchcraft of the West Indies, believed that the child was . . . different. For example, she'd never seen her cry—no, that wasn't true; one night a wolf had been cornered near the President's grounds, and its fearful baying and the quick gunshots made Circumstance burst into tears.

Whenever Jeremy had a day off, he took Circumstance with

him. Carrying the child on his back the way Sacajawea had carried Pomp, he walked one day to the Capitol Building to see the progress. A derelict lurched toward Jeremy as he strode along, the man so besotted with liquor that he could barely stand. He extended his hand, begging for a coin. Ravaged though his face was, Jeremy recognized Blutkopf, the old foreman. He handed him a coin and quickly turned away. Blutkopf was a man who'd hated everybody, Jeremy thought, and now his own hate had consumed him. It was a lesson to be learned.

Diverse people in strange dress strolled along Pennsylvania Avenue, and Jeremy stared at them. With an increasing number of foreign nations sending their representatives to Washington, the city had become noticeably polyglot. He laughed aloud, remembering how the new Turkish minister had requested President Jefferson to supply him with a number of young ladies for his harem. The request was politely refused.

At the Capitol, the air sounded with building noises. Carts loaded with timber and stone rumbled along the roadway, some drawn by oxen, others pulled by slaves. Particles of marble and sawdust filled the air, winches creaked, forges roared, hammers clanged. Sightseers watched the construction, and among them, Jeremy spied Marianne Connaught and her aunt, Victoria. He edged his way closer. Marianne smiled with delight when she recognized him, but Victoria's glance was intended to freeze him. But he refused to be put off.

"Look up there," Marianne said. Stonecutters led by Giuseppe Franzoni and Giovanni Andrei stood on the high scaffolding carving the corn-tassel capitals that had been designed by Latrobe. "Imagine, President Jefferson imported these sculptors all the way from Leghorn," Marianne said. "He says he wants to make Washington every bit as beautiful as Versailles."

"Well, he certainly has a long way to go," Victoria said. "This place will never be anything but the rankest wilderness."

But Jeremy thought otherwise and his blood surged with the progress he saw. He said to Marianne, "Why, in five years, you won't recognize this place; in ten, a whole new city will be here, and in twenty, I see it completed. A new capital for a new nation."

Victoria Connaught flicked her hand in a gesture of dismissal. Then she caught sight of something and lifted her lorgnette.

A troop of Mandan Indians approached, the same people that Meriwether Lewis had brought back to Washington. Jeremy almost didn't recognize them, for their simple, distinctive dress had given way to grander things.

"A decided improvement," Victoria Connaught said. "You see, the good ladies of Washington decided that it was our duty as God-fearing Christians to civilize these savages."

The braves sported frock coats that reached below their knees, trousers, and tall hats, while the squaws wore voluminous bright-colored cambric skirts and hobbled around in high heels.

Victoria hid her laughter behind her fan. "Oh dear, I'm afraid we shall never be able to make silk purses out of them."

Jeremy felt his ears burn and shifted Circumstance on his back. "In their own territory, their clothes suit their lives perfectly."

Victoria raised her eyebrows. "Oh, Marianne, have you heard the latest sport among the young blades in town? Why, they will buy an Indian all the liquor he wants, just to see how quickly he will turn himself into a fool."

"Another good service done by God-fearing Christians?" Jeremy asked evenly.

Victoria lifted her gown and swept up the steps of the Capitol. Much to her consternation, and Marianne's delight, Jeremy fell into step with them. They entered the lobby of the Hall of Representatives, and Jeremy gazed at it in wonder; much of it had been completed during his absence.

"Surely this is the grandest interior in all America," he exclaimed.

"But nothing compared to the great palaces in Europe," Victoria said.

Jeremy's admiration for the architecture was soon blunted by the carryings-on in the lobby. The place had become the resort of youth and fashion for Washingtonians. Couples stood around the open fire in the lobby, since the vast interior space tended to be chilly.

"I see the young men here are imitating the court of France," Marianne said. The men were wearing their hair in curled lovelocks with bangs in front. "Just like Napoleon's."

"Though that little beast does it to hide his baldness," Victoria said.

The ladies paraded by in their most splendid Empire gowns, all designed to show the greatest expanse of their bosoms. Since ladies were permitted on the floor of the House of Representatives, the gallant congressmen vied with each other to give them their seats.

"It seems more like a ballroom than a legislature," Jeremy said, disgust in his voice.

The session was in a momentary recess, and various congressmen flirted outrageously with the Washington beauties.

Victoria Connaught's fan worked the air furiously. "One would never see anything like this in the English parliament. There is some devious quality in an *elected* politician that renders him vulnerable to all the vagaries of the human condition. Now come along, Marianne, we must find some seats. I understand that there's to be an announcement of some momentous news from the west."

"Forgive me, Aunt Victoria, but I think I'll go outside until they resume the session," Marianne said.

Victoria was about to object strenuously, but the expression on her niece's face clearly signaled that she was up to something.

"I shan't be long," Marianne said.

Jeremy and Marianne walked outside and looked at the vista from Capitol Hill. "Seeing you here has made this day more pleasant than I can tell you," he said quietly.

She dropped her gaze, and then forgetting her other motives, said, "And I'm happy to see you again too."

Locked in their embarrassment, they stood in silence for a bit. Then Marianne said, "Your daughter is adorable. I don't think I've ever seen eyes as blue." Then she looked at him earnestly. "I hope you'll forgive my aunt for what she said about . . . Indians."

"Of course. What really upset me was I suddenly saw how difficult Circumstance's life will be."

Marianne gave an abject nod, then said brightly, "Well, in that case, we shall all have to help her."

Jeremy looked at her and a smile broke through his mood.

"I can see that you have a sympathetic heart." He paused for a moment, then said, "Marianne, may I call on you?"

"I'd like nothing better," Marianne said, reaching for his arm. "But for the moment, it can't be. With my mother . . . ill, I live as a ward of my aunt's, and she would refuse. But Washington is not so large that we won't see each other at this function or that. Now I must go to her, or she'll become suspicious."

Jeremy pressed her hand, so fine and soft. Then she disappeared back into the House of Representatives. He stood for a long time, trying to sort out his feelings about this girl, wondering if he was being unfaithful to White Doe's memory, wondering too about Rebecca.

Then a great hubbub came from the chamber and everybody seemed to be rushing about at once. He saw Samuel Smith, the publisher of the *National Intelligencer*, leap onto his horse and gallop away toward the newspaper's offices. And then Marianne Connaught came out, looking pale and stricken.

Jeremy rushed to her. "What is it, what's happened?"

Marianne fought to regain her composure. "Congress just received word that Aaron Burr was arrested near New Orleans."

"Burr? But why?"

"President Jefferson has just had him indicted for treason," she whispered, the word catching in her throat.

"Treason?" he exclaimed, confused. "What did he do?"

"One of the charges is that he tried to foment a war with Mexico. And another is that he tried to split the United States in two, form a separate country reaching from the Appalachian Mountains to the Mississippi River. This is terrible news. I must go."

She stumbled as she started down the steps of the Capitol, and he caught her arm and steadied her. "I don't understand," he said. "What does Burr and a charge of treason have to do with you?"

"Well, you see, he's a great friend of the family's and—" She started to say more, thought better of it, then hurried away, leaving Jeremy to ponder the news, and her distress.

Chapter 35

THE STAGECOACH sped along the dirt road from Washington to Richmond, Virginia. Every twenty-five miles the driver pulled into a way station, the horses were changed, and they were on their way again.

Rebecca held a scented handkerchief to her nose; the motion of the galloping horses and swaying coach had nauseated her. She hadn't wanted to make this journey, but to her shock, Zebulon had been subpoenaed by the Federal government in its trial against Aaron Burr.

She adjusted the bodice of her Empire gown; the high waist suited her, for it hid her pregnancy. Not even Zebulon had guessed, though he'd commented once or twice on her increasing irritability. Nor did she plan on telling him; the longer he didn't know, the better. She knew about his interlude with Tanzy; Washington was too small a town to keep such a secret. Even though he'd sold Tanzy, Rebecca didn't want to give him any excuse to stray from home.

Continuing the argument they'd had throughout the journey, Rebecca said, "If Burr is innocent as he claims, then why did he try to escape?"

"What other choice did he have?" Zebulon snapped. His face looked drawn, and dark circles lined his eyes. "General Wilkenson sent several of his soldiers to kill him, because if he'd reached Washington alive he would have exposed Wilkenson's complicity."

"So Burr says," she said. "With his plot ruined, of course he sees assassins in every corner. But it's Burr who's the killer; let's not forget Alexander Hamilton."

"How can anyone believe Burr planned to overthrow the government when on the day he was arrested, he had only forty-seven men with him?" he exclaimed.

"He would have had more if he'd had his way," she retorted. "That there were so few is a statement of the good sense of our frontiersmen. By all reports, he was fleeing like a common criminal when he was apprehended near Pensacola, and had to be brought to Richmond under guard. You call that the behavior of an innocent man?"

"Suppose the President of the United States had sworn to see you destroyed, had spent his own money gathering evidence against you, evidence you knew to be false. What would you do?"

"Are you telling me that the entire world is out of step, except Burr?" she demanded. "Those who believe him innocent are fools."

Zebulon squared his shoulders irritably. Lord, how he wished she'd shut up. He hadn't yet told her the full implications. "Burr's case will hinge on the testimony of two people, General Wilkenson and William Eaton."

"Eaton?" she repeated, surprised. "The man you served under in Tripoli? Why him?"

Zebulon slammed the side of the coach with his fist. "I don't know why. I only know that Burr's attorneys told me the prosecution planned to call Eaton." He hesitated for a moment, then blurted, "If Burr is convicted, then we're out five thousand dollars."

She snapped her head toward him. "Why?"

"Because I loaned him the money. In return, he promised I would have a position high in the Mexican government."

"You fool! Even if the man was sincere, he's the type who'll always lose at the last throw." Then the ramifications swept over her and she paled. "There's more than money at stake, isn't there? If Burr is convicted of treason . . ."

Zebulon nodded. "We face the distinct possibility that I could be indicted also."

She sat back hard against the leather seat. He glanced at her, but not a word of comfort, not a gesture of support was forthcoming. And why had he done this if not for her? They traveled the rest of the way in silence, each locked in his own misery, Zebulon's mind working to figure all the angles, Rebecca thinking that the father of her child might soon be branded a criminal.

Zebulon had arranged for accommodations at the Golden Eagle Tavern in Richmond, where Burr also was staying. An enormous eagle with a wingspread of eight feet hung over the entrance; the sculpture had been designed and executed by a young artist, Thomas Sully. Rebecca found the accommodations barely adequate; the innkeepers and servants were overworked. Richmond thronged with hundreds of people who'd journeyed for days and weeks to attend the trial. Exhausted from the journey, Rebecca insisted on a light supper in their room; she watched as Zebulon downed a prodigious amount of Madeira.

"Did you see the crowds?" she asked. "Clearly this has become more than a trial for treason."

"We're about to witness a fight to the death between Jefferson on one side, and Burr and Chief Justice Marshall on the other, a battle between the Presidency and the Supreme Court."

"And you were stupid enough to get caught in the middle."

He shrugged off her barb. "Jefferson was very clever in having Burr tried in Virginia, his own state. Anywhere else and Burr would have gone free."

"How did the President manage that?"

"Since the western lands where Burr supposedly hatched his plot are considered part of the Virginia Territory, Jefferson's legal minions had an easy enough time. But Jefferson reckoned without his esteemed cousin, Chief Justice Marshall. Not only is he on the Supreme Court, but he's also a circuit judge of Virginia, and in that capacity is presiding over this trial! Jefferson was nearly apoplectic when he discovered that Marshall had outfoxed him.

"This is Jefferson's chance to destroy the Supreme Court," Zebulon said. "If Marshall shows the slightest partiality toward Burr, if he circumvents the law just *once,* then Jefferson will move to have Marshall impeached, and he'll be able to shape the Supreme Court to his own design."

Rebecca reflected on that. "It can't be so important to Jefferson; after all, he'll leave office shortly."

"Ah, yes, but he's already chosen his successors—all part of the Virginia Dynasty. First little Jemmy Madison, and after him, James Monroe. Think of their power if their hands aren't tied by the Supreme Court. For all his talk about States' Rights, Jefferson's acted more like a monarch than Adams ever did. When he wanted to buy the Louisiana Territory, he bent the Constitution to his will. Would Adams have done that?"

"Of course not," Rebecca said. "Adams would have wheedled and dawdled, sought legal precedent, and in the end we wouldn't own Louisiana. Of the two courses of action, which would you prefer?"

He said nothing, but flung himself on the bed, his eyes merry with Madeira. "There are times when you infuriate me. You're lucky that I love you so. A wife should support her husband in all things."

"Except stupidity," she said.

"We can settle all our arguments on this battlefield," he said, patting the bed. He pulled her close to him and made love to her, his mouth roving over her neck and breasts. He was an expert in the art of making love, and there were times when he moved her. But she could never forget that he considered it a battlefield, and on a battlefield there was always a victor, always a loser.

She felt him heavy on her abdomen and shifted to protect the child, and he, thinking her aroused, rose and plunged harder, faster, until he buried his mouth against her throat to throttle his hoarse cry. They lay panting for a long time, and then she realized he'd fallen asleep.

She ran her hands over her slightly swelling stomach, feeling a flush of pride about her secret, that she had been fertile enough to conceive, to bring new life, new hope into the world. I wonder if it will be a boy or a girl? she thought, and then realized that she didn't care. She knew only that this child would have all the advantages she'd never had. It made her life worth living; it made Zebulon worth bearing, and there were times when it even made her forget Jeremy.

The grand jury was meeting in the State Capitol, a building designed by Jefferson himself, and it seemed to Zebulon that he and Burr were in the very clutches of the President. Zebulon shooed away some chickens and climbed the steps to the Chamber of Delegates, a room with rows of uncomfortable pews, each pew equipped with a box of sand in which tobacco chewers could spit. Virginia was a tobacco state; smoking and chewing were encouraged, since it benefited the economy.

For his defense, Burr had assembled a team of brilliant lawyers, including Henry Clay, and the master of the courtroom, Luther Martin. But Burr planned to be in full control.

As the prosecuting attorney, Jefferson had chosen George Hay. Hay, soon to be married to the daughter of James Monroe, was sure to be loyal to Jefferson.

The Circuit Court for the District of Virginia came to order on May 22, 1807, a little after the noon hour. Zebulon looked around the courtroom jammed with spectators, lawyers, reporters. The landed gentry of Richmond rubbed elbows with frontiersmen in their coonskin caps, leather shirts and breeches.

Andrew Jackson stood near Zebulon, tall and gaunt, with a shock of red hair and a strong thin body that had already earned him the name Old Hickory. He was an abrupt, direct man, with no patience for deceit, no matter how lawyers might try to disguise it with their frills and furbelows. Though Jackson had once supported Burr, even offering to march with him against Mexico, he had disavowed any plan to split the United States in two, and so was still in good favor with Jefferson. However, Jackson had still remained an advocate of Burr's.

Zebulon edged closer to the commanding man. "Burr looks composed, doesn't he?" Zebulon said. "Sometimes I think he enjoys being the center of attention, even if it means being tried for treason."

Jackson's voice rumbled from deep within his chest. "Treason be damned! He was only doing what the entire country wants! To take over all the land on the continent, and make of it one great United States! Burr is a victim of political persecution, and his accuser, General Wilkenson, is a damned liar! Why hell, everybody knows that Wilkenson's been in the pay of the Spanish government for more than fifteen years! When Jefferson sent out the Corps of Discovery to chart the Louisiana Territory, Wilkenson told the Spaniards to intercept them and take them prisoner. Is that the kind of man whose testimony you'd trust?"

Spectators, lawyers, and jury alike listened intently to the evidence. Then it was Burr's turn, and the courtroom reverberated with his ringing defense.

"As to these charges leveled against me, three times in the west I've been tried, and three times I've been found innocent. Yet here we are in court again. Could it be that the man who lives in the President's House is trying to crucify me?"

Couriers carried daily reports of the grand jury's proceedings to Washington. As the case dragged for the prosecution—Marshall was clearly sympathetic to the defense—Jefferson publicly blamed the judicial system, claiming it was acting independently of the will of the people. Jefferson further resurrected his contention that a judge should not hold his position for life, but should be removed at the will of Congress and the President.

"Now we are seeing the true issues," Zebulon said to Rebecca. "Jefferson is after not only Burr, but Marshall. If he can get them both with this trial, so much the better. History is being made right here, and the outcome will affect the relationship between the President and the Supreme Court for generations to come."

"I'm not so much concerned with history as with your going to prison," Rebecca said. "But if Marshall stands firm, there may yet be hope."

During the three weeks the grand jury sat, Aaron Burr had the run of Richmond, and was wined and dined by the gentry, who'd always taken a dim view of Jefferson's leveling "democracy." One day, Burr's chief counsel, John Wickham, gave a dinner party for Burr in his home in the Shockoe Hill District. Rebecca and Zebulon attended, and she was most impressed with the style and grace of these Virginia planters; their manners made Washington seem like a frontier town. Among the guests, Rebecca saw Victoria Connaught and her niece Marianne; the ladies' greetings were gushing.

"But how lovely you look, Rebecca," Marianne said. "Why, you have the serenity of . . . a madonna."

After bouquets of other compliments, they separated. "What are they doing here?" Rebecca asked as she and Zebulon made their way to the punchbowl.

"If the truth were known, it was Connaught money that

helped launch Burr on his scheme, and it's Connaught money that's paying for his defense."

"I've never trusted them," Rebecca said. "If they had their way we'd still be a colony of England's." Zebulon hadn't heard a word she'd said; he was staring after Marianne. Rebecca felt a twinge of jealousy. Both Zebulon and Jeremy fancied this scrawny excuse for a woman, and she couldn't understand why.

Then Rebecca fairly started when she saw Chief Justice Marshall enter the drawing room. He took up a position near the flower-filled hearth of the fireplace, the convex mirror on the wall distorting his features and casting them all over the room. He nodded his greetings to Rebecca and Zebulon.

"I'm no jurist," Zebulon said, "but is it wise for Marshall to attend a dinner with a man whom he'll soon have to judge?"

"I can't think what's in his mind," Rebecca said, surprised herself. "Perhaps he's throwing down the gauntlet, letting Jefferson know that he's not frightened."

The next day, the Republican press clarioned the news, and their editorials immediately called for Marshall to step down from both the trial and the Supreme Court. Marshall remained imperturbable.

The trial proceeded with painstaking detail; the weather grew unbearably hot, but there was never a vacant seat in the courtroom. And then one day Aaron Burr raised a legal point that threw the court into an uproar.

"May it please your honor and the court," he said, "President Jefferson claims to have received certain letters which implicate me in this supposed plot. I've applied to the government for copies but have been unable to obtain them. How can I prepare my defense without the full knowledge of what my accusers have said about me? Therefore, I ask that the President of the United States be subpoenaed and brought to this court."

After a moment of stunned silence, pandemonium broke out. Marshall banged his gavel, shouting, "Order!"

When order was finally restored Burr continued, "I respectfully ask that the right honorable Thomas Jefferson be summoned to Richmond, and bring with him any and all documents relating to this case, so that justice may be served."

The outraged prosecuting attorney, George Hay, could barely make himself heard over the hubbub. "Naturally, I will submit as evidence those letters which the court deems necessary—"

Marshall interrupted, "Sir, how can we determine what is necessary when we have access to nothing? We only know that the President has already prejudiced this case by declaring to Congress, 'Of Burr's guilt, there can be no doubt.' But according to our Constitution, a man is judged innocent until proven guilty, and such guilt or innocence can be decided only by a jury of twelve good and honest men, and not by any one man, not even the President."

Could a President be summoned before a court? The question burned for the next few days. Hay, acting on Jefferson's instructions, admitted that as a private citizen, Jefferson could be called, but as President, the separation of powers guaranteed in the Constitution made his appearance impossible.

Rebecca was caught on the horns of a dilemma. On the one hand, she was dying to set loose the pen of Rebel Thorne. Here was an issue that could well determine the future course of the nation. She loathed Burr, always had, and believed that he was undeniably guilty. Yet if she wrote as her heart dictated, and Burr was convicted of treason, that might help put Zebulon in prison, or worse.

But she also knew that a greater issue had been raised at this trial. Was a President above the law?

If a President was, then during his term of office he might assume the powers of a king or dictator, and could easily subvert the government. Not for a moment did she believe that Jefferson planned to do such a thing. But there might be other Presidents, unprincipled men, who would gladly seize such power.

In the end, discretion demanded that she not write about this matter, and she railed against Zebulon's stupidity that had forced her into this position. All she could do was wait for Jefferson's response to Marshall's demand that he send the Presidential papers to the court.

On June 13, Jefferson's formal answer came and George Hay read it to the grand jury. "The President reserves the right to decide independently of all other authority, judicial or legislative, which of his papers should be placed before the public. The confidential communications of the chief executive are privileged information, and not at the mercy of any court. If the President chooses to deny them, he can. However, those papers which are germaine to this trial will be supplied."

But once again Marshall raised the question, which papers were germaine? The court couldn't possibly judge until it had looked at them, and yet Jefferson was reserving that right for himself. The legal argument seesawed back and forth in static, implacable balance. Burr's own problems seemed insignificant in the light of this new Constitutional crisis.

When Marshall handed down his ruling, his voice rang with all the authority of Chief Justice of the Supreme Court. "Can a President be summoned into court? Yes! Nothing in the Constitution forbids it, or in any statutes that I know, save in the case of a king. But, of course, a President is not entirely like a king. A king can do no wrong and no blame can be imputed to him. But since an elected President is not anointed, and can do wrong, then like any man, he is answerable to the law. On these grounds, I call upon President Jefferson to present himself in this court."

Had a bomb exploded in the courtroom, it couldn't have caused more turmoil. Burr's forces were ecstatic, and Zebulon heard himself whooping and hollering with the rest. In any battle between the virtually inaudible Jefferson and the hypnotic, facile Burr, Burr was sure to win.

In his own way, Marshall had asserted the right of the judiciary to subpoena a President. But he was also canny enough to know that he might not win this battle, so he avoided a further constitutional crisis by stating, "The court will be satisfied with the original letter that General James Wilkenson wrote to President Jefferson. Let the President dispatch that with the related documents. If the court receives this, it will not be necessary for the President to make the tedious journey from Washington."

The usually mild-mannered Jefferson stormed about when he received this directive from Marshall. But he too saw the wisdom in avoiding a crisis that might tear the country apart, so he sent the necessary papers to Richmond. When they arrived, the court found that changes and erasures had been made in the text. Clearly, the evidence had been tampered with, either by somebody in the executive office, or even by the

President himself! But Marshall didn't pursue this; he'd already achieved his most important aim, establishing the supremacy of the Supreme Court.

Then General James Wilkenson appeared in court as a star witness for the prosecution. Zebulon knew that William Eaton would be called next, and he grew increasingly nervous with the thought. But now, he focused his attention on Wilkenson.

Wilkenson looked like a buffoon. Decked out in all his gold braid, spurs, and medals, leather harness and boots, he cut a grotesque figure next to the slight, refined Burr. Wilkenson's principal evidence was a letter Burr had sent him in code, which gave details and conditions of the master plan to conquer Mexico. Under Hay's gentle questioning, Wilkenson acquitted himself tolerably well.

But then Burr's lawyers began to chip away at his testimony. "Isn't it true that alterations have been made in the text of the letter? Isn't it true that the first sentence has been totally erased? And isn't it true that this sentence would make it clear that the letter was in answer to one of your own?"

Wilkenson grew red in the face, mopped his brow, stammered, and contradicted himself to the point of perjury. John Randolph, the foreman of the grand jury—and, incidentally, another cousin of Jefferson's—was so disgusted by Wilkenson that he demanded the general also be indicted for treason!

George Hay hung his head in his hands while the grand jury voted: Seven members voted for an indictment, while only nine voted against. It was a dangerously close vote, and this against one of the government's chief witnesses.

Nevertheless, on June 24, the grand jury indicted Aaron Burr for the misdemeanor of launching an expedition against Spain, and for treason against the United States.

Zebulon fell into a deeply dejected state. Curiously, Rebecca became attentive, conciliatory, and even loving. She couldn't quite understand her new mood; perhaps his own vulnerability brought out hers, or perhaps her condition had softened her. Though he advised her to go home, she elected to stay with him.

The case then went to a trial by jury, and testimony dragged on all during the blistering summer. Next to General Wilkenson, the government's most important witness was William Eaton, and the day he appeared, Zebulon could barely control his anxiety.

Under oath, Eaton told the jury, "Aaron Burr told me that he was going to seize Washington, murder the President, and throw his body in the Potomac. Then he would declare himself Emperor."

The courtroom gasped; this was by far the most damning direct evidence against Burr. Nothing the defense lawyers did could shake Eaton's testimony.

Then Zebulon was summoned to the witness box; he felt the sweat trickling down his back as George Hay began to question him. "Mr. Brand, you were present in the hotel room the night that Aaron Burr made those threats, were you not?"

"I was."

"And to the best of your recollection, is what Mr. Eaton says correct? Remember, you're under oath."

"The words are, perhaps, but the meaning was entirely innocent," Zebulon said.

Hay ordered Zebulon to confine himself to the question, but Chief Justice Marshall said mildly, "The court will allow the witness to continue."

Zebulon tried to sound earnest, straightforward, as he said, "You must understand that we'd all had a great deal to drink, and much of what Mr. Burr said, I thought was said in jest."

The questioning continued for much of the afternoon, and though Zebulon tried hard, in the end he knew that he hadn't convinced the jury.

Later that evening, Zebulon paced the floor of his hotel room. "Burr might have gotten off, except for Eaton's testimony," he said to Rebecca. "But now he stands a good chance of being convicted, and he'll drag us all down with him."

"Is there no way to discredit Eaton's testimony?" Rebecca asked.

"How? Burr *did* say those very things."

"And nobody said anything else that might cast a new light on the testimony?"

He shook his head wearily. At last they went to bed and Zebulon sought solace in making love. In the midst of his passionate assault, he rolled over with a cry, leaving Rebecca wondering what was happening. He threw on his robe and padded down the polished wood hallway to Burr's room and knocked on the door. "It's Zebulon. It's important."

"Can't it wait?" Burr called. "I'm . . . occupied."

"I've found the way to discredit Eaton's testimony!"

Seconds later the door flew open and Zebulon saw a plump form huddled under the covers. Burr looked even slighter in his nakedness, but the reason he'd intrigued so many women was obvious. Burr slipped into a robe and the two men talked hurriedly. Burr stroked his chin. "It might just work. It depends on the way it's handled. Good work; tomorrow will tell."

Zebulon went back to his room, humming.

The following morning, Burr, all smiles, cross-examined William Eaton. "Sir, after your conquest of Derna, did you put in a claim to the United States Government for monies owed you?"

Eaton's eyes narrowed. His glance shifted from Burr to Zebulon, whose face remained perfectly impassive. "I did."

"And how much was that claim?"

"Ten thousand dollars."

A few eyebrows shot up among the jurymen.

Burr continued. "And how long did it take for the government to honor your claim?"

"I don't remember."

"I do. It was almost eighteen months. And has the ten thousand dollars finally been paid?"

"It has, and rightly so."

"And would you tell the court the date it was paid?"

"I don't remember."

"All that money and you don't remember? I remind you, Mr. Eaton, you're under oath."

"In February."

Burr turned first to Marshall and then to the jury. "I ask the court to note that I was arrested on the seventeenth of January. Though Mr. Eaton tried for more than a year and a half to get his money from the government, they didn't pay it until a few days after I was arrested."

Eaton grew red in the face and blurted, "Are you suggesting—?"

"I'm not suggesting anything, merely pointing out that Mr.

Eaton, who *finally* received ten thousand dollars from the government, is now testifying here against me!"

George Hay jumped to his feet and objected strenuously; Marshall, with the mildest expression on his face, sustained it; but Burr had already planted the seeds of doubt in the jury's mind. Zebulon sat back, a look of satisfaction on his face.

In summation, the prosecution maintained that Burr had planned the conspiracy during December of 1806, on Blennerhassett's Island (Blennerhassett had also been indicted as a co-conspirator), but Burr was able to prove conclusively that he hadn't been there on that date.

Then Chief Justice Marshall gave his instructions to the jury. "On the question of treason, the Constitution is exact; two or more persons must witness the alleged traitor in the act of levying war against the United States, or of giving aid and comfort to the enemy. But since Burr wasn't present at the time the government claims the conspiracy took place, at best he could only have *incited* the men to treason, but incitement to treason is no crime under our Constitution. Perhaps there ought to be such a law, but at the moment, there's nothing on the statutes, and so Mr. Burr cannot be held accountable on that level."

George Hay slammed the table top, and Marshall pinned him with a stare. "That this court dares not usurp power is true," Marshall said. "That this court dares not shrink from its duty is no less true!"

Let Jefferson threaten him with impeachment, let him try to break the Supreme Court, Marshall was ready to do battle to preserve the integrity of the judiciary. The trial of Aaron Burr had given the Chief Justice the perfect opportunity to establish the fact that any man, even the President of the United States, was not above the law. The Supreme Court was indeed supreme, and let Jefferson and every future President take note.

With Marshall's instructions sounding in their heads, the jury went out. The following day they returned with their verdict. "We find Burr, not proved to be guilty under this indictment by any evidence submitted to us."

For the next two months Burr stayed in Virginia, but nightly, he and Marshall were burned in effigy. Wherever Burr traveled subsequently—Baltimore, Philadelphia—he found the country shunning him. And then, early in 1808, his grandiose scheme having turned to dust, he sailed for Europe and disappeared from sight.

Zebulon never got his money back, and though Rebecca never mentioned it directly, she managed in subtle ways not to let him forget it.

Chapter 36

THE BIRTH of Suzannah Breech Brand occasioned much celebration in the Brand household. Zebulon, masking his disappointment that it hadn't been a boy, slaughtered a pig for his slaves and gave them an extra ration of rum. He made a circuit of the neighborhood taverns and bought rounds of drinks for everybody. Rebecca named the child after her mother.

It took Rebecca several weeks to recover. The birth had been difficult, with pain so unbearable that she didn't think she could ever have another child. Yet she knew she would; if it took two children, five, she would bear a boy to carry on the Breech-Brand line.

She lay abed, cuddling the tiny creature beside her, with auburn hair as fine as a dandelion, and luminous dark brown eyes so like Zebulon's. Suzannah looked so helpless, and yet so sweet as she fed from her breast. "Well, my love," Rebecca murmured, "you're a woman born into a man's world. But I'll see that you claim your rightful place."

Mathias Breech, grown cantankerous with creeping arthritis, celebrated more than anybody. With a gusto redolent of his former self he partied steadily. One day he came to visit the child loaded down with presents, and Rebecca reprimanded him: "Is this how you'd have your granddaughter know you, as a drunken sot?"

The chastisement struck home. Mathias put himself to bed, didn't touch a drop for a fortnight, and was presentable enough in time for the christening.

Much of Washington and Georgetown turned out for the event. Not that many children were born in the bachelor-ridden community, and Rebecca and Zebulon were popular members of the younger social set. Many legislators attended, but President Jefferson sent his regrets. Dolley, who'd swept into the church with little Jemmy in her wake, confided to Rebecca, "Tom's been suffering from one of his dreadful migraines and begs to be excused."

When Dolley left to take her place in the front pew of the church, Rebecca said to Zebulon, "You see, you've angered Jefferson with your support of Aaron Burr. That's why he didn't come."

"No matter," Zebulon retorted. "In a few weeks there'll be another election, and we'll be rid of the hypocrite. Let him go back to Monticello with his black mistress and bastard children. We've had enough of him, and his lackey Madison is no better. I can't think why you asked the Madisons to stand as Suzannah's godparents."

"I asked them because James Madison is going to be the next President of the United States."

Zebulon's laugh echoed to the vaulted ceiling of the church. "Darling, you're so naïve when it comes to politics. I shudder when I think there are some misguided females like Abigail Adams, who are still agitating for women to have the vote. Why can't you leave such things to men who understand them?"

"I never lost five thousand dollars on a harebrained scheme, nor risked going to jail," she retorted.

Zebulon bit his lip. "Nevertheless, Madison will lose, because the country is fed up to the teeth with Jefferson's milksop policies."

The cries for war had been vociferous when the British warship *Leopard* captured the American merchant ship *Chesapeake* off the coast of Maryland in June of 1807. Jefferson resisted the warmongers, realizing that the nation was far too young to risk the debilitations of another conflict. "One war is more than enough in any man's lifetime," he'd said. However, even such loyal friends as Albert Gallatin and John Quincy Adams disagreed with him.

Jefferson started talks with the British, but failed to get a commitment from them to renounce their impressment of American seamen. Without such a guarantee, all other negotiations seemed hopeless. In November of 1807, the British proclaimed their Orders in Council, a virtual blockade of all

French ports, and asserted their right to search every neutral ship for contraband. Not to be outdone, Napoleon issued his Milan Decree, stating that all vessels that submitted to the British Orders in Council would be considered lawful prizes by the French.

With America caught in the middle, Jefferson tightened his embargo on all British and French goods. But this precipitated an economic depression; the seafaring New England states began agitating for secession from the Union. Fortunes were made and lost in the smuggling trade.

"Just because Thomas Jefferson is a coward, we can't let England and France intimidate us any longer," Zebulon said. "America realizes that, and that's why Jefferson's man will lose."

The church began to fill with guests—the Van Nesses, Captain Tingey, Commodore Barney, the Tayloes, the William Thorntons, and the James Hobans, followed by their four children, with another on the way. A young lawyer and his wife arrived; Francis Scott Key was a new acquaintance of Rebecca's. An aspiring poet, Key had written a number of verses on the occasion of Suzannah's christening.

Then Rebecca saw Jeremy coming down the aisle. His slave woman, Tanzy, walked slightly behind him and she was holding Circumstance by the hand. Rebecca remained rooted, not knowing what to do, what to think.

For his own part, Jeremy had thought long and hard about attending the christening. "I think it's time we rid ourselves of all the ugliness between us. It's gone on too long," he'd told Tanzy. "After all, Suzannah and Circumstance are cousins."

"Best you stay away from them," Tanzy said.

"How can I hold innocent children responsible?" Jeremy asked. And so finally he'd dressed his family in their best and had come to the church.

Three-year-old Circumstance looked like an enchanted child. Her lustrous sable hair fell straight to her shoulders, and her almond-shaped eyes shone a startling blue in her tawny skin. Already she was considered something of an oddity in the small town of Washington; some people knew of her true origins, but newcomers were likely to think she was Tanzy's child by Jeremy. Though responsive to the people around her,

Circumstance also lived in another, stranger world; squirrels ate from her hand, birds perched on her shoulder, and at night, raccoons scratched at her window.

As for Tanzy, she'd blossomed with her new-found freedom, and happiness shone in her face. Each new antic of Circumstance's brought a ready laugh from her, each childhood illness became a cause of great concern. And Circumstance so loved her in return that it slowly muted the pain of her own baby's death.

When the christening was over, Jeremy tentatively approached Rebecca and Zebulon. He'd rarely seen them since their marriage, and then only by accident; the brothers had a tacit agreement to stay clear of each other.

Jeremy gulped, then said haltingly, "My congratulations to you both. Little Suzannah is so beautiful . . . if you'd allow me, I'd like to paint a miniature of her, as a christening present."

Rebecca blinked, taken aback, but since Dolley Madison stood at her side, she was forced to act with some civility. "Why Jeremy, that's kind of you." She searched for a plausible excuse to turn his request down, but before she could find one Jeremy said, "That's wonderful. I'll come by in a week or so."

Behind her, Rebecca could feel Zebulon stirring irritably. She glanced at the people pressing in on her, and the tension began to grow in her own breast. There was the slave Tanzy, who'd been used by Zebulon, and now probably by Jeremy . . . Circumstance, who'd come between her and her one love . . . and this sweet babe in her arms, who should have been Jeremy's child. A sadness swept over her so elemental that it was all she could do to keep from crying out in this house of God, crying out against the cruel cheat that was life itself.

Congratulatory voices continued to buzz about her, and then she heard Jeremy's voice.

"Zebulon, whatever battles we've fought, whatever pain we've visited on each other, surely this is the time to end it." Jeremy had great difficulty saying this, but he gained courage from each word until they were tumbling from him, full of passion and hope. "Zebulon, I can remember years when I loved you. We could have that again . . . be a family once more. Look, we're holding a new generation of children in our arms. We can't, we *mustn't,* let our old feuds contaminate their lives."

Zebulon shifted uneasily from leg to leg, and Jeremy, taking his silence for agreement, reached out impulsively and grasped his hand. Jeremy breathed deeply, feeling that after more than a decade of pain, a great burden had finally been lifted from his soul.

Then he kissed Rebecca on the cheek. A sudden shaft of sunlight lanced through the windows, bathing them all in a golden light. For an impossible moment Rebecca thought that God's grace would overcome everything, and then the light faded.

In the weeks that followed, Jeremy took his brushes and paints and went to the new mansion that Zebulon had built near the Tayloes' Octagon House on New York Avenue and Eighteenth Street. The red-brick building, in a modified Federal style, afforded an unbroken view of the President's House and of Washington, whose homes and buildings were slowly growing along the tendrils of its radial avenues. Mathias had given all the building stone and brick to his daughter as a present, and had already settled a large sum on Suzannah.

The first few times that Jeremy came, Zebulon was at home, and he watched with desultory interest as he sketched his daughter. But then Rebecca decided she didn't want a miniature. "Of what use is it when the child is so young?" Instead, she commissioned Jeremy to paint a portrait of her and Suzannah. Zebulon recognized her mercurial change for what it was, and watching them chatting so easily, choked with jealousy. He didn't trust them alone together, yet it was worse to be with them, doing nothing, so he took to excusing himself from the sittings, claiming pressing business matters.

In part, that was true. Zebulon had taken over the management of the Breech Stone Works, and with Washington in a constant state of building, the company prospered. Zebulon was also outfitting a merchant ship to import the finest marbles from Italy, mahoganies from Africa, and teak from the Orient. True, the French and English blockade would have to be run, but if the ship slipped through, he'd make a fortune. Both public and private buildings in Washington were becoming more elaborate; signs of solid wealth were beginning to appear in the capital. For all its negative qualities Washington was gradually becoming the hub of power in the nation.

But there were times when Zebulon didn't tend to business matters, and instead rode to Jeremy's house. There, he'd check the hours when Tanzy was alone. Once he knocked at the door, but she wouldn't let him in. He felt no guilt about seeking her out; after all, Rebecca had forced him into it.

During the last months of her pregnancy, she'd refused to be touched. Then after Suzannah's birth, she insisted that her doctor advised her not to have relations for at least two months. Thinking to catch her out, Zebulon went to see the doctor, and was surprised when the old fool confirmed what Rebecca said. Still, what was a man to do? God knows there were enough whores in Washington, but with the ever-present danger of disease, Zebulon steered clear of them. He was too smart to bring such a thing home.

But Tanzy . . . she'd once served him in ways no other woman had, and the more he thought about it, the more attractive the prospect became. After all, he told himself, if she's sleeping with my brother, wouldn't she prefer the better man?

After spending an afternoon drinking in Tunnecliff's Tavern, Zebulon felt that his need and alcohol were mixed in proper proportions, and he went to Jeremy's. Once more Tanzy refused to let him in. She'd never told Jeremy about Zebulon's visits; she knew of their deep antagonisms, and didn't want to make it worse. Sooner or later Zebulon would grow weary of the chase and leave her alone. All she had to do was wait, and avoid him.

"Jeremy sent me to get some paints," Zebulon called through the door. "He's run out of cadmium blue, and sienna."

Tanzy was in a quandary: he could be telling the truth, and if she refused, then she'd have to tell Jeremy the reason, and that would bring on all she'd hoped to avoid. She opened the door a crack, and Zebulon bulled his way into the room.

An odor of tobacco and whiskey clung to him; the moment she saw his glittering eyes, she knew. She edged to the fireplace, grabbed the poker, and held it before her.

Zebulon's breath came in short aspirate gasps. That spark of courage in a woman had always been his spur. He advanced on her and lunged. Tanzy made the mistake of not aiming for his head, and her blow caught him on the shoulder. Though one arm went numb, he snatched the poker from her.

Circumstance started to cry and Tanzy exclaimed, "Zebulon, for the love of God, not in front of the child!"

But he seized her arms and pressed his lips against hers. She tried to bite him, but he jerked his head away, and his crooked smile bared his white, even teeth. He toppled her to the floor, his own massive body pinning her, and he toyed with her, running his hand up under her skirts. But he held back from touching her in the places where he knew she hungered to be touched.

Tanzy fought, crying out about the child, crying for reason, and then at last crying out in despair. There were two guards at the entrance to the President's House, not so distant; perhaps they would hear her. But nobody heard, and then gradually her strength ebbed. Zebulon knew that the moment had come. With the alcohol coursing through his blood, he saw all the possibilities, and reveled in them. Whenever Rebecca pleaded one excuse or another, he would have Tanzy.

So engrossed was he that he didn't hear the door swing open. But then a hand grabbed his shoulder and yanked him away from her. He sprawled on the floor, then stared up at his brother. Jeremy's fist smashed into his face, breaking his nose, and blood fountained all over.

Zebulon scrambled to his feet, but stumbled over his loosened breeches, and Jeremy's fist caught him on the back of the neck. He sank to his knees, only to feel another blow almost tear his head away.

Tanzy got up, clutching her torn clothes around her, trying to control her sobbing lest she frighten Circumstance more. "Jeremy, let him go, please, the baby."

Jeremy blinked. The child's crying gradually brought him to his senses. He dragged Zebulon to the door. "Get out," he muttered. "Get out before I kill you."

Zebulon stumbled outside and mounted his horse. "We'll see who kills who," he muttered, as he rode to Tunnecliff's Tavern. His head ached from whiskey and the beating, and he sluiced water from the pump over his head, cleaning up as best he could.

He doubted that Jeremy would say anything to Rebecca. "And even if he does, I don't care," he muttered as he tested a loose tooth. He looked in the mirror and gingerly touched his nose. Broken, no doubt about it. And it would stay that way, a constant reminder for the rest of his life.

A need for revenge grew in him, a need of such magnitude that he realized he'd never be satisfied until he'd ended the feud to his satisfaction. In the deepest reaches of his gut, Zebulon knew that Rebecca still loved his brother. And would go on loving him as long as he remained alive.

Chapter 37

"TAKE A deep breath," Letitia said, and Rebecca pulled in her stomach while her maid hooked up her undergarments. "Shouldn't be so tight in your condition, but you sure look beautiful."

Rebecca slipped into the long-sleeved peach-colored cotton dress; she smoothed her hair and inspected herself in the mirror. Motherhood had agreed with her. The thought that she was fulfilling her duties gave her a great sense of accomplishment. She swore to herself that she was contented. Her social calendar was always full, she did charity work once a week in the poor wards, Zebulon lavished presents on her, and Suzannah was as bright and endearing a child as anyone could wish for. Why then this malaise of her spirit?

With James Madison about to occupy the President's House, and Dolley now hostess in her own right, Rebecca looked forward to a brilliant four years. Plans buzzed in her brain, for this ball, that charity. She thought she might start a school to teach slave children how to read and write, and Dolley was supporting her in this. Most delightful of all, Dolley had asked her to help with the inaugural reception this afternoon, and then the inaugural ball this evening.

"Rebecca, will you hurry?" Zebulon shouted up the stairs.

She swept down the curved staircase and Zebulon caught his breath. Two years of marriage and she could still do this to him. Nightly forays into the mysteries of her flesh hadn't sated his appetite. He could have wished that she were more responsive; there were times when she only suffered his presence, but even that was enough for him, he who long ago had hungered for the thirteen-year-old, naked before her window.

Zebulon extended his arms and lifted her down the final step. "You've got to be careful, you know."

"This one will be a boy," she said. "I want to name him Gunning. It's an old family name. Gunning Breech Brand—it has a wonderful ring to it. A name fit for a President."

He chuckled, but realized she was dead serious. "If it's another girl, will you send her back?"

"It will be a boy," she said matter-of-factly. "A mother knows. From the way I'm carrying, Letitia agrees."

Zebulon snorted. Rebecca couldn't have been more than three months pregnant, yet the ladies, in their infinite wisdom, had already decided on the child's sex.

The Brand home was now tastefully furnished with handsome Sheraton furniture imported from England, Limoges china from France, and a pair of beautiful blue-and-buff oriental rugs. Zebulon's shipping ventures were paying off handsomely. The risk was fierce; sometimes he lost a vessel to the French navy blockading the West Indies, or was boarded by English men-of-war cruising the American coastal waters. But when a ship did manage to slip through, the returns justified the risk. Though he wasn't as rich as the Tayloes or the Connaughts, his prospects couldn't have been brighter. Rebecca and Suzannah wanted for nothing.

Eli helped them into the carriage, and with the liveried slave driving, they proceeded to the Madison house on F Street where the inaugural procession was to form.

Zebulon shook his head. "No matter how much money I spend on Eli's clothes, he still looks like he's just come out of the jungle."

"You should get rid of him. Why harbor somebody who hates you so? One day he'll do you harm."

"Nonsense. I've got to protect my investment. It's taken me this long to train him. He's the best and strongest slave I own. And though he has been rebellious in the past, I've broken him. He'll give us no trouble."

A great many carriages were out and Rebecca said, "Have you ever seen so many people pouring into the city? Why, one innkeeper on the road to Washington swears he saw three stagecoaches pass in a single day!"

"How I curse myself for not holding onto those real-estate

lots," Zebulon said. "They'd be worth a fortune now."

Rebecca didn't respond; she'd grown weary of all the fortunes that Zebulon might have made. With her father so seriously ill, and unable to oversee Zebulon, she'd become increasingly nervous. Zebulon tended to risk everything in order to make that one killing. Lord knows, she hungered as much as anybody to be rich, but in a sensible, orderly manner. If only they'd let *her* run the business! But when she'd suggested it, both Zebulon and her own father had laughed at her.

Shortly before noon on the brisk, brilliant March day, James and Dolley Madison left their house and, escorted by troops and prancing cavalry, proceeded along Pennsylvania Avenue toward the Capitol. Zebulon's carriage fell in line, followed by other carriages, men on horseback, including Jefferson, and hundreds of people on foot.

"Do you know that Madison asked Jefferson to ride with him in his carriage?" Rebecca asked. "But Jefferson refused, saying that he didn't want to divide the honors of the day."

"I've seen that item a half dozen times in the *National Intelligencer,"* Zebulon said. "Really, what fools we are to believe every piece of gossip about our leaders. Divide the honors indeed; everybody knows Madison wouldn't have won without Jefferson."

"You'd best watch your tongue," she said. "The Madisons are supposed to be our friends. And I for one don't believe these Federalist doomsayers. He's not incompetent at all, and he'll make a wonderful President."

"But the man is only five foot four inches tall, and weighs less than a hundred pounds!" Zebulon exclaimed. "Hardly a comforting image as the leader of our country. And of course, he's never been able to give Dolley a child."

"What in heaven's name does that have to do with anything?" Rebecca demanded.

"Oh, Rebecca, be realistic. Despite what we say, we want our leaders to have not only the wisdom of Solomon, but the passions of Bacchus as well. Look at Hamilton and Burr—why, people idolized them, in part because they were famous swordsmen. Even Jefferson, with his bastards sired at a late age, surprised us all, and some people even admired him for it."

Rebecca frowned. "Some day you may understand that a man's worth doesn't depend on his prowess in bed." Then she craned her neck. "My word, will you look at the crowd up ahead?"

Perhaps ten thousand people had congregated around the Capitol Building, and when Madison's carriage came into view, they cheered themselves hoarse.

"And all for a man who's five feet four and weighs less than a hundred pounds," Rebecca said. "I grant you that people may like their leaders lusty, but they aren't so base that they forget their finer qualities. After all, we'd have no Constitution without James Madison."

Promptly at noon, Madison climbed the steps of the Capitol. The House of Representatives had finally been completed, and everybody agreed that this magnificent chamber was the perfect place for the inauguration. Vice-President George Clinton, who'd been reelected (he'd been Jefferson's Vice-President also), was not present to serve as leading officer of the Senate, and so President Pro Tempore John Milledge conducted Madison to his chair. A seat of honor had also been reserved for Jefferson, but he'd refused, saying, "This day I return to the people, and my proper place is among them."

With the invocation, Rebecca clasped her hands and said a very personal, private prayer for the tiny man. With the country in such a turmoil, and the possibility of war with England, or France, or both, he'd need all the help he could get. An idea for a biographical article about him began to form in her head.

The "great little Madison," Aaron Burr had always called him, describing him as no bigger than "half a piece of soap." And like soap, he grew slighter with the years. His marriage to Dolley Payne Todd sixteen years before had been fortuitous; with her all-pervading optimism and infallible social sense, she'd prevented him from following his natural bent and withdrawing further into the background.

In the War for Independence, he'd been too sickly to bear arms, but he'd raised money and written fiery tracts against the tyranny of the British. In addition to being the principal framer of the Constitution, he'd also helped draft the Bill of Rights, and had fought vigorously to have it accepted as the first ten amendments to the Constitution.

Now fifty-seven years old, he still had clear, penetrating blue eyes, a ruddy face, and a voice almost as quiet as Jefferson's. Yet whenever he rose to speak, people strained to listen, for he was acknowledged to be the greatest political theoretician in the country.

Rebecca had a sudden thought and whispered to Zebulon, "Do you realize that not one of our Presidents has been a great orator? They've all won their office by the use of a pen."

When Madison went to the lectern he walked with a quick, bouncing step. He wore his thinning hair in a queue and powdered. For the inauguration, he'd disdained foreign-made clothes, and had chosen a dark brown suit of American-grown Merino wool, spun and tailored in America.

Oh dear, Rebecca thought, he looks just like a little old leprechaun.

Chief Justice Marshall came forward to administer the oath.

"This must rankle Jefferson," Zebulon whispered, "to see his chief rival still in command of the Supreme Court, while he no longer has any power."

"Perhaps, but after eight years in that house, suffering every vilification from the press, and with no private life of his own, he'll be glad to return to Monticello. He said to me at our last dinner, 'Never did a prisoner released from his chains, feel such relief as I shall on shucking off the shackles of power.'"

After the swearing-in ceremony, Madison delivered a short speech, and those who heard it said it was brilliant. Guns were then fired, and amid cheering crowds, the President left the Capitol Building and reviewed nine companies of infantry in full uniform.

Afterward, he returned to his house on F Street, where Dolley Madison, aided by Rebecca and other young matrons of Washington, labored to provide a suitable repast for the well-wishers who jammed the house.

President Madison stood near the door of the drawing room, greeting everybody.

"I notice that our great democrat is not shaking hands," Zebulon said to Rebecca.

"It's not that he doesn't want to," she said, "but Dolley told me that his bones are so fine that the pressing of the flesh made his arm sore."

Dolley was all charm and affability. She wore a plain yellow cambric dress with a long train and a purple velvet bonnet trimmed with white satin and white plumes. As Jefferson's official hostess, she'd practically ruled the President's House, but it had always been by his leave. Now she was about to do it in her own right.

During a momentary respite, Dolley whispered to Rebecca, "Who can know the turn of fate? What if I'd given in to Aaron Burr? Think where I'd be today, wandering through foreign countries, living from hand to mouth. Instead, I'm with my beloved Jemmy, and the wife of the President of the United States!"

Servants wended their way through the crush of people, proffering trays laden with wines and canapés. Dolley had nowhere near enough in help, and her personal maid, Sukie, had been pressed into service. Close friends had sent over their help, and Jeremy had loaned her Tanzy. At one point, when Tanzy came out of the pantry, she almost bumped into Zebulon.

Tanzy's tray rattled, and Zebulon's hand flew instinctively toward his broken nose, and then Tanzy moved away. It hadn't taken more than an instant, but Rebecca had seen it all.

She knew something had happened between Zebulon and Jeremy; the friendliness he'd shown at the christening had evaporated. She suspected it had something to do with the colored slave . . . Then suddenly Victoria Connaught was bearing down on her.

"We waited an hour before we could get into the house!" she complained in an aggrieved tone. "This mob! Why in the Court of St. James's, where they understand protocol, we wouldn't be forced to rub elbows with the rabble."

Marriage had given Rebecca a certain social advantage, and she said sweetly, "I'm sure you'd be happier in the Court of St. James's." Victoria blanched.

If the elder Connaught was here, her ward Marianne was sure to be close behind. Rebecca craned her neck, scanning the room. Then she spied Marianne standing near the butler's pantry, talking to Jeremy. Rebecca's pulse quickened as she watched them. His expression, his smile, the stance of his body—all signaled his interest in her, and the realization coiled through her, constricting her heart.

She turned to Zebulon. "When did the Connaughts get back to Washington?"

"Three weeks ago. I hear they returned especially for the inauguration."

"I can't imagine why. Victoria Connaught hates Dolley—always has, always will. Were they in London again?"

"They tell me they were in New Orleans," Zebulon said. "The Connaughts have extensive holdings there."

"Where don't they have extensive holdings?" Rebecca said. "In England, in Europe, in America . . . the Connaughts are everywhere, like red ants."

That evening, the very first inaugural ball in the history of the United States was held at Long's Hotel on First and A Streets, Southeast. More than four hundred people paid a handsome sum to crowd into the grand ballroom. Even former President Jefferson had come, the first ball he'd attended in more than twenty years, and his presence was a testament of his affection for the Madisons.

The Marine Band struck up "The President's March," and Dolley made a grand entrance on the arm of one of the ball's managers, as the crowd applauded. She looked resplendent in a buff-colored velvet gown, and thin kid slippers laced with beige ribbons. A turban of matching velvet adorned her head, trimmed with white satin and bird-of-paradise plumes. The plumes waved and fluttered almost a foot above everybody else, so one was never at a loss to know Dolley's whereabouts.

The First Lady was followed by her sister, Mrs. Richard Cutts, escorted by President Madison. Zebulon stood on a chair to catch sight of him. He wore a black velvet suit with a ruffled white shirt, his powdered queue tied back with a black velvet ribbon.

Rebecca had taken extra pains with her gown. The periwinkle blue dress had been made by the best couturier in Philadelphia; she'd journeyed there twice for fittings. The rich satin clung to her figure, enhancing the flush of her skin, and highlighting her auburn hair, which had a rope of pearls coiled through it.

"It's an absolutely wonderful ball," she said to Dolley.

"I'd rather be in bed," Madison said.

"Nonsense, Jemmy," Dolley cried gaily. "Don't you realize we're making history? This is the first inaugural ball ever held, and it's my fervent wish that we'll always have one."

The band struck up a lilting melody in three-quarter time, and Rebecca bit her lip as she saw Marianne and Jeremy waltz by. The new dance had just been introduced in America from Vienna. Jeremy's hair had become unruly in the heat and he looked like a teenager; but his navy velvet suit couldn't quite hide the muscles of the man. The casual intimacy with which they waltzed, the abandon of their laughter gnawed away at Rebecca.

For a moment, she feared that she might be sick, and thought desperately, We'll move from Washington. I'll never see him again. I can't stand such torment!

Then Dolley was at her side. "Are you all right? You look so pale."

Rebecca smiled. "Yes, I'm fine."

"Then, my dear, you must dance with the Tunisian ambassador, he's been demanding to know who you are. Chief Justice Marshall threatens to close the hall unless you honor him with a dance, and after that . . ."

Rebecca was swept into the waltz. A thousand candles flickered off the crystal chandeliers, turning the room into a fantasy of light. Never had men looked more handsome, nor women more beautiful. The ballroom fairly blazed with glittering gems: Victoria Connaught wore a river of rubies at her throat, the necklace said to have belonged to Marie Antoinette; Marianne had chosen a simple diamond choker to emphasize her fabulously long neck. But with the new life growing with her, suffusing her body with an inner beauty, no one could compare with Rebecca. The wine, the music, the turn of the dance spiraled her upward and out of her mood.

The musicians stopped for breath, and Rebecca raised a glass of champagne. "Ladies and gentlemen, to the President of the United States, and Dolley!"

An inebriated senator drained his glass, then threw it against the wall. Several revelers followed suit. The room became so hot from the press of bodies, that a cry went up, "Open the windows!"

Men struggled to raise them, but the sashes wouldn't work. Zebulon picked up a chair and heaved it through a transom, then more windows were broken and the room resounded with the shrieks of laughter and the tinkle of broken glass. A rush of cool night air swept through the ballroom, rejuvenating everybody. The band struck up a lively jig.

Zebulon picked up Rebecca and whirled her around. She threw back her head, abandoning herself to the whirling chandelier that looked like a Catherine wheel of fire, and her laughter spun after her. He put her down and she said breathlessly, "I feel as if we are all about to enter a golden age, and you and I shall help make it happen!"

Rebecca clenched her fists, feeling the resolve straighten her spine. No, she would never leave this place. Whatever despair she felt about Jeremy, that too she'd overcome. For Washington fulfilled some deep need in her. To be at the hub of all that was happening in the nation, to be a part of it, perhaps even help influence it... She must stay close to the source of power. It meant her very life.

Chapter 38

IT DIDN'T take long for Rebecca's predictions to come to pass. With Dolley in the President's House, Washington entered a golden era of balls, levees, and parties. Dolley was indefatigable in returning social calls, and in one day set a record by visiting seventeen homes, then that afternoon preparing a state dinner for fifty guests. Legislators and the city's social arbiters flocked to her soon-to-be-famous "groaning board" buffets. More often than not, in the friendly, gay surroundings, political deals advantageous to Madison's administration were consummated.

"Dolley is my secret weapon," Madison said proudly.

Recognizing her as a compelling news item, the *National Intelligencer* and the *Baltimore Sun* reported every bit of gossip, her costumes, quips, likes, and dislikes. Those columns were reprinted by newspapers through the country, and soon she became one of the nation's best-known institutions.

But Dolley's designs had a great deal more to them than mere frivolity. "My dear, I count on you," she said to Rebecca. "We must establish the equivalent of a court here in Washington, albeit a democratic one. We must show the world that we aren't barbarians. In ways of protocol, thank God we have the services of French John Souissat."

Dolley had managed to snatch off the butler who'd been in the employ of the English ambassador, Merry, and French John had become Dolley's master of ceremonies. Rebecca listened avidly to Dolley's plans; she knew Dolley spoke thus to every young matron in Washington, but there was an important difference: she was prepared to take advantage of it.

"Jefferson's taken his furniture back to Monticello with

him," Dolley said, "so we must have funds to furnish the house, make it worthy of its position."

"You know how tight-fisted Congress is," Rebecca said.

"Then we'll just have to deal with Congress," Dolley said, and went off to charm the legislators gulping her claret. No matter how many people were in a room, including strangers first met, the First Lady had the uncanny ability of remembering everybody's name, constituency, and interests. Rebecca watched her intently, learning, absorbing it all.

In an appearance before Congress, Dolley so beguiled the lawmakers that they voted an appropriation of $11,000 to redo the President's House. Madison kept Latrobe on to oversee the new construction, and Jeremy was in charge of all the work crews.

"The first thing we must do is paint the façade," Dolley said, linking her arm through Jeremy's. "I know the original plan was for this house to stand out from the surrounding brick dwellings, but now the building is positively gray. White, white, white!"

Jeremy erected scaffolding, and the crews labored for months to paint the place. Circumstance would come to watch her father, or just to play on the grounds, and Dolley would often invite her in for cookies or let her play with her pet macaw. When the painting was completed, the façade looked so pristine and white, that the citizens gradually fell into the habit of calling it "that white house." Soon the *Baltimore Sun* began referring to the mansion as "The White House."

"We must also finish the East Room," Dolley said to Jeremy. "It's by far the grandest chamber, yet with Jefferson's left-over paraphernalia all about, we can't use it."

Dolley managed to get more work out of the crew than anybody else; her energy was so tireless, so infectious, that workmen often labored past their appointed hours. She also had a large staff of slaves that she treated as equals, for at the core of her being, Dolley remained a Quaker. But no staff was capable of handling the truly grand state occasions, and then Dolley would rent her friends' slaves at thirty-five cents per night, the fee going to the masters.

Often, Tanzy would work at these receptions, and one night

at a dance for Ambassador Erskine, the new minister from England, Tanzy, Sukie, and Letitia were taking a break in the basement kitchen. Two new huge cast-iron stoves had just been put in, modified from a Franklin stove, and the help was having trouble getting used to them.

"I've seen men in love before," Sukie said to Tanzy, "and your boss-man, Jeremy, he's mad for that Marianne Connaught."

"And my Rebecca, she don't like it for nothing," Letitia said.

"She's the kind who doesn't like anything," Tanzy said, "but I don't think Jeremy really likes Marianne."

"Then girl, you don't have eyes," Letitia said. "That Marianne, she be with him in a minute, but that old aunt of hers don't let her out of her sight. Come on, now, time to bring up the next trays."

The slave women, dressed in wide white cotton skirts, their hair tucked under white kerchiefs, circulated the trays among the guests. When she could, Tanzy glanced at Marianne and Jeremy . . . and though it pained her to admit it, Sukie was right.

Weeks later, new furniture arrived from France and England, and the White House reverberated with moving men and painters. "My dear Rebecca," Dolley said, "you must help me with the Oval Parlor. I think it's the most beautiful room in the entire house, and you have such a wonderful eye for these things."

The women tried all sorts of decorating schemes, and finally decided that to give the room the illusion of space, they would hang large mirrors on the walls. Dolley's passion for yellow was reflected in the furniture, yellow satin high-backed sofas and chairs, yellow damask curtains with valances and swags.

"We must have pier tables strategically placed for refreshments, and card tables for loo and whist. And a brand new carpet . . . I know! For being so generous with us, I'll give the old carpet to the House of Representatives."

A punctilious housekeeper, Dolley had breakfast served promptly at nine, and Rebecca might find herself with a light repast of bread and butter and tea. But when her pregnancy became evident, Dolley insisted she have a hearty meal, hot wheat bread, light cakes, a corn loaf, and hashes of chicken or ham. Dinner, served in midafternoon, was the large meal of the day, and usually included several soups, meats, fish, pastries, and puddings. Supper, or high tea, often included baked oysters fished fresh from the Chesapeake Bay.

Dolley always sat at the head of the table, the President at her right. "Jemmy would rather listen than talk," she confided to Rebecca, "so I'm saving him the wear and tear of making conversation. Everybody in the nation wants the President's ear." From a birdstand nearby, Dolley's macaw squawked in agreement.

One blustery, rainy afternoon in late October, Jeremy was working in the attic, trying to locate a leak in the roof. "Damned if I can find it," he said. "It depends on the way the wind drives the rain."

Dolley poked her head up the attic stairs. For once, her expression looked solemn. "Mr. Madison would like to see you in his office." She dabbed at her eyes with a handkerchief.

Jeremy's first thought was that something had happened to Circumstance, and he dashed downstairs. Madison sat in an oversized chair, barely visible over the top of his desk.

"I'm afraid I have some bad news," the President said. "I've just received word that Meriwether Lewis died."

Jeremy sank into a chair. "Dead?" he whispered. "An Indian raid?" Indian tribes in the west had begun forming a loose confederation under the leadership of the Shawnee chief, Tecumseh. White settlers who encroached on territory the Indians considered theirs were massacred.

"It was not Indians," Madison said, compressing his lips. "Lewis was on his way to Washington to report on conditions in the Louisiana Territory, and to put himself at the pleasure of our new administration. Despite some erratic behavior, he was doing a competent job, and I would have insisted that he remain on as governor. One night, traveling through Tennessee, he stopped off at a small town, and there he died."

Jeremy rubbed his forehead. "But how? He was in excellent health. Was there foul play?"

Madison sighed wearily. "We thought there might have been, but that's been ruled out. Naturally, we'll try to keep the matter as quiet as possible, both for his reputation, and the good of the country."

Then the truth came over Jeremy. "My God, he took his own life," he whispered.

"Evidently, he'd made a number of attempts before. This particular night, he'd been drinking heavily, and slashed his wrists. But when the bleeding stopped, he put his own gun to his head," President Madison said.

Jeremy fought back his tears. That a man could be so unhappy in his own body and time as to take his life . . . Shortly after they'd returned from the Northwest Expedition, William Clark had married, and Lewis had become even more vulnerable to the violent swings in his mood. Finally, his own mind had overcome him.

Jeremy walked about in gloom for a week. The news of Lewis's death had also opened all his old wounds about White Doe. It was in this mood that he went to Roger Westman's bookshop on Pennsylvania Avenue one day to pick up a book he'd ordered. Marianne Connaught happened to be there, leafing through a volume of poetry by William Blake. When he greeted her, she couldn't disguise her delight.

"Do you know Blake's poetry?" she asked. "He has such astonishing insights into the duality in man. Sometimes I think he sees into my very soul," she said, and read aloud:

"Tiger, tiger, burning bright
In the forests of the night,
What immortal hand or eye
Could frame thy fearful symmetry?"

"Marianne, I must talk to you," he said.

The urgency in his voice put her on guard. So far, she'd been able to hold him at bay, and she meant to keep it that way. "Jeremy, I can't. My aunt . . ." She pointed outside, where Victoria waited in a splendid black-and-gold coach and four, with the Connaught coat of arms emblazoned in gold leaf on the door. Marianne smiled. "My aunt ordered it from London the moment she learned that Dolley Madison was to have a new red-brown coach with yellow satin curtains at the windows. How silly and vain women can be."

"I'll meet you tonight," Jeremy said.

"Impossible. We're entertaining the British ambassador."

"I'll wait until he leaves, and meet you just outside your gates."

"No!" she said sharply.

"Tonight," he called after as she hurried out.

Later that evening, after he'd heard the town crier announce nine o'clock, Jeremy rode out to the Connaught estate in the hills. He didn't know if Marianne would come, he knew only that he had to ease his own confusion about her. He saw the guests leave, saw the Connaught mansion go dark. The galleon moon marked the passage of time, moving through a cloudless sky. Then he saw a dark figure approach.

Marianne hurried to him. "I can only stay a moment." She leaned against a silver birch. Her cloak fell open and he saw the crisp linen and lace of her night clothes. "Everyone thinks I've gone to bed," she said nervously.

"Marianne, we can't go on this way," he said urgently. "It's inhuman, especially when two people care about each other as we do."

"You must understand," she whispered. "For more than a decade I've lived with a daily dose of hatred for the name Brand."

He reached through the darkness and gripped her arm. "I can't accept that, and I won't let you accept it either. Would you spend the rest of your life hating? Don't you know what that would do to you?"

He braced his hand against the birch and leaned close to her. "I know you care for me, I see it in your eyes, I hear it in your laugh. Marianne, for years I was like a walking dead man. Oh, I managed to go to work and to class and maybe attended an occasional party, but I had no interest in anyone. I resigned myself to being alone for the rest of my days. Then I met you."

"Stop, please," she murmured, tears starting to her eyes. "You mustn't say any more, I can't bear it. I can't go against every member of my family. I can't!"

He dug his fingers into her shoulders. "You must hear me. I won't be cheated twice by fate. I beg you, don't listen to your family, listen only to your heart." He placed his hand on her breast. "Hear it, so strong, yearning to be free. And only you can free it, Marianne—not I, nor your aunt. Only you."

Tears trickled from the corners of her eyes and he kissed them away. And then his lips found hers, warm, sweet, yielding, and all the stored passions of the past years burst forth in him.

"I love you," he whispered, as his arms went around her, and he heard his words echoed back. He spread his cloak on the ground and with a gentle motion drew her down. His hands moved lovingly over her young, chaste flesh, and his words, coming from a place unknown to him, wove a web of enchantment around them. Too far gone to heed the warnings of her family, Marianne trembled in fear and anticipation.

After endless endearments and kisses that inflamed their bodies, he moved to become one with her. She cried out once in pain, and a thought wrenched through her at that moment, that she'd abandoned her vow. But something more important was happening within her soul. She clung to him as he carried her to a place where nothing mattered, not her father's death, nor her mother's madness. Nothing mattered except that he'd placed his brand on her.

When passion was spent, they lay on the grass in blissful lassitude. "I feel as though I've been bled of all my poisons," she murmured.

He leaned over and kissed her lightly. "We'll marry as soon as possible. I'll talk to your aunt—"

She shivered and he drew the edge of her cloak around her. "Jeremy, you must give me time. I need to tell my family as gently as possible."

"How much time?" he asked.

"In a few years my aunt will no longer be my guardian, and we can do whatever we want."

"Years?" he repeated, sitting up abruptly. "Neither of us could stand such torment."

"But we'll see each other often," she said hastily.

"When can we meet again?" he asked, reaching for her.

"I don't know. Next week?"

"Sooner," he said.

"Jeremy, this is so new to me. There are things I must learn, precautions to take."

Fearing that pressing her further might frighten her away, he agreed. "All right, next week, at this time. But if I must wait that long . . ."

They made love again, this time he was less hurried, more responsive to her needs, and whatever fears she'd had melted in his embrace. She'd fallen in love, hopelessly in love, and with a man she'd sworn to destroy.

Every week for the next month, Jeremy and Marianne met. He resented the secrecy of these stolen moments, but forgot that when he was in her arms. He worked better, slept better; hope and energy and life once more burgeoned within him, for she had given him back his manhood.

At the balls and levees where they met, Victoria Connaught watched them gravitate to each other. Once during an intermission of *She Stoops to Conquer,* she leaned to Marianne, "You're paying entirely too much attention to Jeremy Brand."

Her heart skipped but she said gaily, "But you see, Aunt Victoria, he's just joined the militia, the unit charged with the defense of Washington. And as you know, he's in that White House daily, and is privy to all sorts of information. Do you know that the Navy Yard is putting in more gun emplacements?"

"How many?" Victoria asked.

"I don't know yet, but in time. Who knows, we may stumble on the overall plan for the defense of Washington, something we've been trying to learn for months."

Victoria grudgingly agreed that Marianne might continue to see Jeremy. With each meeting their love grew, but at the same time, she passed along every scrap of information she learned from him, as though trying to assuage her guilt. Marianne suffered from this wrenching duality in her life, but as the months passed, she convinced herself that she would win Jeremy to her cause. The war in Europe was going badly for the English, and the fate of the free world hung in the balance. Napoleon had to be stopped! That meant America must be prevented from starting a diversionary war against England. And thus persuaded that she was acting in the cause of the greater good, Marianne continued her perilous course.

Chapter 39

THE CENSUS of 1810 revealed that the nation had grown by an astonishing rate; the United States now boasted a population of 7,000,000, up one-third since the turn of the century. This count included 1,300,000 slaves and 145,000 freed Negroes. New York and Philadelphia had in excess of 100,000 people, and Washington, D.C., claimed 8,000 inhabitants.

But due to the blockades from the British and French, the severe economic depression continued to grip the country; people were going hungry, if not outright starving.

When Gunning Breech Brand was born, Mathias celebrated the birth of his grandson with such abandon that a massive stroke felled him. With relentless devotion, Rebecca tried to nurse him back to health.

"I never realized how much he meant in my life," she said wearily to Letitia, who'd come to spell her.

"Best you get some rest," Letitia murmured, "or you'll be getting sick yourself."

In spite of everything the doctors did, Mathias succumbed. Not having the one person she'd counted on all her life left a gaping void in Rebecca's life; though she knew his flaws only too well, she had loved him. And suddenly she no longer had a buffer between Zebulon and herself.

She was bereft for months, but when the British captured one of Zebulon's ships, causing severe losses to the Breech-Brand Enterprises, Rebecca pulled herself from her melancholy mood and tried to salvage the business.

"If I leave everything in Zebulon's hands," she said to Letitia, "we'll all soon be ruined."

• • •

"I think we should relocate," Zebulon said. "There aren't enough people in Washington to start a major business. What about Philadelphia? I've always wanted to try publishing. The press is beginning to exert a powerful influence in the country."

"What do you know of publishing?" she asked, frowning.

"Or I'd go to New York, talk to the Schuylers and Astors, get in on the ground floor of the banking business."

If she wasn't so angry she would have laughed at his silly flights of fancy. "Our future lies in neither of those cities; those industries are already controlled. The same is true in New England, where they've set up those cotton mills and shoe factories. But I've heard some interesting stories about Pittsburgh."

Zebulon shrugged. "That wilderness? I understand that they're going to build iron mills and tool-and-die shops, but nothing will come of it."

"What about this Robert Fulton?"

"The mad inventor they call 'Toot'?" Zebulon laughed derisively. "They say he's working on a new steamboat and hopes to get a monopoly on the Ohio and Mississippi Rivers—the way he did on the Hudson, for all the good it did him."

"Do you think the future is in steam?" she asked.

"It's a frivolous invention, capricious at best. It will never replace the sail. The boats blow up all the time and scare the livestock onshore. Of the thirteen hundred cargo boats now plying the Potomac, not one is steam."

"Well, that leaves us with very few options," Rebecca said. "One day, the federal government will control everything that happens in this nation. Why not be a part of that?"

Zebulon's eyes narrowed. "Run for office?"

"That would have been the simplest way," she said, "but I've already made inquiries among the members of both parties; though your Tripoli service might have helped, the reputation you gained in your early years makes you too vulnerable a candidate. That original speculation about the city's real estate lots, the bastard children you have running about, and the scandal about the death of Devroe Connaught are all too much to overcome. But there are other ways to build a base of power.

You must get on the board of directors of a bank, join the militia, do charity work, raise money for the new St. John's Church. In short, if you want the Brands to amount to anything, if you want Gunning to have some advantage in life, you must give up your gambling and your drinking and become a pillar of the community. With the War Hawks in control of Congress, war is certain to come, and in such volatile times, a man can do much to advance himself."

The War Hawks, so called because of their constant, strident call to arms, were led by Henry Clay of Kentucky and John Calhoun of South Carolina. In the 1810 elections, more than one half of the pacifist legislators had lost their seats, a great blow for Madison, who'd hoped to continue the peaceful course set by Jefferson.

"War will come," Zebulon said, "and it should be with the French."

Rebecca shrugged. "Who can say? Though Napoleon harasses us as much as the English, I doubt we'll go to war with the French. We've still too much goodwill toward them for helping us in our revolution. From what Dolley tells me, Madison is being forced toward war with the English."

"That's suicidal!" Zebulon exclaimed. "The British Navy is the most powerful in the world. They have fifty times as many ships as we do."

"That may be, but there's an even more important consideration. Canada. Our War Hawks won't be satisfied until they've driven the English completely out of North America, and annexed that vast territory."

In 1811, a disastrous confrontation inflamed Americans even more against the British. President Madison called a meeting of the heads of the War Department and of the Washington militia, to alert them to the disquieting news from the west. Present in the Cabinet Room were Major General Van Ness, commander of the militia; Zebulon, who'd somehow managed to wrangle a lieutenancy; and Jeremy, risen to a captain in the outfit. A cold November mizzle swept in from the Potomac, and a fire crackled in the hearth. Jeremy was pleased to see that the draft was finally working properly.

Madison went to a map of the Indiana Territory, and pointed

to a region just north of the Ohio River. "Here, at the junction of the Wabash River and Tippecanoe Creek, is a large concentration of Indians. Our settlers in the area were fearful that the British were inciting the Indians against them, and protested to Governor Harrison."

Jeremy knew of Harrison and his reputation; at thirty-eight, he was both a canny frontier fighter and politician. He governed the Indiana Territory with a strong hand.

Madison continued, "After a number of Indian provocations, Harrison marched into the area hoping to subdue the Shawnees. Their chief, Tecumseh, was away, trying to form a federation of tribes to force our settlers out. Tecumseh left his brother, Tenskwatawa, the Prophet, in charge."

Everybody in the room, if not in America, had heard of the Prophet. A one-eyed man, intensely mystical, the Prophet could fall into trances at will and see visions. The Indians believed that the Great Spirit, in taking one of his eyes, had compensated him by giving him the gift of prophecy. Tenskwatawa had accurately predicted an eclipse of the sun, and lately had given the "stamped foot" warnings, predicting that severe earthquakes would rock the country. When in that year a series of powerful quakes had jolted Tennessee and Kentucky, and were felt as far away as Washington, D.C., the Prophet's fame was assured. He further predicted that he would defeat any American force sent against him.

"When General Harrison arrived at Tippecanoe, the Shawnees attacked. Harrison managed to fight them off, but great losses were suffered by both sides."

Madison shuffled some papers nervously and said, "There's one more thing. Harrison's sent me a message about some silly curse the Prophet made. You see, he was smarting from his defeat, and wanted to win his adherents back." He opened a notepaper and read, "Any American elected President in a year that ends with zero, will never live to finish out his term of office. This curse shall stand for all time."

"Surely you don't believe that drivel," Zebulon exclaimed. "More important, what's happened to Tecumseh?"

"He did manage to form a federation of Indian nations, thirty-two in all, and if they ally themselves with the British, it could mean the end of our westward expansion. One final note: After the battle of Tippecanoe, Harrison found British weapons all over the field of battle."

The room exploded in rage, a rage experienced by the rest of the nation when the news was made known. The War Hawks, eager to annex Canada, led the call for war, and in Congress, Henry Clay roared, "I prefer the troubled ocean of war . . . with all its calamities . . . to the tranquil and putrescent pool of ignominious peace!"

As the war talk heated up, a series of meetings were held at the homes of prominent citizens. One such gathering was at the Connaught town house. Amid the shouting and the calls for order, Victoria's voice called out with insistent authority.

"I find it the height of calumny, that a so-called republic, boasting of its freedom, can stoop so low as to aid and abet Napoleon's monstrous ambitions. That this so-called republic wants to plunge the patricidal weapon into the heart of the very country from whence we all sprang—that, my fellow citizens, is conduct so loathsome, that I know God will give us the chastisement we so richly deserve."

A cry of protest greeted that, but Victoria overrode the shouts, her jeweled fan weaving endless patterns around her bewigged face. "Great Britain has been fighting for freedom, everybody's freedom, and we must somehow persuade that little gnome Madison and his silly wife that we're embarked on a ruinous course. All intelligent, concerned citizens must speak out!"

Madison himself tried desperately to avoid war. New Englanders were dead set against it, and both Massachusetts and Connecticut threatened to secede from the Union. But events moved inexorably forward, and finally Madison was forced to ask Congress to declare war against Great Britain. The vote in the Senate was narrow indeed, nineteen to thirteen, and the unpopular conflict immediately became known as "Mr. Madison's War."

PART FIVE

Chapter 40

THE WAR affected the citizens of Washington in many ways. Zebulon suddenly saw the means to make a quick killing. A serious wheat-crop failure in the United States had forced prices sky-high. But smugglers were still doing a brisk business with Canada, so Zebulon sent one of his ships there to buy wheat. He didn't consider it war profiteering; after all, wasn't he bringing food to a hungry nation? But he did decide to keep this particular venture secret from Rebecca.

For her part, Rebecca had turned into a raging patriot. Vitalized by the war and what she considered its moral foundations, she furiously wrote article after article defending Madison and calling the nation to arms.

But in her investigations Rebecca learned very quickly just how unprepared the nation was for war and tried to alert one and all to the dangers.

"During his term in office," Rebel Thorne wrote, "President Jefferson so downgraded our navy, that our total fleet consists of seven frigates and twelve sloops. The British fleet outnumbers us by fifty to one. Jefferson also advocated a civilian militia, believing they would appear in time of crisis, fight off an invading enemy, then return to their peaceful pursuits. Consequently, our army is in a woefully unprepared state.

"I reveal no secrets when I say that our regular army numbers about 6,700 officers and men, but they are poorly trained, poorly outfitted, and poorly led. Major General Dearborn, known as 'Granny' to his men, commands the Eastern armies; it's true that he's a veteran of our War for Independence, but he's gotten so fat that he can't mount his horse! Major General William Hull commands the Western sector, but has a reputation of being frightened of his own shadow. And General Wilkenson, the buffoon who testified at Aaron Burr's trial and who commands Louisiana, has degenerated further into a gross, addlepated hypochondriac.

"Still, despite all these negatives, President Madison had no recourse but to declare war on Great Britain. If the truth be known, by her blockades and impressment of our seamen, Britain has waged war on us for the past two decades! But if we are so unprepared, then why declare war now, in this summer of 1812? Because Napoleon is marching on Moscow! And if, as expected, he conquers Russia, then England will have her hands full fighting Napoleon. That will leave us free to win our war in the New World, and to show Great Britain once and for all that we are a free and independent nation."

As the preparations for war got under way, Jeremy said to Tanzy, "If anything should happen to me, I want to make sure you're free. I've signed the papers for your freedom, and I'm having my lawyer, Francis Scott Key, register them."

"Thank you," Tanzy murmured. "I want you to know that not for one day have you made me feel like a slave. And I'd like to go on working for you, taking care of Circumstance."

Jeremy broke into a broad grin. "Nothing would please me more!"

In July of 1812, the American forces struck all along the Canadian border. Everybody believed it would be a quick and easy victory, but battle after battle was lost to the superior British army, and to incredible American bungling. Tecumseh and a thousand of his fiercest braves joined the British and wreaked havoc behind the American lines. General Hull was so frightened of him that when the British warned they would set Tecumseh on Detroit, Hull surrendered that city without firing a shot.

The only positive note was the performance of the tiny United States Navy. The *Essex,* under Captain David Porter, led the British fleet a merry chase. In August, the *Constitution* sank the *Guerriere* off the coast of Maine. And in December the *Constitution* also sank the British frigate *Java,* off the coast of Brazil.

With the war going badly, Madison appeared doomed to certain defeat in the election held at the end of 1812. The Federalists, with their huge campaign coffers, backed New York Mayor Dewitt Clinton, who tried to have something for everybody. Clinton's campaign was managed by the shrewd Martin Van Buren, rumored to be the illegitimate son of Aaron Burr. But the President had a far better campaign manager. Dolley was everywhere, and so popular, that even Madison's staunchest enemies hesitated to say anything against her. She was the guest of honor aboard the *Constellation* to celebrate United States naval victories, and on the festooned quarterdeck ablaze with lanterns, Washington's elite, including Rebecca and Zebulon, danced far into the night. Following Decatur's capture of the *Macedonia*, a huge celebration took place at Tomlinson's Hotel, and Decatur presented Dolley with the *Macedonia*'s flag. Dolley held the flag aloft and said, "Great Britain *stamped* us into independent states, *counciled* us into a manufacturing people, and is now *fighting* us into a maritime power!" The crowd cheered itself hoarse.

The final electoral vote: Clinton, 87; Madison, 128.

By the beginning of 1813, it became evident that the war would be long and drawn out, and the victor in doubt. The British blockade was being felt with increasing strength, custom receipts were down to one-tenth of normal. Yet the Canadian cities of York and Halifax grew rich on the brisk illegal trade with renegade New England shippers. New England then refused to help finance the war, and only the intercession of New Yorker John Jacob Astor, who floated a loan of twenty-six million dollars, kept the government solvent.

Notwithstanding, Washington grew more frenetic than ever, with an endless round of balls, levees, dinners, weddings, and embassy functions. Gilded coaches bumped along Pennsylvania Avenue in increasing numbers, ladies' dresses were more ornate, and the number of colorful uniforms magnified the city's revelry.

It became so blatant that preachers thundered against the wild parties, the delivery of mail on the Sabbath, and the wickedness of Washington in general. Reverend Breckenridge shouted from the pulpit, "Your temples and palaces shall be burned to the ground!" But war called for frantic entertainments. "After all," Zebulon told Rebecca, "one could be dead with the next battle."

At the White House, Rebecca helped Dolley plan her "fringe parties." The young ladies of Washington society no longer indulged in idle gossip and petit point, these days they talked solemnly about the battles around the Great Lakes, while they sewed fringes for their boyfriends' epaulets.

"With all you carry on your shoulders, I can't imagine how you remain so cheerful," Rebecca told Dolley.

"But my dear, I *am* beside myself. When Mr. Madison became so ill with Potomac fever, and there was talk that Henry Clay planned to seize the government, why every night I went to bed quaking. But I kept my courage, gave Jemmy his quinine, and a merciful Lord helped him recover. It does no good to show distress. It would only worry Jemmy further, and believe me, he has much to worry about. If one keeps up a cheerful front, well, then perhaps that's the way things will work out."

Years earlier, when Rebecca first met Dolley, she'd thought her a bit flighty, and laughed at the costumes she'd affected, the turbans she'd practically invented as her trademark. But she saw that beneath that seemingly frivolous façade, there dwelt a woman of rare sensibilities. When she married Madison, it couldn't have been a love match; he was seventeen years her senior and half her size. Yet she'd become his staunchest ally, his dearest friend. In peace or war, her devotion had been so great that it could be called no other name but love.

And then quite suddenly Rebecca saw a glimmer of hope for herself and Zebulon. "I will make it work," she whispered. "I will. If only he'll give me a chance."

One day, Jeremy received a summons from Madison to attend a cabinet meeting, already in progress. Present were James Monroe, the secretary of state; George Armstrong, the opinionated, self-absorbed New Yorker recently appointed secretary of war; and assorted military personnel.

Madison said to Jeremy, "We've asked you here because of your experience in the western territories. We'd have sent for William Clark, but as he is now the governor of the Missouri Territory, and engaged in the Indian Wars, we thought it best to leave him at his post."

Madison's hand trembled as he poured a glass of water. Jeremy thought he looked awful. He had the soul and character of a philosopher, rather than a soldier, and was more suited to the debates in the political chambers than in leading his nation in war.

Madison went on. "Through reports of enemy activity and other considerations, we think that the Louisiana Territory might turn into the soft underbelly of the nation. Since you have firsthand knowledge of this area, would you be good enough to repeat what you've already told me?"

Jeremy said, "When we were on the Northwest Expedition, Meriwether Lewis always warned us that the British intended to capture New Orleans. That force would work its way up the Mississippi, while another English army would descend from Canada, capture the Great Lakes, and join up with the southern force. Once the Louisiana Territory was conquered, their combined armies would sweep eastward with but one thought, to drive us into the sea. I believe the British plan to do this right now."

Armstrong threw back his head and laughed harshly. "That is the most ludicrous thing I've ever heard. Pray tell, where will the British get the men to conquer New Orleans?"

"I understand Napolcon has been forced to retreat from Moscow, and that he's lost most of his army," Jeremy said.

"A momentary setback," Armstrong said, waving his larded arm. "Napoleon is invincible."

Jeremy set his jaw. He didn't like this patrician blowhard, but he kept his peace because of President Madison. "I believe the soundest policy would be for us to depend on our own efforts, rather than counting on others. Outside of a few sparse settlements, such as New Orleans and St. Louis, the territory is mostly uninhabited. At best, we could only muster a thin corps of frontiersmen. And if the British should manage to further inflame the Indians against our settlers, then they're lost."

Madison nodded gravely. "We've received reports that British agents have been infiltrating the territory, stirring up the Creek Indians. We've already alerted General Andrew Jackson."

This elicited such a harangue from Secretary of War Armstrong, including a veiled threat of resignation, that Madison abandoned the subject. He shuffled some papers, and Jeremy knew he'd been dismissed. With a slight bow, he left the Cabinet Room.

Later that night, after he'd put Circumstance to bed, Jeremy rode out to the Connaught estate. Marianne met him at the old abandoned barn on the outskirts of the property. After they'd made love, they lay in each other's arms, and she caressed his bare chest. "You seem so far away, darling."

He told her about the meeting with Madison, of Armstrong's supercilious attitude, and when he mentioned New Orleans, she stiffened.

"What's the matter?" he asked.

"Nothing, just the dampness in this hay."

Then he said, "Here I am worried about New Orleans, when Washington itself is even more vulnerable. The Chesapeake Bay has almost become a British lake; their war ships cruise about as they please, burning, pillaging, raping. Hampton Bay and Havre de Grace have been leveled to the ground."

"Suppose the British do invade. Are we prepared?" Marianne asked tentatively.

"I think not. Some people say that Armstrong hates Washington so much that he would gladly see it burned. Then the government would have to move to a real city like Philadelphia, or New York."

"But surely the militia will protect the city," she said.

"With the exception of Joshua Barney's men from the Navy Yard, there isn't a decent fighting unit in all Washington."

"I wish the fighting would stop!" she exclaimed. "I don't care who wins!"

He gazed at her intently, trying to fathom what was going on in her mind.

She saw the look in his eyes and put her head against his chest, kissing his rigid nipples. "After searching all my life for someone to love, I couldn't bear it if anything happened to you. Am I so mistaken to hate war?"

"Every man of sound mind hates war," he said. "But you must understand, Marianne, the British intend to crush us, force us back into their empire. It's no longer a war to prevent the impressment of our seamen, nor to break the British blockade that's strangled us for years. Marianne, this is nothing less than our Second War for Independence, and unless we have firm resolve, we shall lose it!"

Chapter 41

THE WARM June weather gave way to the stultifying heat of July. Many Washingtonians left for the watering places in the mountains of Virginia and Maryland, but the President and his cabinet remained in the capital. More British vessels were reported in Chesapeake Bay, but the *National Intelligencer* kept up a continued cheerful front, insisting that there was no danger.

Jeremy crumpled the paper into a ball and threw it across the room. "How can those idiots on the paper keep saying that?" he demanded.

Tanzy and Circumstance listened to him in silence as he paced the confines of the room, slamming pieces of furniture with his fist to emphasize his anger. "The British have entered Paris! They've forced Napoleon to abdicate! That means they've freed thousands of their troops to battle here! And still Armstrong does nothing to defend Washington. How can Madison and Monroe be so blind? Have we all gone mad?"

At the Connaught estate, Victoria had just received a secret communiqué from a British vessel prowling the Chesapeake. "Marianne, come quickly!" she cried.

Marianne came in from the sewing room, where she'd been with her mother, and hurried to her aunt. "What is it?"

"I thank the merciful Lord that he's allowed me to see this day," Victoria exclaimed, her face wreathed in smiles. "This calls for a glass of sherry." She poured two glasses and handed one to Marianne. "My dear, I've just received the most momentous news. Ten thousand of Wellington's crack troops have sailed from England for Canada. Once they arrive there, they'll cross the border and invade!"

"Oh my God," Marianne whispered.

"It is wonderful, isn't it?" Victoria said, completely misinterpreting her niece's response. "And that's not all. At the same time, other British forces under the command of General Ross and Admiral Cockburn—remember we met them the last time we were in London? Well, they're preparing to land an army in the Chesapeake area. If all goes as planned, they'll march on Washington and take the city!"

"No, it can't be," Marianne murmured, shaking her head.

Victoria leaned forward and grasped her hands. "Child, I know it appears too good to be true. We've waited so long for this, put aside our personal lives, but now at last our efforts are about to be rewarded. Marianne, I've saved the best for last. Your cousin Sean will be commanding one of the intelligence units landing here."

Marianne felt the blood leave her face and she reeled, spilling some of her sherry.

This time, Victoria couldn't misinterpret the mood. "Well, my dear, you don't seem too pleased. What's wrong?"

Marianne took a deep breath and managed to say, "The same thing that's been wrong all along. More killing, more lives ruined. Will it never end?"

Victoria's eyes narrowed. "You sound as if you've been listening to subversives."

"There are those who say that we're the subversives," Marianne said. "We *do* live in this land; we *are* Americans."

"Never! We're English, and we'll be English again just as soon as this rabble nation is crushed. All your strange ideas . . . You've been listening to Jeremy Brand, haven't you?"

Though Marianne had long ago reached the age where her aunt no longer had any legal control over her, she hadn't been able to tell her family the way she felt about Jeremy. The outbreak of the war had further complicated matters. But she could contain herself no longer. "And what if I have been talking to Jeremy? I've never met a more decent human being!"

"He's a peasant, a commoner," Victoria spat.

Marianne refused to flinch under Victoria's rheumy gaze. "Then you must brand me that also," she said.

"This is unspeakable!" Victoria shouted. "Have you forgotten what they did? They murdered your father! Have you no shame?"

"Jeremy didn't do that," Marianne shouted back.

The two women whirled as the drawing room doors flew open. Hearing the raised voices, Elizabeth Connaught had come in from the sewing room. Her only sign of age was her graying hair. Her eyes still had the clearness of youth, but they saw little; the shutters were shut, no light might pass. In her hand, she clutched a ten-foot-long panel of petit point she'd been stitching.

"Marianne? You must help me with this," Elizabeth said, holding out the panel. Almost twenty years of labor had made it a monumental canvas of the old Federal City, with quaint figures on horseback, autumnal forests, snakes writhing at the bank of the river, and the sky aflame. As Marianne came to her mother, Elizabeth grasped her arm. "We must finish it, and very soon."

Marianne gently loosened her mother's fingers. "We'll do some more tomorrow."

Elizabeth shook her head. "No, not tomorrow. The fire has eaten tomorrow."

With a strangled cry, Marianne called for the maid; she came running in and led Elizabeth out of the drawing room. Marianne slumped to the settee, tears spilling from her eyes. Her anguished face was drained of all color and she seemed on the verge of fainting. That canvas . . . as she'd watched her mother through the years, every single one of those stitches had gone like a needle through Marianne's heart.

Victoria pressed the glass of sherry into her hands. "Are you all right?"

She nodded.

"Child, by all that's sacred, by all the love I hold for you, I beg you, don't throw away all we've worked for. Our way is better. You know I'm speaking the truth. Do you need any greater proof than that sad poor creature?"

With the vision of her mother in her tear-swollen eyes, Marianne nodded imperceptibly.

"Excellent, excellent. Remember, you're a Connaught." Victoria raised her glass. "We shall crush these rebellious colonies once and for all. I drink to victory."

Marianne felt the wine burn as it went down her throat. "To victory," she whispered.

At seven in the evening of August 18, Major Hiram Blackwell sent a courier racing from Smith Point at the mouth of the Potomac to the White House. When President Madison read the message, he immediately sent runners to summon his cabinet and the other men vital to the defense of Washington.

Armstrong, the secretary of war, grumbled about being interrupted at supper, and James Monroe complained about the late hour. General Winder, recently appointed by Madison to oversee the defense of Washington, hurried to the White House, as did Major General Van Ness, commander of the Washington militia, and his second in command, Jeremy Brand.

Madison looked close to exhaustion. "Twenty-two more British vessels have sailed into the Chesapeake. They include three warships of the line, a brig, a topsail schooner, several frigates, and at least nine troop transports. They've joined forces with the British ships already in the bay, and now the enemy fleet numbers fifty-one vessels."

Dead silence greeted this piece of news, and then Jeremy said, "The troop transports are a clear signal that the British intend to strike at Washington."

"That's exactly what they want us to think," Armstrong exclaimed. "Any strategist can see that there's nothing to be gained by invading this—this sheep walk! The British are after Baltimore, where they can cut our lines of communication to Philadelphia, New York, and Boston."

Though James Monroe usually feuded with Armstrong over the slightest matter—Monroe's overweening ambition threw him into the center of any argument—in this case he agreed with him. "If the British did land here, they'd be wiped out completely."

Van Ness disagreed vehemently. "This is sheer madness, not to protect one's capital. We must build breastworks at vital roads, outfit our militia, protect the heart of the nation!"

"Are you suggesting that we waste money that we don't have?" Armstrong demanded.

Van Ness swore and threw his hands in the air. Then General Winder requested arms and men for his unit and Armstrong turned him down too. After considerably more shouting President Madison managed to restore some order. "I've met with such resistance and vacillation from all of you that I've devised my own defense plans. I'll station three thousand men at a point midway between Washington and Baltimore, so that they can defend either city. An additional ten thousand men will be stationed in nearby states, ready to strike wherever they're needed."

"That sounds like an excellent plan," Jeremy said. He was surprised, and suddenly felt very proud of his tiny President.

Armstrong began paring his nails. "The only difficulty is that I can't put those additional ten thousand men on active duty."

"Why not?" Jeremy asked.

"The government simply doesn't have the money to pay them."

Hours later, the cabinet meeting broke up without anything being resolved.

In the dead of the night, a slave named Benjamin held a secret meeting in the basement of an abandoned warehouse on the Potomac. Some fifteen Negroes had managed to slip away from their quarters and had gathered there; among them was Eli.

"All we have to do is revolt," Benjamin said. "Then we join up with the British. They set up a place for us on Tangier Island in the Chesapeake Bay and we all be free men."

The whites of Eli's eyes flashed in his dark face. "Who told you this?"

"Everybody know it. The British been telling us since this war started. Revolt. Be free. You seen this?" He passed out the propaganda leaflets the British had flooded the area with.

Eli's voice rumbled with anger. "When I was captured in my land and put on a ship, that ship flew the British flag. When we made our first stop, it was Liverpool, England. English ships transported millions of our people from Africa to the new world, and the English grew rich on our blood. And now you ask me to believe that the very same nation would set us free?"

"But that's what they promise. All we have to do—"

"Don't be a fool," Eli interrupted. "Can't you see you're

being used again? If there's freedom for us anywhere in this country, then it will come from the North." For a moment, his mind flashed back through the years to John and Abigail Adams, and how outspoken they'd been about the abolition of slavery.

"Look at those Presidents," Benjamin hissed. "Thomas Jefferson owns slaves and makes babies with them, but says we ain't equal to whites. And Madison owns slaves."

Eli studied Benjamin; the slave could neither read nor write. Somebody must have drilled these thoughts into his head. That somebody must have been his owners, the Connaughts.

"Benjamin, if you think that *any* white man will willingly give us our freedom, then you're a worse fool than I thought. One day when we're stronger, better organized, we'll fight for it. But that day isn't now."

"You run scared if you want," Benjamin said with a wave of his hand. "But them of us who ain't cowards, we revolt the minute the British soldiers land. Couple of days now, I hears. Then we be free."

With the news that a massive British fleet was cruising in the Chesapeake, panic hit Washington. Once more Victoria Connaught tried to influence opinion among the powerful families in Washington, and at a hastily convened town-hall meeting, she was addressing the crowd. Victoria was now more than eighty, and cataracts blurred her vision, but her presence and passion held the audience rapt. Many were even sympathetic to her.

"The situation has become impossible," she said. "New England is ready to secede from the Union, and Maryland, the supposed protector of this city, would sign a peace treaty with the British tomorrow if it had the choice. Now is the time for thinking people to act responsibly, and I say we must sue for peace."

Rebecca fidgeted in her chair. "Damn the old fool!"

Zebulon shushed her. "Let her finish."

Victoria Connaught continued. "In England, I made the acquaintance of Rear Admiral Cockburn, who commands the British fleet. Let me assure you, in peace he's a perfect gentleman, but in war I understand that he can be a veritable Attila."

Unable to contain herself another second, Rebecca called out, "Yes, we saw that when Cockburn burned and pillaged Hampton and Havre de Grace."

"That was in retaliation for American troops setting fire to the parliament buildings in York," Victoria said. "As I've always maintained, violence begets violence. Admiral Cockburn's men are the best in the world, and he is so beloved that they will follow him anywhere."

"I've yet to meet a commander who's not beloved by his men," Rebecca said sarcastically. "And if he *is* so beloved, why do British sailors constantly desert?"

Victoria turned the full force of her weighted gaze on her. "Mark me, Madam Brand, if we persist in this madness, then Cockburn will level this city. Do you want your homes burned, your possessions destroyed? No. Then speak out now, and end this madness. The war is lost anyway."

Victoria Connaught almost had the audience believing her when Jeremy jumped to his feet. "Madam, you appeal for reason, yet we all know the terms that John Quincy Adams brought back from the peace conference in Russia. The British demand that we return the Louisiana Territory to Spain. Is that reasonable? The British insist on the exclusion of American vessels from the fisheries off Newfoundland. You call that reasonable? And they would prohibit us from trading with anybody save England. How can anybody in his right mind believe that these demands are reasonable?"

Marianne, sitting near her aunt, dug her fingers into her palms. She loathed being here, trapped between her family and her lover. When will this dreadful war be over? she thought desperately.

Jeremy went on. "The sole British aim is to crush our nation and place us under the domination of the crown. Our experiment, a democracy of the people, faces certain extinction, and the United States will be no more . . . born 1776, died 1814."

Though she knew it to be a piece of insanity, Victoria Connaught was so enraged that she couldn't help but speak out. "Who can say but that God wills it so?"

A chair fell over with a clatter as Rebecca pushed her way to where Victoria sat. "I cannot believe that, I won't believe that! Madam Connaught, I know that Washington abounds with people who feel as you do, but I'll tell you this. If the British should land and march on Washington, and if any of my fellow citizens raised one finger to help them, I would personally take my pistol, place it at the traitor's heart, and pull the trigger!"

"How dare you say such a thing?" Victoria Connaught demanded. "Have we degenerated into savages?"

"I dare say it because this is my country, built on the dreams and aspirations of all the people I call brother." Rebecca's eyes swept over the hall and locked with Jeremy's. In that instant, understanding and admiration flowed between them, for in this matter, they knew their souls were joined. And somewhere deep within them, both mourned that it couldn't have been more.

"And now instead of sitting here talking," Rebecca said, "it's time we were rounding up ammunition, digging ditches! Time we did *something* instead of just wasting time." She swept from the meeting hall, and most of the people followed her.

Later that evening, Victoria Connaught carefully folded some papers and put them in a waterproof packet. "Well, we did our best to have the city spared, but they wouldn't listen. They've brought it on their own heads." Her wattles shook delicately as she shuddered. "Those Brand people, they're as disgusting as any common criminals."

A deep weariness hung heavily on Marianne's shoulders, and she pressed her fingers to her temples. Would they never be able to extricate themselves from this labyrinth of hate?

"You're to take these papers to Mr. Hopewell at Drum Point," Victoria said, handing them to her. "The roads are being watched, so it will create less suspicion if a woman goes."

Marianne mounted her black gelding and rode hard for the peninsula. She arrived at the small cabin a little after dusk, her horse in a lather. She gave the packet to Mr. Hopewell. The Tory sympathizer had been passing information to the British ever since the war began. Marianne had turned to go when a tall balding man stepped from behind a curtain and blocked her path.

"Sean!"

Her cousin smiled and embraced her. Mr. Hopewell brought

them a bottle of wine and Sean raised his glass. "Here's to seeing you again, and to the success of our mission."

Marianne looked at him over the rim of her glass. Even out of uniform he cut a fine figure. His body had the thick solidity of a man of thirty-eight. He'd recently lost his wife to tuberculosis, leaving him with two young children.

"I'd never expected to see you here," she said. "Isn't it dangerous? If you were caught out of uniform you could be shot as a spy."

"Dangerous it is, but all of war is a risk. Since I knew the area well, I volunteered for the assignment, and Providence rewarded me by sending you."

She twitched uneasily with the compliment. During her last trip to England, when his wife had been so very ill, he'd paid much attention to her. She knew he had designs, ones that her aunt had encouraged, and lest he go further with this line of talk, she hurriedly opened the papers and pointed to a map of the Washington area.

"The American flotilla will sail up the Patuxent River," she said. "Joshua Barney and his men plan to anchor the ships above the tidewater for safety."

"Which is where the stupid Americans should have built their capital in the first place," he said. "That way, we could never have outflanked the city, as we're about to do. What about gun emplacements around Washington?"

"None, really. There are two cannon in front of the White House, but they're more decorative than useful. The only really fortified place is the Navy Yard."

"Ah, yes, and the Navy Yard is vital to our plans," he said. "There are ships there, and naval stores to replenish our own dwindling supplies." He straightened and grasped her hand in his. "Marianne, at last the grand design is falling into place. If all goes well with our Washington campaign, then we strike at Baltimore. And then administer the coup de grâce at New Orleans. We'll sail there to support our invasion force which is scheduled to land at the end of this year. But first we must deliver a punishing blow to Washington."

"That shouldn't be difficult," she said. "There's no leadership; everybody works at cross-purposes. Monroe and Armstrong do nothing but quarrel, and General Winder, in charge of the city's overall defense, does nothing but ride aimlessly through the countryside."

"All that works for us," he said. "How many men can they put into the field?"

"About four thousand, I think. But most of them are ragged and ill-equipped."

"Extraordinary. What can be in their minds? Do they *want* to lose their capital? No discipline whatsoever, and where there's no discipline, a nation must fall. Is there any one general or good fighting force that we should eliminate at the outset?"

Remembering what Jeremy had told her about Joshua Barney's unit, Marianne's throat tightened. With his predilection for getting into things, Jeremy would probably take it into his head to fight alongside Barney, and so she said nothing.

"And what of this planned slave insurrection?" Sean asked. "It's imperative that a revolt break out the moment our troops land. There are more than one and a half million Negroes in America. If they were to rise up against their masters victory would be ours."

"We've tried in every way possible to foment unrest," she said. "But we've no clear sign of success."

Sean cracked his knuckles one by one. "It's been our greatest disappointment. We've guaranteed every Negro his freedom, but so far only a handful have joined us. But I'm sure it will be different once we've landed."

"It will be dark shortly. I must go," Marianne said.

He led her to the door. "What news of the Brand brothers?"

She clasped her hands to keep them from trembling. "I don't know. I rarely see them."

Sean reflected on that; it wasn't what his aunt had written to him. He smiled at her. "Well, I've a feeling that I'll meet them soon enough. When I do, there'll be old scores to settle." With an impulsive move he took her in his arms, holding her long enough for her to sense his pleasure.

"Marianne, when this is over . . ."

She pulled free before he could say more. "But it's not over. And right now, I can think of nothing else."

He held onto her arms, so many thoughts on his mind. She regarded him. His strong face and character, his deportment, everything about him marked him as a superior man, one that any woman could love. But God had seen fit to twist her emotions and her life, seen fit to make her love Jeremy. There were times when she envied her mother's ability to block out the real world, for with the vital maps and plans in Sean's hands, she now felt that she had committed a terrible crime. She had betrayed her country, she had betrayed Jeremy.

Chapter 42

BY FRIDAY, August 19, Washington was rife with rumors: that the British would attack the capital, that they possessed a terrible, secret weapon. Armstrong discounted it all. "If the British had a secret weapon, we would know about it. And Baltimore is their goal; it's a much more important military target."

"But they've landed only fifteen miles from Washington," Jeremy said. "They're heading toward Bladensburg now."

"A diversionary feint," Armstrong insisted.

Though the call went out to the surrounding states for men and weapons, the immediate source of help lay in the city's own militia. Jeremy tried to get the men organized as they assembled at the foot of Capitol Hill.

"How do they look?" Major General Van Ness asked.

Jeremy shook his head. "We've only been able to muster about a thousand men. Most of them are in terrible shape, some have no clothes or shoes, others have no rifles, and those that do lack powder and shot."

"Have the supplies we requested from the War Department arrived?" Van Ness demanded.

"Armstrong refused our requisition on the grounds that he doesn't have enough for the regular army."

Van Ness's curses colored the air. "The idiot *wants* the British to take the capital! Well, we've known all along that he didn't have any love for our city." He looked ruefully at the rag-tag company of men before him. "Where is Jefferson's civilian militia now that the British are bearing down on us?"

Van Ness cornered Armstrong and read him out in no uncertain terms. Madison, under intense pressure from Armstrong, revoked Van Ness's orders, leaving General Winder in full charge. Outraged, Van Ness quit in disgust, and the civilian militia fell apart.

Later that night while Jeremy was cleaning his gun, Tanzy asked, "What will you do now?"

"Join forces with Joshua Barney's sailors. They're the only ones who know what they're doing."

"I'm worried about Circumstance," Tanzy said. "Would it be better to leave the city?"

Jeremy considered that. "If we run, then the British are sure to capture it. I think we've got to make a stand. All we need is the will and we can beat them."

"Mrs. Madison told me that if things got real bad then I should bring Circumstance over there. The President is going to post a guard around the White House."

"That's a good idea, Tanzy. My mind's easier knowing that you're watching out for her. How in the world did I ever get along without you?"

He smiled at her and she felt her pulse quicken. But then he began cleaning his rifle and the moment passed. He paused and said, "Tanzy, if you do go to the White House, will you take my drawings with you for safekeeping? There's a bin in the basement you can store them in." He shook his head. "You'd think that President Jefferson's so-called scientific commission in Philadelphia would have called for them by now. Well, I guess that's always the way with bureaucratic red tape."

"Papa, can I go to the front with you?" Circumstance asked.

He scooped her up in his arms and nuzzled her. "No, this is one journey I've got to make alone. But I'll come back, I promise." And then suddenly he was overcome with an unbidden memory . . . Many years ago, he'd made exactly the same promise to her mother.

To prevent the American flotilla from falling into the hands of the British, Commodore Joshua Barney sailed his vessels up the Patuxent River. Admiral Cockburn's fleet sailed after them in hot pursuit.

Barney had sixteen gunboats and thirteen trading vessels, but they were no match for the British men-of-war, bristling with scores of cannon. Rather than have the British capture the flotilla, Barney blew the lot up.

After firing the ships, Barney and his men joined General Winder's force just nine miles north of Washington, and it was there that Jeremy attached himself to the swashbuckling old salt with his five-hundred-odd men.

James Monroe was in the field also, countermanding everybody's orders, and at nine that evening he dashed off a communiqué to the White House. "The enemy is advancing six miles on the road. Our troops were on the march to meet them but in too small a body to engage. General Winder proposes to retire, till he can collect them in a body. The enemy is in full march toward Washington. Have the materials prepared to destroy the bridges. And you had better remove the records to a safe place."

Monday evening, August 21, harassed clerks at the State Department hurriedly packed up important documents, including George Washington's commission, the papers of the Revolutionary Government, the secret journals of Congress, and the Declaration of Independence.

As the clerks struggled with the cartons of papers, Armstrong paused in the doorway long enough to shout, "The British aren't going to attack Washington, they're going to Baltimore!"

The clerks continued packing. Clearly, the man was suffering from some kind of aberration; all along he'd maintained that the British would never land, and now they were less than ten miles distant, encircling Bladensburg. The government papers were secreted in Edgar Patterson's gristmill across the Potomac, two miles above Georgetown.

The only man in Washington with diplomatic immunity was the French minister, Louis Serurier. After Napoleon's defeat, the English had been instrumental in placing Louis XVIII on the throne, and so naturally they would respect that monarch's ambassador. Colonel Tayloe, owner of the fabulous Octagon House a few blocks from the White House, devised an ingenious scheme to save his mansion. He asked Ambassador Serurier to move into the Octagon House for the duration of the war, and the French minister agreed.

• • •

"You and the children have to get out of Washington," Zebulon said to Rebecca. "The militia has fallen apart, and there isn't a hope in hell that they'll be able to defend the city."

"I'm not leaving," Rebecca said. "I've told you before and I don't want to argue. I'm staying right here."

"I blame this entire thing on Madison," Zebulon said, pouring himself a heavy shot of brandy. "He doesn't know the first thing about leadership. The Tories in southern Maryland are giving the British food, ammunition, and information. God knows how many British sympathizers there are in Washington, boring from within."

Rebecca unhooked the crystal drops from the sconces and packed them away, along with all the other breakables. "I know of one family," she muttered. "Victoria Connaught would gladly see the city fall—nay, the entire country. Then she'd be a bona fide duchess again. Lord knows what other nightmarish dreams figure in her twisted mind."

"Mayor Blake's enforced a ten o'clock curfew," Zebulon said. "Be sure you're not out on the streets then. Watch out especially for the slaves. There are all sorts of rumors about an insurrection."

For a moment, seeing him standing there ramrod straight with his saber buckled to his side, pistols stuck in his belt, Rebecca loved him. She turned and looked out the leaded-glass windows and saw the White House a few blocks away, standing on its small rise of ground. Outside, wagons rolled along New York Avenue, loaded down with furniture and bedding, chairs upended, children sitting on top of it all. Other people had simply locked up their homes and fled.

"Sometimes I wonder how we ever won the Revolution," she said. "Was it by default? Look at these cowards run. And from an invader with stretched supply lines. Don't they realize that if we all made a stand, fought the British from the rooftops, from the streets and the forests, that we'd win the day? Have we become so soft a nation that we can't see that?"

Zebulon swept her into his arms and kissed her full on the mouth. The tension had made him hunger for her, and she wasn't far from the same mood. But she brushed his searching hand aside when Suzannah came running into the room, carrying Gunning along. She was almost six years old and a delicate miniature version of Zebulon with his dark good looks. Gunning, dressed in a little sailor suit, favored Rebecca, with the same titian hair and hazel eyes. Zebulon picked up the children, one in each arm.

"I must go now," he said, kissing them.

"Where?" Suzannah asked.

"I'm in charge of moving the government's papers from the Capitol. We'll store some in Tomlinson's Hotel, and the rest in nearby houses." Zebulon put the children down and kissed Rebecca. "I'll make arrangements for you to stay at Ambassador Serurier's in the Octagon House. You'll be safe there."

Rebecca nodded absently. She might send the children there if things really became dangerous, but she had no intention of leaving her own house. Despite the British inducements, only a handful of slaves had gone over to them, and Negroes were working alongside white people, digging ditches to fortify the city. But Rebecca, a consummate realist, knew that their loyalties could change in an instant if their masters fled, and she'd worked too long and too hard to risk having her home go up in smoke.

Chapter 43

AT THE White House on Tuesday evening, President and Dolley Madison fidgeted through supper. Madison read and reread the dispatches from the front, searching vainly for words of comfort. "I can't bear the suspense of this harrowing evening," he said. "Dolley, I don't know if there's anything I can do, but it's my duty as Commander in Chief to be with my men. My dear, if I were to go, do you have the courage, the firmness, to remain here? I'll return as soon as humanly possible."

"My only fear is for you and the success of our army," she said.

He kissed her on the cheek. "Take care then, and if anything should happen, save the cabinet papers. Oh, and I promised the Custis grandchildren that I would look after the portrait of General Washington."

"Don't worry, my dear, I'll see to it," she said.

Madison, in the company of his aides, headed for Long Old Fields, some eight miles east of Washington, where the American army was encamped. When they got there, they found the army in hopeless confusion.

"What happened?" Madison demanded of General Winder.

"A grazing cow blundered into our camp in the darkness," Winder said. "The men thought the British were attacking, and fired their muskets at anything that moved. It's a wonder no one was killed. The cow's fine also."

Eight miles to the north of Long Old Fields, Rear Admiral Cockburn, General Ross, Captain Sean Connaught, and the crack troops of the British army were spending a quiet night in preparation for the morning's engagement.

General Ross studied the map that Marianne Connaught had given Sean several days before. "With the Americans fielding about five thousand men, both our armies are now evenly matched."

"But they're an undisciplined, leaderless lot," Sean said. "They're the scum of the earth, the rejects of Europe."

"Nevertheless, I believe we're too far from our supply ships. To go further south and strike at Washington would put our troops in even greater jeopardy. Particularly since we don't know the terrain," General Ross said.

"But I know this place like the back of my hand," Sean said. He clenched his fist. "Sir, we have Washington within our grasp. We could give it such a punishing blow that it might well make the Americans sue for peace."

"I agree completely," Admiral Cockburn said. "General, we mustn't give up this golden opportunity. It's what every soldier ever dreams of, capturing the enemy's capital. And we haven't come across a single bit of resistance worth noting. I submit that *not* to strike at Washington would mark us as cowards."

After careful consideration, and continuous urging from both Sean and Cockburn, General Ross agreed. At two o'clock the following day, August 23, all the forces of the British army and marines, along with every available sailor from the British warships, had congregated and began the march towards Bladensburg. The road at Bladensburg led directly to Washington.

Exactly at that hour, James Madison, reassured that the Americans had gotten hold of themselves and were ready to fend off any enemy attack, returned to the White House and called another meeting with his cabinet.

Armstrong had finally come up with some sort of contingency plan for Washington. "If the British do march here—I'm certain that they won't, but just in case—we should barricade all our forces in the Capitol Building. Once the British charge is spent, we then rush out and decimate them." Armstrong placed his hand over his heart, "On the success of this plan, I would pledge both my life and my reputation."

Another officer thought it best to blow up the Capitol so as not to give the British that satisfaction, but Madison said, "No, it would be better if the British did that. Such an act might inflame our people and make them fight the harder."

Leaving Captain Carroll with a force of one hundred men to guard the White House, once more Madison and his cabinet rode for the front. An hour later they learned that the situation had deteriorated, and Madison sent a courier galloping back to the White House.

Dolley ripped open the message. "Be ready at a moment's warning to get your carriage and be ready to flee the city. The enemy is reported now stronger than first thought. They might attack the city and destroy it."

When Dolley informed Captain Carroll and the staff, they were stunned. Dolley then sent Sukie running to Jeremy's house to get Circumstance and Tanzy. "They aren't safe alone now," she said. She turned to her butler, French John Souissat. "We must salvage as much as we can," she said, and she began to cram everything of value into her trunks.

French John said, "Madame, it would be easy to lay a trail of powder leading to explosives that would ignite when the British entered the house."

Dolley gasped. "Gladly would I defend this house if I had a cannon at every window! For this is the home of the President of the United States, and whoever attacks it attacks every single American. But hidden explosives? Never! War is horrible, but even in war some things aren't done."

Having packed all the important papers, and seen to the safety of the servants and of the guests who'd been visiting, including one of her sisters, Dolley waited for further word. The hours dragged by, and to keep her mind from horrible thoughts, she penned letter after letter to another sister, an hour-by-hour account of all that was happening.

The British troops, aptly nicknamed Wellington's Invincibles, five thousand strong, were on the road to Bladensburg. The town afforded access to the only bridge that crossed the Eastern Branch of the Potomac north of Washington.

Jeremy, along with Joshua Barney's men, had taken up positions on the Washington side of the bridge. "Why doesn't

General Winder give the command to blow up the bridge?" Jeremy demanded. "If the British manage to cross here, they'll have a clear road directly south to the capital. Doesn't Winder understand that?"

"I think not," Barney said, spitting out tobacco juice. "I believe those months he spent as a British prisoner of war addled his brains. He claims the ammunition wagons haven't arrived from Washington."

"We could set fire to it," Jeremy said.

"Of course! But Winder is a nincompoop, and he'll cost us this battle and this day. Never have I seen such a thing. Our defenses are confounded by every high and mighty general in the government thinking that he and he alone is in command," Barney exclaimed. "Even Colonel Monroe, who hasn't fought in a battle in twenty-five years, fancies himself as some kind of Caesar!"

Amidst all the confusion, President Madison and Armstrong finally arrived at the south bank of the river. At almost the same moment, the British army occupied the north bank, their red tunics and the flashing steel of their bayonets reflecting the sun.

The President's party galloped toward the Bladensburg bridge and would have crossed it if they hadn't been stopped by a lone American scout, William Simmons. "Don't cross!" Simmons cried, waving his arms.

"Out of our way, man," Armstrong ordered.

"Mr. President, the British have occupied Bladensburg," Simmons cried, grabbing the bridle of Madison's horse.

"The enemy in Bladensburg?" Madison echoed faintly. The entire party wheeled their horses and turned back.

The indomitable British war machine advanced; the perfect cadence of feet against the hard-packed earth sounded through the still countryside. Victorious in every major arena in the world, strengthened by the knowledge that they'd defeated Napoleon, the scourge of Europe, they moved forward. What were these silly Americans to them? The British foot soldiers reached their side of the bridge, and at a command from their officer, stopped. On the other side, the Americans waited, ready to fire.

In the little stone town of Bladensburg, the British marines worked to set up some sort of contraption. "Can you make out what they're doing?" Joshua Barney asked Jeremy, who held the spyglass to his eye.

"I've never seen anything like that device before," Jeremy said. Suddenly a series of whooshes sounded over the heads of the Americans, followed by explosions off to the left.

The men looked at each other. "It's not a cannon, I can tell you that," Barney said, and ducked as more explosions peppered their positions.

President Madison was in a dilemma. He was the Commander in Chief of the army, and it was his constitutional duty to lead his men in battle. Yet he could see that he and his cabinet would only be in the way. He turned to Armstrong and Monroe and said, "Come, we must leave the battlefield to the commanding general."

When a few more missiles tore across the sky and exploded all about them, Madison and the others retreated farther behind the lines. The American artillery scored a few hits on the ranks of the advancing British foot soldiers, but their glee was short-lived, for the British barrage became even more fierce.

The Americans couldn't have known that the new British weapon was the rocket. It hadn't been fully developed or perfected, and the British gunners depended more on a barrage than accuracy, but when the projectiles began to burst in the American breastwork defenses, the soldiers broke ranks and scrambled to get out.

The British advanced across the bridge, and Barney's artillery raked them, but before the gunners had a chance to reload, the British had raced across and fanned out, outflanking the American lines.

"They're like an unstoppable machine," Jeremy shouted, as he watched the redcoated ranks advance. If one soldier fell, another immediately stepped into his place. General Winder's attempt to rally his forces succeeded momentarily, until another fusillade of rockets whizzed overhead, and then the entire regiment of Americans dissolved in the face of this awesome weapon. They broke and ran, carrying everything before them.

"We must retreat also!" Barney shouted to his men. "Otherwise, we'll be cut off by the damned redcoats!"

Jeremy knew that if the American line had held, they could

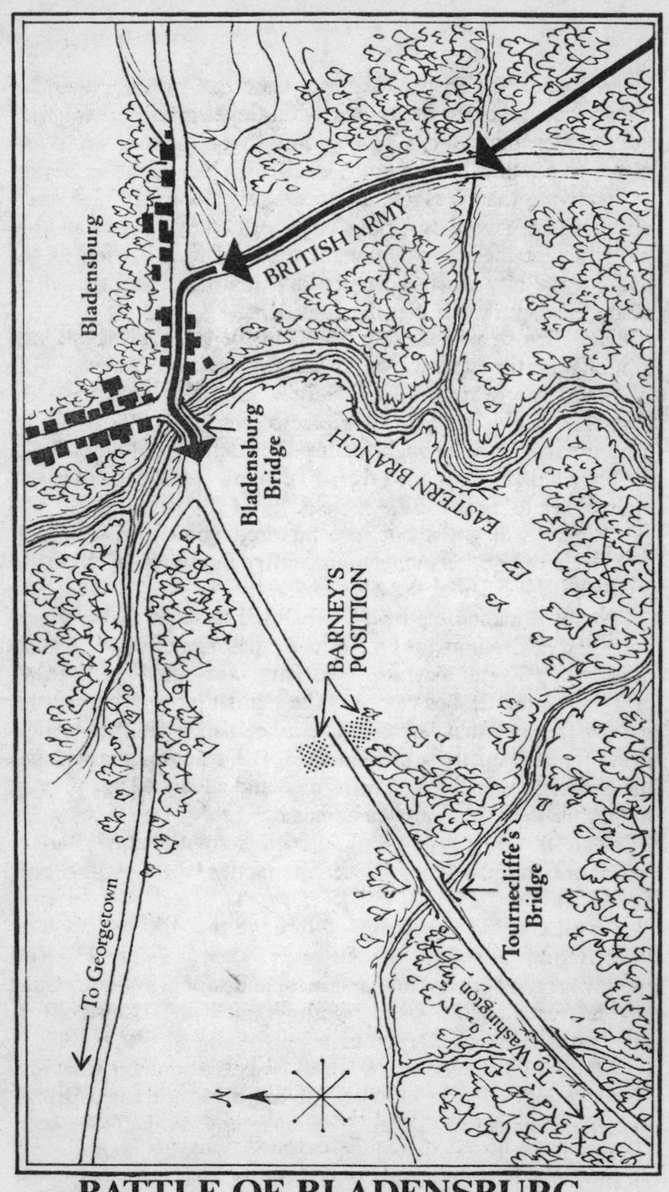

BATTLE OF BLADENSBURG

have stopped the British, but the panic had hit the American lines so quickly that the retreat would ever after be known as the "Bladensburg Races." By midafternoon the rout was complete; in less than half an hour, the British had been victorious.

Knowing that Washington was surely doomed, Madison's only concern now was for the safety of Dolley, and he and his party fought their way along the clogged road, trying to get back to the city. Joshua Barney and his men, also retreating along the same road, met the President.

"The British will capture Madison for sure unless we buy him enough time to get away," Jeremy said to Barney.

"Aye, you're right there," Barney said, and shouted to his gunners, "Move those artillery pieces over here. We've got to hold the road long enough for the President to get away."

The gunners positioned their five small cannon to cover the approaches to Tournecliffe's creek.

"We've still got about five hundred good men," Barney said, "and the British number almost five thousand. Well, that's ten to one, just about the right odds."

Jeremy watched the road that wound through the stands of alder and oak. Almost twenty minutes passed before the British appeared. "There they are," Jeremy whispered to Barney, pointing to the flashes of red as the British moved through the forest. The men that Jeremy and Barney had positioned behind stone fences and trees opened fire. The cannons roared, and the British line buckled. It re-formed and advanced again, only to stagger under the next cannonade.

"This is the way we should have fought them," Barney yelled waving his sword. "Guerrilla tactics, the way our forefathers did."

Another artillery blast ripped through the British lines, and then Barney raised his sword and shouted, "Charge!" The motley array of boatswains, marines, and sailors swept forward and in fierce hand-to-hand fighting routed the British. Then both sides fell back to regroup.

Admiral Cockburn and General Ross sent in their reserves. Under a heavy rocket barrage, the impeccably trained British once more managed to outflank the Americans, and they scattered. One rocket exploded near Jeremy; he felt a tearing blow hit his left arm. He touched it gingerly; it was broken. Another piece of shrapnel had torn open his forehead. Though waves of dizziness overcame him he managed to bind up his wounds.

Jeremy searched the shell-pocked glen and finally found Commodore Barney propped against a tree. A rocket shell had broken his leg. "We'll fight on," Barney said, and tried to rally his men.

"Look there, the ammunition wagons are leaving!" Jeremy shouted, as he saw them disappearing down the road. The civilian drivers hadn't counted on being this close to the conflict, and with the British charge, they fled for their lives, taking the ammunition wagons with them.

"We can't fight for long without ammunition," Barney said to Jeremy. "Can you walk, man?"

"I think so," he said, struggling to his feet. He tried to lift Barney, but the commodore shook his head. "I wouldn't get very far with this broken leg. It's more important for you to get away."

"I won't leave you here," Jeremy said.

"Listen to me, Jeremy, this is an order. You must get back to Washington. Tell Captain Tingey that he's got to blow up the Navy Yard. Everything—the warehouses, the ships at anchor. Nothing must fall into the hands of the British. Their supplies are limited, but if they replenish them from our own stores, then we're lost. Now get going, man. Remember, tell Tingey to destroy everything."

Jeremy tried to clear his head. He couldn't bear the thought of leaving Barney here, but even in his stunned state he knew the importance of the Navy Yard. He scrambled up a rise of hill just as the British regulars reached the tree where Barney sat. Jeremy looked back and saw two men helping the commodore to his feet. He could only pray that the British would treat Barney decently. A bullet whizzed close by to his head and Jeremy took off.

It's only five miles to Washington, he told himself as he put one foot in front of the other. Blood trickled down his face, and a dull pain radiated from his arm, seeming to throb in time with his heartbeat. "I've got to reach the Navy Yard before the British do, I've got to," he whispered as he drove himself along.

Chapter 44

DOLLEY MADISON stood on the roof of the White House, spyglass in hand, searching frantically through the pall of dust and smoke that rolled along the road from Bladensburg. "I can get no sense of the battle," she said.

French John Souissat stood on the roof with her, along with Sukie and Tanzy; Sukie was more petrified of the height than of anything else.

"I see somebody coming!" Dolley cried. "He's wearing a tricorn hat, so he must be an American. And he's a Negro. Hurry, we must go downstairs and see who it is."

Dolley rushed down from the roof, with Sukie and Tanzy following hard after. Downstairs in the State Dining Room, Madison's servant boy, Paul Jennings, was busily setting the table. Madison had told him that the cabinet, some generals, and several aides would be dining there that evening, perhaps forty people in all, and Jennings arranged the table accordingly. Dolley had sent all the other servants away for their safety.

The doors flew open and the horseman Dolley had seen stumbled into the house. It was Jim Smith, the President's freed manservant.

"Clear out!" Jim shouted. "General Armstrong's ordered a full retreat. The British will be here soon!"

Dolley leaned against the table for support. "And the President, is he safe?" she asked anxiously.

"He is," Jim said. "He sent you this," and handed Dolley a note.

She tore open the envelope and read, "The battle is lost, fly at once. I will meet you, god willing, at the Reverend Maffitt's estate, Salona."

The note trembled in Dolley's hand, but conscious that all eyes were on her, she composed herself. "Hurry, we must go, but first save whatever you can. The silver," she said to Tanzy.

Tanzy took all the official silverware and loaded it into the creaky wagon that had been commandeered. Horses and wagons were worth their weight in gold. Sukie packed a small clock, a favorite of Dolley's, and some rare books that Jefferson had left to start a White House collection. At Dolley's orders, Tanzy yanked down the red velvet curtains from the drawing room. In minutes, the wagon was loaded and on its way to the Bank of Maryland, safely beyond the city limits.

"The portrait!" Dolley cried, rushing to the full-length painting of General Washington that Gilbert Stuart had done. "We can't let that fall into the hands of the British!"

Suddenly the entire battle, even the fate of the Union, seemed to hang on whether they'd be able to save the painting. French John tugged and twisted at the frame, but it had been solidly screwed into the wall. Captain Carroll, who'd gone to get Dolley's carriage, returned to find them still fussing with the painting.

"Madam, please," he insisted. "Leave it, or we'll all be taken prisoner."

Then Tanzy came running in from the woodshed with an axe.

"Break the frame," Dolley said to French John. "But carefully."

He chopped the frame to bits, took out the canvas still on its stretcher, and laid it on the dining-room floor. Dolley turned to Jacob Barker, and to another New Yorker, Robert de Peyster, who'd been guests at the White House.

"Save that picture," she said. "Save it if humanly possible. If you cannot, then destroy it. But under no circumstances must the British be allowed to capture it."

Then she rushed back into the drawing room and rescued some ornamental eagles and a few remaining boxes of Madison's papers, including his original copies of the Declaration of Independence, and his first rough drafts of the Constitution. "Now quickly, ladies, we must flee!" she said, and as she ran from the room, she stuffed a few more pieces of silver into her reticule.

Dolley ran down the White House steps and threw herself into her carriage. Sukie got in beside her. "Let the child come with me," she called to Tanzy, who held Circumstance by the hand.

"That's all right," Tanzy said, "I'll take care of her." She'd promised Jeremy she'd look after Circumstance, and she would. Reflexively, her hand moved to the dagger she kept strapped to her leg. She'd carried it there ever since Zebulon had attacked her.

A second carriage carried off some of Dolley's guests; a wagon driven by John Freeman, another of Madison's servants, took Tanzy and Circumstance.

"But what about Papa?" Circumstance asked. "Where is he? How will he know where to find us?"

"Don't worry, we'll find your father tomorrow, or he'll find us," she said. As he had instructed her, Tanzy had hidden Jeremy's folios of drawings in a bin in the White House basement, thinking that they'd be safest there. But now she wasn't so sure and had half a mind to run back and get them.

But just then John Freeman lashed the horses and the carriage started off, moving out of the White House driveway.

"John, wait!" Tanzy cried, as they turned on to Pennsylvania Avenue.

"Oh, look over there!" Circumstance said, pointing.

A runaway horse galloped along Pennsylvania Avenue, frightened by the noise and the press of people. The mob fled screaming before the horse's hooves. John Freeman fought to control their own rearing mare, but she bolted, dragging the wagon along the ruts and potholes of Pennsylvania Avenue. The wheels hit an exposed root, and the wagon thundered down, breaking the axle. Tanzy tried to cushion the child's fall, and had the wind knocked out of her.

"Are you all right?" Circumstance asked anxiously.

Tanzy gasped for breath and then nodded. The mob had descended on their wagon like vultures, ripping the contents from it, and carrying off the mare, with John Freeman chasing them. Tanzy looked for Dolley's carriage, but it had been swallowed by the crowd.

"Come on," she said to Circumstance. "We'll have to get away on our own."

The stream of refugees moved at a snail's pace under the

setting August sun. Wagons broke down, horses died under their loads, and the approach to the bridge across the Potomac to Virginia was hopelessly snarled.

"We'll never get across here," Tanzy said. "If we head across the town to the Navy Yard, we can take the ferry to the Virginia side."

A rider galloped through the streets shouting, "The British are a half-mile from the city!"

"Hurry, child, hurry!" Tanzy said, as they ran.

With the onset of twilight the air turned oppressive and still, and Tanzy looked anxiously at the sky. "Something's wrong," she said.

Circumstance gazed at her quizzically.

Then Tanzy felt the heaviness in her lungs. When she'd lived in the West Indies, such a stillness always meant the calm before the storm. "Pray not," she said to Circumstance, "but I think there's a hurricane coming."

Could such a thing be? Tanzy wondered. An invasion and a hurricane at the same time? Surely the fates were conspiring against them. A gust of wind whipped through the streets and the bough of an elm snapped and crashed down close by to them. "It will be too dangerous to cross the river now," she said. "We must find a safe place here."

When Circumstance stumbled, Tanzy swept her into her arms and continued running.

About two hours after Dolley had fled from the White House, President Madison arrived. By now, the slight, ailing President was near collapse. He sank into a chair, heaving for breath, and his words were short, aspirate gasps. "I'd always thought, like Jefferson, that a democratic citizen fighting for his own home would be much more than a match for the paid hireling of some foreign foe. But this day I've been sorely disabused of that notion. If this has taught us anything, it's that we must have a strong regular army for the defense of our nation."

The aides said nothing. Hindsight was not the quality most sought for in a leader.

"Unless we leave, we shall be trapped here by the British," an aide said.

Madison stood up and his aides helped him outside. He

mounted up and rode hard for Virginia, hoping to meet Dolley there.

With the city empty of American troops, a mob began to rampage through the streets, looting the government buildings. They came to the White House, broke in, and started to help themselves to anything not nailed down. But before they could do serious damage, the cry went up in the streets that the British had entered the city and were on their way there. The mob scattered, leaving the front door of the White House open and banging in the wind.

Chapter 45

AS HE stumbled along the road, Jeremy saw the buildings of Washington rising before him in the gathering darkness. Distracted by pain and weariness, he could barely keep his wits about him. But he had only one purpose in mind—to reach the Navy Yard and deliver Commodore Barney's orders to Captain Tingey. At last he dragged his way to the southernmost tip of the city and was helped inside the Navy Yard gate by a sailor.

"Man, you're bleeding like a stuck pig," Captain Tingey said when he saw Jeremy.

"Never mind that," he said. "You've got to blow up the Navy Yard. And everything in it. Barney says the British mustn't capture anything."

Tingey's face set. "Aye, we were getting ready to do it ourselves, but you've just made it official." He glanced at the clock. "Eight-fifteen now. I'll give the order to blow it all in five more minutes."

Jeremy had known Captain Tingey practically all his adult life. Not only had he designed most of the facilities here in 1800, but during his fifteen years as commander, he'd made the Navy Yard the best in the nation.

"I know this must be a bitter blow to you, sir," Jeremy said.

"Aye, and old John Adams will have a fit when he hears of it," Tingey said. "This Navy Yard was his idea. But sad as it is, it would be worse if our supplies fell into the hands of the British and were used to kill fellow Americans."

With a final glance around Tingey shouted, "All right then, light your fuses!"

Sailors raced to the buildings, throwing lighted torches everywhere; warehouses caught fire, then the sail lofts erupted. The flames leapt to the paint supplies, and from there to the lumberyard and sawmill, and a tongue of fire arced to the new frigate *Columbia,* about to be launched, and to the sloop of war *Argus*. The fire reached the ammunition dump and a great explosion turned night into day and sent out shock waves that rocked the city.

Jeremy recoiled from the blast of heat as the orange-and-red fireball roared into the sky. He rubbed his eyes wearily. Now he would go and find Circumstance and Tanzy.

General Ross and Admiral Cockburn rode into Washington at the head of their troops. "Extraordinary that our casualties have been so light," Cockburn said. "I've sent a platoon ahead to the Navy Yard, and—"

Suddenly a gigantic explosion sent a rush of air sweeping over them and plumes of fire flared into the sky. Explosion after explosion tore the Navy Yard asunder. Cockburn's face hardened. "Well, the Yankees beat us to it. We'll have to make the best of it."

Sean Connaught came galloping up to the two leaders. "Sir, the Capitol is that building straight ahead. My scouts have already been through it, and it's deserted."

They rode closer, and Ross squinted through the darkness at the two wings which were still connected by a wooden walkway. "It's not an unhandsome building," he said.

"But what it symbolizes is anathema," Cockburn said. "If we allowed every colony to get away with rebellion, we would soon lose the Empire. Besides, we must remember, an eye for an eye. The Americans *did* burn the Canadian Parliament Building at York, so this is just retaliation." Then Cockburn slapped his thigh, and a grin spread across his handsome features. "General Ross, do you realize that we've captured the enemy's capital?"

As they came within two hundred yards of the building, a shot rang out. Ross's horse whinnied and then fell over, dead. More shots were fired, and four British soldiers took fatal bullets.

"It came from that building!" Sean Connaught shouted. Taking a detachment of men, he rode for Tomlinson's Hotel.

Inside the hotel, Zebulon and some militiamen had been hiding cartons of the congressional records in the basement storerooms. But when Zebulon saw the British approaching, he'd been unable to resist giving the order to fire on them. Too late, he realized his tactical error. "They know we're here for sure," he shouted. "Everybody out of the hotel!"

Just as the British swarmed through the front door, Zebulon and his men escaped through the back and scattered into the darkness.

Sean Connaught tramped through the building, finding guns and ammunition stored everywhere. "I want this building leveled!" he ordered, and his demolition crew set fires on every floor.

Then Sean rejoined the rest of the British force and the soldiers broke open the doors of the Capitol and methodically began to ransack it. One enterprising redcoat cut down the portraits of Louis XVI and Marie Antoinette that hung in the room adjoining the Senate chamber.

Cockburn appraised the Capitol. "These limestone walls are so thick that I believe the only way to destroy the building is to blow it up."

"I doubt we can spare that much powder from our dwindling supply," Ross said. "If we'd captured the Navy Yard intact, it would've been a very different matter."

"Sir," Sean Connaught interrupted with a stiff salute, "if I may be permitted, I can have our demolition team set fire to the place. With this quick wind, I think we can provide a merry blaze for your amusement."

Cockburn smiled. "Carry on, Captain."

Sean called the demolition crew to attention. "Chop all that woodwork into kindling," he ordered. "Pile the furniture together and sprinkle it liberally with rocket powder."

In a short time the crew was done, and Sean, with a glint of madness in his eyes, said to Admiral Cockburn, "You have no idea how much pleasure this gives me."

"Then you shall have the honor of lighting the first match," Cockburn said.

Sean lit the trail of powder, watched it race toward the center of the room and then mushroom into flame.

In the House of Representatives section of the building, other British troops were firing rockets into the roof, hoping to set the rafters ablaze. "We can't seem to get it started," a midshipman told Sean.

"The roof is covered with sheet iron," he said. He had them repeat the procedure that had set the Senate afire.

Now both wings of the Capitol were ablaze, the flames visible through the windows. Everything inside was burning, with the thick limestone walls acting like an oven: The secret journals of the House, the law library, the 740 books purchased in 1802 by Jefferson as a start for a Library of Congress, the gilt eagle surmounting the clock over the Speaker of the House's chair. The hands of the clock stopped at ten o'clock as the flames reached it. Up shot the flames, roaring through the broken windows and open doors, finally melting the sheet-iron roof, which fell in flaming molten globules to the marble floor.

Borne on the increasingly strong winds, the sparks quickly ignited four other houses near the Capitol, including two that General Washington had built nearby as an expression of his faith in the city. Some of the records of the House of Representatives had been stored in those two buildings, and they went up in flames.

"All right men, on to the President's Mansion, or as these colonials call it, the White House," Admiral Cockburn said. "I promise you, it won't be white for long!"

Whichever way Tanzy turned, she was confronted by burning buildings. She clutched Circumstance to her and tried to think of a safe place to go. The British had sealed off all roads out of the city, and fire raged all along the waterfront. She and Circumstance had been wandering hither and yon throughout the city for hours, and she was ready to drop from exhaustion. She ran to a house and pounded on the door. No answer came from within.

Then she saw British soldiers running through the streets, their bayonets at the ready. With Circumstance in hand, Tanzy hurried to another house. This time the door was opened, but by a grinning redcoat. Tanzy turned and fled, but the soldier followed her outside. Strong hands grabbed her and threw her to the ground. The leering soldier straddled her. Circumstance flung herself at the man, but with a backhand swipe he knocked her aside.

Tanzy screamed and raked for the man's eyes with her fingernails, but a sharp blow to the chin stunned her. Circumstance sprang at the soldier again, pummeling him with her tiny fists, while he tried to loosen his belt. The delay allowed Tanzy to regain her senses. She struggled under the soldier's weight, and with a wrench, managed to free one of her hands. She drew her knife from under her skirts and with a sharp jab plunged it into the soldier's side. She scrambled out from under the wounded redcoat, grabbed Circumstance, and ran.

But the soldier cried out, "Stop her, she stabbed me!"

Other redcoats raced after Tanzy, and this time there were too many of them to fight off. "Pray that the soldier lives," an officer said to Tanzy. "Otherwise, Admiral Cockburn will see that you hang. Take her to headquarters!" he shouted, and Tanzy and Circumstance were hustled off to the campaign post that the British had set up at Rhode's Tavern on F and Fifteenth Streets, chosen because of its proximity to the White House.

"Hurry, get those buckets up to the roof!" Rebecca ordered Eli and Letitia. They carried the sloshing pails up through the attic. "That's it," she said, "pour the water over the shingles."

Sparks carried on the wind flew all about her. Some landed on the wet shingles, sputtered, and died. Her eyes flinched from the blazing city before her. Flames leapt from the Capitol Building, drawing air up into a flaming vortex. At the river's edge, occasional explosions still rocked the Navy Yard, and the night air reeked of turpentine and resin. Here and there a private home fell victim to the leaping fire. "Well, that won't happen to my house," Rebecca said resolutely. "Keep wetting that roof down. Go and get more water."

Thank God they'd built the house of brick. If the wind didn't shift, perhaps they'd be spared. But the wind was growing in intensity, a storm was brewing.

Rebecca went to the children's room. Suzannah and Gunning ran to her and clutched her skirts.

"It's all right," she said soothingly. "Mamma's here. No harm's going to come to you." She noticed that Gunning was sniveling, but Suzannah looked at her with her huge dark eyes, and not a sound escaped her. "Good girl," she said, stroking her daughter's dark silken hair. She had a momentary thought that the backbone in this family might have been passed on through the female line.

Suddenly the door burst open and Zebulon stumbled into the room. His face was grimed with dirt and his uniform was torn. "I've killed some soldiers," he whispered. "They may have followed me here. I've got to hide."

"In the root cellar," she said, opening the door to the basement. He stumbled down the darkened steps and she locked the door after him. Then she went to the window, edged the curtains aside, and peered out. Her heart sank when she saw troops of British soldiers, their red coats seemingly aflame in the reflected firelight, heading toward the house. There were perhaps a hundred and fifty men, led by an officer on a prancing white charger. He was decked out in the braid of an admiral and was wearing an admiral's hat; that much she could make out through her spy glass. "That must be Admiral Cockburn," she whispered.

What an unthinking fool Zebulon had been to have led them here and jeopardized the children!

She held her breath and then released it slowly when the soldiers marched right by her house. Obviously, they were after something more important. She watched with sinking heart as they continued on their way to the White House.

Chapter 46

FALLING, LURCHING forward, and falling again, Jeremy finally reached his house. "Circumstance!" he shouted. But the house was empty, a shutter banged in the wind. He held his head in his hands and tried to think where they'd go. Then he remembered that Dolley said she'd watch out for them. He climbed the low fence surrounding the President's grounds, and staggered across the lawn to the White House. In the play of firelight and shadow the house wavered in his vision. The pain in his arm became so intense that he must have passed out momentarily, for when he regained his senses, he found himself lying on the front steps.

He dragged his way into the house. The entrance hall looked bare, the drawing room strangely denuded of its red velvet curtains; yet in the dining room, the table was set, as if the guests would be arriving momentarily. Again and again he shouted Circumstance's name, but all he got back was an echo. Dazed and reeling from pain, he lit a candle and climbed the stairs to the second floor.

"Where is everybody?" he shouted.

The house remained silent, brooding, waiting. He searched the upper rooms. There wasn't a soul in the entire house. Then he glanced out of the upper story window and saw redcoats marching along Pennsylvania Avenue, led by a man on a white charger.

He knew he could still make it out the south entrance and escape across the lawn, but something held him rooted. Waves of faintness were interspersed with a thousand thoughts. I've worked on this house for more than twenty years, he thought. I know every room, every nook and cranny. I've seen three

Presidents live within these walls, witnessed their weaknesses and strengths, broken bread with them, and shared their aspirations for the glory of this great nation.

And now the enemy in their red coats were coming to destroy it.

He heard voices, distinct English accents, and then the sound of footsteps on the stairway. Unless he hid, he'd be captured for certain. Where? The roof? Then it came to him. The clothes closet that he'd built for President Jefferson! The rack worked on a swivel so that only one section at a time needed to be exposed, while the other section of the rack fit into a cedar-lined well. A thought came to him as he wedged his way into the double-gated clothes well: Jefferson's ingenuity might well save his life this night.

The voices became muffled, but Jeremy could tell that there were many soldiers in the house, searching through every room on every floor, including this one. He held his breath and waited.

On the main floor, Admiral Cockburn, General Ross, and Sean Connaught tramped through the rooms. "I say, will you look at this," Cockburn said to Sean. "This dining table is set for scores of people." The winebottles lay in coolers that had been packed with ice, which had melted in the August heat.

"I expect that little Jemmy Madison thought he'd be victorious at Bladensburg," Sean chortled. "This was to be his celebration dinner."

"Most hospitable for Jemmy to set the table for us, wouldn't you say?" Cockburn said, as he sampled a generous helping of cold cuts that a soldier brought up from the kitchen.

The officers poured themselves a round of Madeira. "I propose a toast," Cockburn said. "To the health of the Prince Regent, and success to His Majesty's arms by land and sea."

"It's not every day that we capture the capital of the enemy," General Ross said.

"We must have some souvenirs to recall the occasion," Cockburn said, and began to forage through the rooms. "I shall take this old stovepipe hat of Jemmy's, the one he wore to make him appear taller. And this pillow from Mrs. Madison's chair: I shall take that too, so that I may always be reminded of Dolley's . . . ah, seat."

The British soldiers ransacked the house, crying out each time they found another treasure—a pair of rhinestone buckles from Madison's shoes, turbans galore with foot-high ostrich plumes. Then one of the subalterns brought in the President's medicine chest jammed with dozens of prescriptions from his physician in Washington, Dr. Ewell, and even some of Dr. Rush's famous "thunder pills."

"With all this medication, it's a wonder that the man could govern at all," Sean laughed.

"Our situation here proves that he hasn't!" Admiral Cockburn said gleefully, and they drank another toast.

Sean Connaught looked around the East Room. He saw nothing in the way of souvenirs that interested him. He wouldn't need anything to remind him of this triumph. But his clothes were so sweat-stained that they clung to his back. "I'd like nothing better than some clean linen," he said to Cockburn.

"Perhaps Jemmy will loan you some," he said with a laugh.

Whistling "God Save the King," Sean went upstairs to President Madison's bedroom.

Inside the closet, Jeremy drew his pistol. He might have to kill the man, for he heard him coming closer. The door creaked open and a razor-thin shaft of light cut the darkness. Jeremy saw a hand reach for a shirt, the groping fingers were so close that he could see the man's ring, with a seal that looked familiar. He couldn't place it, yet he knew that he'd seen that insignia before.

The man chose a shirt, stripped and changed garments, leaving his dirty clothes behind. Then he was gone. Jeremy slumped with relief. But it was a relief that didn't last long.

With the food eaten and the wine drunk, a soldier swept the remaining silver and plates into a tablecloth and carried it off as booty. In the Oval Room, considered by many in America to be the most beautiful room in the White House, Admiral Cockburn ordered his men to pile the furniture in the center of the floor.

"Sean, the preparations are done, and now the honors are yours," Cockburn said with a flourish. "See if you can't give us as merry a blaze as you did with the Capitol."

Sean's dark-blue eyes narrowed. "I stood in this room years ago and swore I would see this house destroyed. Truly, this proves there is a God!"

He stove in a barrel of gunpowder with the butt of his pistol and sprinkled it on the heaped furniture. Then the squad raced from room to room, throwing lighted torches on the pyres. Upstairs, Jeremy smelled smoke. He fought his way out of the closet and edged over to the staircase. Dense smoke curled upwards.

"They've set the house afire!" he gasped.

These so-called civilized men were destroying just for the sake of destroying. They were no better than Vandals! Somehow, Jeremy felt that he himself was being violated. His rage was so monumental that he knew he had to do something lest he lose his mind. Something to let these Huns know that there were Americans who would fight to the death for their country, fight to the death for their belief in freedom.

He checked his pistols; loaded and ready.

The wound in his temple reopened, and fresh blood coursed down his face. He might have lost consciousness save that the pain in his arm kept prying him back to reality. The seasoned wood paneling caught fire, the windows shattered from the heat, and the air sucked in from the outside fanned the flames into a roaring blaze. As the fire licked at the walls and at the banister railing, Jeremy stole downstairs. He smelled the acrid odor of burning hair, then realized that it was his own. He slapped at the back of his head, blinked the sweat from his eyes, as the grand entrance foyer seemed to melt in his swimming vision.

Suddenly a voice called out, "Who's there?" and Jeremy whirled to see Sean Connaught confronting him at the foot of the staircase. Neither man recognized the other. Sean Connaught raised his pistol, but Jeremy fired his pistol first. The bullet passed through Sean's shoulder; he reeled and the impact carried him through the front doors.

Jeremy dropped to the floor to escape the intense heat and crawled through the doorway. Outside he felt the blessed relief of the night air. The man he'd shot lay nearby, groaning and momentarily stunned. Clutching at the sandstone, Jeremy inched himself to his feet until he stood at full height. In the driveway he saw a man in the uniform of a naval officer mount a white charger and took him to be Admiral Cockburn. With the roaring of the fire all about them, the British had been unaware of the shooting.

Jeremy drew his other pistol and shouted, "Admiral!"

Cockburn wheeled his horse and looked at the dark figure limned against the roaring inferno of the White House.

"Draw your pistol, sir!" Jeremy cried. "You shall not go unpunished!"

Cockburn reached for his gun.

Jeremy steadied his arm and fired, just as Sean Connaught threw himself at him, deflecting his aim. The bullet passed harmlessly through Cockburn's hat. Then Jeremy collapsed.

A half dozen soldiers rushed him with fixed bayonets, but didn't shoot, fearing to hit Connaught, who was tangled with him.

"Is he dead?" Cockburn demanded.

"Close enough," Sean said, stemming the blood from his own wound. He rolled the man over with his foot and then he recognized him. "Jeremy Brand!" He wished it could have been Zebulon; that would have made his revenge complete.

"Admiral, I think we'd better bring the American with us," Sean said. "Obviously, he was hiding in the White House while we were there and may have overheard our plans."

Cockburn agreed. Jeremy was slung over a horse and carried to the British headquarters at Rhode's Tavern. There he was turned over to the ship's doctors, who'd set up an aid station for the wounded in the tavern's back room. After the British casualties had been cared for, a doctor examined Jeremy. Sean Connaught stood nearby.

"Broken arm, lost a lot of blood, concussion due to a gunshot wound to the head. He's still unconscious, but I think he'll live."

Sean Connaught's thin wet lips twitched with suppressed anger. He thought of that long-ago day when he'd seen his uncle murdered before his eyes, and by this man's brother. He thought of his Aunt Elizabeth, consigned forever to a life of the living dead. Surely the crimes of the Brands cried out to heaven for vengeance, and a just God had given him the opportunity to avenge the family name. Zebulon Brand's turn would come also.

Sean gripped the doctor's arm. "I charge you, make sure you tend to him. I want him alive. The man is a spy, and I intend to have him hanged."

Chapter 47

THE BRITISH had converted the outbuildings and stables of Rhode's Tavern into prisons to hold captured militiamen, suspected snipers, and other Americans who'd fought them. Among the hostages were Circumstance and Tanzy.

Admiral Cockburn sat at a table in the tavern's main room, meting out justice. A decanter of wine stood before him. "Burning makes one deucedly thirsty, wouldn't you say?" he asked Sean. "Who's next?"

Sean, his arm bound in a sling, shoved Tanzy and Circumstance forward. "My aide tells me that this colored slave tried to murder one of our soldiers."

Tanzy glared at him. "I'm not a slave! Your soldier tried to rape me."

Circumstance nodded her head vigorously. "I saw him."

"Be quiet, child," Sean ordered.

"But it's true," Circumstance began.

Tanzy gripped her shoulders. "Don't say anything, it won't do us any good."

Suddenly the shutters flew open and a great gust of wind swept into the room, blowing papers about and extinguishing the candles. "Bolt the doors and windows," Cockburn ordered. When the candles were relit, he regarded Tanzy impatiently. "Do you always have such infernal weather in this city?"

Tanzy remained silent, but Circumstance stepped forward. "This storm has been sent by the Lord to drive out the invaders who would destroy our land."

Taken aback, Cockburn let out a short, harsh laugh, but Sean reached out and slapped her. "Don't be impertinent."

Tanzy sprang at him, but another soldier held her arms.

Circumstance stared at the man without flinching; she memorized every detail of his face. She would never forget him. "We'll win," she whispered. "The rain will put out all the fires you've set. It's a sure sign that the Lord wills it. We'll win."

"Get them out of my sight," Cockburn said. "They can't do us any harm."

Circumstance and Tanzy were locked up with the other prisoners in the outbuildings.

About an hour later, Marianne Connaught, her face hidden beneath a dark cloak, swept into Rhode's Tavern on a gust of wind-driven rain.

"Marianne, you shouldn't have come here," Sean said. "It's too dangerous."

"I know, but the situation is so serious that I had to warn you," she said. "News of your presence in Washington has reached the surrounding states, and a large force of the regular army is heading here."

"When will they get here?" Cockburn asked.

"Two days, three at the latest," Marianne said.

Cockburn drummed his fingers on the table. "Without the stores from their Navy Yard, I'm afraid we can't engage their army. We must retreat back to our ships. But this weather . . ."

"My aunt says there's a hurricane heading this way. She's lived through one of these before," Marianne said.

Sean took her arm. "Marianne, I've some good news for you. We captured somebody earlier whom I know will interest you." He led her to the rear room where Jeremy lay. His arm had been set and bandaged, but he was still unconscious.

Marianne would have fainted if Sean hadn't caught her. "Brandy!" he shouted to a soldier, who quickly brought it. The drink revived her and color returned to her cheeks.

"You know this man then?" Admiral Cockburn asked.

She nodded. "He's . . . an acquaintance of mine."

"She's entirely too modest," Sean said. "Jeremy Brand means a great deal more to the Connaughts than that."

"Well, my dear, you should know that this night, your . . . acquaintance not only wounded your cousin, but almost cost me my life."

Marianne fought to keep her voice from trembling. She

knelt beside Jeremy, whose breathing seemed labored and shallow. "He's seriously wounded, isn't he?" She looked up at Admiral Cockburn. "Oh, please, let me take him to my doctor."

"Marianne!" Sean exclaimed, caught by surprise.

She turned her brimming eyes to her cousin. "You don't understand. Jeremy had nothing to do with my father's death, nothing. Am I to hate him because he bears the same name as his brother? In the years that I've known him, he's shown me nothing but kindness, and recently . . ." Her voice caught but she managed to finish. ". . . well, he's done me a personal service. I owe this to him. Please, I beg you—"

Sean's face hardened. By the degree of her concern, she'd given herself away. Before she could say any more, he said to Cockburn, "Surely you can see that what my cousin asks is impossible. This man was spying on us in the White House. He cannot be set free, or even allowed to remain in Washington."

"Quite right," Cockburn said. He patted Marianne's arm. "My dear, rest assured that whatever you believe you owe this man, it will be faithfully discharged by us. Our own shipboard doctors will see to him. And now you'd best go. I've been on the high seas long enough to know that this storm will hit us before too long, and you mustn't be trapped here."

He helped her on with her cloak. "One last thing. Will you alert our supporters that we strike at Baltimore shortly? And as soon as we've leveled that city, then part of the fleet will sail on to New Orleans, where, God willing, we shall all meet."

Marianne stared at Jeremy lying there, his long blond hair matted with blood, his craggy face twitching as if in a nightmare. Cockburn would send him to one of the navy's infernal prison ships, where if he didn't die of his wounds, he would surely perish of mistreatment or disease. And there was nothing she could do about it. Suddenly, the victory she'd worked for all these years seemed hollow, overshadowed by her love. With a final, heart-wrenching look at him, she left. As she fought her way through the storm she thought desperately, I must do something!

Dawn broke several hours later, though with Washington now in the grip of the storm, the sky remained dark and lowering. The White House, the Capitol, and other government buildings had burned steadily during the night, and though the walls of the White House and Capitol hadn't yet collapsed, the intense heat would surely buckle them soon.

The British troops made ready to depart. "It's madness to go out in this weather," Admiral Cockburn said, "but we've no alternative. We just can't sit here and allow the American army to cut us off from our ships."

Since traveling would be difficult in the extreme, only the most important prisoners were taken along, so Circumstance, Tanzy, and scores of other people were let go. One wagon held prisoners chained together, and another wagon held the wounded, including Jeremy. Cockburn gave the order to march, and the files of soldiers and wagons started out.

The storm struck with its full fury, howling along the wide avenues, uprooting trees, and lashing everything with torrents of rain. The beat of rain against his face revived Jeremy. As the wagon bumped along Pennsylvania Avenue, all that had happened slowly came back to him. He raised himself on his elbow and strained for one last look at Washington. He prayed that Tanzy and Circumstance were safe. And then he saw it, the fire-blackened ruin of the White House. His heart contracted and it was all he could do to keep from screaming aloud.

Fire and storm battered at the remains of the building, the roof had fallen in, the interior was gutted. But the walls, the massive Aquia sandstone walls, were still standing. And then he noticed the clouds of smoke—and something else, what?—was it steam? The torrential downpour was putting out the fire! And to Jeremy, it seemed like an omen.

"It will rise again, I swear it," he whispered. "If I have to rebuild it with my own hands, it will rise again!"

Selected Bibliography

IT WOULD be impossible to list all the reference material used in the research for *The American Palace* series, Book I, *Bless This House*. What follows is a selected bibliography.

Wherever possible, primary sources were investigated; the Columbia Historical Society, the Library of Congress, the Smithsonian Institution, the Office of the Architect of the Capitol, and the Office of the Curator of the White House were all invaluable sources of information.

Believing that there is no substitute for the actual experience, I retraced the route of the Lewis and Clark Expedition, some eight thousand miles by car, foot, boat, and horseback. Several museums along the way all have excellent written material and artifacts pertaining to the expedition, notably the Museum of Westward Expansion in St. Louis, and the state museums at Pierre, South Dakota; Bismarck, North Dakota; Helena, Montana; and the National Memorial at Fort Clatsop, Oregon. For the adventurous among you, a warning—the mountain passes in the Bitterroot Range are usually snowed in by early October and don't reopen until late June.

And for actually placing oneself in the setting of this novel, there's nothing like a tour through the White House, the Capitol, the Octagon House, the Stephen Decatur House, the former Dolley Madison House on Lafayette Square, and Rhode's Tavern. Finally, many of the quaint cobbled streets of Georgetown still reflect the atmosphere and architecture of Washington, D.C., in the early 1800s.

The White House

Aikman, Lonnelle. *The Living White House*. Washington, D.C.: White House Historical Association and National Geographic, 1966.

Coleman, Edna. *Seventy-five Years of White House Gossip*. Garden City, N.Y.: Doubleday, 1926.

Frary, I. T. *They Built the White House*. Freeport, N.Y.: Books for Libraries, 1969.

Furman, Bess. *White House Profile*. Indianapolis: Bobbs-Merrill, 1951.

Harris, P. Baker. *Laying the Cornerstone of the White House*. Washington, D.C.: Potomac Lodge Number Five, 1949.

Hoban file. Office of the Architect of the Capitol.

Hurd, Charles. *The White House*. New York: Hawthorne, 1966.

Jensen, Amy. *The White House and Its Thirty-four Families*. New York: McGraw-Hill, 1958.

Kimball, Fiske, and Wells Bennett. "The Competition for the Federal Buildings," *Journal of the American Institute of Architecture*, 1919, Vol. VII, Nos. 1, 3, 5, 8, and 12.

Latrobe, Benjamin. *The Journal of Latrobe*. 1905. Reprint. New York: B. Franklin, 1971.

Lewis, Ethel. *The White House*. New York: Dodd, Mead, 1937.

Ryan, William, and Desmond Guinness. *The White House*. New York: McGraw-Hill, 1981.

The White House: An Historic Guide. Washington, D.C.: White House Historical Association and National Geographic, 1979.

Wolff, Sidney Perry. *A Tour of the White House with Mrs. John F. Kennedy*. Garden City, N.Y.: Doubleday, 1962.

The City of Washington, D.C.

Some of these books and articles are not widely available; those marked with an asterisk (*) can be found at the Columbia Historical Society, 1307 New Hampshire Avenue, N.W., Washington, D.C. 20038.

Adler, Bill, ed. *Washington: A Reader*. New York: Meredith Press, 1967.

*Bryan, Wilhelmus. *A History of the National Capital*, 2 vols. New York: Macmillan, 1914–16.

**The City of Washington*. Washington, D.C.: Junior League and Columbia Historical Society, n.d.

*Fisher, Perry G. *Materials for the Study of Washington: A Selected Annotated Bibliography*. Washington, D.C.: George Washington University, 1974.

*Green, Constance. *Washington, a History of the Capital, 1800–1950*. Vol. I, Village and Capital. Princeton: Princeton University Press, 1976.

Gutheim, Frederick. *Worthy of the Nation*. Washington, D.C.: National Capital Planning Commission and Smithsonian, 1977.

Gutheim, Frederick and Wilcomb E. Washburn. *The Federal City: Plans and Realities*. Washington, D.C.: National Capital Planning Commission and Smithsonian, 1976.

*Hines, Christian. *Early Recollections of Washington City*. Washington, D.C.: Chronicle, 1866.

Jefferson, Thomas, et al. *Thomas Jefferson and the National Capital*, ed. Saul K. Padover. Washington, D.C.: U.S. Government Printing Office, 1946. (Correspondence between Jefferson, Latrobe, L'Enfant, Ellicott, Washington, et al., about the disposition of the nation's capital.)

Josephy, Alvin, Jr. *History of the Congress of the United States*. New York: American Heritage, 1975.

"Laying of the Cornerstone of the Capitol," *Columbia Mirror and Alexandria Gazette*, Sept. 25, 1793. Microfilm, Library of Congress.

Maury, William M. *Washington, D.C.: Past and Present*. New York: C.B.S. Publications, 1975.

Pictorial History of the Capitol and the Congress, 7th ed. Washington, D.C.: U.S. Congress, 1980.

Porter, John Addison. *The City of Washington, Its Origins and Administration*. Baltimore: Johns Hopkins, 1885.

Smith, Margaret Bayard. *Washington, D.C., Social Life and Customs: The First Forty Years of Washington Society*, ed. Gaillard Hunt. New York: Scribner's, 1906.

Thames, Bill, and Phyllis Thames. *Natural Washington*. New York: Holt, Rinehart and Winston, 1980.

*Thornton, Mrs. William. "Diary of Mrs. William Thornton," *Records of the Columbia Historical Society*, Vol. 10.

The Presidents and the First Ladies

Works by Presidents Washington, Adams, Jefferson, and Madison printed in America before 1801 are available in the Readex Microprint Edition of Early American Imprints published by the American Antiquarian Society.

General

Bassett, Margaret. *Profiles and Portraits of American Presidents and Their Wives*. Freeport, Me.: Bond Wheelwright, 1969.

Borden, Morton, ed. *America's Ten Greatest Presidents*. Chicago: Rand McNally, 1961.

Durbin, Louisa. *Inaugural Cavalcade*. New York: Dodd, Mead, 1972.

Every Four Years. Washington, D.C.: Smithsonian, 1980.

Freidel, Frank. *The Presidents of the United States of America*. Washington, D.C.: White House Historical Association and National Geographic, 1978.

Hughes, Emmet John. *The Living Presidency*. New York: Coward, McCann & Geoghegan, 1973.

Kahler, James G. *Hail to the Chief*. Princeton: Pyne Press, 1972.

Klapthor, Margaret B. *The First Ladies*. Washington, D.C.: White House Historical Association and National Geographic, 1978.

Lorant, Stephen. *The Glorious Burden*. Lenox, Mass.: Author's Edition, 1976.

Roseboom, Eugene H., and Alfred E. Eckes, Jr. *A History of Presidential Elections*. New York: Collier, 1979.

Washington

Kite, Elizabeth S. *L'Enfant and Washington*. Baltimore: Johns Hopkins, 1929.

Washington, George. *The Writings of George Washington,* 12 vols., ed. Jared Sparks. Boston: American Stationers, 1834–37.

Washington, Man and Monument. Washington, D.C.: White House Historical Association and National Geographic, 1978.

Adams

Adams, John. *The Works of John Adams,* 10 vols., ed. Charles F. Adams. Boston: Little, Brown, 1856.

Akers, Charles W. *Abigail Adams: An American Woman*. Boston: Little, Brown, 1980.

Jefferson

Boardman, Fon W. *America and the Virginia Dynasty*. New York: Walck, 1974.

Brodie, Fawn. *Thomas Jefferson: An Intimate Biography*. New York: Norton, 1974.

Jefferson, Isaac. *Memoirs of a Monticello Slave*. Charlottesville, Va.: University Press of Virginia, 1951.

Malone, Dumas. *Jefferson and His Time,* Vol. 4: Jefferson the President, First Term, 1801–1805; Vol. 5: Jefferson the President, Second Term, 1805–1809. Boston: Little, Brown, 1970, 1974.

Madison

Hunt-Jones, Conover: *Dolley and the Great Little Madison*. Washington, D.C.: American Institute of Architects Foundation, 1977.

Madison, James. *James Madison in His Own Words,* 2 vols., ed. Merrill D. Peterson. New York: Newsweek, 1974.

Moore, Virginia. *The Madisons: A Biography*. New York: McGraw-Hill, 1979.

Thane, Elswyth. *Dolley Madison, Her Life and Times*. New York: Crowell-Collier, 1970.

The Lewis and Clark Expedition

Burroughs, Raymond D., ed. *The Natural History of the Lewis and Clark Expedition*. East Lansing, Mich.: Michigan State, 1961.

Coues, Elliott, ed. *History of the Lewis and Clark Expedition*. 1893. Reprint, 3 vols. New York: Dover, n.d.

Clarke, Charles. *The Men of the Lewis and Clark Expedition: Biographical Roster of the Fifty-one Members of the Expedition*. Glendale, Calif.: Arthur H. Clark, 1970.

Ferris, Robert. *Lewis and Clark*. Washington, D.C.: U.S. Department of the Interior, National Park Service, 1975.

Hawke, David Freeman. *Those Tremendous Mountains*. New York: Norton, 1980.

Lewis, Meriwether, and William Clark. *The Journals of Lewis and Clark,* 8 vols., ed. Reuben Gold Thwaites. 1904–5. Reprint. New York: Arno, 1969.

Tompkins, Calvin. *The Lewis and Clark Trail*. New York: Harper and Row, 1965.

General History

The American Heritage History of the United States, 22 vols. New York: American Heritage, 1976.

Dos Passos, John. *The Shackles of Power*. Garden City, N.Y.: Doubleday, 1966.

Forester, C. S. *The Age of Fighting Sail*. Garden City, N.Y.: Doubleday, 1956.

Ganoe, William A. *A History of the United States Army*. 1942. Reprint. Ashton, Md.: Eric Lundberg, 1964.

Garitee, Jerome R. *The Republic's Private Navy*. Middletown, Conn.: Wesleyan for Mystic Seaport, 1977.

Historical Statistics of the United States, 2 vols. Washington, D.C.: U.S. Department of Commerce, 1975.

Icenhower, Joseph. *American Sea Heroes*. Maplewood, N.J.: Hammond, 1970.

Lloyd, Alan. *The Scorching of Washington*. Washington, D.C.: Robert B. Luce, 1975.

Lord, Walter. *The Dawn's Early Light*. New York: Norton, 1972.

200 Years: A Bicentennial History of the United States. Washington, D.C.: U.S. News and World Report, 1976.

Tully, Andrew. *When They Burned the White House*. New York: Simon and Schuster, 1961.

I love this country. I love its people, and I cherish its political form of government. When I began to work on *The American Palace* series, I naturally expected to be fascinated by Washington and its political intrigues, fascinated by the Presidents and their families who had occupied the White House—our American Palace. But what I discovered beggared any of my expectations.

Along with my research in Washington, I also set out across America and traveled more than ten thousand miles gathering material. In one such journey I followed the Lewis and Clark Expedition, by car, horseback, canoe, and foot. What I learned in my travels reaffirmed my belief in the basic goodness of our people.

My hope for this series is that it will effectively portray some of the magnificence of our heritage, and perhaps indicate an even greater magnificence in our future. I believe it can be ours if we but remain true to the dreams and aspirations of our forefathers.

Evan H. Rhodes